I0577494

HORROR HISTORIA

VIOLET

HORROR HISTORIA brings together the most influential monsters and original gothic stories in one blood-curdling collection.

Collect each volume and complete the ultimate nightmare pantheon.

Horror Historia Black
Nightmares and boogeymen of the phantasmagoria.

Horror Historia Brown
Werewolves, hellhounds, and other supernatural beasts.

Horror Historia Green
Carnivorous and lethal vegetation.

Horror Historia Indigo
Practitioners of sorcery and witchcraft.

Horror Historia Pink
Murderers, ghouls, and other monsters of the flesh.

Horror Historia Red
Bloodsuckers and vampire variants.

Horror Historia Violet
Magical beings of folklore and mythology.

Horror Historia White
Ghosts, phantoms, and visitants.

Horror Historia Yellow
Mummies and nightmares of the Nile.

VIOLET

31 Essential Faerie Tales and 4 Mystical Poems

curated and edited by
C.S.R. Calloway

HORROR HISTORIA VIOLET

Published by CSRC Storytelling
Los Angeles, California

ISBNs:
Hardcover: 978-1-955382-73-1
Paperback: 978-1-955382-74-8
Ebook: 978-1-955382-75-5

Cover designed by Mena Bo

This compilation © 2023 CSRC Storytelling

Introduction, selection, and notes © 2023 C.S.R. Calloway

No part of this book may be reproduced or copied in any form without written permission from the publisher.

CONTENTS

LEXICON ETHEREA

It is important to note that folklore surrounding each of these creatures can vary, with different regional variations and interpretations. In some traditions and stories, any of these creatures may be associated with specific fae beings or connected to other supernatural entities. Representations in modern media may incorporate elements of traditional folklore while also incorporating new imaginative elements.

BANSHEES (*singular: banshee*) are supernatural beings from Irish folklore associated with death and the foretelling of imminent demise. They are often depicted as female spirits who wail or keen in a mournful manner, typically near the residences of those about to die. Banshees are believed to be connected to specific families and appear as an omen or warning of death. *Classification: non-fae.*

BOGGARTS (*singular: boggart*) are mischievous supernatural creatures found in English folklore. They are often associated with household spirits or bogeymen, known for playing tricks and causing disturbances. Boggarts are known to hide in dark corners, closets, or under beds, and their mischievous actions can range from simple pranks to more disruptive behavior. *Classification: fae.*

BROWNIES (*singular: brownie*) are mythical creatures from Scottish and English folklore. They are believed to be household spirits or helpful beings that assist with domestic tasks, particularly during the night. Brownies are often depicted as small, brown-skinned creatures, with friendly dispositions. They are generally seen as benevolent beings, although they can become mischievous if they feel unappreciated or mistreated. Brownies are known for their diligent work in exchange for small gifts or acts of kindness. They are said to be particularly fond of offerings of food, such as milk or honey. *Classification: fae.*

CHANGELINGS (*singular: changeling*) are beings from folklore, particularly in European cultures including Irish, Scottish, and Scandinavian folklore, believed to be substitutions for a human child by the fae. According to the legends, fairies would secretly exchange a human baby with a changeling, typically an elderly fairy or a fairy child with deformities or illnesses. The changeling would then be raised by human parents, while the human child was taken away by the fairies. Changelings were believed to possess characteristics that differed from human children, such as abnormal behavior, physical appearance, or slow development. The presence of a changeling was often seen as a hardship for the human family, and various rituals and methods were employed to try and retrieve the original child or force the fairies to return the changeling. *Classification: fae.*

DEVAS (*singular: deva*) are spiritual beings or divine entities found in various Eastern religions and mythologies, such as Hinduism, Buddhism, and Jainism. In Hinduism, devas are often described as celestial beings with great power and are associated with different aspects of the natural world or specific functions in the cosmic order. *Classification: non-fae.*

DRYADS (*singular: dryad*) are nymphs in Greek mythology who are specifically associated with trees and forests. See **nymphs** for further information. *Classification: non-fae.*

DWARVES (*singular: dwarf*) are mythical beings that are commonly associated with Germanic and Norse folklore. They are often depicted as short and stout creatures, skilled in craftsmanship and mining. Dwarves are known for their expertise in metalworking and are often portrayed as living in underground dwellings or mountains. *Classification: non-fae.*

ELVES (*singular: elf*) are mythical creatures prominent in folklore and mythology, particularly in Germanic and Scandinavian traditions. They are often depicted as tall, slender beings with pointed ears and otherworldly beauty. Elves are known for their magical abilities and their association with forests and woodlands, often portrayed as skilled craftsmen and artisans. Elves are believed to have their own realms or dwellings separate from the human world, including underground or in the depths of mountains. *Classification: fae.*

FAIRIES (*singular: fairy*) are supernatural creatures that are often depicted as small, magical beings with human-like features. They are often, but not always, portrayed with wings, which enable them to fly. They are believed to possess abilities such as casting spells, granting wishes, and manipulating natural elements. Possessing the abilities of enchantment, glamour, and the ability to control or influence their surroundings, fairies are closely associated with the natural world and believed to inhabit forests, meadows, and other natural landscapes while guarding plants, animals, and natural resources. Fairies can exhibit a range of personalities, from mischievous tricksters to kind and helpful beings. In some stories, fairies enjoy playing pranks on humans, while in others, they assist those in need or offer guidance and wisdom. They are often said to have their own realms existing parallel to the human world. These fairylands are believed to be enchanted and inaccessible to humans except under certain circumstances. *Classification: fae.*

GNOMES (*singular: gnome*) are mythical creatures often depicted as small, humanoid beings associated with the earth and underground realms. Typically portrayed as wise, industrious, and skilled in various crafts and trades, gnomes are commonly depicted wearing pointed hats and are known for their affinity for gardens and nature. *Classification: fae.*

GOBLINS (*singular: goblin*) are mythical creatures that are often portrayed as mischievous, cunning, and sometimes malicious. They are typically depicted as small, grotesque humanoid beings with pointed ears, sharp teeth, and a penchant for causing trouble. Goblins are commonly associated with dark places such as caves, forests, or abandoned structures. *Classification: fae.*

GREMLINS (*singular: gremlin*) are mischievous creatures that have their origins in British folklore. They are typically depicted as small, impish beings known for causing disruptions and mechanical failures, most notably sabotaging aircraft. *Classification: non-fae.*

IMPS (*singular: imp*) are supernatural creatures that have been depicted in various mythologies and folklore. They are often portrayed as mischievous, small, and often troublesome beings. Imps are known for their playful and sometimes malicious behavior, often causing mischief or playing pranks on humans. They are often associated with witchcraft and are believed to be familiars or servants of witches. They are sometimes depicted as minor demons or spirits that assist witches in their magical practices. *Classification: non-fae.*

KELPIES (*singular: kelpie*) are mythological creatures found in Scottish folklore that are said to inhabit bodies of water such as lochs and rivers. They are typically depicted as shape-shifting water spirits that appear as horses, often with a sleek and beautiful appearance. Kelpies are known for their allure and their ability to draw victims to their watery domain and drown or devour them. *Classification: non-fae.*

KOBOLDS (*singular: kobold*) are mythological creatures found in Germanic folklore. They are typically described as small, impish beings associated with the underground or hidden places such as mines, caves, or households. Kobolds are often depicted as helpful or protective towards their human inhabitants, but they can also be mischievous or even malevolent if offended or mistreated. They may take on various forms, from small humanoid creatures to animals or even inanimate objects. Kobolds are believed to bring both good fortune and trouble to those they interact with, and they are often associated with tasks such as maintaining household chores or protecting treasures. *Classification: fae.*

LEPRECHAUNS (*singular: leprechaun*) are mythological creatures from Irish folklore. They are often depicted as small, mischievous beings, usually around 2 or 3 feet tall and typically dressed in green with pointed shoes, a hat, and a coat. Associated with good luck, leprechauns are said to hide their pots of gold at the end of the rainbow. Leprechauns, frequently shown to be skilled shoemakers, appear as old men with beards and skilled shoemakers. *Classification: fae.*

MERFOLK (*singular: merperson, mermaid, merman*) are mythological creatures that are often depicted as having the upper body of a human and the lower body of a fish. They are associated with bodies of water, particularly the ocean, and are renowned for their beauty and captivating voices, often luring sailors and fishermen with their enchanting songs and appearances. *Classification: either.*

NAIADS (*singular: naiad*) are nymphs in Greek mythology who are associated with bodies of fresh water such as springs, fountains, rivers, and lakes. See **nymphs** for further information. *Classification: non-fae.*

NYMPHS (*singular: nymph*) are mythological creatures found in various cultures and mythologies, often associated with nature and natural features such as forests, mountains, springs, and groves. In Greek mythology, nymphs were believed to be minor deities or spirits of nature who embodied the vitality and essence of their respective domains, most especially forests (dryads), mountains (oreads), and springs (naiads). Often depicted as beautiful, youthful maidens, they were believed to possess the power to bestow blessings or curses upon those who encountered them. Nymphs were known for their association with fertility, beauty, and the preservation of their natural habitats. *Classification: non-fae.*

PAN is a prominent figure in Greek mythology associated with nature, music, and the wild. In Greek mythology, Pan is known as a satyr, a creature with the upper body of a man and the lower body of a goat. Pan is often depicted as a mischievous and playful deity who roams the forests and mountains, playing his pan flute and engaging in revelry. The music of Pan was believed to have the power to inspire both fear and joy, and it was said that his melodies could captivate both mortals and immortals alike, appealing to the inherent wildness and instinctual nature within humanity. *Classification: non-fae.*

PIXIES (*singular: pixie*) are small, mythical creatures commonly associated with Celtic folklore and are typically depicted as small, winged beings with a human-like appearance. They are believed to reside in forests, meadows, and other natural environments, influencing the growth of plants and flowers. Pixies are known for their love and skill of music and dancing. Sometimes blamed for causing disturbances, stealing small household items, or leading travelers astray in the woods, pixies are generally seen as mischievous rather than malevolent, and their pranks are often more playful than harmful, though they can be fickle and easily offended. *Classification: fae.*

The **SEELIE COURT** is a concept in fae folklore that represents a faction or group of fairies associated with benevolence, beauty, and light. The members of the Seelie Court are known for their enchanting beauty, and they often engage in acts of goodwill towards mortals. They may provide aid, protection, or blessings to humans who show respect and reverence towards the fae. However, despite their seemingly benevolent nature, the fairies of the Seelie Court are known to have their own rules and codes of conduct, which can be capricious with a strict sense of justice. *Classification: fae.*

SELKIES (*singular: selkie*) are creatures associated with the sea and originating from Celtic folklore, particularly from the traditions of Scotland and Ireland. They are often depicted as seals that can shed their skin and transform into human form. They are gentle and beautiful beings with enchanting singing voices and the ability to shift between their seal form and human form by donning or removing their sealskin. Legend has it that if a human finds and hides a selkie's sealskin, the selkie becomes bound to them and may even marry them. However, if the selkie ever finds their hidden sealskin, they will return to the sea, leaving their human family behind. *Classification: non-fae.*

SIRENS (*singular: siren; also: lorelei*) are mythological creatures from Greek mythology, depicted as bird-women with the ability to lure sailors to their demise in treacherous waters with their irresistible songs. *Classification: non-fae.*

THE SLUAGH is a supernatural entity from Irish and Scottish mythology, sometimes referred to as "the Host of the Unforgiven Dead." In some accounts, the Sluagh are depicted as malevolent spirits or ghosts of the dead who fly through the air in large flocks, seeking to steal the souls of the living. They are said to be particularly active around Samhain (Halloween) and the Feast of the Dead, and are often associated with dark, foreboding landscapes such as abandoned graveyards or haunted forests. In other accounts, the Sluagh are portrayed as more neutral or even helpful beings, guiding lost travelers or offering warnings of impending danger, seen as a kind of intermediary between the living and the dead, or between the human and supernatural worlds. *Classification: non-fae.*

SPRITES (*singular: sprite*) are often depicted as small, supernatural beings with a connection to the elements of air and water, often found near bodies of water such as streams, lakes, or waterfalls. Sprites are typically portrayed as playful and mischievous creatures. They are known to frolic in the natural world, engaging in dances, singing, and other joyful activities. They have an ethereal and ephemeral quality, often appearing as shimmering or glowing figures. Sprites are sometimes associated with specific natural phenomena, such as the sprites that are said to appear during thunderstorms or the water sprites that dwell in underwater realms. *Classification: fae.*

SYLPHS (*singular: sylph, sylphid*) are elemental spirits often depicted as delicate creatures that inhabit the skies and embody the qualities of air such as lightness and grace. They are often described as invisible or transparent, and their presence is believed to be felt through gentle breezes or rustling sounds. In some traditions, sylphs are also associated with protecting and guarding the purity of the air and maintaining the balance of the natural world. *Classification: non-fae.*

TROLLS (*singular: troll*) are mythical creatures that have origins in Scandinavian folklore. They are often depicted as large, strong, and sometimes grotesque beings with a variety of physical characteristics. Trolls, usually depicted as solitary creatures, are typically associated with mountains, caves, and forests. They are known for their strength, trickery, and sometimes malevolent behavior. *Classification: non-fae.*

The **UNSEELIE COURT** is a concept in fae folklore and mythology that represents a faction of fairies associated with darkness, malevolence, and chaos. Members of the Unseelie Court are often depicted as creatures of darkness, dwelling in hidden places like deep forests, caves, or other secluded areas. They may engage in activities that bring misfortune or harm to humans, such as leading travelers astray, causing nightmares, or stealing children. The fairies of the Unseelie Court may have eerie features, twisted forms, or even monstrous attributes. Despite their malevolent nature, they are believed to have their own sense of honor and may adhere to their own set of rules and customs. *Classification: fae.*

WATER GUARDIAN FAIRIES are often associated with bodies of water such as rivers, lakes, and oceans. These entities are believed to have a connection to the water element and are often depicted as supernatural beings or spirits that inhabit and protect these aquatic environments. In Irish mythology, the water guardian fairies assist Manannán mac Lir in his role as a guardian of the sea. *Classification: fae.*

The **WILL O' THE WISP**, also known as Will-o'-Wisp or Ignis Fatuus, is a phenomenon found in folklore and mythology referring to a mysterious phosphorescent glow that appears at night, often over marshy areas or swamps. The light, associated with mischievous spirits or supernatural beings, seems to dance or flicker, appearing and disappearing, potentially leading people deeper into the wilderness or into treacherous terrain. The phenomenon has been attributed to various natural explanations, such as the combustion of marsh gases or the reflection of moonlight on wet surfaces. *Classification: non-fae.*

Witches (*singular: witch*) are often depicted as practitioners of magic, typically associated with the casting of spells, potions, and engaging in various mystical practices. They are commonly portrayed as individuals, usually women, who possess supernatural abilities and knowledge of the occult. *Classification: non-fae.*

Introduction to the Volume

"Come, faeries, take me out of this dull house!
Let me have all the freedom I have lost—
Work when I will and idle when I will!
Faeries, come take me out of this dull world,
For I would ride with you upon the wind,
Run on the top of the disheveled tide,
And dance upon the mountains like a flame!"

— W. B. Yeats,
The Land of Heart's Desire

When it comes to classifying supernatural beings, fae present an intriguing case. Fairies serve as the foundational archetype, though their portrayal in modern depictions varies greatly. While commonly presented as winged and diminutive, their defining traits in fiction are their mischievous and magical nature, often bordering on malevolence. However, the classification of fae expands beyond fairies, encompassing an array of creatures depending on cultural and authorial whims. This taxonomy may include sprites, pixies, elves, leprechauns, dwarves, gnomes, trolls, goblins, brownies, boggarts, banshees, changelings, sylphs, the Sluagh, nymphs (such as dryads and naiads), sirens, mermaids, kelpies, and even witches on rare occasions[1]—just to scratch the surface. While all fairies are fae, not all fae are fairies, and the realm of magical spirits and creatures extends well beyond the fae. The rich tapestry of folklore and storytelling intertwines and blends the many variations, casting a wide net that encompasses legendary creatures of both ethereal and corporeal nature. While certain beings like imps and gremlins share fairy-like qualities, they are distinct from the traditional fair folk themselves. For the purposes of this collection, what holds utmost importance is the role these creatures— whether fae or fae adjacent—play in the story, rather than their individual categorization.

Deeply rooted in Celtic tradition, folklore, and mythology, fairies occupy a unique space within the realm of mythical creatures. Unlike iconic horror

---

[1] For a compendium devoted entirely to witches, wizards, and sorcerers, *Horror Historia Indigo* serves as a marvelous companion to this collection.

figures like vampires, werewolves, and zombies, fairies aren't typically categorized as outright malevolent beings. In fact, their nature is multifaceted, as they are just as likely to grant wishes and bestow blessings as they are to mete out malicious retribution. However, in the pages of literary horror, fairies and fae often take on a distinctly harmful persona. These dangerous and alluring creatures are depicted as capable of luring unsuspecting humans into their realm, ensnaring them forever. As beings imbued with immense power, fairies and their literary ilk pose a significant danger to humans, even if they don't outright manifest as horrific monsters.

Some of the longest surviving folktales incorporating fairies include the ballad of Tam Lin, who was captured by the Queen of Fairies before falling in love with and impregnating a mortal woman. Edmund Spenser's epic poem *The Faerie Queene* (1590) serves as a Reformation allegory, celebrating the Tudor dynasty and Elizabeth I, the then-current queen of England. In 1597, the renowned playwright William Shakespeare introduced Queen Mab in his tragedy *Romeo and Juliet*. After a century, Queen Mab reemerged in later stories and poems as the Queen of Fairies, despite her initial portrayal as "the fairies' midwife."

In the early 19th century, the Brothers Grimm published their famed collection of fairy tales, which included stories about fairies and other supernatural beings. Grimm's fairy tales were often dark and cautionary, warning readers about the dangers of consorting with fairies or breaking taboos.

Irish antiquary Thomas Crofton Croker published his collection *Fairy Legends and Traditions of the South of Ireland* in 1825. One of the featured stories, "The Legend of Knockgrafton," tells of a man who, after making contributions to a song sung by nearby fairies, is magically relieved of the hump on his back.[2] Situated in County Tipperary, Ireland, Knockgrafton finds itself in close proximity to another site that sparked inspiration in Richard D'Alton Williams for his poem "The Fairies of Knockshegowna."

> They glide along o'er the dewy banks,
>   On their viewless filmy wings,
> And anon and again from their restless ranks
>   Their fairy laughter rings.

In 1887, James Bowker published *Goblin Tales of Lancashire*, which featured an eerie procession of a fairy funeral that, quite horrifyingly, foreshadowed the death of one of the two protagonists.

---

[2] The story that inspired "The Legend of Knockgrafton" has lived on in variations for generations. Comedian T.P. Hearn included a popular joke in his stand-up routine— popularized and frequently replayed on the American television series *Comic View* in the 1990s—where, instead of fairies, the afflicted man spoke with the Devil, showing how interchangeable the role of a fairy in folklore is with that of an archfiend.

...standing together against the trunk of a large tree, they gazed at the miniature being stepping so lightly over the road, mottled by the stray moonbeams. It was a dainty little object; but although neither Adam nor Robin could comprehend the burden of the song it sang, the unmistakable croon of grief with which each stave ended told the listeners that the fairy was singing a requiem. The men kept perfectly silent, and in a little while the figure paused and turned round, as though in expectation, continuing, however, its mournful notes. By-and-by the voices of other singers were distinguished, and as they grew louder the fairy standing in the roadway ceased to render the verse, and sang only the refrain, and a few minutes afterwards Adam and Robin saw a marvelous cavalcade pass through the gateway. A number of figures, closely resembling the one to which their attention had first been drawn, walked two by two, and behind them others with their caps in their hands, bore a little black coffin, the lid of which was drawn down so as to leave a portion of the contents uncovered. Behind these again others, walking in pairs, completed the procession. All were singing in inexpressibly mournful tones, pausing at regular intervals to allow the voice of the one in advance to be heard, as it chanted the refrain of the song, and when the last couple had passed into the avenue, the gates closed as noiselessly as they had opened.

In the late 19th and early 20th centuries, writers such as Lord Dunsany and Arthur Machen explored the darker side of fairy folklore in their works of horror fiction. In Dunsany's 1905 novel *The King of Elfland's Daughter*, a mortal man becomes entranced by the fairy queen Lirazel and is drawn into the world of the fairies, where he is forced to confront the perilous and unpredictable nature of their realm. Machen's *The Great God Pan* (1894) and *The White People* (1904) both feature supernatural beings that resemble fairies at their most sinister. *Pan* in particular features a nefarious supernatural being named Helen Vaughan, who is described both as a "fairy" and a "daughter of Pan."

Pan, the Greek god of the wild, was frequently portrayed in horror literature as a dark, mischievous figure with the power to seduce and corrupt humans. In Victorian-era and early 20th-century horror literature, Pan and fairies often overlapped in terms of their depiction as alluring, but capricious and unpredictable creatures. In this period, fairies were often depicted as having the power to enchant humans and lure them into their realm, where they might be subjected to terrifying ordeals or trapped there forever.

In the 1920s and 1930s, pulp magazines that were popular at the time began to feature stories about fae as well. These stories often combined elements of horror and fantasy, depicting these magical creatures as both alluring and terrifying. Authors such as Clark Ashton Smith and Manly Wade Wellman wrote stories that included fairies and other supernatural beings, creating a rich tapestry of horror fiction drawing on folklore and mythology from around the world.

Many modern day horror tales continue to utilize the world and creatures of fae in their telling, including: *The Call* by Peadar Ó Guilín, a young adult novel set in a world where teenagers are taken to the fairy world to fight for their lives in a deadly game; *The Folk of the Air* trilogy by Holly Black, a young adult series that follows a mortal girl who is raised in the fairy world and becomes embroiled in the politics and power struggles of the fae; *The Hazel Wood* by Melissa Albert, a young adult novel that blends fairy tales and horror as a teenage girl discovers the truth about her grandmother's mysterious past; and *The Changeling* by Victor LaValle, a novel exploring the horror of losing a child and the lengths a parent will go to get them back. In film and television, examples of modern-day fairy horror include the series *Carnival Row* and its collection of refugee fae; Corin Hardy and Felipe Marino's film *The Hallow*, whose titular creatures are a class of "fairies, banshees, and baby stealers;" and Guillermo del Toro's glorious *Pan's Labyrinth*, which has a horrific depiction of a faun who may or may not be the famous mythological figure. Even after centuries, Queen Mab herself persists, revealing her presence to those who seek their amusement where light dances and shadows whisper.

C.S.R. CALLOWAY

NOTES ON THE COLLECTION

Gothic grotesqueries, penny dreadfuls, pulp magazines, and other darkly inventive publications have produced a dread allure across the world, infiltrating culture and influencing language, becoming the source for multiple adaptations across all forms of media. HORROR HISTORIA brings together the most influential monsters and original gothic stories in distinctive blood-curdling collections, existing not as an exhaustive tome or panoptic omnibus, but as one hell of a starter kit for the archetypes, conventions and motifs necessary to build the ultimate nightmare pantheon.

To make HORROR HISTORIA texts more accessible to the contemporary reader, minor changes have been made with spelling, punctuation, capitalization, italicization, hyphenation, and spacing. British spellings ("colour" instead of "color") have been altered throughout. Obvious typographical errors in the original texts have been corrected. Many of these stories contain depictions common during their day among writers from systemically majoritized backgrounds and cultures, though any outright slurs have been altered or removed. Neither the publisher nor the editor endorses any characterizations, depictions, or language which would be considered ableist, racist, xenophobic, or otherwise offensive.

Each book in the HORROR HISTORIA collection is dedicated to **Gerardo Maravilla** and this *VIOLET* entry in addition is specially dedicated to **Ariel Landrum, LMFT**.

1

Frank Martin and the Fairies

William Carleton

first published in the *Irish Penny Journal*, as part of an article titled "Irish Superstitions: No. III. Ghosts and Fairies" (February 1841)

Martin was a thin, pale man, when I saw him, of a sickly look, and a constitution naturally feeble. His hair was a light auburn, his beard mostly unshaven, and his hands of a singular delicacy and whiteness, owing, I dare say, as much to the soft and easy nature of his employment as to his infirm health. In everything else he was as sensible, sober, and rational as any other man; but on the topic of fairies, the man's mania was peculiarly strong and immovable. Indeed, I remember that the expression of his eyes was singularly wild and hollow, and his long narrow temples sallow and emaciated.

Now, this man did not lead an unhappy life, nor did the malady he labored under seem to be productive of either pain or terror to him, although one might be apt to imagine otherwise. On the contrary, he and the fairies maintained the most friendly intimacy, and their dialogues—which I fear were woefully one-sided ones—must have been a source of great pleasure to him, for they were conducted with much mirth and laughter, on his part at least.

"Well, Frank, when did you see the fairies?"

"Whist! there's two dozen of them in the shop (the weaving shop) this minute. There's a little ould fellow sittin' on the top of the sleys, an' all to be rocked while I'm weavin'. The sorrow's in them, but they're the greatest little skamers alive, so they are. See, there's another of them at my dressin' noggin.[3] Go out o' that, you *shingawn*; or, bad cess to me, if you don't, but I'll lave you a mark. Ha! cut, you thief you!"

"Frank, am't you afeard o' them?"

---

[3] The dressings are a species of sizy flummery, which is brushed into the yam to keep the thread round and even, and to prevent it from being frayed by the friction of the reed.

"Is it me! Arra, what ud' I be afeard o' them for? Sure they have no power over me."

"And why haven't they, Frank?"

"Because I was baptized against them."

"What do you mean by that?"

"Why, the priest that christened me was tould by my father, to put in the proper prayer against the fairies—an' a priest can't refuse it when he's asked—an' he did so. Begorra, it's well for me that he did—(let the tallow alone, you little glutton—see, theres a weeny thief o' them aitin' my tallow)—becaise, you see, it was their intention to make me king o' the fairies."

"Is it possible?"

"Devil a lie in it. Sure you may ax them, an' they'll tell you."

"What size are they, Frank?"

"Oh, little wee fellows, with green coats, an' the purtiest little shoes ever you seen. There's two of them—both ould acquaintances o' mine—runnin' along the yarn-beam. That ould fellow with the bob-wig is called Jim jam, an' the other chap, with the three-cocked hat, is called Nickey Nick. Nickey plays the pipes. Nickey, give us a tune, or I'll malivogue you—come now, 'Lough Erne Shore'. Whist, now—listen!"

The poor fellow, though weaving as fast as he could all the time, yet bestowed every possible mark of attention to the music, and seemed to enjoy it as much as if it had been real.

But who can tell whether that which we look upon as a privation may not after all be a fountain of increased happiness, greater, perhaps, than any which we ourselves enjoy? I forget who the poet is who says—

> "Mysterious are thy laws;
>   The vision's finer than the view;
>   Her landscape Nature never drew
> So fair as Fancy draws."

Many a time, when a mere child, not more than six or seven years of age, have I gone as far as Frank's weaving-shop, in order, with a heart divided between curiosity and fear, to listen to his conversation with the good people. From morning till night his tongue was going almost as incessantly as his shuttle; and it was well known that at night, whenever he awoke out of his sleep, the first thing he did was to put out his hand, and push them, as it were, off his bed.

"Go out o' this, you thieves, you—go out o' this now, an' let me alone. Nickey, is this any time to be playing the pipes, and me wants to sleep? Go off, now—troth if yez do, you'll see what I'll give yez tomorrow. Sure I'll be makin' new dressin's; and if yez behave decently, maybe I'll lave yez the scrapin' o' the pot. There now. Och! poor things, they're dacent crathurs. Sure they're all gone, barrin' poor Red-cap, that doesn't like to lave me." And then the harmless monomaniac would fall back into what we trust was an innocent slumber.

About this time there was said to have occurred a very remarkable circumstance, which gave poor Frank a vast deal of importance among the neighbors. A man named Frank Thomas, the same in whose house Mickey M'Rorey held the first dance at which I ever saw him, as detailed in a former sketch; this man, I say, had a child sick, but of what complaint I cannot now remember, nor is it of any importance. One of the gables of Thomas's house was built against, or rather into, a Forth or Rath, called Towny, or properly Tonagh Forth. It was said to be haunted by the fairies, and what gave it a character peculiarly wild in my eyes was, that there were on the southern side of it two or three little green mounds, which were said to be the graves of unchristened children, over which it was considered dangerous and unlucky to pass. At all events, the season was mid-summer; and one evening about dusk, during the illness of the child, the noise of a hand-saw was heard upon the Forth. This was considered rather strange, and, after a little time, a few of those who were assembled at Frank Thomas's went to see who it could be that was sawing in such a place, or what they could be sawing at so late an hour, for every one knew that nobody in the whole country about them would dare to cut down the few white-thorns that grew upon the Forth. On going to examine, however, judge of their surprise, when, after surrounding and searching the whole place, they could discover no trace of either saw or sawyer. In fact, with the exception of themselves, there was no one, either natural or supernatural, visible. They then returned to the house, and had scarcely sat down, when it was heard again within ten yards of them. Another examination of the premises took place, but with equal success. Now, however, while standing on the Forth, they heard the sawing in a little hollow, about a hundred and fifty yards below them, which was completely exposed to their view. but they could see nobody. A party of them immediately went down to ascertain, if possible, what this singular noise and invisible labour could mean; but on arriving at the spot, they heard the sawing, to which were now added hammering, and the driving of nails upon the Forth above, whilst those who stood on the Forth continued to hear it in the hollow. On comparing notes, they resolved to send down to Billy Nelson's for Frank Martin a distance of only about eighty or ninety yards. He was soon on the spot, and without a moment's hesitation solved the enigma.

"'Tis the fairies," said he. 'I see them, and busy crathurs they are."

"But what are they sawing, Frank?"

"They are makin' a child's coffin," he replied; "they have the body already made, an' they're now nailin' the lid together."

That night the child died, and the story goes that on the second evening afterwards, the carpenter who was called upon to make the coffin brought a table out from Thomas's house to the Forth, as a temporary bench; and, it is said, that the sawing and hammering necessary for the completion of his task were precisely the same which had been heard the evening but one before—

neither more nor less. I remember the death of the child myself, and the making of its coffin, but I think the story of the supernatural carpenter was not heard in the village for some months after its interment.

Frank had every appearance of a hypochondriac about him. At the time I saw him, he might be about thirty-four years of age, but I do not think, from the debility of his frame and infirm health, that he has been alive for several years. He was an object of considerable interest and curiosity, and often have I been present when he was pointed out to strangers as "the man that could see the good people."

THE WIFE OF KONG TOLV:
A FAIRY TALE OF SCANDINAVIA[4]

Dinah Maria Mulock Craik

first published in *Sharpe's London Magazine* (June 1850)

Hyldreda Kalm stood at the door of her cottage, and looked abroad into the quietness of the Sabbath morn. The village of Skjelskör lay at a little distance down the vale, lighted by the sunshine of a Zealand summer, which, though brief, is glowing and lovely even as that of the south. Hyldreda had looked for seventeen years upon this beautiful scene, the place where she was born. Sunday after Sunday she had stood thus and listened for the distant tinkle of the church bell. A stranger, passing by, might have said, how lovely were her face and form; but the widowed mother, whose sole stay she was, and the little delicate sister, who had been her darling from the cradle, would have answered, that if none were so fair, none were likewise so good as Hyldreda; and that all the village knew. If she did love to bestow greater taste and care on her Sunday garments than most young damsels of her class, she had a right—for was she not beautiful as any lady? And did not the eyes of Esbern Lynge say so, when, week after week, he came up the hilly road, and descended again to the little chapel, supporting the feeble mother's slow steps, and watching his betrothed as she bounded on before, with little Resa in her hand?

"Is Esbern coming?" said the mother's voice within.

"I know not—I did not look," answered Hyldreda, with a girlish willfulness. "I saw only the sun shining on the river, and the oak-wood waving in the breeze."

"Look down the road, child; the time passes. Go quickly."

"She is gone already," said Resa, laughing merrily. "She is standing under the great elder-tree to wait for Esbern Lynge."

---

[4] The idea of this story is partly taken from a Danish *Visa*, or legendary ballad, entitled "Proud Margaret." - AUTHOR

"Call her back—call her back!" cried the mother, anxiously. "To stand beneath an elder-tree, and this night will be St. John's Eve! On Sunday, too, and she a Sunday child! Call her quickly, Resa."

The little child lifted up her voice, "Hyld—"

"Not her name—utter not her name!" And the widow Kalm went on muttering to herself, "Perhaps the Hyldemoer will not have heard.[5] Alas the day! when my child was born under an elder-tree, and I, poor desolate mother! was terrified into giving my babe that name. Great Hyldemoer, be propitiated! Holy Virgin!" and the widow's prayer became a curious mingling of superstition and piety, "Blessed Mary! let not the elves have power over my child! HaveI not kept her heart from evil? does not the holy cross lie on her pure breast day and night? Do I not lead her every Sunday, winter and summer, in storm, sunshine, or snow, to the chapel in the valley? And this day I will say for her a double prayer."

The mother's counted beads had scarce come to an end when Hyldreda stood by her side, and, following the light-footed damsel, came Esbern Lynge.

"Child, why didst thou linger under the tree?" said the widow. "It does not become a young maiden to stand flaunting outside her door. Who wert thou watching so eagerly?"

"Not thee, Esbern," laughed the girl, shaking her head at her betrothed, who interposed with a happy conscious face; "I was looking at a grand train that wound along the road, and thinking how pleasant it would be to dress on a Sunday like the lady of the castle, and recline idly behind four prancing horses instead of trudging on in these clumsy shoes."

The mother frowned, and Esbern Lynge looked sorrowful.

"I wish I could give her all she longs for," sighed the young man, as they proceeded on their way, his duteous arm supporting the widow, while Hyldreda and Resa went bounding onward before them; "She is as beautiful as a queen—I would that I could make her one."

"Wish rather, Esbern, that Heaven may make her a pious, lowly-hearted maid, and, in good time, a wife; that she may live in humility and content, and die in peace among her own people."

Esbern said nothing—he could not think of death and *her* together. So he and the widow Kalm walked on silently—and so slowly that they soon lost sight of the two blithe sisters.

Hyldreda was talking merrily of the grand sight she had just seen, and describing to little Resa the gilded coach, the prancing horses, with glittering harness. "Oh! but it was a goodly train, as it swept down toward the river. Who knows? Perhaps it may have been the king and queen themselves."

---

[5] *Hyldemoer*, elder-mother, is the name of a Danish elf inhabiting the elder-tree. *Eda* signifies a grandmother or female ancestor. Children born on Sundays were especially under the power of the elves.

"No," said little Resa, rather fearfully, "you know Kong Tolv never lets any mortal king pass the bridge of Skjelskör."[6]

"*Kong Tolv!* what, more stories about Kong Tolv!" laughed the merry maiden; "I never saw him; I wish I could see him, for then I might believe in thy tales, little one."

"Hush, hush!—But mother told me never to speak of these things to thee," answered Resa; "unsay the wish, or some harm may come."

"I care not! who would heed these elfin tales on such a lovely day? Look, Resa, down that sunny meadow, where there is a cloud shadow dancing on the grass; a strange cloud it is too, for it almost resembles a human form."

"It is Kong Tolv rolling himself in the sunshine," cried the trembling child; "Look away, my sister, lest he should hear us."

Again Hyldreda's fearless laugh made music through the still air, and she kept looking back until they passed from the open road into the gloom of the oak wood.

"It is strange that thou shouldst be so brave," said Resa once more. "I tremble at the very thought of the Elle-people of whom our villagers tell, while thou hast not a single fear. Why is it, sister?"

"I know not, save that I never yet feared any thing," answered Hyldreda, carelessly. "As for Kong Tolv, let him come, I care not."

While she spoke, a breeze swept through the oak wood, the trees began to bend their tops, and the under branches were stirred with leafy murmurings, as the young girl passed beneath. She lifted her fair face to meet them. "Ah 'tis delicious, this soft scented wind; it touches my face like airy kisses; it makes the leaves seem to talk to me in musical whispers. Dost thou not hear them too, little Resa? and dost thou not—?"

Hyldreda suddenly stopped, and gazed eagerly down the road.

"Well, sister," said Resa, "what art dreaming of now? Come, we shall be late at church, and mother will scold." But the elder sister stood motionless. "How strange thine eyes look; what dost thou see, Hyldreda."

"Look—what is there!"

"Nothing, but a cloud of dust that the wind sweeps forward. Stand back, sister, or it will blind thee."

Still Hyldreda bent forward with admiring eyes, muttering, "Oh! the grand golden chariot, with its four beautiful white horses! And therein sits a man—surely it is the king! and the lady beside him is the queen. See, she turns—"

Hyldreda paused, dumb with wonder, for despite the gorgeous show of jeweled attire, she recognized that face. It was the same she had looked at an hour before in the little cracked mirror. The lady in the carriage was the exact counterpart of herself!

---

[6] Kong Tolv, or *King Twelve,* is one of the Elle-kings who divide the fairy sovereignty of Zealand.

The pageant came and vanished. Little Resa turned round and wiped her eyes—she, innocent child, had seen nothing but a cloud of dust. Her elder sister answered not her questionings, but remained silent, oppressed by a nameless awe. It passed not, even when the chapel was reached, and Hyldreda knelt to pray. Above the sound of the hymn she heard the ravishing music of the leaves in the oak wood, and instead of the priest she seemed to behold the two dazzling forms which had sat side by side in the golden chariot.

When service was ended, and all went homewards, she lingered under the trees where the vision, or reality, whichever it was, had met her sight, half longing for its reappearance. But her mother whispered something to Esbern, and they hurried Hyldreda away.

She laid aside her Sunday mantle, the scarlet woof which to spin, weave, and fashion, had cost her a world of pains. How coarse and ugly it seemed! She threw it contemptuously aside, and thought how beautiful looked the purple-robed lady, who was so like herself.

"And why should I not be as fair as she? I should, if I were only dressed as fine. Heaven might as well have made me a lady, instead of a poor peasant girl."

These repinings entered the young heart hitherto so pure and happy. They haunted her even when she rejoined her mother, Resa, and Esbern Lynge. She prepared the noonday meal, but her step was heavy and her hand unwilling. The fare seemed coarse, the cottage looked dark and poor. She wondered what sort of a palace home was that owned by the beautiful lady; and whether the king, if king the stranger were, presided at his banquet table as awkwardly as did Esbern Lynge at the mean board here.

At the twilight, Hyldreda did not steal out as usual to talk with her lover beneath the rose-porch. She went and hid herself out of his sight, under the branches of the great elder-tree, which to her had always a strange charm, perhaps because it was the spot of all others where she was forbidden to stay. However, this day Hyldreda began to feel herself to be no longer a child, but a woman whose will was free.

She sat under the dreamy darkness of the heavy foliage. Its faint sickly odor overpowered her like a spell. Even the white bunches of elder flowers seemed to grow alive in the twilight, and to change into faces, looking at her whithersoever she turned. She shut her eyes, and tried to summon back the phantom of the golden chariot, and especially of the king-like man who sat inside. Scarce had she seen him clearly, but she felt he looked a king. If wishing could bring to her so glorious a fortune, she would almost like to have, in addition to the splendors of rich dress and grand palaces, such a noble-looking man for her lord and husband.

And the poor maiden was rudely awakened from her dream, by feeling on her delicate shoulders the two heavy hands of Esbern Lynge.

Haughtily she took them off. Alas! he, loving her so much, had ever been lightly loved in return! today he was not loved at all. He came at an ill time, for the moment his hand put aside the elder branches, all the dazzling fancies of his betrothed vanished in air. He came, too, with an ill-wooing, for he implored her to trifle no more, but to fulfill her mother's hope and his, and enter as mistress at the little blacksmith's forge. She, who had just been dreaming of a palace home! Not a word she answered at first, and then cold, cruel words, worse than silence. So Esbern, who, though a lover, was a manly-hearted youth, and thought it shame to be mocked by a girl's light tongue, left her there and went away, not angry, but very sorrowful.

Little Resa came to summon her sister. But Hyldreda trembled before the gathering storm, for widow Kalm, though a tender mother, was one who well knew how to rule. Her loud, severe voice already warned the girl of the reproof that was coming. To avoid it only for a little, until her own proud spirit was calmed. Hyldreda told Resa she would not come in until after she had taken a little walk down the moonlight road. As she passed from under the elder-tree, she heard a voice, like her mother's, and yet not her mother's— no, it could never be, for it shouted after her,

"Come now, or come no more!"

Some evil impulse goaded the haughty girl to assert her womanly right of free action, and she passed from her home, flying with swift steps. A little, only a little absence, to show her indignant pride, and she would be back again, to heal all strife. Nevertheless, ere she was aware, Hyldreda had reached the oak-wood, beneath which she had seen the morning's bewildering sight.

And there again, brighter in the moonlight than it had ever seemed in the day, came sweeping by the stately pageant. Its torches flung red shadows on the trees, its wheels resounded through the night's quiet with a music as of silver bells. And sitting in his state alone, grand but smiling, was the lord of all this splendor.

The chariot stopped, and he dismounted. Then the whole train vanished, and, shorn of all his glories, except a certain brightness which his very presence seemed to shed, the king, if he were indeed such, stood beside the trembling peasant maid.

He did not address her, but looked in her face inquiringly, until Hyldreda felt herself forced to be the first to speak.

"My lord, who art thou, and what is thy will with me?"

He smiled. "Thanks, gentle maiden, for thy question has taken off the spell. Otherwise it could not be broken, even by Kong Tolv."

Hyldreda shuddered with fear. Her fingers tried to seize the cross which always lay on her breast, but no! she had thrown aside the coarse black wooden crucifix, while dreaming of ornaments of gold. And it was St. John's Eve, and she stood beneath the haunted oak-wood. No power had she to fly, and her prayers died on her lips, for she knew herself in the Hill-king's power.

Kong Tolv began to woo, after the elfin fashion, brief and bold. "Fair maiden, the Dronningstolen is empty, and 'tis thou must fill it. Come and enter my palace under the hill."[7]

---

[7] Dronningstolen, or Queen's Chair.

But the maiden sobbed out that she was too lowly to sit on a queen's chair, and that none of mortals, save the dead, made their home underground. And she prayed the Elle-king to let her go back to her mother and little Resa.

He only laughed. "Wouldst be content, then, with the poor cottage, and the black bread, and the labor from morn till eve. Didst thou not of thyself wish for a palace and a lord like me? And did not the Hyldemoer waft me the wish, so that I came to meet and welcome thee under the hill?"

Hyldreda made one despairing effort to escape, but she heard again Kong Tolv's proud laugh, and looking up, she saw that the thick oak-wood had changed to an army. In place of every tree stood a fierce warrior, ready to guard every step. She thought it must be all a delirious dream that would vanish with the morning. Suddenly she heard the far village clock strike the hour. Mechanically she counted—one—two—three—four—up to *twelve*.

As she pronounced the last word, Kong Tolv caught her in his arms, saying, "Thou hast named me and art mine."

Instantly all the scene vanished, and Hyldreda found herself standing on the bleak side of a little hill, alone in the moonlight. But very soon the clear night darkened, and a heavy storm arose. Trembling, she looked around for shelter, and saw in the hill-side a tiny door, which seemed to invite her to enter. She did so! In a moment she stood dazzled by a blaze of light—a mortal amidst the festival of the elves. She heard the voice of Kong Tolv, half-speaking, half-singing,

> "Welcome, maiden, fair and free,
> Thou hast come of thyself in the hill to me;
> Stay thou here, nor thy fate deplore;
> Thou hast come of thyself in at my door."

And bewildered by the music, the dance, and the splendor, Hyldreda remembered no more the cottage, with its one empty chair, nor the miserable mother, nor the little sister straining her weeping eyes along the lonely road.

The mortal maiden became the Elle-king's bride, and lived in the hill for seven long years; at least, so they seemed in Elfinland, where time passes like the passing of a strain of music, that dies but to be again renewed. Little thought had she of the world above ground, for in the hill-palace was continual pleasure, and magnificence without end. No remembrance of lost kindred troubled her, for she sat in the Dronningstolen, and all the elfin people bowed down before the wife of the mighty Kong Tolv.

She might have lived so always, with no desire ever to go back to earth, save that one day she saw trickling down through the palace roof a pearly stream. The elves fled away, for they said it was some mortal weeping on the grassy hill overhead. But Hyldreda staid and looked on until the stream settled into a clear, pellucid pool. A sweet mirror it made, and the Hill-king's bride ever loved to see her own beauty. So she went and gazed down into the shining water.

There she beheld—not the image of the elfin-queen, but of the peasant maid, with her mantle of crimson wool, her coarse dress, and her black crucifix. She turned away in disgust, but soon her people brought her elfin mirrors, wherein she could see her present self, gorgeously clad, and a thousand times more fair. It kindled in her heart a proud desire.

She said to her lord, "Let me go back for a little while to my native village, and my ancient home, that I may show them all my splendor, and my greatness. Let me enter, sitting in my gilded chariot, with the four white horses, and feel myself as queen-like as the lady I once saw beneath the oak-wood."

Kong Tolv laughed, and assented. "But," he said, "keep thy own proud self the while. The first sigh, the first tear, and I carry thee back into the hill with shame."

So Hyldreda left the fairy-palace, sweeping through the village, with a pageant worthy a queen. Thus in her haughtiness, after seven years had gone by, she came to her mother's door.

Seven years, none of which had cast one shadow on the daughter's beauty. But time and grief together had bowed the mother almost to the verge of the grave. The one knew not the other, until little Resa came between; little Resa, who looked her sister's olden self, blooming in the sweetness of seventeen. Nothing to her was the magnificence of the beautiful guest; she only saw Hyldreda, the lost and found.

"Where hast thou been?" said the mother, doubtfully, when in answer to all their caresses, the stately lady only looked on them with a proud smile; "Who gave thee those grand dresses, and put the matron's vail upon thy hair?"

"I am the Hill-king's wife," said Hyldreda. "I dwell in a gorgeous palace, and sit on a queen's throne."

"God preserve thee!" answered the mother. But Hyldreda turned away, for Kong Tolv had commanded her never to hear or utter the holy Name. She began to inquire about her long-forgotten home, but half-carelessly, as if she had no interest in it now.

"And who was it," she asked, "that wept on the hill-side until the tears dropped through, staining my palace walls?"

"I," answered Resa, blushing; and then Hyldreda perceived that, young as she was, the girl wore the matron's head-tire. "I, sitting there with my babe, wept to think of my poor sister who died long ago, and never knew the sweetness of wifehood and motherhood. And almost it grieved me, to think that my love had blotted out the bitterness of her memory even from the heart of Esbern Lynge."

At the name, proudly laughed the elder sister, "Take thy husband, and be happy, girl; I envy thee not; I am the wife of the great Hill-king."

"And does thy lord love thee? Does he sit beside thee at eve, and let thee lean thy tired head on his breast, as Esbern does with me? And hast thou young children dancing about thy feet, and a little blue-eyed one to creep dove-like to thy heart at nights, as mine does? Say, dear sister, art thou as happy as I?"

Hyldreda paused. Earth's sweet ties arose before her, and the grandeur of her lot seemed only loneliness. Forgetting her lord's command, she sighed, she even wept one regretful tear; and that moment in her presence stood Kong Tolv.

"Kill me, but save my mother, my sister," cried the wife, with a broken heart. The prayer was needless; *they* saw not the Elle-king, and he marked not them—he only bore away Hyldreda, singing mockingly in her ear something of the same rhyme which had bound her his:

> "Complainest thou here all drearily—
>   Camest thou not of thyself in the hill to me?
>   And stayest thou here thy lot to deplore?
>   Camest thou not of thyself in at my door?"

When the mother and sister of Hyldreda lifted up their eyes, they saw nothing but a cloud of dust sweeping past the cottage-door, they heard nothing but the ancient elder-tree howling aloud as its branches were tossed about in a gust of wintry wind.

Kong Tolv took back to the hill his mortal bride. There he set her in a golden chair, and brought to her to drink a silver horn of elfin-wine, in the which he had dropped an ear of wheat. At the first draught, she forgot the village where she had dwelt—at the second, she forgot the sister who had been her darling—at the third, she forgot the mother who bore her. Again she rejoiced in the glories of the fairy-palace, and in the life of never-ceasing pleasure.

Month after month rolled by—by her scarce counted, or counted only in jest, as she would number a handful of roses, all held so fast and sure, that none could fall or fade; or as she would mark one by one the little waves of a rivulet whose source was eternally flowing.

Hyldreda thought no more of any earthly thing, until there came, added to her own, a young, new life. When her beautiful babe, half-elf, half-mortal, nestled in her woman's breast, it wakened there the fountain of human love, and of long-forgotten memories.

"Oh! let me go home once—once more," she implored of her lord. "Let me go to ask my mother's forgiveness, and above all, to crave the church's blessing on this my innocent babe."

Kong Tolv frowned, and then looked sad. For it is the one great sorrow of the Elle-people, that they, with all others of the elfin race, are shut out from Heaven's mercy. Therefore do they often steal mortal wives, and strive to have their children christened according to holy rite, in order to participate in the blessings granted to the offspring of Adam.

"Do as thou wilt," the Hill-king answered; "but know, there awaits a penalty. In exchange for a soul, must be given a life."

His dark saying fell coldly on the heart of the young mother. It terrified her for a time, but soon the sweet strange wiles of her elfin-babe beguiled her into renewed happiness; so that her longing faded away.

The child grew not like a mortal child. An unearthly beauty was in its face; wondrous precocious signs marked it from its birth. Its baby-speech was very wisdom. Its baby-smile was full of thought. The mother read her olden soul— the pure soul that was hers of yore—in her infant's eyes.

One day when Hyldreda was following the child in its play, she noticed it disappear through what seemed the outlet of the fairy-palace, which outlet she herself had never been able to find. She forgot that her boy was of elfin as well as of mortal race. Out it passed, the mother eagerly pursuing, until she found herself with the child in a meadow near the village of Skjelskör, where years ago she had often played. It was on a Sunday morning, and cheerfully yet solemnly rang out the chapel-bells. All the sounds and sights of earth came back upon her, with a longing that would not be restrained.

In the white frozen grass, for it was wintertime, knelt the wife of Kong Tolv, holding fast to her bosom the elfin babe, who shivered at every blast of wind, yet, shivering, seemed to smile. Hyldreda knelt, until the chapel-bells ceased at service-time. And then there came bursting from her lips the long-sealed prayers, the prayers of her childhood. While she breathed them, the rich fairy garments crumbled from her, and she remained clad in the coarse dress she wore when Kong Tolv carried her away; save that it hung in miserable tatters, as if worn for years, and through its rents the icy wind pierced her bosom, so that the heart within might have sunk and died, but for the ever-abiding warmth of maternal love.

That told her how in one other mother's heart there must be warmth still.

"I will go home," she murmured, "I will say, 'Mother, take me in and save me, or else I die!'" And so, when the night closed, and all the villagers were safe at home, and none could mock at her and her misery, the poor desolate one crept to her mother's door.

It had been open to her even when she came in her pride; how would it be closed against her sorrow and humility? And was there ever a true mother's breast, that while life yet throbbed there, was not a refuge for a repentant child?

Hyldreda found shelter and rest. But the little elfin babe, unused to the air of earth, uttered continual moanings. At night, the strange eyes never closed, but looked at her with a dumb entreaty. And tenfold returned the mother's first desire, that her darling should become a "christened child."

Much the old grandame gloried in this, looking with distrust on the pining, withered babe. But keenly upon Hyldreda's memory came back the saying of Kong Tolv, that for a soul would be exchanged a life. It must be *hers*. That, doubtless, was the purchase; and thus had Heaven ordained the expiation of her sin. If so, meekly she would offer it, so that Heaven would admit into its mercy her beloved child.

It was in the night—in the cold white night, that the widow Kalm, with her daughter and the mysterious babe, came to the chapel of Skjelskör. All the way thither they had been followed by strange, unearthly noises; and as they passed beneath the oak-wood, it seemed as if the overhanging branches were transformed into giant hands, that evermore snatched at the child. But in vain; for the mother held it fast, and on its little breast she had laid the wooden cross which she herself used to wear when a girl. Bitterly the infant had wailed, but when they crossed the threshold of the chapel, it ceased, and a smile broke over its face—a smile pure and saintly, such as little children wear, lying in a sleep so beautiful that the bier seems like the cradle.

The mother beheld it, and thought, What if her foreboding should be true; that the moment which opened the gate of Heaven's mercy unto her babe, should close upon herself life and life's sweetnesses? But she felt no fear.

"Let me kiss thee once again, my babe, my darling!" she murmured; "perhaps I may never kiss thee more. Even now, I feel as if my eyes were growing dark, and thy little face were gliding from my sight. But I can let thee go, my sweet! God will take care of thee, and keep thee safe, even amidst this bitter world."

She clasped and kissed the child once more, and, kneeling, calm, but very pale, she awaited whatever might be her doom.

The priest, performing by stealth what he almost deemed a desecration of the hallowed rite, began to read the ceremony over the fairy babe. All the while, it looked at him with those mysterious eyes, so lately opened to the world, yet which seemed to express the emotions of a whole existence. But when the sprinkled water touched them, they closed, softly, slowly, like a blue flower at night.

The mother, still living, and full of thankful wonder that she did live, took from the priest's arms her recovered treasure, her Christian child. It lay all smiling, but it lifted not its eyes: the color was fading on its lips, and its little hands were growing cold. For it—not for her, had been the warning. It had rendered up its little life, and received an immortal soul.

For years after this, there abode in the village of Skjelskör a woman whom some people thought was an utter stranger, for none so grave, and at the same time so good, was ever known among the light-hearted people of Zealand. Others said that if any one could come back alive from fairy land, the woman must be Hyldreda Kalm. But as later generations arose, they mocked at the story of Kong Tolv and the palace under the hill, and considered the whole legend but an allegory, the moral of which they did not fail to preach to their fair young daughters continually.

Nevertheless, this woman had surely once lived, for her memory, embalmed by its own rich virtues, long lingered in the place where she had dwelt. She must have died there, too, for they pointed out her grave, and a smaller one beside it, though whose that was, none knew. There was a tradition that when she died—it was on a winter night, and the clock was just striking twelve—there arose a stormy wind which swept through the neighboring oak-wood, laying every tree prostrate on the ground. And from that hour there was no record of the Elle-people or the mighty Kong Tolv having been ever again seen in Zealand.

THE SHINING PYRAMID

Arthur Machen

first published in *The Unknown World* (May 1895)

1. THE ARROW-HEAD CHARACTER

"Haunted, you said?"

"Yes, haunted. Don't you remember, when I saw you three years ago, you told me about your place in the west with the ancient woods hanging all about it, and the wild, domed hills, and the ragged land? It has always remained a sort of enchanted picture in my mind as I sit at my desk and hear the traffic rattling in the Street in the midst of whirling London. But when did you come up?"

"The fact is, Dyson, I have only just got out of the train. I drove to the station early this morning and caught the 10.45."

"Well, I am very glad you looked in on me. How have you been getting on since we last met? There is no Mrs. Vaughan, I suppose?"

"No," said Vaughan, "I am still a hermit, like yourself. I have done nothing but loaf about."

Vaughn had lit his pipe and sat in the elbow chair, fidgeting and glancing about him in a somewhat dazed and restless manner. Dyson had wheeled round his chair when his visitor entered and sat with one arm fondly reclining on the desk of his bureau, and touching the litter of manuscript.

"And you are still engaged in the old task?" said Vaughan, pointing to the pile of papers and the teeming pigeon-holes.

"Yes, the vain pursuit of literature, as idle as alchemy, and as entrancing. But you have come to town for some time I suppose; what shall we do tonight?"

"Well, I rather wanted you to try a few days with me down in the west. It would do you a lot of good. I'm sure."

"You are very kind, Vaughan, but London in September is hard to leave. Doré could not have designed anything more wonderful and mystic than Oxford Street as I saw it the other evening; the sunset flaming, the blue haze transmuting the plain street into a road 'far in the spiritual city.'"

"I should like you to come down though. You would enjoy roaming over our hills. Does this racket go on all day and night? It quite bewilders me; I wonder how you can work through it. I am sure you would revel in the great peace of my old home among the woods."

Vaughan lit his pipe again, and looked anxiously at Dyson to see if his inducements had had any effect, but the man of letters shook his head, smiling, and vowed in his heart a firm allegiance to the streets.

"You cannot tempt me," he said.

"Well, you may be right. Perhaps, after all, I was wrong to speak of the peace of the country. There, when a tragedy does occur, it is like a stone thrown into a pond; the circles of disturbance keep on widening, and it seems as if the water would never be still again."

"Have you ever any tragedies where you are?"

"I can hardly say that. But I was a good deal disturbed about a month ago by something that happened; it may or may not have been a tragedy in the usual sense of the word."

"What was the occurrence?"

"Well, the fact is a girl disappeared in a way which seems highly mysterious. Her parents, people of the name of Trevor, are well-to-do farmers, and their eldest daughter Annie was a sort of village beauty; she was really remarkably handsome. One afternoon she thought she would go and see her aunt, a widow who farms her own land, and as the two houses are only about five or six miles apart, she started off, telling her parents she would take the short cut over the hills. She never got to her aunt's, and she never was seen again. That's putting it in a few words."

"What an extraordinary thing! I suppose there are no disused mines, are there, on the hills? I don't think you quite run to anything so formidable as a precipice?"

"No; the path the girl must have taken had no pitfalls of any description; it is just a track over wild, bare hillside, far, even from a byroad. One may walk for miles without meeting a soul, but it is perfectly safe."

"And what do people say about it?"

"Oh, they talk nonsense—among themselves. You have no notion as to how superstitious English cottagers are in out-of-the-way parts like mine. They are as bad as the Irish, every whit, and even more secretive."

"But what do they say?"

"Oh, the poor girl is supposed to have 'gone with the fairies,' or to have been 'taken by the fairies.' Such stuff!" he went on, "one would laugh if it were not for the real tragedy of the case."

Dyson looked somewhat interested.

"Yes," he said, "'fairies' certainly strike a little curiously on the ear in these days. But what do the police say? I presume they do not accept the fairy-tale hypothesis?"

"No; but they seem quite at fault. What I am afraid of is that Annie Trevor must have fallen in with some scoundrels on her way. Castletown is a large seaport, you know, and some of the worst of the foreign sailors occasionally desert their ships and go on the tramp up and down the country.

Not many years ago a Spanish sailor named Garcia murdered a whole family for the sake of plunder that was not worth sixpence. They are hardly human, some of these fellows, and I am dreadfully afraid the poor girl must have come to an awful end."

"But no foreign sailor was seen by anyone about the country?"

"No; there is certainly that; and of course country people are quick to notice anyone whose appearance and dress are a little out of the common. Still it seems as if my theory were the only possible explanation."

"There are no data to go upon," said Dyson, thoughtfully. "There was no question of a love affair, or anything of the kind, I suppose?"

"Oh, no, not a hint of such a thing. I am sure if Annie were alive she would have contrived to let her mother know of her safety."

"No doubt, no doubt. Still it is barely possible that she is alive and yet unable to communicate with her friends. But all this must have disturbed you a good deal."

"Yes, it did; I hate a mystery, and especially a mystery which is probably the veil of horror. But frankly, Dyson, I want to make a clean breast of it; I did not come here to tell you all this."

"Of course not," said Dyson, a little surprised at Vaughan's uneasy manner. "You came to have a chat on more cheerful topics."

"No, I did not. What I have been telling you about happened a month ago, but something which seems likely to affect me more personally has taken place within the last few days, and to be quite plain, I came up to town with the idea that you might be able to help me. You recollect that curious case you spoke to me about on our last meeting; something about a spectacle-maker."

"Oh, yes, I remember that. I know I was quite proud of my acumen at the time; even to this day the police have no idea why those peculiar yellow spectacles were wanted. But, Vaughan, you really look quite put out; I hope there is nothing serious?"

"No, I think I have been exaggerating, and I want you to reassure me. But what has happened is very odd."

"And what has happened?"

"I am sure that you will laugh at me, but this is the story. You must know there is a path, a right of way, that goes through my land, and to be precise, close to the wall of the kitchen garden. It is not used by many people; a woodman now and again finds it useful, and five or six children who go to school in the village pass twice a day. Well, a few days ago I was taking a walk about the place before breakfast, and I happened to stop to fill my pipe just by the large doors in the garden wall. The wood, I must tell you, comes to within a few feet of the wall, and the track I spoke of runs right in the shadow of the trees. I thought the shelter from a brisk wind that was blowing rather pleasant, and I stood there smoking with my eyes on the ground. Then something caught my attention. Just under the wall, on the short grass; a number of small flints were arranged in a pattern; something like this": and

Mr. Vaughan caught at a pencil and piece of paper, and dotted down a few strokes.

"You see," he went on, "there were, I should think, twelve little stones neatly arranged in lines, and spaced at equal distances, as I have shown it on the paper. They were pointed stones, and the points were very carefully directed one way."

"Yes," said Dyson, without much interest, "no doubt the children you have mentioned had been playing there on their way from school. Children, as you know, are very fond of making such devices with oyster shells or flints or flowers, or with whatever comes in their way."

"So I thought; I just noticed these flints were arranged in a sort of pattern and then went on. But the next morning I was taking the same round, which, as a matter of fact, is habitual with me, and again I saw at the same spot a device in flints. This time it was really a curious pattern; something like the spokes of a wheel, all meeting at a common centre, and this centre formed by a device which looked like a bowl; all, you understand done in flints."

"You are right," said Dyson, "that seems odd enough. Still it is reasonable that your half-a-dozen school children are responsible for these fantasies in stone."

"Well, I thought I would set the matter at rest. The children pass the gate every evening at half-past five, and I walked by at six, and found the device just as I had left it in the morning. The next day I was up and about at a quarter to seven, and I found the whole thing had been changed. There was a pyramid outlined in flints upon the grass. The children I saw going by an hour and a half later, and they ran past the spot without glancing to right or left. In the evening I watched them going home, and this morning when I got to the gate at six o'clock there was a thing like a half moon waiting for me."

"So then the series runs thus: firstly ordered lines, then, the device of the spokes and the bowl, then the pyramid, and finally, this morning, the half moon. That is the order, isn't it?"

"Yes; that is right. But do you know it has made me feel very uneasy? I suppose it seems absurd, but I can't help thinking that some kind of signaling is going on under my nose, and that sort of thing is disquieting."

"But what have you to dread? You have no enemies?"

"No; but I have some very valuable old plate."

"You are thinking of burglars then?" said Dyson, with an accent of considerable interest, "but you must know your neighbors. Are there any suspicious characters about?"

"Not that I am aware of. But you remember what I told you of the sailors."

"Can you trust your servants?"

"Oh, perfectly. The plate is preserved in a strong room; the butler, an old family servant, alone knows where the key is kept. There is nothing wrong there. Still, everybody is aware that I have a lot of old silver, and all country folks are given to gossip. In that way information may have got abroad in very undesirable quarters."

"Yes, but I confess there seems something a little unsatisfactory in the burglar theory. Who is signaling to whom? I cannot see my way to accepting such an explanation. What put the plate into your head in connection with these flints signs, or whatever one may call them?"

"It was the figure of the Bowl," said Vaughan. "I happen to possess a very large and very valuable Charles II punch-bowl. The chasing is really exquisite, and the thing is worth a lot of money. The sign I described to you was exactly the same shape as my punch-bowl."

"A queer coincidence certainly. But the other figures or devices: you have nothing shaped like a pyramid?"

"Ah, you will think that queerer. As it happens, this punch-bowl of mine, together with a set of rare old ladles, is kept in a mahogany chest of a pyramidal shape. The four sides slope upwards, the narrow towards the top."

"I confess all this interests me a good deal," said Dyson. "let us go on then. What about the other figures; how about the Army, as we may call the first sign, and the Crescent or Half moon?"

"Ah, there is no reference that I can make out of these two. Still, you see I have some excuse for curiosity at all events. I should be very vexed to lose any of the old plate; nearly all the pieces have been in the family for generations. And I cannot get it out of my head that some scoundrels mean to rob me, and are communicating with one another every night."

"Frankly," said Dyson, "I can make nothing of it; I am as much in the dark as yourself. Your theory seems certainly the only possible explanation, and yet the difficulties are immense."

He leaned back in his chair, and the two men faced each other, frowning, and perplexed by so bizarre a problem.

"By the way," said Dyson, after a long pause, "what is your geological formation down there?"

Mr. Vaughan looked up, a good deal surprised by the question.

"Old red sandstone and limestone, I believe," he said. "We are just beyond the coal measures, you know."

"But surely there are no flints either in the sandstone or the limestone?"

"No, I never see any flints in the fields. I confess that did strike me as a little curious."

"I should think so! It is very important. By the way, what size were the flints used in making these devices?"

"I happen to have brought one with me; I took it this morning."

"From the Half moon?"

"Exactly. Here it is."

He handed over a small flint, tapering to a point, and about three inches in length.

Dyson's face blazed up with excitement as he took the thing from Vaughan.

"Certainly," he said, after a moment's pause, "you have some curious neighbors in your country. I hardly think they can harbor any designs on your punch-bowl. Do you know this is a flint arrowhead of vast antiquity, and not only that, but an arrow-head of a unique kind? I have seen specimens from all parts of the world, but there are features about this thing that are quite peculiar." He laid down his pipe, and took out a book from a drawer.

"We shall just have time to catch the 5.45 to Castletown," he said.

2. THE EYES ON THE WALL

Mr. Dyson drew in a long breath of the air of the hills and felt all the enchantment of the scene about him. It was very early morning, and he stood on the terrace in the front of the house.

Vaughan's ancestor had built on the lower slope of a great hill, in the shelter of a deep and ancient wood that gathered on three sides about the house, and on the fourth side, the southwest, the land fell gently away and sank to the valley, where a brook wound in and out in mystic esses, and the dark and gleaming alders tracked the stream's course to the eye. On the terrace in the sheltered place no wind blew, and far beyond, the trees were still. Only one sound broke in upon the silence, and Dyson heard the noise of the brook singing far below, the song of clear and shining water rippling over the stones, whispering and murmuring as it sank to dark deep pools.

Across the stream, just below the house, rose a grey stone bridge, vaulted and buttressed, a fragment of the Middle Ages, and then beyond the bridge the hills rose again, vast and rounded like bastions, covered here and there with dark woods and thickets of undergrowth, but the heights were all bare of trees, showing only grey turf and patches of bracken, touched here and there with the gold of fading fronds; Dyson looked to the north and south, and still he saw the wall of the hills, and the ancient woods, and the stream drawn in and out between them; all grey and dim with morning mist beneath a grey sky in a hushed and haunted air.

Mr. Vaughan's voice broke in upon the silence.

"I thought you would be too tired to be about so early," he said. "I see you are admiring the view. It is very pretty, isn't it, though I suppose old Meyrick Vaughan didn't think much about the scenery when he built the house. A queer grey, old place, isn't it?"

"Yes, and how it fits into the surroundings; it seems of a piece with the grey hills and the grey bridge below."

"I am afraid I have brought you down on false pretenses, Dyson," said Vaughan, as they began to walk up and down the terrace. "I have been to the place, and there is not a sign of anything this morning."

"Ah, indeed. Well, suppose we go round together."

They walked across the lawn and went by a path through the ilex shrubbery to the back of the house. There Vaughan pointed out the track leading down to the valley and up to the heights above the wood, and presently they stood beneath the garden wall, by the door.

"Here, you see, it was," said Vaughan, pointing to a spot on the turf. "I was standing just where you are now that morning I first saw the flints."

"Yes, quite so. That morning it was the Army, as I call it; then the Bowl, then the Pyramid, and, yesterday, the Half moon. What a queer old stone that is," he went on, pointing to a block of limestone rising out of the turf just beneath the wall. 'It looks like a sort of dwarf pillar, but I suppose it is natural."

"Oh, yes, I think so. I imagine it was brought here, though, as we stand on the red sandstone. No doubt it was used as a foundation stone for some older building."

"Very likely," Dyson was peering about him attentively, looking from the ground to the wall, and from the wall to the deep wood that hung almost over the garden and made the place dark even in the morning.

"Look here," said Dyson at length, "it is certainly a case of children this time. Look at that." He was bending down and staring at the dull red surface of the mellowed bricks of the wall.

Vaughan came up and looked hard where Dyson's finger was pointing, and could scarcely distinguish a faint mark in deeper red.

"What is it?" he said. "I can make nothing of it."

"Look a little more closely. Don't you see it is an attempt to draw the human eye?"

"Ah, now I see what you mean. My sight is not very sharp. Yes, so it is, it is meant for an eye, no doubt, as you say. I thought the children learnt drawing at school."

"Well, it is an odd eye enough. Do you notice the peculiar almond shape; almost like the eye of a Chinaman?"

Dyson looked meditatively at the work of the undeveloped artist, and scanned the wall again, going down on his knees in the minuteness of his inquisition.

"I should like very much," he said at length, "to know how a child in this out of the way place could have any idea of the shape of the Mongolian eye. You see the average child has a very distinct impression of the subject; he draws a circle, or something like a circle, and put a dot in the centre. I don't think any child imagines that the eye is really made like that; it's just a convention of infantile art. But this almond-shaped thing puzzles me extremely. Perhaps it may be derived from a gilt Chinaman on a tea-canister in the grocer's shop. Still that's hardly likely."

"But why are you so sure it was done by a child?"

"Why! Look at the height. These old-fashioned bricks are little more than two inches thick; there are twenty courses from the ground to the sketch if we call it so; that gives a height of three and a half feet. Now, just imagine you are going to draw something on this wall. Exactly; your pencil, if you had one, would touch the wall somewhere on the level with your eyes, that is, more than five feet from the ground. It seems, therefore, a very simple deduction to conclude that this eye on the wall was drawn by a child about ten years old."

"Yes, I had not thought of that. Of course one of the children must have done it."

"I suppose so; and yet as I said, there is something singularly unchildlike about those two lines, and the eyeball itself, you see, is almost an oval. To my mind, the thing has an odd, ancient air; and a touch that is not altogether pleasant. I cannot help fancying that if we could see a whole face from the same hand it would not be altogether agreeable. However, that is nonsense, after all, and we are not getting farther in our investigations. It is odd that the flint series has come to such an abrupt end."

The two men walked away towards the house, and as they went in at the porch there was a break in the grey sky, and a gleam of sunshine on the grey hill before them.

All the day Dyson prowled meditatively about the fields and woods surrounding the house. He was thoroughly and completely puzzled by the trivial circumstances he proposed to elucidate, and now he again took the flint arrow-head from his pocket, turning it over and examining it with deep attention. There was something about the thing that was altogether different from the specimens he had seen at the museums and private collections; the shape was of a distinct type, and around the edge there was a line of little punctured dots, apparently a suggestion of ornament. Who, thought Dyson, could possess such things in so remote a place; and who, possessing the flints, could have put them to the fantastic use of designing meaningless figures under Vaughan's garden wall? The rank absurdity of the whole affair offended him unutterably; and as one theory after another rose in his mind only to be rejected, he felt strongly tempted to take the next train back to town. He had seen the silver plate which Vaughan treasured, and had inspected the punch-bowl, the gem of the collection, with close attention; and what he saw and his interview with the butler convinced him that a plot to rob the strong box was out of the limits of enquiry. The chest in which the bowl was kept, a heavy piece of mahogany, evidently dating from the beginning of the century, was certainly strongly suggestive of a pyramid, and Dyson was at first inclined to the inept maneuvers of the detective, but a little sober thought convinced him of the impossibility of the burglary hypothesis, and he cast wildly about for something more satisfying. He asked Vaughan if there were any gipsies in the neighborhood, and heard that the Romany had not been seen for years. This dashed him a good deal, as he knew the gipsy habit of leaving queer hieroglyphics on the line of march, and had been much elated when the thought occurred to him. He was facing Vaughan by the old-fashioned hearth when he put the question, and leaned back in his chair in disgust at the destruction of his theory.

"It is odd," said Vaughan, "but the gipsies never trouble us here. Now and then the farmers find traces of fires in the wildest part of the hills, but nobody seems to know who the fire-lighters are."

"Surely that looks like gipsies?"

"No, not in such places as those. Tinkers and gipsies and wanderers of all sorts stick to the roads and don't go very far from the farmhouses."

"Well, I can make nothing of it. I saw the children going by this afternoon, and, as you say, they ran straight on. So we shall have no more eyes on the wall at all events."

"No, I must waylay them one of these days and find out who is the artist."

The next morning when Vaughan strolled in his usual course from the lawn to the back of the house he found Dyson already awaiting him by the garden door, and evidently in a state of high excitement, for he beckoned furiously with his hand, and gesticulated violently.

"What is it?" asked Vaughan. "The flints again?"

"No; but look here, look at the wall. There; don't you see it?"

"There's another of those eyes!"

"Exactly. Drawn, you see, at a little distance from the first, almost on the same level, but slightly lower."

"What on earth is one to make of it? It couldn't have been done by the children; it wasn't there last night, and they won't pass for another hour. What can it mean?"

"I think the very devil is at the bottom of all this," said Dyson. "Of course, one cannot resist the conclusion that these infernal almond eyes are to be set down to the same agency as the devices in the arrow-heads; and where that conclusion is to lead us is more than I can tell. For my part, I have to put a strong check on my imagination, or it would run wild."

"Vaughan," he said, as they turned away from the wall, "has it struck you that there is one point—a very curious point—in common between the figures done in flints and the eyes drawn on the wall?"

"What is that?" asked Vaughan, on whose face there had fallen a certain shadow of indefinite dread.

"It is this. We know that the signs of the Army, the Bowl, the Pyramid, and the Half moon must have been done at night. Presumably they were meant to be seen at night. Well, precisely the same reasoning applies to those eyes on the wall."

"I do not quite see your point."

"Oh, surely. The nights are dark just now, and have been very cloudy, I know, since I came down. Moreover, those overhanging trees would throw that wall into deep shadow even on a clear night."

"Well?"

"What struck me was this. What very peculiarly sharp eyesight, they, whoever 'they' are, must have to be able to arrange arrow-heads in intricate order in the blackest shadow of the wood, and then draw the eyes on the wall without a trace of bungling, or a false line."

"I have read of persons confined in dungeons for many years who have been able to see quite well in the dark," said Vaughan.

"Yes," said Dyson, "there was the abbé in Monte Cristo. But it is a singular point."

3. The Search for the Bowl

"Who was that old man that touched his hat to you just now?" said Dyson, as they came to the bend of the lane near the house.

"Oh, that was old Trevor. He looks very broken, poor old fellow."

"Who is Trevor?"

"Don't you remember? I told you the story that afternoon I came to your rooms—about a girl named Annie Trevor, who disappeared in the most inexplicable manner about five weeks ago. That was her father."

"Yes, yes, I recollect now. To tell the truth I had forgotten all about it. And nothing has been heard of the girl?"

"Nothing whatever. The police are quite at fault."

"I am afraid I did not pay very much attention to the details you gave me. Which way did the girl go?"

"Her path would take her right across those wild hills above the house: the nearest point in the track must be about two miles from here."

"Is it near that little hamlet I saw yesterday?"

"You mean Croesyceiliog, where the children came from? No; it goes more to the north."

"Ah, I have never been that way."

They went into the house, and Dyson shut himself up in his room, sunk deep in doubtful thought, but yet with the shadow of a suspicion growing within him that for a while haunted his brain, all vague and fantastic, refusing to take definite form. He was sitting by the open window and looking out on the valley and saw, as if in a picture, the intricate winding of the brook, the grey bridge, and the vast hills rising beyond; all still and without a breath of wind to stir the mystic hanging woods, and the evening sunshine glowed warm on the bracken, and down below a faint mist, pure white, began to rise from the stream. Dyson sat by the window as the day darkened and the huge bastioned hills loomed vast and vague, and the woods became dim and more shadowy: and the fancy that had seized him no longer appeared altogether impossible. He passed the rest of the evening in a reverie, hardly hearing what Vaughan said; and when he took his candle in the hall, he paused a moment before bidding his friend good-night.

"I want a good rest," he said. "I have got some work to do tomorrow."

"Some writing, you mean?"

"No. I am going to look for the Bowl."

"The Bowl! If you mean my punch-bowl, that is safe in the chest."

"I don't mean the punch-bowl. You may take my word for it that your plate has never been threatened. No; I will not bother you with any suppositions. We shall in all probability have something much stronger than suppositions before long. Good-night, Vaughan."

The next morning Dyson set off after breakfast. He took the path by the garden wall, and noted that there were now eight of the weird almond eyes dimly outlined on the brick.

"Six days more," he said to himself, but as he thought over the theory he had formed, he shrank, in spite of strong conviction, from such a wildly incredible fancy. He struck up through the dense shadows of the wood, and at length came out on the bare hillside, and climbed higher and higher over the slippery turf, keeping well to the north, and following the indications given him by Vaughan. As he went on, he seemed to mount ever higher above the world of human life and customary things; to his right he looked at a fringe of orchard and saw a faint blue smoke rising like a pillar; there was the hamlet from which the children came to school, and there the only sign of life, for the woods embowered and concealed Vaughan's old grey house. As he reached what seemed the summit of the hill, he realized for the first time the desolate loneliness and strangeness of the land; there was nothing but grey sky and grey hill, a high, vast plain that seemed to stretch on for ever and ever, and a faint glimpse of a blue-peaked mountain far away and to the north. At length he came to the path, a slight track scarcely noticeable, and from its position and by what Vaughan had told him he knew that it was the way the lost girl, Annie Trevor, must have taken. He followed the path on the bare hill-top, noticing the great limestone rocks that cropped out of the turf, grim and hideous, and of an aspect as forbidding as an idol of the South Seas; and suddenly he halted, astonished, although he had found what he searched for.

Almost without warning the ground shelved suddenly away on all sides, and Dyson looked down into a circular depression, which might well have been a Roman amphitheater, and the ugly crags of limestone rimmed it round as if with a broken wall. Dyson walked round the hollow, and noted the position of the stones, and then turned on his way home.

"This," he thought to himself, "is more than curious. The Bowl is discovered, but where is the Pyramid?"

"My dear Vaughan," he said, when he got back, "I may tell you that I have found the Bowl, and that is all I shall tell you for the present. We have six days of absolute inaction before us; there is really nothing to be done."

4. The Secret of the Pyramid

"**I** have just been round the garden," said Vaughan one morning. "I have been counting those infernal eyes, and I find there are fourteen of them. For heaven's sake, Dyson, tell me what the meaning of it all is."

"I should be very sorry to attempt to do so. I may have guessed this or that, but I always make it a principle to keep my guesses to myself. Besides, it is really not worth while anticipating events; you will remember my telling you that we had six days of inaction before us? Well, this is the sixth day, and the last of idleness. Tonight, I propose we take a stroll."

"A stroll! Is that all the action you mean to take?"

"Well, it may show you some very curious things. To be plain, I want you to start with me at nine o'clock this evening for the hills. We may have to be out all night, so you had better wrap up well, and bring some of that brandy."

"Is it a joke?" asked Vaughan, who was bewildered with strange events and strange surmises.

"No, I don't think there is much joke in it. Unless I am much mistaken we shall find a very serious explanation of the puzzle. You will come with me, I am sure?"

"Very good. Which way do you want to go?"

"By the path you told me of; the path Annie Trevor is supposed to have taken."

Vaughan looked white at the mention of the girl's name.

"I did not think you were on that track," he said. "I thought it was the affair of those devices in flint and of the eyes on the wall that you were engaged on. It's no good saying any more, but I will go with you."

At a quarter to nine that evening the two men set out, taking the path through the wood, and up the hill-side. It was a dark and heavy night, the sky was thick with clouds, and the valley full of mist, and all the way they seemed to walk in a world of shadow and gloom, hardly speaking, and afraid to break the haunted silence. They came out at last on the steep hill-side, and instead of the oppression of the wood there was the long, dim sweep of the turf, and higher, the fantastic limestone rocks hinted horror through the darkness, and the wind sighed as it passed across the mountain to the sea, and in its passage beat chill about their hearts. They seemed to walk on and on for hours, and the dim outline of the hill still stretched before them, and the haggard rocks still loomed through the darkness, when suddenly Dyson whispered, drawing his breath quickly, and coming close to his companion:

"Here," he said, "we will lie down. I do not think there is anything yet."

"I know the place," said Vaughan, after a moment. "I have often been by in the daytime. The country people are afraid to come here, I believe; it is supposed to be a fairies' castle, or something of the kind. But why on earth have we come here?"

"Speak a little lower," said Dyson. "It might not do us any good if we are overheard."

"Overheard here! There is not a soul within three miles of us."

"Possibly not; indeed, I should say certainly not. But there might be a body somewhat nearer."

"I don't understand you in the least," said Vaughan, whispering to humor Dyson, "but why have we come here?"

"Well, you see this hollow before us is the Bowl. I think we had better not talk even in whispers."

They lay full length upon the turf; the rock between their faces and the Bowl, and now and again, Dyson, slouching his dark, soft hat over his forehead, put out the glint of an eye, and in a moment drew back, not daring to take a prolonged view. Again he laid an ear to the ground and listened, and the hours went by, and the darkness seemed to blacken, and the faint sigh of the wind was the only sound.

Vaughan grew impatient with this heaviness of silence, this watching for indefinite terror; for to him there was no shape or form of apprehension, and he began to think the whole vigil a dreary farce.

"How much longer is this to last?" he whispered to Dyson, and Dyson who had been holding his breath in the agony of attention put his mouth to Vaughan's ear and said:

"Will you listen?" with pauses between each syllable, and in the voice with which the priest pronounces the awful words.

Vaughan caught the ground with his hands, and stretched forward, wondering what he was to hear. At first there was nothing, and then a low and gentle noise came very softly from the Bowl, a faint sound, almost indescribable, but as if one held the tongue against the roof of the mouth and expelled the breath. He listened eagerly and presently the noise grew louder, and became a strident and horrible hissing as if the pit beneath boiled with fervent heat, and Vaughan, unable to remain in suspense any longer, drew his cap half over his face in imitation of Dyson, and looked down to the hollow below.

It did, in truth, stir and seethe like an infernal caldron. The whole of the sides and bottom tossed and writhed with vague and restless forms that passed to and fro without the sound of feet, and gathered thick here and there and seemed to speak to one another in those tones of horrible sibilance, like the hissing of snakes, that he had heard. It was as if the sweet turf and the cleanly earth had suddenly become quickened with some foul writhing growth. Vaughan could not draw back his face, though he felt Dyson's finger touch him, but he peered into the quaking mass and saw faintly that there were things like faces and human limbs, and yet he felt his inmost soul chill with the sure belief that no fellow soul or human thing stirred in all that tossing and hissing host. He looked aghast, choking back sobs of horror, and at length the loathsome forms gathered thickest about some vague object in the middle of the hollow, and the hissing of their speech grew more venomous, and he saw in the uncertain light the abominable limbs, vague and yet too plainly seen, writhe and intertwine, and he thought he heard, very faint, a low human moan striking through the noise of speech that was not of man. At his heart something seemed to whisper ever "the worm of corruption, the worm that dieth not," and grotesquely the image was pictured to his imagination of a piece of putrid offal stirring through and through with bloated and horrible creeping things. The writhing of the dusky limbs continued, they seemed clustered round the dark form in the middle of the hollow, and the sweat dripped and poured off Vaughan's forehead, and fell cold on his hand beneath his face.

Then, it seemed done in an instant, the loathsome mass melted and fell away to the sides of the Bowl, and for a moment Vaughan saw in the middle of the hollow the tossing of human arms.

But a spark gleamed beneath, a fire kindled, and as the voice of a woman cried out loud in a shrill scream of utter anguish and terror, a great pyramid of flame spired up like a bursting of a pent fountain, and threw a blaze of light upon the whole mountain. In that instant Vaughan saw the myriads beneath; the things made in the form of men but stunted like children hideously deformed, the faces with the almond eyes burning with evil and unspeakable lusts; the ghastly yellow of the mass of naked flesh and then as if by magic the place was empty, while the fire roared and crackled, and the flames shone abroad.

"You have seen the Pyramid," said Dyson in his ear, "the Pyramid of fire."

5. The Little People

"Then you recognize the thing?"

"Certainly. It is a brooch that Annie Trevor used to wear on Sundays; I remember the pattern. But where did you find it? You don't mean to say that you have discovered the girl?"

"My dear Vaughan, I wonder you have not guessed where I found the brooch. You have not forgotten last night already?"

"Dyson," said the other, speaking very seriously, "I have been turning it over in my mind this morning while you have been out. I have thought about what I saw, or perhaps I should say about what I thought I saw, and the only conclusion I can come to is this, that the thing won't bear recollection. As men live, I have lived soberly and honestly, in the fear of God, all my days, and all I can do is believe that I suffered from some monstrous delusion, from some phantasmagoria of the bewildered senses. You know we went home together in silence, not a word passed between us as to what I fancied I saw; had we not better agree to keep silence on the subject? When I took my walk in the peaceful morning sunshine, I thought all the earth seemed full of praise, and passing by that wall I noticed there were no more signs recorded, and I blotted out those that remained. The mystery is over, and we can live quietly again. I think some poison has been working for the last few weeks; I have trod on the verge of madness, but I am sane now."

Mr. Vaughan had spoken earnestly, and bent forward in his chair and glanced at Dyson with something of entreaty.

"My dear Vaughan," said the other, after a pause, "what's the use of this? It is much too late to take that tone; we have gone too deep. Besides you know as well as I that there is no delusion in the case; I wish there were with all my heart. No, in justice to myself I must tell you the whole story, so far as I know it."

"Very good," said Vaughan with a sigh, "if you must, you must."

"Then," said Dyson, "we will begin with the end if you please. I found this brooch you have just identified in the place we have called the Bowl. There was a heap of grey ashes, as if a fire had been burning, indeed, the embers were still hot, and this brooch was lying on the ground, just outside the range of the flame. It must have dropped accidentally from the dress of the person who was wearing it. No, don't interrupt me; we can pass now to the beginning, as we have had the end. Let us go back to that day you came to see me in my rooms in London. So far as I can remember, soon after you came in you mentioned, in a somewhat casual manner, that an unfortunate and mysterious incident had occurred in your part of the country; a girl named Annie Trevor had gone to see a relative, and had disappeared. I confess freely that what you said did not greatly interest me; there are so many reasons which may make it extremely convenient for a man and more especially a woman to vanish from the circle of their relations and friends. I suppose, if we were to consult the police, one would find that in London somebody disappears mysteriously every other week, and the officers would, no doubt, shrug their shoulders, and tell you that by the law of averages it could not be otherwise. So I was very culpably careless to your story, and besides, here is another reason for my lack of interest; your tale was inexplicable. You could only suggest a blackguard sailor on the tramp, but I discarded the explanation immediately.

"For many reasons, but chiefly because the occasional criminal, the amateur in brutal crime, is always found out, especially if he selects the country as the scene of his operations. You will remember the case of that Garcia you mentioned; he strolled into a railway station the day after the murder, his trousers covered with blood, and the works of the Dutch clock, his loot, tied in a neat parcel. So rejecting this, your only suggestion, the whole tale became, as I say, inexplicable, and, therefore, profoundly uninteresting. Yes, therefore, it is a perfectly valid conclusion. Do you ever trouble your head about problems which you know to be insoluble? Did you ever bestow much thought on the old puzzle of Achilles and the tortoise? Of course not, because you knew it was a hopeless quest, and so when you told me the story of a country girl who had disappeared I simply placed the whole thing down in the category of the insoluble, and thought no more about the matter. I was mistaken, so it has turned out; but if you remember, you immediately passed on to an affair which interested you more intensely, because personally, I need not go over the very singular narrative of the flint signs, at first I thought it all trivial, probably some children's game, and if not that a hoax of some sort; but your showing me the arrow-head awoke my acute interest. Here, I saw, there was something widely removed from the commonplace, and matter of real curiosity; and as soon as I came here I set to work to find the solution, repeating to myself again and again the signs you had described. First came the sign we have agreed to call the Army; a number of serried lines of flints, all pointing in the same way. Then the lines, like the spokes of a wheel, all converging towards the figure of a Bowl, then the triangle or Pyramid, and last of all the Half moon. I confess that I exhausted conjecture in my efforts to unveil this mystery, and as you will understand it was a duplex or rather triplex problem. For I had not merely to ask myself: what do these figures mean? but also, who can possibly be responsible for the designing of them? And again, who can possibly possess such valuable things, and knowing their value thus throw them down by the wayside? This line of thought led me to suppose that the person or persons in question did not know the value of unique flint arrow-heads, and yet this did not lead me far, for a well-educated man might easily be ignorant on such a subject. Then came the complication of the eye on the wall, and you remember that we could not avoid the conclusion that in the two cases the same agency was at work. The peculiar position of these eyes on the wall made me inquire if there was such a thing as a dwarf anywhere in the neighborhood, but I found that there was not, and I knew that the children who pass by every day had nothing to do with the matter. Yet I felt convinced that whoever drew the eyes must be from three and a half to four feet high, since, as I pointed out at the time, anyone who draws on a perpendicular surface chooses by instinct a spot about level with his face. Then again, there was the question of the peculiar shape of the eyes; that marked Mongolian character of which the English countryman could have no conception, and for a final cause of confusion the obvious fact that the designer or designers must be able practically to see in the dark. As you remarked, a man who has been confined for many years in an extremely dark cell or dungeon might acquire that power; but since the days of Edmond Dantès, where would such a prison be found in Europe? A sailor, who had been immured for a considerable period in some horrible Chinese oubliette, seemed the individual I was in search of, and though it looked improbable, it was not absolutely impossible that a sailor or, let us say, a man employed on shipboard, should be a dwarf. But how to account for my imaginary sailor being in possession of prehistoric arrow-heads? And the possession granted, what was the meaning and object of these mysterious signs of flint, and the almond-shaped eyes? Your theory of a contemplated burglary I saw, nearly from the first, to be quite untenable, and I confess I was utterly at a loss for a working hypothesis. It was a mere accident which put me on the track; we passed poor old Trevor, and your mention of his name and of the disappearance of his daughter, recalled the story which I had forgotten, or which remained unheeded. Here, then, I said to myself, is another problem, uninteresting, it is true, by itself; but what if it prove to be in relation with all these enigmas which torture me? I shut myself in my room, and endeavored to dismiss all prejudice from my mind, and I went over everything de novo, assuming for theory's sake that the disappearance of Annie Trevor had some connection with the flint signs and the eyes on the wall. This assumption did not lead me very far, and I was on the point of giving the whole problem up in despair, when a possible significance of the Bowl struck me. As you know there is a 'Devil's Punch-bowl' in Surrey, and I saw that the symbol might refer to some feature in the country. Putting the two extremes together, I determined to look for the Bowl near the path which the lost girl had taken, and you know how I found it. I interpreted the sign by what I knew, and read the first, the Army, thus:

"'there is to be a gathering or assembly at the Bowl in a fortnight (that is the Half moon) to see the Pyramid, or to build the Pyramid.'

"The eyes, drawn one by one, day by day, evidently checked off the days, and I knew that there would be fourteen and no more. Thus far the way seemed pretty plain; I would not trouble myself to inquire as to the nature of the assembly, or as to who was to assemble in the loneliest and most dreaded place among these lonely hills. In Ireland or China or the West of America the question would have been easily answered; a muster of the disaffected, the meeting of a secret society; vigilantes summoned to report: the thing would be simplicity itself; but in this quiet corner of England, inhabited by quiet folk, no such suppositions were possible for a moment. But I knew that I should have an opportunity of seeing and watching the assembly, and I did not care to perplex myself with hopeless research; and in place of reasoning a wild fancy entered into judgment: I remembered what people had said about Annie Trevor's disappearance, that she had been 'taken by the fairies.' I tell you, Vaughan, I am a sane man as you are, my brain is not, I trust, mere vacant space to let to any wild improbability, and I tried my best to thrust the fantasy away. And the hint came of the old name of fairies, 'the little people,' and the very probable belief that they represent a tradition of the prehistoric Turanian inhabitants of the country, who were cave dwellers: and then I realized with a shock that I was looking for a being under four feet in height, accustomed to live in darkness, possessing stone instruments, and familiar with the Mongolian cast of features! I say this, Vaughan, that I should be ashamed to hint at such visionary stuff to you, if it were not for that which you saw with your very eyes last night, and I say that I might doubt the evidence of my senses, if they were not confirmed by yours. But you and I cannot look each other in the face and pretend delusion; as you lay on the turf beside me I felt your flesh shrink and quiver, and I saw your eyes in the light of the flame. And so I tell you without any shame what was in my mind last night as we went through the wood and climbed the hill, and lay hidden beneath the rock.

"There was one thing that should have been most evident that puzzled me to the very last. I told you how I read the sign of the Pyramid; the assembly was to see a pyramid, and the true meaning of the symbol escaped me to the last moment. The old derivation from 'up, fire,' though false, should have set me on the track, but it never occurred to me.

"I think I need say very little more. You know we were quite helpless, even if we had foreseen what was to come. Ah, the particular place where these signs were displayed? Yes, that is a curious question. But this house is, so far as I can judge, in a pretty central situation amongst the hills; and possibly, who can say yes or no, that queer, old limestone pillar by your garden wall was a place of meeting before the Celt set foot in Britain. But there is one thing I must add: I don't regret our inability to rescue the wretched girl. You saw the appearance of those things that gathered thick and writhed in the Bowl; you may be sure that what lay bound in the midst of them was no longer fit for earth."

"So?" said Vaughan.

"So she passed in the Pyramid of Fire," said Dyson, "and they passed again to the underworld, to the places beneath the hills."

/

THE STOLEN CHILD

W. B. Yeats

from *The Wanderings of Oisin and Other Poems* (1889)

Where dips the rocky highland
Of Sleuth Wood in the lake,
There lies a leafy island
Where flapping herons wake
The drowsy water rats;
There we've hid our faery vats,
Full of berries
And of reddest stolen cherries.
    Come away, O human child!
    To the waters and the wild
    With a faery, hand in hand,
    For the world's more full of weeping than you can understand.

Where the wave of moonlight glosses
The dim gray sands with light,
Far off by furthest Rosses
We foot it all the night,
Weaving olden dances
Mingling hands and mingling glances
Till the moon has taken flight;
To and fro we leap
And chase the frothy bubbles,
While the world is full of troubles
And anxious in its sleep.
    Come away, O human child!
    To the waters and the wild
    With a faery, hand in hand,
    For the world's more full of weeping than you can understand.

Where the wandering water gushes
From the hills above Glen-Car,
In pools among the rushes
That scarce could bathe a star,
We seek for slumbering trout
And whispering in their ears
Give them unquiet dreams;
Leaning softly out
From ferns that drop their tears
Over the young streams.
 Come away, O human child!
 To the waters and the wild
 With a faery, hand in hand,
 For the world's more full of weeping than you can understand.

Away with us he's going,
The solemn-eyed:
He'll hear no more the lowing
Of the calves on the warm hillside
Or the kettle on the hob
Sing peace into his breast,
Or see the brown mice bob
Round and round the oatmeal chest.
 For he comes, the human child,
 To the waters and the wild
 With a faery, hand in hand,
 For the world's more full of weeping than he can understand.

THE CHILD THAT WENT WITH THE FAIRIES

J. Sheridan Le Fanu

first published in *All the Year Round* (February 1870)

Eastward of the old city of Limerick, about ten Irish miles under the range of mountains known as the Slieveelim hills, famous as having afforded Sarsfield a shelter among their rocks and hollows, when he crossed them in his gallant descent upon the cannon and ammunition of King William, on its way to the beleaguering army, there runs a very old and narrow road. It connects the Limerick road to Tipperary with the old road from Limerick to Dublin, and runs by bog and pasture, hill and hollow, straw-thatched village, and roofless castle, not far from twenty miles.

Skirting the healthy mountains of which I have spoken, at one part it becomes singularly lonely. For more than three Irish miles it traverses a deserted country. A wide, black bog, level as a lake, skirted with copse, spreads at the left, as you journey northward, and the long and irregular line of mountain rises at the right, clothed in heath, broken with lines of grey rock that resemble the bold and irregular outlines of fortifications, and riven with many a gully, expanding here and there into rocky and wooded glens, which open as they approach the road.

A scanty pasturage, on which browsed a few scattered sheep or kine, skirts this solitary road for some miles, and under shelter of a hillock, and of two or three great ash-trees, stood, not many years ago, the little thatched cabin of a widow named Mary Ryan.

Poor was this widow in a land of poverty. The thatch had acquired the grey tint and sunken outlines, that show how the alternations of rain and sun have told upon that perishable shelter.

But whatever other dangers threatened, there was one well provided against by the care of other times. Round the cabin stood half a dozen mountain ashes, as the rowans, inimical to witches, are there called. On the worn planks of the door were nailed two horse-shoes, and over the lintel and spreading along the thatch, grew, luxuriant, patches of that ancient cure for many maladies, and prophylactic against the machinations of the evil one, the house-leek. Descending into the doorway, in the chiaroscuro of the interior, when your eye grew sufficiently accustomed to that dim light, you might discover, hanging at the head of the widow's wooden-roofed bed, her beads and a phial of holy water.

Here certainly were defenses and bulwarks against the intrusion of that unearthly and evil power, of whose vicinity this solitary family were constantly reminded by the outline of Lisnavoura, that lonely hillhaunt of the "Good people," as the fairies are called euphemistically, whose strangely dome-like summit rose not half a mile away, looking like an outwork of the long line of mountain that sweeps by it.

It was at the fall of the leaf, and an autumnal sunset threw the lengthening shadow of haunted Lisnavoura, close in front of the solitary little cabin, over the undulating slopes and sides of Slieveelim. The birds were singing among the branches in the thinning leaves of the melancholy ash-trees that grew at the roadside in front of the door. The widow's three younger children were playing on the road, and their voices mingled with the evening song of the birds. Their elder sister, Nell, was "within in the house," as their phrase is, seeing after the boiling of the potatoes for supper.

Their mother had gone down to the bog, to carry up a hamper of turf on her back. It is, or was at least, a charitable custom—and if not disused, long may it continue—for the wealthier people when cutting their turf and stacking it in the bog, to make a smaller stack for the behoof of the poor, who were welcome to take from it so long as it lasted, and thus the potato pot was kept boiling, and hearth warm that would have been cold enough but for that good-natured bounty, through wintry months.

Moll Ryan trudged up the steep "bohereen" whose banks were overgrown with thorn and brambles, and stooping under her burden, re-entered her door, where her dark-haired daughter Nell met her with a welcome, and relieved her of her hamper.

Moll Ryan looked round with a sigh of relief, and drying her forehead, uttered the Munster ejaculation:

"Eiah, wisha! It's tired I am with it, God bless it. And where's the craythurs, Nell?"

"Playin' out on the road, mother; didn't ye see them and you comin' up?"

"No; there was no one before me on the road," she said, uneasily; "not a soul, Nell; and why didn't ye keep an eye on them?"

"Well, they're in the haggard, playin' there, or round by the back o' the house. Will I call them in?"

"Do so, good girl, in the name o' God. The hens is comin' home, see, and the sun was just down over Knockdoulah, an' I comin' up."

So out ran tall, dark-haired Nell, and standing on the road, looked up and down it; but not a sign of her two little brothers, Con and Bill, or her little sister, Peg, could she see. She called them; but no answer came from the little haggard, fenced with straggling bushes. She listened, but the sound of their voices was missing. Over the stile, and behind the house she ran—but there all was silent and deserted.

She looked down toward the bog, as far as she could see; but they did not appear. Again she listened—but in vain. At first she had felt angry, but now a different feeling overcame her, and she grew pale. With an undefined boding she looked toward the heathy boss of Lisnavoura, now darkening into the deepest purple against the flaming sky of sunset.

Again she listened with a sinking heart, and heard nothing but the farewell twitter and whistle of the birds in the bushes around. How many stories had she listened to by the winter hearth, of children stolen by the fairies, at nightfall, in lonely places! With this fear she knew her mother was haunted.

No one in the country round gathered her little flock about her so early as this frightened widow, and no door "in the seven parishes" was barred so early.

Sufficiently fearful, as all young people in that part of the world are of such dreaded and subtle agents, Nell was even more than usually afraid of them, for her terrors were infected and redoubled by her mother's. She was looking towards Lisnavoura in a trance of fear, and crossed herself again and again, and whispered prayer after prayer. She was interrupted by her mother's voice on the road calling her loudly. She answered, and ran round to the front of the cabin, where she found her standing.

"And where in the world's the craythurs—did ye see sight o' them anywhere?" cried Mrs. Ryan, as the girl came over the stile.

"Arrah! mother, 'tis only what they're run down the road a bit. We'll see them this minute coming back. It's like goats they are, climbin' here and runnin' there; an' if I had them here, in my hand, maybe I wouldn't give them a hiding all round."

"May the Lord forgive you, Nell! the childhers gone. They're took, and not a soul near us, and Father Tom three miles away! And what'll I do, or who's to help us this night? Oh, wirristhru, wirristhru! The craythurs is gone!"

"Whisht, mother, be aisy: don't ye see them comin' up?"

And then she shouted in menacing accents, waving her arm, and beckoning the children, who were seen approaching on the road, which some little way off made a slight dip, which had concealed them. They were approaching from the westward, and from the direction of the dreaded hill of Lisnavoura.

But there were only two of the children, and one of them, the little girl, was crying. Their mother and sister hurried forward to meet them, more alarmed than ever.

"Where is Billy—where is he?" cried the mother, nearly breathless, so soon as she was within hearing.

"He's gone—they took him away; but they said he'll come back again," answered little Con, with the dark brown hair.

"He's gone away with the grand ladies," blubbered the little girl.

"What ladies—where? Oh, Leum, asthora! My darlin', are you gone away at last? Where is he? Who took him? What ladies are you talkin' about? What way did he go?" she cried in distraction.

"I couldn't see where he went, mother; 'twas like as if he was going to Lisnavoura."

With a wild exclamation the distracted woman ran on towards the hill alone, clapping her hands, and crying aloud the name of her lost child.

Scared and horrified, Nell, not daring to follow, gazed after her, and burst into tears; and the other children raised high their lamentations in shrill rivalry.

Twilight was deepening. It was long past the time when they were usually barred securely within their habitation. Nell led the younger children into the cabin, and made them sit down by the turf fire, while she stood in the open door, watching in great fear for the return of her mother.

After a long while they did see their mother return. She came in and sat down by the fire, and cried as if her heart would break.

"Will I bar the door, mother?" asked Nell.

"Ay, do—didn't I lose enough, this night, without lavin' the doore open, for more o' yez to go; but first take an' sprinkle a dust o' the holy waters over ye, acuishla, and bring it here till I throw a taste iv it over myself and the craythurs; an' I wondher, Nell, you'd forget to do the like yourself, lettin' the craythurs out so near nightfall. Come here and sit on my knees, asthora, come to me, mavourneen, and hould me fast, in the name o' God, and I'll hould you fast that none can take yez from me, and tell me all about it, and what it was —the Lord between us and harm—an' how it happened, and who was in it."

And the door being barred, the two children, sometimes speaking together, often interrupting one another, often interrupted by their mother, managed to tell this strange story, which I had better relate connectedly and in my own language.

The Widow Ryan's three children were playing, as I have said, upon the narrow old road in front of her door. Little Bill or Leum, about five years old, with golden hair and large blue eyes, was a very pretty boy, with all the clear tints of healthy childhood, and that gaze of earnest simplicity which belongs not to town children of the same age. His little sister Peg, about a year older, and his brother Con, a little more than a year elder than she, made up the little group.

Under the great old ash-trees, whose last leaves were falling at their feet, in the light of an October sunset, they were playing with the hilarity and eagerness of rustic children, clamoring together, and their faces were turned toward the west and storied hill of Lisnavoura.

Suddenly a startling voice with a screech called to them from behind, ordering them to get out of the way, and turning, they saw a sight, such as they never beheld before. It was a carriage drawn by four horses that were pawing and snorting, in impatience, as it just pulled up. The children were almost under their feet, and scrambled to the side of the road next their own door.

This carriage and all its appointments were old-fashioned and gorgeous, and presented to the children, who had never seen anything finer than a turf car, and once, an old chaise that passed that way from Killaloe, a spectacle perfectly dazzling.

Here was antique splendor. The harness and trappings were scarlet, and blazing with gold. The horses were huge, and snow white, with great manes, that as they tossed and shook them in the air, seemed to stream and float sometimes longer and sometimes shorter, like so much smoke—their tails were long, and tied up in bows of broad scarlet and gold ribbon. The coach itself was glowing with colors, gilded and emblazoned. There were footmen in gay liveries, and three-cocked hats, like the coachman's; but he had a great wig, like a judge's, and their hair was frizzed out and powdered, and a long thick "pigtail," with a bow to it, hung down the back of each.

All these servants were diminutive, and ludicrously out of proportion with the enormous horses of the equipage, and had sharp, sallow features, and small, restless fiery eyes, and faces of cunning and malice that chilled the children. The little coachman was scowling and showing his white fangs under his cocked hat, and his little blazing beads of eyes were quivering with fury in their sockets as he whirled his whip round and round over their heads, till the lash of it looked like a streak of fire in the evening sun, and sounded like the cry of a legion of "fillapoueeks" in the air.

"Stop the princess on the highway!" cried the coachman, in a piercing treble.

"Stop the princess on the highway!" piped each footman in turn, scowling over his shoulder down on the children, and grinding his keen teeth.

The children were so frightened they could only gape and turn white in their panic. But a very sweet voice from the open window of the carriage reassured them, and arrested the attack of the lackeys.

A beautiful and "very grand-looking" lady was smiling from it on them, and they all felt pleased in the strange light of that smile.

"The boy with the golden hair, I think," said the lady, bending her large and wonderfully clear eyes on little Leum.

The upper sides of the carriage were chiefly of glass, so that the children could see another woman inside, whom they did not like so well.

This was a black woman, with a wonderfully long neck, hung round with many strings of large variously-colored beads, and on her head was a sort of turban of silk striped with all the colors of the rainbow, and fixed in it was a golden star.[8]

This black woman had a face as thin almost as a death's-head, with high cheekbones, and great goggle eyes, the whites of which, as well as her wide range of teeth, showed in brilliant contrast with her skin, as she looked over the beautiful lady's shoulder, and whispered something in her ear.

"Yes; the boy with the golden hair, I think," repeated the lady.

And her voice sounded sweet as a silver bell in the children's ears, and her smile beguiled them like the light of an enchanted lamp, as she leaned from the window with a look of ineffable fondness on the golden-haired boy, with the large blue eyes; insomuch that little Billy, looking up, smiled in return with a wondering fondness, and when she stooped down, and stretched her jeweled arms towards him, he stretched his little hands up, and how they touched the other children did not know; but, saying, "Come and give me a kiss, my darling," she raised him, and he seemed to ascend in her small fingers as lightly as a feather, and she held him in her lap and covered him with kisses.

Nothing daunted, the other children would have been only too happy to change places with their favored little brother. There was only one thing that was unpleasant, and a little frightened them, and that was the black woman, who stood and stretched forward, in the carriage as before. She gathered a rich silk and gold handkerchief that was in her fingers up to her lips, and seemed to thrust ever so much of it, fold after fold, into her capacious mouth, as they thought to smother her laughter, with which she seemed convulsed, for she was shaking and quivering, as it seemed, with suppressed merriment; but her eyes, which remained uncovered, looked angrier than they had ever seen eyes look before.

But the lady was so beautiful they looked on her instead, and she continued to caress and kiss the little boy on her knee; and smiling at the other children she held up a large russet apple in her fingers, and the carriage began to move slowly on, and with a nod inviting them to take the fruit, she dropped it on the road from the window; it rolled some way beside the wheels, they following, and then she dropped another, and then another, and so on. And the same thing happened to all; for just as either of the children who ran beside had caught the rolling apple, somehow it slipt into a hole or ran into a ditch, and looking up they saw the lady drop another from the window, and so the chase was taken up and continued till they got, hardly knowing how far they had gone, to the old cross-road that leads to Owney. It seemed that there the horses' hoofs and carriage wheels rolled up a wonderful

---

[8] Le Fanu would not use "black" here to describe a person of African descent, though otherness due to culture, race imperialism are clearly implied, so the character could be what a modern writer would categorize as "Black." Notably, and perhaps tellingly, an analogous character is introduced briefly in his vampire novella *Carmilla*, in a strikingly similar scenario.

dust, which being caught in one of those eddies that whirl the dust up into a column, on the calmest day, enveloped the children for a moment, and passed whirling on towards Lisnavoura, the carriage, as they fancied, driving in the centre of it; but suddenly it subsided, the straws and leaves floated to the ground, the dust dissipated itself, but the white horses and the lackeys, the gilded carriage, the lady and their little golden-haired brother were gone.

At the same moment suddenly the upper rim of the clear setting sun disappeared behind the hill of Knockdoula, and it was twilight. Each child felt the transition like a shock—and the sight of the rounded summit of Lisnavoura, now closely overhanging them, struck them with a new fear.

They screamed their brother's name after him, but their cries were lost in the vacant air. At the same time they thought they heard a hollow voice say, close to them, "Go home."

Looking round and seeing no one, they were scared, and hand in hand— the little girl crying wildly, and the boy white as ashes, from fear, they trotted homeward, at their best speed, to tell, as we have seen, their strange story.

Molly Ryan never more saw her darling. But something of the lost little boy was seen by his former playmates.

Sometimes when their mother was away earning a trifle at haymaking, and Nelly washing the potatoes for their dinner, or "beatling" clothes in the little stream that flows in the hollow close by, they saw the pretty face of little Billy peeping in archly at the door, and smiling silently at them, and as they ran to embrace him, with cries of delight, he drew back, still smiling archly, and when they got out into the open day, he was gone, and they could see no trace of him anywhere.

This happened often, with slight variations in the circumstances of the visit. Sometimes he would peep for a longer time, sometimes for a shorter time, sometimes his little hand would come in, and, with bended finger, beckon them to follow; but always he was smiling with the same arch look and wary silence—and always he was gone when they reached the door. Gradually these visits grew less and less frequent, and in about eight months they ceased altogether, and little Billy, irretrievably lost, took rank in their memories with the dead.

One wintry morning, nearly a year and a half after his disappearance, their mother having set out for Limerick soon after cockcrow, to sell some fowls at the market, the little girl, lying by the side of her elder sister, who was fast asleep, just at the grey of the morning heard the latch lifted softly, and saw little Billy enter and close the door gently after him. There was light enough to see that he was barefoot and ragged, and looked pale and famished. He went straight to the fire, and cowered over the turf embers, and rubbed his hands slowly, and seemed to shiver as he gathered the smoldering turf together.

The little girl clutched her sister in terror and whispered, "Waken, Nelly, waken; here's Billy come back!"

Nelly slept soundly on, but the little boy, whose hands were extended close over the coals, turned and looked toward the bed, it seemed to her, in fear, and she saw the glare of the embers reflected on his thin cheek as he turned toward her. He rose and went, on tiptoe, quickly to the door, in silence, and let himself out as softly as he had come in.

After that, the little boy was never seen any more by any one of his kindred.

"Fairy doctors," as the dealers in the preternatural, who in such cases were called in, are termed, did all that in them lay—but in vain. Father Tom came down, and tried what holier rites could do, but equally without result. So little Billy was dead to mother, brother, and sisters; but no grave received him. Others whom affection cherished, lay in holy ground, in the old churchyard of Abington, with headstone to mark the spot over which the survivor might kneel and say a kind prayer for the peace of the departed soul. But there was no landmark to show where little Billy was hidden from their loving eyes, unless it was in the old hill of Lisnavoura, that cast its long shadow at sunset before the cabin-door; or that, white and filmy in the moonlight, in later years, would occupy his brother's gaze as he returned from fair or market, and draw from him a sigh and a prayer for the little brother he had lost so long ago, and was never to see again.

BECKWITH'S CASE

Maurice Hewlett

from *Lore of Proserpine* (1913)

The facts were as follows. Mr. Stephen Mortimer Beckwith was a young man living at Wishford in the Amesbury district of Wiltshire. He was a clerk in the Wilts and Dorset Bank at Salisbury, was married and had one child. His age at the time of the experience here related was twenty-eight. His health was excellent.

On the 30th November, 1887, at about ten o'clock at night, he was returning home from Amesbury where he had been spending the evening at a friend's house. The weather was mild, with a rain-bearing wind blowing in squalls from the south-west. It was three-quarter moon that night, and although the sky was frequently overcast it was at no time dark. Mr. Beckwith, who was riding a bicycle and accompanied by his fox-terrier Strap, states that he had no difficulty in seeing and avoiding the stones cast down at intervals by the road-menders; that flocks of sheep in the hollows were very visible, and that, passing Wilsford House, he saw a barn owl quite plainly and remarked its heavy, uneven flight.

A mile beyond Wilsford House, Strap, the dog, broke through the quick-set hedge upon his right-hand side and ran yelping up the down, which rises sharply just there. Mr. Beckwith, who imagined that he was after a hare, whistled him in, presently calling him sharply, "Strap, Strap, come out of it." The dog took no notice, but ran directly to a clump of gorse and bramble half-way up the down, and stood there in the attitude of a pointer, with uplifted paw, watching the gorse intently, and whining. Mr. Beckwith was by this time dismounted, observing the dog. He watched him for some minutes from the road. The moon was bright, the sky at the moment free from cloud.

He himself could see nothing in the gorse, though the dog was undoubtedly in a high state of excitement. It made frequent rushes forward, but stopped short of the object that it saw and trembled. It did not bark outright but rather whimpered—"a curious, shuddering, crying noise," says Mr. Beckwith. Interested by the animal's persistent and singular behavior, he now sought a gap in the hedge, went through on to the down, and approached the clumped bushes. Strap was so much occupied that he barely noticed his master's coming; it seemed as if he dared not take his eyes for one second from what he saw in there.

Beckwith, standing behind the dog, looked into the gorse. From the distance at which he still stood he could see nothing at all. His belief then was that there was either a tramp in a drunken sleep, possibly two tramps, or a hare caught in a wire, or possibly even a fox. Having no stick with him he did not care, at first, to go any nearer, and contented himself with urging on his terrier. This was not very courageous of him, as he admits, and was quite unsuccessful. No verbal excitations would draw Strap nearer to the furze-bush. Finally the dog threw up his head, showed his master the white arcs of his eyes and fairly howled at the moon. At this dismal sound Mr. Beckwith owned himself alarmed. It was, as he describes it—though he is an Englishman—"uncanny." The time, he owns, the aspect of the night, loneliness of the spot (midway up the steep slope of a chalk down), the mysterious shroud of darkness upon shadowed and distant objects and flood of white light upon the foreground—all these circumstances worked upon his imagination.

He was indeed for retreat; but here Strap was of a different mind. Nothing would excite him to advance, but nothing either could induce him to retire. Whatever he saw in the furze-bush Strap must continue to observe. In the face of this Beckwith summoned up his courage, took it in both hands and went much nearer to the furze-bushes, much nearer, that is, than Strap the terrier could bring himself to go. Then, he tells us, he did see a pair of bright eyes far in the thicket, which seemed to be fixed upon his, and by degrees also a pale and troubled face. Here, then, was neither fox nor drunken tramp, but some human creature, man, woman, or child, fully aware of him and of the dog.

Beckwith, who now had surer command of his feelings, spoke aloud asking, "What are you doing there? What's the matter?" He had no reply. He went one pace nearer, being still on his guard, and spoke again. "I won't hurt you," he said. "Tell me what the matter is." The eyes remained unwinkingly fixed upon his own. No movement of the features could be discerned. The face, as he could now make it out, was very small—"about as big as a big wax doll's," he says, "of a longish oval, very pale." He adds, "I could see its neck now, no thicker than my wrist; and where its clothes began. I couldn't see any arms, for a good reason. I found out afterward that they had been bound behind its back. I should have said immediately, 'That's a girl in there,' if it had not been for one or two plain considerations. It had not the size of what we call a girl, nor the face of what we mean by a child. It was, in fact, neither fish, flesh, nor fowl. Strap had known that from the beginning, and now I was of Strap's opinion myself."

Advancing with care, a step at a time, Beckwith presently found himself within touching distance of the creature. He was now standing with furze half-way up his calves, right above it, stooping to look closely at it; and as he stooped and moved, now this way, now that, to get a clearer view, so the crouching thing's eyes gazed up to meet his, and followed them about, as if safety lay only in that never-shifting, fixed regard. He had noticed, and states in his narrative, that Strap had seemed quite unable, in the same way, to take his eyes off the creature for a single second.

He could now see that, of whatever nature it might be, it was, in form and features, most exactly a young woman. The features, for instance, were regular and fine. He remarks in particular upon the chin. All about its face, narrowing the oval of it, fell dark glossy curtains of hair, very straight and glistening with wet. Its garment was cut in a plain circle round the neck, and short off at the shoulders, leaving the arms entirely bare. This garment, shift, smock or gown, as he indifferently calls it, appeared thin, and was found afterward to be of a grey color, soft and clinging to the shape. It was made loose, however, and gathered in at the waist. He could not see the creature's legs, as they were tucked under her. Her arms, it has been related, were behind her back. The only other things to be remarked upon were the strange stillness of one who was plainly suffering, and might well be alarmed, and appearance of expectancy, a dumb appeal; what he himself calls rather well "an ignorant sort of impatience, like that of a sick animal."

"Come," Beckwith now said, "let me help you up. You will get cold if you sit here. Give me your hand, will you?" She neither spoke nor moved; simply continued to search his eyes. Strap, meantime, was still trembling and whining. But now, when he stooped yet lower to take her forcibly by the arms, she shrank back a little way and turned her head, and he saw to his horror that she had a great open wound in the side of her neck—from which, however, no blood was issuing. Yet it was clearly a fresh wound, recently made.

He was greatly shocked. "Good God," he said, "there's been foul play here," and whipped out his handkerchief. Kneeling, he wound it several times round her slender throat and knotted it as tightly as he could; then, without more ado, he took her up in his arms, under the knees and round the middle, and carried her down the slope to the road. He describes her as of no weight at all. He says it was "exactly like carrying an armful of feathers about." "I took her down the hill and through the hedge at the bottom as if she had been a pillow."

Here it was that he discovered that her wrists were bound together behind her back with a kind of plait of thongs so intricate that he was quite unable to release them. He felt his pockets for his knife, but could not find it, and then recollected suddenly that he should have a new one with him, the third prize in a whist tournament in which he had taken part that evening. He found it wrapped in paper in his overcoat pocket, with it cut the thongs and set the little creature free. She immediately responded—the first sign of animation which she had displayed—by throwing both her arms about his body and clinging to him in an ecstasy. Holding him so that, as he says, he felt the shuddering go all through her, she suddenly lowered her head and touched his wrist with her cheek. He says that instead of being cold to the touch, "like a fish," as she had seemed to be when he first took her out of the furze, she was now "as warm as a toast, like a child."

So far he had put her down for "a foreigner," convenient term for defining something which you do not quite understand. She had none of his language, evidently; she was undersized, some three feet six inches by the look of her, and yet perfectly proportioned.9 She was most curiously dressed in a frock cut to the knee, and actually in nothing else at all. It left her bare-legged and bare-armed, and was made, as he puts it himself, of stuff like cobweb: "those dusty, drooping kind which you put on your finger to stop bleeding." He could not recognize the web, but was sure that it was neither linen nor cotton. It seemed to stick to her body wherever it touched a prominent part: "you could see very well, to say nothing of feeling, that she was well made and well nourished." She ought, as he judged, to be a child of five years old, "and a feather-weight at that"; but he felt certain that she must be "much more like sixteen." It was that, I gather, which made him suspect her of being something outside experience. So far, then, it was safe to call her a foreigner: but he was not yet at the end of his discoveries.

Heavy footsteps, coming from the direction of Wishford, in due time proved to be those of Police Constable Gulliver, a neighbor of Beckwith's and guardian of the peace in his own village. He lifted his lantern to flash it into the traveler's eyes, and dropped it again with a pleasant "good evening." He added that it was inclined to be showery, which was more than true, as it was at the moment raining hard. With that, it seems, he would have passed on.

But Beckwith, whether smitten by self-consciousness of having been seen with a young woman in his arms at a suspicious hour of the night by the village policeman, or bursting perhaps with the importance of his affair, detained Gulliver. "Just look at this," he said boldly. "Here's a pretty thing to have found on a lonely road. Foul play somewhere, I'm afraid," he then exhibited his burden to the lantern light.

To his extreme surprise, however, the constable, after exploring the beam of light and all that it contained for some time in silence, reached out his hand for the knife which Beckwith still held open. He looked at it on both sides, examined the handle and gave it back. "Foul play, Mr. Beckwith?" he said laughing. "Bless you, they use bigger tools than that. That's just a toy, the like of that. Cut your hand with it, though, already, I see." He must have noticed the handkerchief, for as he spoke the light from his lantern shone full upon the face and neck of the child, or creature, in the young man's arms, so clearly that, looking down at it, Beckwith himself could see the clear grey of its intensely watchful eyes, and the very pupils of them, diminished to specks of black. It was now, therefore, plain to him that what he held was a foreigner indeed, since the parish constable was unable to see it. Strap had smelt it,

---

9 Her exact measurements are stated to have been as follows: height from crown to sole, 3 feet 5 inches. Round waist, 15 inches; round bust, 21 inches; round wrist, 3-1/2 inches; round neck, 7-1/2 inches. - AUTHOR

then seen it, and he, Beckwith, had seen it; but it was invisible to Gulliver. "I felt now," he says in his narrative, "that something was wrong. I did not like the idea of taking it into the house; but I intended to make one more trial before I made up my mind about that. I said good night to Gulliver, put her on my bicycle and pushed her home. But first of all I took the handkerchief from her neck and put it in my pocket. There was no blood upon it, that I could see."

His wife, as he had expected, was waiting at the gate for him. She exclaimed, as he had expected, upon the lateness of the hour. Beckwith stood for a little in the roadway before the house, explaining that Strap had bolted up the hill and had had to be looked for and fetched back. While speaking he noticed that Mrs. Beckwith was as insensible to the creature on the bicycle as Gulliver the constable had been. Indeed, she went much further to prove herself so than he, for she actually put her hand upon the handle-bar of the machine, and in order to do that drove it right through the centre of the girl crouching there. Beckwith saw that done. "I declare solemnly upon my honor," he writes, "that it was as if Mary had drilled a hole clean through the middle of her back. Through gown and skin and bone and all her arm went; and how it went I don't know. To me it seemed that her hand was on the handle-bar, while her upper arm, to the elbow, was in between the girl's shoulders. There was a gap from the elbow downwards where Mary's arm was inside the body; then from the creature's diaphragm her lower arm, wrist and hand came out. And all the time we were speaking the girl's eyes were on my face. I was now quite determined that I wouldn't have her in the house for a mint of money."

He put her, finally, in the dog-kennel. Strap, as a favorite, lived in the house; but he kept a greyhound in the garden, in a kennel surrounded by a sort of run made of iron poles and galvanized wire. It was roofed in with wire also, for the convenience of stretching a tarpaulin in wet weather. Here it was that he bestowed the strange being rescued from the down.

It was clever, I think, of Beckwith to infer that what Strap had shown respect for would be respected by the greyhound, and certainly bold of him to act upon his inference. However, events proved that he had been perfectly right. Bran, the greyhound, was interested, highly interested in his guest. The moment he saw his master he saw what he was carrying. "Quiet, Bran, quiet there," was a very unnecessary adjuration. Bran stretched up his head and sniffed, but went no further; and when Beckwith had placed his burden on the straw inside the kennel, Bran lay down, as if on guard, outside the opening and put his muzzle on his forepaws. Again Beckwith noticed that curious appearance of the eyes which the fox-terrier's had made already. Bran's eyes were turned upward to show the narrow arcs of white.

Before he went to bed, he tells us, but not before Mrs. Beckwith had gone there, he took out a bowl of bread and milk to his patient. Bran he found to be still stretched out before the entry; the girl was nestled down in the straw, as if asleep or prepared to be so, with her face upon her hand. Upon an afterthought he went back for a clean pocket handkerchief, warm water and a sponge. With these, by the light of a candle, he washed the wound, dipped the rag in hazeline,[10] and applied it. This done, he touched the creature's head, nodded a good night and retired. "She smiled at me very prettily," he says. "That was the first time she did it."

There was no blood on the handkerchief which he had removed.

Early in the morning following upon the adventure Beckwith was out and about. He wished to verify the overnight experiences in the light of refreshed intelligence. On approaching the kennel he saw at once that it had been no dream. There, in fact, was the creature of his discovery playing with Bran the greyhound, circling sedately about him, weaving her arms, pointing her toes, arching her graceful neck, stooping to him, as if inviting him to sport, darting away—"like a fairy," says Beckwith, "at her magic, dancing in a ring." Bran, he observed, made no effort to catch her, but crouched rather than sat, as if ready to spring. He followed her about with his eyes as far as he could; but when the course of her dance took her immediately behind him he did not turn his head, but kept his eye fixed as far backward as he could, against the moment when she should come again into the scope of his vision. "It seemed as important to him as it had the day before to Strap to keep her always in his eye. It seemed—and always seemed so long as I could study them together—intensely important." Bran's mouth was stretched to "a sort of grin"; occasionally he panted. When Beckwith entered the kennel and touched the dog (which took little notice of him) he found him trembling with excitement. His heart was beating at a great rate. He also drank quantities of water.

Beckwith, whose narrative, hitherto summarized, I may now quote, tells us that the creature was indescribably graceful and light-footed. "You couldn't hear the fall of her foot: you never could. Her dancing and circling about the cage seemed to be the most important business of her life; she was always at it, especially in bright weather. I shouldn't have called it restlessness so much as busyness. It really seemed to mean more to her than exercise or irritation at confinement. It was evident also that she was happy when so engaged. She used to sing. She sang also when she was sitting still with Bran; but not with such exhilaration.

"Her eyes were bright—when she was dancing about—with mischief and devilry. I cannot avoid that word, though it does not describe what I really mean. She looked wild and outlandish and full of fun, as if she knew that she was teasing the dog, and yet couldn't help herself. When you say of a child that he looks wicked, you don't mean it literally; it is rather a compliment than not. So it was with her and her wickedness. She did look wicked, there's no mistake—able and willing to do wickedly; but I am sure she never meant to hurt Bran. They were always firm friends, though the dog knew very well who was master.

---

[10] an alcoholic distillate from the leaves and twigs of witch-hazel

"When you looked at her you did not think of her height. She was so complete; as well made as a statuette. I could have spanned her waist with my two thumbs and middle fingers, and her neck (very nearly) with one hand. She was pale and inclined to be dusky in complexion, but not so dark as a gipsy; she had grey eyes, and dark-brown hair, which she could sit upon if she chose. Her gown you could have sworn was made of cobweb; I don't know how else to describe it. As I had suspected, she wore nothing else, for while I was there that first morning, so soon as the sun came up over the hill she slipped it off her and stood up dressed in nothing at all. She was a regular little Venus—that's all I can say. I never could get accustomed to that weakness of hers for slipping off her frock, though no doubt it was very absurd. She had no sort of shame in it, so why on earth should I?

"The food, I ought to mention, had disappeared: the bowl was empty. But I know now that Bran must have had it. So long as she remained in the kennel or about my place she never ate anything, nor drank either. If she had I must have known it, as I used to clean the run out every morning. I was always particular about that. I used to say that you couldn't keep dogs too clean. But I tried her, unsuccessfully, with all sorts of things: flowers, honey, dew—for I had read somewhere that fairies drink dew and suck honey out of flowers. She used to look at the little messes I made for her, and when she knew me better would grimace at them, and look up in my face and laugh at me.

"I have said that she used to sing sometimes. It was like nothing that I can describe. Perhaps the wind in the telegraph wire comes nearest to it, and yet that is an absurd comparison. I could never catch any words; indeed I did not succeed in learning a single word of her language. I doubt very much whether they have what we call a language—I mean the people who are like her, her own people. They communicate with each other, I fancy, as she did with my dogs, inarticulately, but with perfect communication and understanding on either side. When I began to teach her English I noticed that she had a kind of pity for me, a kind of contempt perhaps is nearer the mark, that I should be compelled to express myself in so clumsy a way. I am no philosopher, but I imagine that our need of putting one word after another may be due to our habit of thinking in sequence. If there is no such thing as Time in the other world it should not be necessary there to frame speech in sentences at all. I am sure that Thumbeline (which was my name for her—I never learned her real name) spoke with Bran and Strap in flashes which revealed her whole thought at once. So also they answered her, there's no doubt. So also she contrived to talk with my little girl, who, although she was four years old and a great chatterbox, never attempted to say a single word of her own language to Thumbeline, yet communicated with her by the hour together. But I did not know anything of this for a month or more, though it must have begun almost at once.

"I blame myself for it, myself only. I ought, of course, to have remembered that children are more likely to see fairies than grown-ups; but then—why did Florrie keep it all secret? Why did she not tell her mother, or me, that she had seen a fairy in Bran's kennel? The child was as open as the day, yet she concealed her knowledge from both of us without the least difficulty. She seemed the same careless, laughing child she had always been; one could not have supposed her to have a care in the world, and yet, for nearly six months she must have been full of care, having daily secret intercourse with Thumbeline and keeping her eyes open all the time lest her mother or I should find her out. Certainly she could have taught me something in the way of keeping secrets. I know that I kept mine very badly, and blame myself more than enough for keeping it at all. God knows what we might have been spared if, on the night I brought her home, I had told Mary the whole truth! And yet—how could I have convinced her that she was impaling some one with her arm while her hand rested on the bar of the bicycle? Is not that an absurdity on the face of it? Yes, indeed; but the sequel is no absurdity. That's the terrible fact.

"I kept Thumbeline in the kennel for the whole winter. She seemed happy enough there with the dogs, and, of course, she had had Florrie, too, though I did not find that out until the spring. I don't doubt, now, that if I had kept her in there altogether she would have been perfectly contented.

"The first time I saw Florrie with her I was amazed. It was a Sunday morning. There was our four-year-old child standing at the wire, pressing herself against it, and Thumbeline close to her. Their faces almost touched; their fingers were interlaced; I am certain that they were speaking to each other in their own fashion, by flashes, without words. I watched them for a bit; I saw Bran come and sit up on his haunches and join in. He looked from one to another, and all about; and then he saw me.

"Now that is how I know that they were all three in communication; because, the very next moment, Florrie turned round and ran to me, and said in her pretty baby-talk, 'Talking to Bran. Florrie talking to Bran.' If this was willful deceit it was most accomplished. It could not have been better done. 'And who else were you talking to, Florrie?' I said. She fixed her round blue eyes upon me, as if in wonder, then looked away and said shortly, 'No one else.' And I could not get her to confess or admit then or at any time afterward that she had any cognizance at all of the fairy in Bran's kennel, although their communications were daily, and often lasted for hours at a time. I don't know that it makes things any better, but I have thought sometimes that the child believed me to be as insensible to Thumbeline as her mother was. She can only have believed it at first, of course, but that may have prompted her to a concealment which she did not afterwards care to confess to.

"Be this as it may, Florrie, in fact, behaved with Thumbeline exactly as the two dogs did. She made no attempt to catch her at her circlings and wheelings about the kennel, nor to follow her wonderful dances, nor (in her presence) to imitate them. But she was (like the dogs) aware of nobody else when under the spell of Thumbeline's personality; and when she had got to know her she seemed to care for nobody else at all. I ought, no doubt, to have foreseen that and guarded against it.

"Thumbeline was extremely attractive. I never saw such eyes as hers, such mysterious fascination. She was nearly always good-tempered, nearly always happy; but sometimes she had fits of temper and kept herself to herself. Nothing then would get her out of the kennel, where she would lie curled up like an animal with her knees to her chin and one arm thrown over her face. Bran was always wretched at these times, and did all he knew to coax her out. He ceased to care for me or my wife after she came to us, and instead of being wild at the prospect of his Saturday and Sunday runs, it was hard to get him along. I had to take him on a lead until we had turned to go home; then he would set off by himself, in spite of hallooing and scolding, at a long steady gallop and one would find him waiting crouched at the gate of his run, and Thumbeline on the ground inside it, with her legs crossed like a tailor, mocking and teasing him with her wonderful shining eyes. Only once or twice did I see her worse than sick or sorry; then she was transported with rage and another person altogether. She never touched me—and why or how I had offended her I have no notion—but she buzzed and hovered about me like an angry bee.11 She appeared to have wings, which hummed in their furious movement; she was red in the face, her eyes burned; she grinned at me and ground her little teeth together. A curious shrill noise came from her, like the screaming of a gnat or hover fly; but no words, never any words. Bran showed me his teeth too, and would not look at me. It was very odd.

"When I looked in, on my return home, she was as merry as usual, and as affectionate. I think she had no memory.

"I am trying to give all the particulars I was able to gather from observation. In some things she was difficult, in others very easy to teach. For instance, I got her to learn in no time that she ought to wear her clothes, such as they were, when I was with her. She certainly preferred to go without them, especially in the sunshine; but by leaving her the moment she slipped her frock off I soon made her understand that if she wanted me she must behave herself according to my notions of behavior. She got that fixed in her little head, but even so she used to do her best to hoodwink me. She would slip out one shoulder when she thought I wasn't looking, and before I knew where I was half of her would be gleaming in the sun like satin. Directly I noticed it I used to frown, and then she would pretend to be ashamed of herself, hang her head, and wriggle her frock up to its place again. However, I never could teach her to keep her skirts about her knees. She was as innocent as a baby about that sort of thing.

"I taught her some English words, and a sentence or two. That was toward the end of her confinement to the kennel, about March. I used to touch parts of her, or of myself, or Bran, and peg away at the names of them. Mouth, eyes,

---

11 "I have sometimes thought," he adds in a note, "that it may have been jealousy. My wife had been with me in the garden and had stuck a daffodil in my coat."- AUTHOR

ears, hands, chest, tail, back, front: she learned all those and more. Eat, drink, laugh, cry, love, kiss, those also. As for kissing (apart from the word) she proved herself to be an expert. She kissed me, Florrie, Bran, Strap indifferently, one as soon as another, and any rather than none, and all four for choice.

"I learned some things myself, more than a thing or two. I don't mind owning that one thing was to value my wife's steady and tried affection far above the wild love of this unbalanced, unearthly little creature, who seemed to be like nothing so much as a woman with the conscience left out. The conscience, we believe, is the still small voice of the Deity crying to us in the dark recesses of the body; pointing out the path of duty; teaching respect for the opinion of the world, for tradition, decency and order. It is thanks to conscience that a man is true and a woman modest. Not that Thumbeline could be called immodest, unless a baby can be so described, or an animal. But could I be called 'true'? I greatly fear that I could not—in fact, I know it too well. I meant no harm; I was greatly interested; and there was always before me the real difficulty of making Mary understand that something was in the kennel which she couldn't see. It would have led to great complications, even if I had persuaded her of the fact. No doubt she would have insisted on my getting rid of Thumbeline—but how on earth could I have done that if Thumbeline had not chosen to go? But for all that I know very well that I ought to have told her, cost what it might. If I had done it I should have spared myself lifelong regret, and should only have gone without a few weeks of extraordinary interest which I now see clearly could not have been good for me, as not being founded upon any revealed Christian principle, and most certainly were not worth the price I had to pay for them.

"I learned one more curious fact which I must not forget. Nothing would induce Thumbeline to touch or pass over anything made of zinc.12 I don't know the reason of it; but gardeners will tell you that the way to keep a plant from slugs is to put a zinc collar round it. It is due to that I was able to keep her in Bran's run without difficulty. To have got out she would have had to pass zinc. The wire was all galvanized.

"She showed her dislike of it in numerous ways: one was her care to avoid touching the sides or top of the enclosure when she was at her gambols. At such times, when she was at her wildest, she was all over the place, skipping high like a lamb, twisting like a leveret, wheeling round and round in circles like a young dog, or skimming, like a swallow on the wing, above ground. But she never made a mistake; she turned in a moment or flung herself backward if there was the least risk of contact. When Florrie used to converse with her from outside, in that curious silent way the two had, it would always be the child that put its hands through the wire, never Thumbeline. I once tried to

---

12 This is a curious thing, unsupported by any other evidence known to me. I asked Despoina about it, but she would not, or she did not, answer. She appeared not to understand what zinc was, and I had none handy. - AUTHOR

put her against the roof when I was playing with her. She screamed like a shot hare and would not come out of the kennel all day. There was no doubt at all about her feelings for zinc. All other metals seemed indifferent to her.

"With the advent of spring weather Thumbeline became not only more beautiful, but wilder, and exceedingly restless. She now coaxed me to let her out, and against my judgment I did it; she had to be carried over the entry; for when I had set the gate wide open and pointed her the way into the garden she squatted down in her usual attitude of attention, with her legs crossed, and watched me, waiting. I wanted to see how she would get through the hateful wire, so went away and hid myself, leaving her alone with Bran. I saw her creep to the entry and peer at the wire. What followed was curious. Bran came up wagging his tail and stood close to her, his side against her head; he looked down, inviting her to go out with him. Long looks passed between them, and then Bran stooped his head, she put her arms around his neck, twined her feet about his foreleg, and was carried out. Then she became a mad thing, now bird, now moth; high and low, round and round, flashing about the place for all the world like a humming-bird moth, perfectly beautiful in her motions (whose ease always surprised me), and equally so in her coloring of soft grey and dusky-rose flesh. Bran grew a puppy again and whipped about after her in great circles round the meadow. But though he was famous at coursing, and has killed his hares single-handed, he was never once near Thumbeline. It was a wonderful sight and made me late for business.

"By degrees she got to be very bold, and taught me boldness too, and (I am ashamed to say) greater degrees of deceit. She came freely into the house and played with Florrie up and down stairs; she got on my knee at meal-times, or evenings when my wife and I were together. Fine tricks she played me, I must own. She spilled my tea for me, broke cups and saucers, scattered my Patience cards, caught poor Mary's knitting wool and rolled it about the room. The cunning little creature knew that I dared not scold her or make any kind of fuss. She used to beseech me for forgiveness occasionally when I looked very glum, and would touch my cheek to make me look at her imploring eyes, and keep me looking at her till I smiled. Then she would put her arms round my neck and pull herself up to my level and kiss me, and then nestle down in my arms and pretend to sleep. By-and-by, when my attention was called off her, she would pinch me, or tweak my necktie, and make me look again at her wicked eye peeping out from under my arm. I had to kiss her again, of course, and at last she might go to sleep in earnest. She seemed able to sleep at any hour or in any place, just like an animal.

"I had some difficulty in arranging for the night when once she had made herself free of the house. She saw no reason whatever for our being separated; but I circumvented her by nailing a strip of zinc all round the door; and I put one round Florrie's too. I pretended to my wife that it was to keep out draughts. Thumbeline was furious when she found out how she had been tricked. I think she never quite forgave me for it. Where she hid herself at night I am not sure. I think on the sitting-room sofa; but on mild mornings I used to find her out-doors, playing round Bran's kennel.

"Strap, our fox-terrier, picked up some rat poison towards the end of April and died in the night. Thumbeline's way of taking that was very curious. It shocked me a good deal. She had never been so friendly with him as with Bran, though certainly more at ease in his company than in mine. The night before he died I remember that she and Bran and he had been having high games in the meadow, which had ended by their all lying down together in a heap, Thumbeline's head on Bran's flank, and her legs between his. Her arm had been round Strap's neck in a most loving way. They made quite a picture for a Royal Academician; 'Tired of Play,' or 'The End of a Romp,' I can fancy he would call it. Next morning I found poor old Strap stiff and staring, and Thumbeline and Bran at their games just the same. She actually jumped over him and all about him as if he had been a lump of earth or a stone. Just some such thing he was to her; she did not seem able to realise that there was the cold body of her friend. Bran just sniffed him over and left him, but Thumbeline showed no consciousness that he was there at all. I wondered, was this heartlessness or obliquity? But I have never found the answer to my question.13

"Now I come to the tragical part of my story, and wish with all my heart that I could leave it out. But beyond the full confession I have made to my wife, the County Police and the newspapers, I feel that I should not shrink from any admission that may be called for of how much I have been to

---

13 I have observed this frequently for myself, and can answer Beckwith's question for him. I would refer the reader in the first place to my early experience of the boy (to call him so) with the rabbit in the wood. There was an act of shocking cruelty, done idly, almost unconsciously. I was not shocked at all, child as I was, and quickly moved to pity and terror, because I knew that the creature was not to be judged by our standards. From this and other things of the sort which I have observed, and from this tale of Beckwith's, I judge, that, to the fairy kind, directly life ceases to be lived at the full, the object, be it fairy, or animal, or vegetable, is not perceived by the other to exist. Thus, if a fairy should die, the others would not know that its accidents were there; if a rabbit (as in the case cited) should be caught it would therefore cease to be rabbit. We ourselves have very much the same habit of regard toward plant life. Our attitude to a tree or a growing plant ceases the moment that plant is out of the ground. It is then, as we say, *dead*—that is, it ceases to be a plant. So also we never scruple to pluck the flowers, or the whole flower-scape from a plant, to put it in our buttonhole or in the bosom of our friend, and thereafter to cease our interest in the plant as such. It now becomes a memory, a *gage d'amour*, a token or a sudden glory— what you will. This is the habit of mankind; but I know of rare ones, both men and women, who never allow dead flowers to be thrown into the draught, but always give them decent burial, either cremation or earth to earth. I find that admirable, yet don't condemn their neighbors, nor consider fairies cruel who torture the living and disregard the maimed or the dead. - AUTHOR

blame. In May, on the 13th of May, Thumbeline, Bran, and our only child, Florrie, disappeared.

"It was a day, I remember well, of wonderful beauty. I had left them all three together in the water meadow, little thinking of what was in store for us before many hours. Thumbeline had been crowning Florrie with a wreath of flowers. She had gathered cuckoo-pint and marsh marigolds and woven them together, far more deftly than any of us could have done, into a chaplet. I remember the curious winding, wandering air she had been singing (without any words, as usual) over her business, and how she touched each flower first with her lips, and then brushed it lightly across her bosom before she wove it in. She had kept her eyes on me as she did it, looking up from under her brows, as if to see whether I knew what she was about.

"I don't doubt now but that she was bewitching Florrie by this curious performance, which every flower had to undergo separately; but, fool that I was, I thought nothing of it at the time, and bicycled off to Salisbury leaving them there.

"At noon my poor wife came to me at the Bank distracted with anxiety and fatigue. She had run most of the way, she gave me to understand. Her news was that Florrie and Bran could not be found anywhere. She said that she had gone to the gate of the meadow to call the child in, and not seeing her, or getting any answer, she had gone down to the river at the bottom. Here she had found a few picked wild flowers, but no other traces. There were no footprints in the mud, either of child or dog. Having spent the morning with some of the neighbors in a fruitless search, she had now come to me.

"My heart was like lead, and shame prevented me from telling her the truth as I was sure it must be. But my own conviction of it clogged all my efforts. Of what avail could it be to inform the police or organise search-parties, knowing what I knew only too well? However, I did put Gulliver in communication with the head-office in Sarum, and everything possible was done. We explored a circuit of six miles about Wishford; every fold of the hills, every spinney,[14] every hedgerow was thoroughly examined. But that first night of grief had broken down my shame: I told my wife the whole truth in the presence of Reverend Richard Walsh, the Congregational minister, and in spite of her absolute incredulity, and, I may add, scorn, next morning I repeated it to Chief Inspector Notcutt of Salisbury. Particulars got into the local papers by the following Saturday; and next I had to face the ordeal of the *Daily Chronicle*, *Daily News*, *Daily Graphic*, *Star*, and other London journals. Most of these newspapers sent representatives to lodge in the village, many of them with photographic cameras. All this hateful notoriety I had brought upon myself, and did my best to bear like the humble, contrite Christian which I hope I may say I have become. We found no trace of our dear one, and never have to this day. Bran, too, had completely vanished. I have not cared to keep a dog since.

---

[14] a small area of foliage, usually trees and bushes

"Whether my dear wife ever believed my account I cannot be sure. She has never reproached me for wicked thoughtlessness, that's certain. Mr. Walsh, our respected pastor, who has been so kind as to read this paper, told me more than once that he could hardly doubt it. The Salisbury police made no comments upon it one way or another. My colleagues at the Bank, out of respect for my grief and sincere repentance, treated me with a forbearance for which I can never be too grateful. I need not add that every word of this is absolutely true. I made notes of the most remarkable characteristics of the being I called Thumbeline *at the time of remarking them*, and those notes are still in my possession."

Here, with the exception of a few general reflections which are of little value, Mr. Beckwith's paper ends. It was read, I ought to say, by the Rev. Richard Walsh at the meeting of the South Wilts Folklore Society and Field Club held at Amesbury in June 1892, and is to be found in the published transactions of that body (Vol. IV. New Series, pp. 305 *seq.*).

THE WHITE PEOPLE

Arthur Machen

first published in *Horlick's Magazine* (January 1904)

PROLOGUE

"**S**orcery and sanctity," said Ambrose, "these are the only realities. Each is an ecstasy, a withdrawal from the common life."

Cotgrave listened, interested. He had been brought by a friend to this mouldering house in a northern suburb, through an old garden to the room where Ambrose the recluse dozed and dreamed over his books.

"Yes," he went on, "magic is justified of her children. There are many, I think, who eat dry crusts and drink water, with a joy infinitely sharper than anything within the experience of the 'practical" epicure.'"

"You are speaking of the saints?"

"Yes, and of the sinners, too. I think you are falling into the very general error of confining the spiritual world to the supremely good; but the supremely wicked, necessarily, have their portion in it. The merely carnal, sensual man can no more be a great sinner than he can be a great saint. Most of us are just indifferent, mixed-up creatures; we muddle through the world without realizing the meaning and the inner sense of things, and, consequently, our wickedness and our goodness are alike second-rate, unimportant."

"And you think the great sinner, then, will be an ascetic, as well as the great saint?"

"Great people of all kinds forsake the imperfect copies and go to the perfect originals. I have no doubt but that many of the very highest among the saints have never done a 'good action' (using the words in their ordinary sense). And, on the other hand, there have been those who have sounded the very depths of sin, who all their lives have never done an 'ill deed.'"

He went out of the room for a moment, and Cotgrave, in high delight, turned to his friend and thanked him for the introduction.

"He's grand," he said. "I never saw that kind of lunatic before."

Ambrose returned with more whisky and helped the two men in a liberal manner. He abused the teetotal sect with ferocity, as he handed the seltzer, and pouring out a glass of water for himself, was about to resume his monologue, when Cotgrave broke in—

"I can't stand it, you know," he said, "your paradoxes are too monstrous. A man may be a great sinner and yet never do anything sinful! Come!"

"You're quite wrong," said Ambrose. "I never make paradoxes; I wish I could. I merely said that a man may have an exquisite taste in Romanée Conti, and yet never have even smelt four ale. That's all, and it's more like a truism than a paradox, isn't it? Your surprise at my remark is due to the fact that you haven't realized what sin is. Oh, yes, there is a sort of connexion between Sin with the capital letter, and actions which are commonly called sinful: with murder, theft, adultery, and so forth. Much the same connexion that there is between the A, B, C and fine literature. But I believe that the misconception—it is all but universal—arises in great measure from our looking at the matter through social spectacles. We think that a man who does evil to us and to his neighbors must be very evil. So he is, from a social standpoint; but can't you realize that Evil in its essence is a lonely thing, a passion of the solitary, individual soul? Really, the average murderer, quâ murderer, is not by any means a sinner in the true sense of the word. He is simply a wild beast that we have to get rid of to save our own necks from his knife. I should class him rather with tigers than with sinners."

"It seems a little strange."

"I think not. The murderer murders not from positive qualities, but from negative ones; he lacks something which non-murderers possess. Evil, of course, is wholly positive—only it is on the wrong side. You may believe me that sin in its proper sense is very rare; it is probable that there have been far fewer sinners than saints. Yes, your standpoint is all very well for practical, social purposes; we are naturally inclined to think that a person who is very disagreeable to us must be a very great sinner! It is very disagreeable to have one's pocket picked, and we pronounce the thief to be a very great sinner. In truth, he is merely an undeveloped man. He cannot be a saint, of course; but he may be, and often is, an infinitely better creature than thousands who have never broken a single commandment. He is a great nuisance to us, I admit, and we very properly lock him up if we catch him; but between his troublesome and unsocial action and evil—Oh, the connexion is of the weakest."

It was getting very late. The man who had brought Cotgrave had probably heard all this before, since he assisted with a bland and judicious smile, but Cotgrave began to think that his "lunatic" was turning into a sage.

"Do you know," he said, "you interest me immensely? You think, then, that we do not understand the real nature of evil?"

"No, I don't think we do. We over-estimate it and we under-estimate it. We take the very numerous infractions of our social 'bylaws'—the very necessary and very proper regulations which keep the human company together—and we get frightened at the prevalence of 'sin' and 'evil.' But this is really nonsense. Take theft, for example. Have you any horror at the thought of Robin Hood, of the Highland caterans of the seventeenth century, of the moss-troopers, of the company promoters of our day?

"Then, on the other hand, we underrate evil. We attach such an enormous importance to the 'sin' of meddling with our pockets (and our wives) that we have quite forgotten the awfulness of real sin."

"And what is sin?" said Cotgrave.

"I think I must reply to your question by another. What would your feelings be, seriously, if your cat or your dog began to talk to you, and to dispute with you in human accents? You would be overwhelmed with horror. I am sure of it. And if the roses in your garden sang a weird song, you would go mad. And suppose the stones in the road began to swell and grow before your eyes, and if the pebble that you noticed at night had shot out stony blossoms in the morning?

"Well, these examples may give you some notion of what sin really is."

"Look here," said the third man, hitherto placid, "you two seem pretty well wound up. But I'm going home. I've missed my tram, and I shall have to walk."

Ambrose and Cotgrave seemed to settle down more profoundly when the other had gone out into the early misty morning and the pale light of the lamps.

"You astonish me," said Cotgrave. "I had never thought of that. If that is really so, one must turn everything upside down. Then the essence of sin really is—"

"In the taking of heaven by storm, it seems to me," said Ambrose. "It appears to me that it is simply an attempt to penetrate into another and higher sphere in a forbidden manner. You can understand why it is so rare. There are few, indeed, who wish to penetrate into other spheres, higher or lower, in ways allowed or forbidden. Men, in the mass, are amply content with life as they find it. Therefore there are few saints, and sinners (in the proper sense) are fewer still, and men of genius, who partake sometimes of each character, are rare also. Yes; on the whole, it is, perhaps, harder to be a great sinner than a great saint."

"There is something profoundly unnatural about sin? Is that what you mean?"

"Exactly. Holiness requires as great, or almost as great, an effort; but holiness works on lines that *were* natural once; it is an effort to recover the ecstasy that was before the Fall. But sin is an effort to gain the ecstasy and the knowledge that pertain alone to angels, and in making this effort man becomes a demon. I told you that the mere murderer is not *therefore* a sinner; that is true, but the sinner is sometimes a murderer. Gilles de Raiz is an instance. So you see that while the good and the evil are unnatural to man as he now is—to man the social, civilized being—evil is unnatural in a much deeper sense than good. The saint endeavors to recover a gift which he has lost; the sinner tries to obtain something which was never his. In brief, he repeats the Fall."

"But are you a Catholic?" said Cotgrave.

"Yes; I am a member of the persecuted Anglican Church."

"Then, how about those texts which seem to reckon as sin that which you would set down as a mere trivial dereliction?"

"Yes; but in one place the word 'sorcerers' comes in the same sentence, doesn't it? That seems to me to give the key-note. Consider: can you imagine for a moment that a false statement which saves an innocent man's life is a sin? No; very good, then, it is not the mere liar who is excluded by those words; it is, above all, the 'sorcerers' who use the material life, who use the failings incidental to material life as instruments to obtain their infinitely wicked ends. And let me tell you this: our higher senses are so blunted, we are so drenched with materialism, that we should probably fail to recognize real wickedness if we encountered it."

"But shouldn't we experience a certain horror—a terror such as you hinted we would experience if a rose tree sang—in the mere presence of an evil man?"

"We should if we were natural: children and women feel this horror you speak of, even animals experience it. But with most of us convention and civilization and education have blinded and deafened and obscured the natural reason. No, sometimes we may recognize evil by its hatred of the good —one doesn't need much penetration to guess at the influence which dictated, quite unconsciously, the 'Blackwood' review of Keats—but this is purely incidental; and, as a rule, I suspect that the Hierarchs of Tophet pass quite unnoticed, or, perhaps, in certain cases, as good but mistaken men."

"But you used the word 'unconscious' just now, of Keats' reviewers. Is wickedness ever unconscious?"

"Always. It must be so. It is like holiness and genius in this as in other points; it is a certain rapture or ecstasy of the soul; a transcendent effort to surpass the ordinary bounds. So, surpassing these, it surpasses also the understanding, the faculty that takes note of that which comes before it. No, a man may be infinitely and horribly wicked and never suspect it. But I tell you, evil in this, its certain and true sense, is rare, and I think it is growing rarer."

"I am trying to get hold of it all," said Cotgrave. "From what you say, I gather that the true evil differs generically from that which we call evil?"

"Quite so. There is, no doubt, an analogy between the two; a resemblance such as enables us to use, quite legitimately, such terms as the 'foot of the mountain' and the 'leg of the table.' And, sometimes, of course, the two speak, as it were, in the same language. The rough miner, or 'puddler,' the untrained, undeveloped 'tiger-man,' heated by a quart or two above his usual measure, comes home and kicks his irritating and injudicious wife to death. He is a murderer. And Gilles de Raiz was a murderer. But you see the gulf that separates the two? The 'word,' if I may so speak, is accidentally the same in each case, but the 'meaning' is utterly different. It is flagrant 'Hobson Jobson' to confuse the two, or rather, it is as if one supposed that Juggernaut and the Argonauts had something to do etymologically with one another. And no doubt the same weak likeness, or analogy, runs between all the 'social' sins and the real spiritual sins, and in some cases, perhaps, the lesser may be 'schoolmasters' to lead one on to the greater—from the shadow to the reality. If you are anything of a Theologian, you will see the importance of all this."

"I am sorry to say," remarked Cotgrave, "that I have devoted very little of my time to theology. Indeed, I have often wondered on what grounds theologians have claimed the title of Science of Sciences for their favorite study; since the 'theological' books I have looked into have always seemed to me to be concerned with feeble and obvious pieties, or with the kings of Israel and Judah. I do not care to hear about those kings."

Ambrose grinned.

"We must try to avoid theological discussion," he said. "I perceive that you would be a bitter disputant. But perhaps the 'dates of the kings' have as much to do with theology as the hobnails of the murderous puddler with evil."

"Then, to return to our main subject, you think that sin is an esoteric, occult thing?"

"Yes. It is the infernal miracle as holiness is the supernal. Now and then it is raised to such a pitch that we entirely fail to suspect its existence; it is like the note of the great pedal pipes of the organ, which is so deep that we cannot hear it. In other cases it may lead to the lunatic asylum, or to still stranger issues. But you must never confuse it with mere social misdoing. Remember how the Apostle, speaking of the 'other side,' distinguishes between 'charitable' actions and charity. And as one may give all one's goods to the poor, and yet lack charity; so, remember, one may avoid every crime and yet be a sinner."

"Your psychology is very strange to me," said Cotgrave, "but I confess I like it, and I suppose that one might fairly deduce from your premises the conclusion that the real sinner might very possibly strike the observer as a harmless personage enough?"

"Certainly; because the true evil has nothing to do with social life or social laws, or if it has, only incidentally and accidentally. It is a lonely passion of the soul—or a passion of the lonely soul—whichever you like. If, by chance, we understand it, and grasp its full significance, then, indeed, it will fill us with horror and with awe. But this emotion is widely distinguished from the fear and the disgust with which we regard the ordinary criminal, since this latter is largely or entirely founded on the regard which we have for our own skins or purses. We hate a murderer, because we know that we should hate to be murdered, or to have any one that we like murdered. So, on the 'other side,' we venerate the saints, but we don't 'like' them as we like our friends. Can you persuade yourself that you would have 'enjoyed' St. Paul's company? Do you think that you and I would have 'got on' with Sir Galahad?

"So with the sinners, as with the saints. If you met a very evil man, and recognized his evil; he would, no doubt, fill you with horror and awe; but there is no reason why you should 'dislike' him. On the contrary, it is quite possible that if you could succeed in putting the sin out of your mind you might find the sinner capital company, and in a little while you might have to reason yourself back into horror. Still, how awful it is. If the roses and the lilies suddenly sang on this coming morning; if the furniture began to move in procession, as in De Maupassant's tale!"

"I am glad you have come back to that comparison," said Cotgrave, "because I wanted to ask you what it is that corresponds in humanity to these imaginary feats of inanimate things. In a word—what is sin? You have given me, I know, an abstract definition, but I should like a concrete example."

"I told you it was very rare," said Ambrose, who appeared willing to avoid the giving of a direct answer. "The materialism of the age, which has done a good deal to suppress sanctity, has done perhaps more to suppress evil. We find the earth so very comfortable that we have no inclination either for ascents or descents. It would seem as if the scholar who decided to 'specialize' in Tophet, would be reduced to purely antiquarian researches. No paleontologist could show you a *live* pterodactyl."

"And yet you, I think, have 'specialized,' and I believe that your researches have descended to our modern times."

"You are really interested, I see. Well, I confess, that I have dabbled a little, and if you like I can show you something that bears on the very curious subject we have been discussing."

Ambrose took a candle and went away to a far, dim corner of the room. Cotgrave saw him open a venerable bureau that stood there, and from some secret recess he drew out a parcel, and came back to the window where they had been sitting.

Ambrose undid a wrapping of paper, and produced a green pocket-book.

"You will take care of it?" he said. "Don't leave it lying about. It is one of the choicer pieces in my collection, and I should be very sorry if it were lost."

He fondled the faded binding.

"I knew the girl who wrote this," he said. "When you read it, you will see how it illustrates the talk we have had tonight. There is a sequel, too, but I won't talk of that."

"There was an odd article in one of the reviews some months ago," he began again, with the air of a man who changes the subject. "It was written by a doctor—Dr. Coryn, I think, was the name. He says that a lady, watching her little girl playing at the drawing-room window, suddenly saw the heavy sash give way and fall on the child's fingers. The lady fainted, I think, but at any rate the doctor was summoned, and when he had dressed the child's wounded and maimed fingers he was summoned to the mother. She was groaning with pain, and it was found that three fingers of her hand, corresponding with those that had been injured on the child's hand, were swollen and inflamed, and later, in the doctor's language, purulent sloughing set in."

Ambrose still handled delicately the green volume.

"Well, here it is," he said at last, parting with difficulty, it seemed, from his treasure.

"You will bring it back as soon as you have read it," he said, as they went out into the hall, into the old garden, faint with the odor of white lilies.

There was a broad red band in the east as Cotgrave turned to go, and from the high ground where he stood he saw that awful spectacle of London in a dream.

The Green Book

The morocco binding of the book was faded, and the color had grown faint, but there were no stains nor bruises nor marks of usage. The book looked as if it had been bought "on a visit to London" some seventy or eighty years ago, and had somehow been forgotten and suffered to lie away out of sight. There was an old, delicate, lingering odour about it, such an odor as sometimes haunts an ancient piece of furniture for a century or more. The end-papers, inside the binding, were oddly decorated with colored patterns and faded gold. It looked small, but the paper was fine, and there were many leaves, closely covered with minute, painfully formed characters.

I found this book (the manuscript began) in a drawer in the old bureau that stands on the landing. It was a very rainy day and I could not go out, so in the afternoon I got a candle and rummaged in the bureau. Nearly all the drawers were full of old dresses, but one of the small ones looked empty, and I found this book hidden right at the back. I wanted a book like this, so I took it to write in. It is full of secrets. I have a great many other books of secrets I have written, hidden in a safe place, and I am going to write here many of the old secrets and some new ones; but there are some I shall not put down at all. I must not write down the real names of the days and months which I found out a year ago, nor the way to make the Aklo letters, or the Chian language, or the great beautiful Circles, nor the Mao Games, nor the chief songs. I may write something about all these things but not the way to do them, for peculiar reasons. And I must not say who the Nymphs are, or the Dôls, or Jeelo, or what voolas mean. All these are most secret secrets, and I am glad when I remember what they are, and how many wonderful languages I know, but there are some things that I call the secrets of the secrets of the secrets that I dare not think of unless I am quite alone, and then I shut my eyes, and put my hands over them and whisper the word, and the Alala comes. I only do this at night in my room or in certain woods that I know, but I must not describe them, as they are secret woods. Then there are the Ceremonies, which are all of them important, but some are more delightful than others— there are the White Ceremonies, and the Green Ceremonies, and the Scarlet Ceremonies. The Scarlet Ceremonies are the best, but there is only one place where they can be performed properly, though there is a very nice imitation which I have done in other places. Besides these, I have the dances, and the

Comedy, and I have done the Comedy sometimes when the others were looking, and they didn't understand anything about it. I was very little when I first knew about these things.

When I was very small, and mother was alive, I can remember remembering things before that, only it has all got confused. But I remember when I was five or six I heard them talking about me when they thought I was not noticing. They were saying how queer I was a year or two before, and how nurse had called my mother to come and listen to me talking all to myself, and I was saying words that nobody could understand. I was speaking the Xu language, but I only remember a very few of the words, as it was about the little white faces that used to look at me when I was lying in my cradle. They used to talk to me, and I learnt their language and talked to them in it about some great white place where they lived, where the trees and the grass were all white, and there were white hills as high up as the moon, and a cold wind. I have often dreamed of it afterwards, but the faces went away when I was very little. But a wonderful thing happened when I was about five. My nurse was carrying me on her shoulder; there was a field of yellow corn, and we went through it, it was very hot. Then we came to a path through a wood, and a tall man came after us, and went with us till we came to a place where there was a deep pool, and it was very dark and shady. Nurse put me down on the soft moss under a tree, and she said: "She can't get to the pond now." So they left me there, and I sat quite still and watched, and out of the water and out of the wood came two wonderful white people, and they began to play and dance and sing. They were a kind of creamy white like the old ivory figure in the drawing-room; one was a beautiful lady with kind dark eyes, and a grave face, and long black hair, and she smiled such a strange sad smile at the other, who laughed and came to her. They played together, and danced round and round the pool, and they sang a song till I fell asleep. Nurse woke me up when she came back, and she was looking something like the lady had looked, so I told her all about it, and asked her why she looked like that. At first she cried, and then she looked very frightened, and turned quite pale. She put me down on the grass and stared at me, and I could see she was shaking all over. Then she said I had been dreaming, but I knew I hadn't. Then she made me promise not to say a word about it to anybody, and if I did I should be thrown into the black pit. I was not frightened at all, though nurse was, and I never forgot about it, because when I shut my eyes and it was quite quiet, and I was all alone, I could see them again, very faint and far away, but very splendid; and little bits of the song they sang came into my head, but I couldn't sing it.

I was thirteen, nearly fourteen, when I had a very singular adventure, so strange that the day on which it happened is always called the White Day. My mother had been dead for more than a year, and in the morning I had lessons, but they let me go out for walks in the afternoon. And this afternoon I walked a new way, and a little brook led me into a new country, but I tore my frock getting through some of the difficult places, as the way was through many bushes, and beneath the low branches of trees, and up thorny thickets on the hills, and by dark woods full of creeping thorns. And it was a long, long way. It seemed as if I was going on for ever and ever, and I had to creep by a place like a tunnel where a brook must have been, but all the water had dried up, and the floor was rocky, and the bushes had grown overhead till they met, so that it was quite dark. And I went on and on through that dark place; it was a long, long way. And I came to a hill that I never saw before. I was in a dismal thicket full of black twisted boughs that tore me as I went through them, and I cried out because I was smarting all over, and then I found that I was climbing, and I went up and up a long way, till at last the thicket stopped and I came out crying just under the top of a big bare place, where there were ugly grey stones lying all about on the grass, and here and there a little twisted, stunted tree came out from under a stone, like a snake. And I went up, right to the top, a long way. I never saw such big ugly stones before; they came out of the earth some of them, and some looked as if they had been rolled to where they were, and they went on and on as far as I could see, a long, long way. I looked out from them and saw the country, but it was strange. It was winter time, and there were black terrible woods hanging from the hills all round; it was like seeing a large room hung with black curtains, and the shape of the trees seemed quite different from any I had ever seen before. I was afraid. Then beyond the woods there were other hills round in a great ring, but I had never seen any of them; it all looked black, and everything had a voor over it. It was all so still and silent, and the sky was heavy and grey and sad, like a wicked voorish dome in Deep Dendo. I went on into the dreadful rocks. There were hundreds and hundreds of them. Some were like horrid-grinning men; I could see their faces as if they would jump at me out of the stone, and catch hold of me, and drag me with them back into the rock, so that I should always be there. And there were other rocks that were like animals, creeping, horrible animals, putting out their tongues, and others were like words that I could not say, and others like dead people lying on the grass. I went on among them, though they frightened me, and my heart was full of wicked songs that they put into it; and I wanted to make faces and twist myself about in the way they did, and I went on and on a long way till at last I liked the rocks, and they didn't frighten me any more. I sang the songs I thought of; songs full of words that must not be spoken or written down. Then I made faces like the faces on the rocks, and I twisted myself about like the twisted ones, and I lay down flat on the ground like the dead ones, and I went up to one that was grinning, and put my arms round him and hugged him. And so I went on and on through the rocks till I came to a round mound in the middle of them. It was higher than a mound, it was nearly as high as our house, and it was like a great basin turned upside down, all smooth and round and green, with one stone, like a post, sticking up at the top. I climbed up the sides, but they were so steep I had to stop or I should have rolled all the way down again, and I should have knocked against the stones at the bottom, and perhaps been killed. But I wanted to get up to the very top of the big round mound, so I lay down flat on my face, and took hold of the grass with my hands and drew myself up, bit by bit, till I was at the top. Then I sat down on the stone in the middle, and looked all round about. I felt I had come such a long, long way, just as if I were a hundred miles from home, or in some other country, or in one of the strange places I had read about in the *Tales of the Genie* and the *Arabian Nights*, or as if I had gone across the sea, far away, for years and I had found another world that nobody had ever seen or heard of before, or as if I had somehow flown through the sky and fallen on one of the stars I had read about where everything is dead and cold and grey, and there is no air, and the wind doesn't blow. I sat on the stone and looked all round and down and round about me. It was just as if I was sitting on a tower in the middle of a great empty town, because I could see nothing all around but the grey rocks on the ground. I couldn't make out their shapes any more, but I could see them on and on for a long way, and I looked at them, and they seemed as if they had been arranged into patterns, and shapes, and figures. I knew they couldn't be, because I had seen a lot of them coming right out of the earth, joined to the deep rocks below, so I looked again, but still I saw nothing but circles, and small circles inside big ones, and pyramids, and domes, and spires, and they seemed all to go round and round the place where I was sitting, and the more I looked, the more I saw great big rings of rocks, getting bigger and bigger, and I stared so long that it felt as if they were all moving and turning, like a great wheel, and I was turning, too, in the middle. I got quite dizzy and queer in the head, and everything began to be hazy and not clear, and I saw little sparks of blue light, and the stones looked as if they were springing and dancing and twisting as they went round and round and round. I was frightened again, and I cried out loud, and jumped up from the stone I was sitting on, and fell down. When I got up I was so glad they all looked still, and I sat down on the top and slid down the mound, and went on again. I danced as I went in the peculiar way the rocks had danced when I got giddy, and I was so glad I could do it quite well, and I danced and danced along, and sang extraordinary songs that came into my head. At last I came to the edge of that great flat hill, and there were no more rocks, and the way went again through a dark thicket in a hollow. It was just as bad as the other one I went through climbing up, but I didn't mind this one, because I was so glad I had seen those singular dances and could imitate them. I went down, creeping through the bushes, and a tall nettle stung me on my leg, and made me burn, but I didn't mind it, and I tingled with the boughs and the thorns, but I only laughed and sang. Then I got out of the thicket into a close valley, a little secret place like a dark passage that nobody ever knows of, because it was so narrow and deep and the woods were so thick round it. There is a steep bank with trees hanging over it, and there the ferns keep green all through the winter, when they are dead and brown upon the hill, and the ferns there have a sweet, rich smell like what oozes out of fir trees. There was a little stream of water running down this valley, so small that I could easily step across it. I drank the water with my hand, and it tasted like bright, yellow wine, and it sparkled and bubbled as it ran down over beautiful red and yellow and green stones, so that it seemed alive and all colors at once. I drank it, and I drank more with my hand, but I couldn't drink enough, so I lay down and bent my head and sucked the water up with my lips. It tasted much better, drinking it that way, and a ripple would come up to my mouth and give me a kiss, and I laughed, and drank again, and pretended there was a nymph, like the one in the old picture at home, who lived in the water and was kissing me. So I bent low down to the water, and put my lips softly to it, and whispered to the nymph that I would come again. I felt sure it could not be common water, I was so glad when I got up and went on; and I danced again and went up and up the valley, under hanging hills. And when I came to the top, the ground rose up in front of me, tall and steep as a wall, and there was nothing but the green wall and the sky. I thought of "for ever and for ever, world without end, Amen"; and I thought I must have really found the end of the world, because it was like the end of everything, as if there could be nothing at all beyond, except the kingdom of Voor, where the light goes when it is put out, and the water goes when the sun takes it away. I began to think of all the long, long way I had journeyed, how I had found a brook and followed it, and followed it on, and gone through bushes and thorny thickets, and dark woods full of creeping thorns. Then I had crept up a tunnel under trees, and climbed a thicket, and seen all the grey rocks, and sat in the middle of them when they turned round, and then I had gone on through the grey rocks and come down the hill through the stinging thicket and up the dark valley, all a long, long way. I wondered how I should get home again, if I could ever find the way, and if my home was there anymore, or if it were turned and everybody in it into grey rocks, as in the *Arabian Nights*. So I sat down on the grass and thought what I should do next. I was tired, and my feet were hot with walking, and as I looked about I saw there was a wonderful well just under the high, steep wall of grass. All the ground round it was covered with bright, green, dripping moss; there was every kind of moss there, moss like beautiful little ferns, and like palms and fir trees, and it was all green as jewelry, and drops of water hung on it like diamonds. And in the middle was the great well, deep and shining and beautiful, so clear that it looked as if I could touch the red sand at the bottom, but it was far below. I stood by it and looked in, as if I were looking in a glass. At the bottom of the well, in the middle of it, the red grains of sand were moving and stirring all the time, and I saw how the water bubbled up, but at the top it was quite smooth, and full and brimming. It was a great well, large like a bath, and with the shining, glittering green moss about it, it looked like a great white jewel, with green jewels all round. My feet were so hot and tired that I took off my boots and stockings, and let my feet down into the water, and the water was soft and cold, and when I got up I wasn't tired any more, and I felt I must go on, farther and farther, and see what was on the other side of the wall. I climbed up it very slowly, going sideways all the time, and when I got to the top and looked over, I was in the queerest country I had seen, stranger even than the hill of the grey rocks. It looked as if earth-children had been playing there with their spades, as it was all hills and hollows, and castles and walls made of earth and covered with grass. There were two mounds like big beehives, round and great and solemn, and then hollow basins, and then a steep mounting wall like the ones I saw once by the seaside where the big guns and the soldiers were. I nearly fell into one of the round hollows, it went away from under my feet so suddenly, and I ran fast down the side and stood at the bottom and looked up. It was strange and solemn to look up. There was nothing but the grey, heavy sky and the sides of the hollow; everything else had gone away, and the hollow was the whole world, and I thought that at night it must be full of ghosts and moving shadows and pale things when the moon shone down to the bottom at the dead of the night, and the wind wailed up above. It was so strange and solemn and lonely, like a hollow temple of dead heathen gods. It reminded me of a tale my nurse had told me when I was quite little; it was the same nurse that took me into the wood where I saw the beautiful white people. And I remembered how nurse had told me the story one winter night, when the wind was beating the trees against the wall, and crying and moaning in the nursery chimney. She said there was, somewhere or other, a hollow pit, just like the one I was standing in, everybody was afraid to go into it or near it, it was such a bad place. But once upon a time there was a poor girl who said she would go into the hollow pit, and everybody tried to stop her, but she would go. And she went down into the pit and came back laughing, and said there was nothing there at all, except green grass and red stones, and white stones and yellow flowers. And soon after people saw she had most beautiful emerald earrings, and they asked how she got them, as she and her mother were quite poor. But she laughed, and said her earrings were not made of emeralds at all, but only of green grass. Then, one day, she wore on her breast the reddest ruby that any one had ever seen, and it was as big as a hen's egg, and glowed and sparkled like a hot burning coal of fire. And they asked how she got it, as she and her mother were quite poor. But she laughed, and said it was not a ruby at all, but only a red stone. Then one day she wore round her neck the loveliest necklace that any one had ever seen, much finer than the queen's finest, and it was made of great bright diamonds, hundreds of them, and they shone like all the stars on a night in June. So they asked her how she got it, as she and her mother were quite poor. But she laughed, and said they were not diamonds at all, but only white stones. And one day she went to the Court, and she wore on her head a crown of pure angel-gold, so nurse said, and it shone like the sun, and it was much more splendid than the crown the king was wearing himself, and in her ears she wore the emeralds, and the big ruby was the brooch on her breast, and the great diamond necklace was sparkling on her neck. And the king and queen thought she was some great princess from a long way off, and got down from their thrones and went to meet her, but somebody told the king and queen who she was, and that she was quite poor. So the king asked why she wore a gold crown, and how she got it, as she and her mother were so poor. And she laughed, and said it wasn't a gold crown at all, but only some yellow flowers she had put in her hair. And the king thought it was very strange, and said she should stay at the Court, and they would see what would happen next. And she was so lovely that everybody said that her eyes were greener than the emeralds, that her lips were redder than the ruby, that her skin was whiter than the diamonds, and that her hair was brighter than the golden crown. So the king's son said he would marry her, and the king said he might. And the bishop married them, and there was a great supper, and afterwards the king's son went to his wife's room. But just when he had his hand on the door, he saw a tall, black man, with a dreadful face, standing in front of the door, and a voice said—

> Venture not upon your life,
> This is mine own wedded wife.

Then the king's son fell down on the ground in a fit. And they came and tried to get into the room, but they couldn't, and they hacked at the door with hatchets, but the wood had turned hard as iron, and at last everybody ran away, they were so frightened at the screaming and laughing and shrieking and crying that came out of the room. But next day they went in, and found there was nothing in the room but thick black smoke, because the black man had come and taken her away. And on the bed there were two knots of faded grass and a red stone, and some white stones, and some faded yellow flowers. I remembered this tale of nurse's while I was standing at the bottom of the deep hollow; it was so strange and solitary there, and I felt afraid. I could not see any stones or flowers, but I was afraid of bringing them away without knowing, and I thought I would do a charm that came into my head to keep the black man away. So I stood right in the very middle of the hollow, and I made sure that I had none of those things on me, and then I walked round the place, and touched my eyes, and my lips, and my hair in a peculiar manner, and whispered some queer words that nurse taught me to keep bad things away. Then I felt safe and climbed up out of the hollow, and went on through all those mounds and hollows and walls, till I came to the end, which was high above all the rest, and I could see that all the different shapes of the earth were arranged in patterns, something like the grey rocks, only the pattern was different. It was getting late, and the air was indistinct, but it looked from where I was standing something like two great figures of people lying on the grass. And I went on, and at last I found a certain wood, which is too secret to be described, and nobody knows of the passage into it, which I found out in a very curious manner, by seeing some little animal run into the wood through it. So I went after the animal by a very narrow dark way, under thorns and bushes, and it was almost dark when I came to a kind of open place in the middle. And there I saw the most wonderful sight I have ever seen, but it was only for a minute, as I ran away directly, and crept out of the wood by the passage I had come by, and ran and ran as fast as ever I could, because I was afraid, what I had seen was so wonderful and so strange and beautiful. But I wanted to get home and think of it, and I did not know what might not happen if I stayed by the wood. I was hot all over and trembling, and my heart was beating, and strange cries that I could not help came from me as I ran from the wood. I was glad that a great white moon came up from over a round hill and showed me the way, so I went back through the mounds and hollows and down the close valley, and up through the thicket over the place of the grey rocks, and so at last I got home again. My father was busy in his study, and the servants had not told about my not coming home, though they were frightened, and wondered what they ought to do, so I told them I had lost my way, but I did not let them find out the real way I had been. I went to bed and lay awake all through the night, thinking of what I had seen. When I came out of the narrow way, and it looked all shining, though the air was dark, it seemed so certain, and all the way home I was quite sure that I had seen it, and I wanted to be alone in my room, and be glad over it all to myself, and shut my eyes and pretend it was there, and do all the things I would have done if I had not been so afraid. But when I shut my eyes the sight would not come, and I began to think about my adventures all over again, and I remembered how dusky and queer it was at the end, and I was afraid it must be all a mistake, because it seemed impossible it could happen. It seemed like one of nurse's tales, which I didn't really believe in, though I was frightened at the bottom of the hollow; and the stories she told me when I was little came back into my head, and I wondered whether it was really there what I thought I had seen, or whether any of her tales could have happened a long time ago. It was so queer; I lay awake there in my room at the back of the house, and the moon was shining on the other side towards the river, so the bright light did not fall upon the wall. And the house was quite still. I had heard my father come upstairs, and just after the clock struck twelve, and after the house was still and empty, as if there was nobody alive in it. And though it was all dark and indistinct in my room, a pale glimmering kind of light shone in through the white blind, and once I got up and looked out, and there was a great black shadow of the house covering the garden, looking like a prison where men are hanged; and then beyond it was all white; and the wood shone white with black gulfs between the trees. It was still and clear, and there were no clouds on the sky. I wanted to think of what I had seen but I couldn't, and I began to think of all the tales that nurse had told me so long ago that I thought I had forgotten, but they all came back, and mixed up with the thickets and the grey rocks and the hollows in the earth and the secret wood, till I hardly knew what was new and what was old, or whether it was not all dreaming. And then I remembered that hot summer afternoon, so long ago, when nurse left me by myself in the shade, and the white people came out of the water and out of the wood, and played, and danced, and sang, and I began to fancy that nurse told me about something like it before I saw them, only I couldn't recollect exactly what she told me. Then I wondered whether she had been the white lady, as I remembered she was just as white and beautiful, and had the same dark eyes and black hair; and sometimes she smiled and looked like the lady had looked, when she was telling me some of her stories, beginning with "Once on a time," or "In the time of the fairies." But I thought she couldn't be the lady, as she seemed to have gone a different way into the wood, and I didn't think the man who came after us could be the other, or I couldn't have seen that wonderful secret in the secret wood. I thought of the moon: but it was afterwards when I was in the middle of the wild land, where the earth was made into the shape of great figures, and it was all walls, and mysterious hollows, and smooth round mounds, that I saw the great white moon come up over a round hill. I was wondering about all these things, till at last I got quite frightened, because I was afraid something had happened to me, and I remembered nurse's tale of the poor girl who went into the hollow pit, and was carried away at last by the black man. I knew I had gone into a hollow pit too, and perhaps it was the same, and I had done something dreadful. So I did the charm over again, and touched my eyes and my lips and my hair in a peculiar manner, and said the old words from the fairy language, so that I might be sure I had not been carried away. I tried again to see the secret wood, and to creep up the passage and see what I had seen there, but somehow I couldn't, and I kept on thinking of nurse's stories. There was one I remembered about a young man who once upon a time went hunting, and all the day he and his hounds hunted everywhere, and they crossed the rivers and went into all the woods, and went round the marshes, but they couldn't find anything at all, and they hunted all day till the sun sank down and began to set behind the mountain. And the young man was angry because he couldn't find anything, and he was going to turn back, when just as the sun touched the mountain, he saw come out of a brake in front of him a beautiful white stag. And he cheered to his hounds, but they whined and would not follow, and he cheered to his horse, but it shivered and stood stock still, and the young man jumped off the horse and left the hounds and began to follow the white stag all alone. And soon it was quite dark, and the sky was black, without a single star shining in it, and the stag went away into the darkness. And though the man had brought his gun with him he never shot at the stag, because he wanted to catch it, and he was afraid he would lose it in the night. But he never lost it once, though the sky was so black and the air was so dark, and the stag went on and on till the young man didn't know a bit where he was. And they went through enormous woods where the air was full of whispers and a pale, dead light came out from the rotten trunks that were lying on the ground, and just as the man thought he had lost the stag, he would see it all white and shining in front of him, and he would run fast to catch it, but the stag always ran faster, so he did not catch it. And they went through the enormous woods, and they swam across rivers, and they waded through black marshes where the ground bubbled, and the air was full of will-o'-the-wisps, and the stag fled away down into rocky narrow valleys, where the air was like the smell of a vault, and the man went after it. And they went over the great mountains and the man heard the wind come down from the sky, and the stag went on and the man went after. At last the sun rose and the young man found he was in a country that he had never seen before; it was a beautiful valley with a bright stream running through it, and a great, big round hill in the middle. And the stag went down the valley, towards the hill, and it seemed to be getting tired and went slower and slower, and though the man was tired, too, he began to run faster, and he was sure he would catch the stag at last. But just as they got to the bottom of the hill, and the man stretched out his hand to catch the stag, it vanished into the earth, and the man began to cry; he was so sorry that he had lost it after all his long hunting. But as he was crying he saw there was a door in the hill, just in front of him, and he went in, and it was quite dark, but he went on, as he thought he would find the white stag. And all of a sudden it got light, and there was the sky, and the sun shining, and birds singing in the trees, and there was a beautiful fountain. And by the fountain a lovely lady was sitting, who was the queen of the fairies, and she told the man that she had changed herself into a stag to bring him there because she loved him so much. Then she brought out a great gold cup, covered with jewels, from her fairy palace, and she offered him wine in the cup to drink. And he drank, and the more he drank the more he longed to drink, because the wine was enchanted. So he kissed the lovely lady, and she became his wife, and he stayed all that day and all that night in the hill where she lived, and when he woke he found he was lying on the ground, close to where he had seen the stag first, and his horse was there and his hounds were there waiting, and he looked up, and the sun sank behind the mountain. And he went home and lived a long time, but he would never kiss any other lady because he had kissed the queen of the fairies, and he would never drink common wine any more, because he had drunk enchanted wine. And sometimes nurse told me tales that she had heard from her great-grandmother, who was very old, and lived in a cottage on the mountain all alone, and most of these tales were about a hill where people used to meet at night long ago, and they used to play all sorts of strange games and do queer things that nurse told me of, but I couldn't understand, and now, she said, everybody but her great-grandmother had forgotten all about it, and nobody knew where the hill was, not even her great-grandmother. But she told me one very strange story about the hill, and I trembled when I remembered it. She said that people always went there in summer, when it was very hot, and they had to dance a good deal. It would be all dark at first, and there were trees there, which made it much darker, and people would come, one by one, from all directions, by a secret path which nobody else knew, and two persons would keep the gate, and every one as they came up had to give a very curious sign, which nurse showed me as well as she could, but she said she couldn't show me properly. And all kinds of people would come; there would be gentle folks and village folks, and some old people and boys and girls, and quite small children, who sat and watched. And it would all be dark as they came in, except in one corner where some one was burning something that smelt strong and sweet, and made them laugh, and there one would see a glaring of coals, and the smoke mounting up red. So they would all come in, and when the last had come there was no door any more, so that no one else could get in, even if they knew there was anything beyond. And once a gentleman who was a stranger and had ridden a long way, lost his path at night, and his horse took him into the very middle of the wild country, where everything was upside down, and there were dreadful marshes and great stones everywhere, and holes underfoot, and the trees looked like gibbet-posts, because they had great black arms that stretched out across the way. And this strange gentleman was very frightened, and his horse began to shiver all over, and at last it stopped and wouldn't go any farther, and the gentleman got down and tried to lead the horse, but it wouldn't move, and it was all covered with a sweat, like death. So the gentleman went on all alone, going farther and farther into the wild country, till at last he came to a dark place, where he heard shouting and singing and crying, like nothing he had ever heard before. It all sounded quite close to him, but he couldn't get in, and so he began to call, and while he was calling, something came behind him, and in a minute his mouth and arms and legs were all bound up, and he fell into a swoon. And when he came to himself, he was lying by the roadside, just where he had first lost his way, under a blasted oak with a black trunk, and his horse was tied beside him. So he rode on to the town and told the people there what had happened, and some of them were amazed; but others knew. So when once everybody had come, there was no door at all for anybody else to pass in by. And when they were all inside, round in a ring, touching each other, some one began to sing in the darkness, and some one else would make a noise like thunder with a thing they had on purpose, and on still nights people would hear the thundering noise far, far away beyond the wild land, and some of them, who thought they knew what it was, used to make a sign on their breasts when they woke up in their beds at dead of night and heard that terrible deep noise, like thunder on the mountains. And the noise and the singing would go on and on for a long time, and the people who were in a ring swayed a little to and fro; and the song was in an old, old language that nobody knows now, and the tune was queer. Nurse said her great-grandmother had known some one who remembered a little of it, when she was quite a little girl, and nurse tried to sing some of it to me, and it was so strange a tune that I turned all cold and my flesh crept as if I had put my hand on something dead. Sometimes it was a man that sang and sometimes it was a woman, and sometimes the one who sang it did it so well that two or three of the people who were there fell to the ground shrieking and tearing with their hands. The singing went on, and the people in the ring kept swaying to and fro for a long time, and at last the moon would rise over a place they called the Tole Deol, and came up and showed them swinging and swaying from side to side, with the sweet thick smoke curling up from the burning coals, and floating in circles all around them. Then they had their supper. A boy and a girl brought it to them; the boy carried a great cup of wine, and the girl carried a cake of bread, and they passed the bread and the wine round and round, but they tasted quite different from common bread and common wine, and changed everybody that tasted them. Then they all rose up and danced, and secret things were brought out of some hiding place, and they played extraordinary games, and danced round and round and round in the moonlight, and sometimes people would suddenly disappear and never be heard of afterwards, and nobody knew what had happened to them. And they drank more of that curious wine, and they made images and worshipped them, and nurse showed me how the images were made one day when we were out for a walk, and we passed by a place where there was a lot of wet clay. So nurse asked me if I would like to know what those things were like that they made on the hill, and I said yes. Then she asked me if I would promise never to tell a living soul a word about it, and if I did I was to be thrown into the black pit with the dead people, and I said I wouldn't tell anybody, and she said the same thing again and again, and I promised. So she took my wooden spade and dug a big lump of clay and put it in my tin bucket, and told me to say if any one met us that I was going to make pies when I went home. Then we went on a little way till we came to a little brake growing right down into the road, and nurse stopped, and looked up the road and down it, and then peeped through the hedge into the field on the other side, and then she said, "Quick!" and we ran into the brake, and crept in and out among the bushes till we had gone a good way from the road. Then we sat down under a bush, and I wanted so much to know what nurse was going to make with the clay, but before she would begin she made me promise again not to say a word about it, and she went again and peeped through the bushes on every side, though the lane was so small and deep that hardly anybody ever went there. So we sat down, and nurse took the clay out of the bucket, and began to knead it with her hands, and do queer things with it, and turn it about. And she hid it under a big dock-leaf for a minute or two and then she brought it out again, and then she stood up and sat down, and walked round the clay in a peculiar manner, and all the time she was softly singing a sort of rhyme, and her face got very red. Then she sat down again, and took the clay in her hands and began to shape it into a doll, but not like the dolls I have at home, and she made the queerest doll I had ever seen, all out of the wet clay, and hid it under a bush to get dry and hard, and all the time she was making it she was singing these rhymes to herself, and her face got redder and redder. So we left the doll there, hidden away in the bushes where nobody would ever find it. And a few days later we went the same walk, and when we came to that narrow, dark part of the lane where the brake runs down to the bank, nurse made me promise all over again, and she looked about, just as she had done before, and we crept into the bushes till we got to the green place where the little clay man was hidden. I remember it all so well, though I was only eight, and it is eight years ago now as I am writing it down, but the sky was a deep violet blue, and in the middle of the brake where we were sitting there was a great elder tree covered with blossoms, and on the other side there was a clump of meadowsweet, and when I think of that day the smell of the meadowsweet and elder blossom seems to fill the room, and if I shut my eyes I can see the glaring blue sky, with little clouds very white floating across it, and nurse who went away long ago sitting opposite me and looking like the beautiful white lady in the wood. So we sat down and nurse took out the clay doll from the secret place where she had hidden it, and she said we must "pay our respects," and she would show me what to do, and I must watch her all the time. So she did all sorts of queer things with the little clay man, and I noticed she was all streaming with perspiration, though we had walked so slowly, and then she told me to "pay my respects," and I did everything she did because I liked her, and it was such an odd game. And she said that if one loved very much, the clay man was very good, if one did certain things with it, and if one hated very much, it was just as good, only one had to do different things, and we played with it a long time, and pretended all sorts of things. Nurse said her great-grandmother had told her all about these images, but what we did was no harm at all, only a game. But she told me a story about these images that frightened me very much, and that was what I remembered that night when I was lying awake in my room in the pale, empty darkness, thinking of what I had seen and the secret wood. Nurse said there was once a young lady of the high gentry, who lived in a great castle. And she was so beautiful that all the gentlemen wanted to marry her, because she was the loveliest lady that anybody had ever seen, and she was kind to everybody, and everybody thought she was very good. But though she was polite to all the gentlemen who wished to marry her, she put them off, and said she couldn't make up her mind, and she wasn't sure she wanted to marry anybody at all. And her father, who was a very great lord, was angry, though he was so fond of her, and he asked her why she wouldn't choose a bachelor out of all the handsome young men who came to the castle. But she only said she didn't love any of them very much, and she must wait, and if they pestered her, she said she would go and be a nun in a nunnery. So all the gentlemen said they would go away and wait for a year and a day, and when a year and a day were gone, they would come back again and ask her to say which one she would marry. So the day was appointed and they all went away; and the lady had promised that in a year and a day it would be her wedding day with one of them. But the truth was, that she was the queen of the people who danced on the hill on summer nights, and on the proper nights she would lock the door of her room, and she and her maid would steal out of the castle by a secret passage that only they knew of, and go away up to the hill in the wild land. And she knew more of the secret things than any one else, and more than any one knew before or after, because she would not tell anybody the most secret secrets. She knew how to do all the awful things, how to destroy young men, and how to put a curse on people, and other things that I could not understand. And her real name was the Lady Avelin, but the dancing people called her Cassap, which meant somebody very wise, in the old language. And she was whiter than any of them and taller, and her eyes shone in the dark like burning rubies; and she could sing songs that none of the others could sing, and when she sang they all fell down on their faces and worshipped her. And she could do what they called shib-show, which was a very wonderful enchantment. She would tell the great lord, her father, that she wanted to go into the woods to gather flowers, so he let her go, and she and her maid went into the woods where nobody came, and the maid would keep watch. Then the lady would lie down under the trees and begin to sing a particular song, and she stretched out her arms, and from every part of the wood great serpents would come, hissing and gliding in and out among the trees, and shooting out their forked tongues as they crawled up to the lady. And they all came to her, and twisted round her, round her body, and her arms, and her neck, till she was covered with writhing serpents, and there was only her head to be seen. And she whispered to them, and she sang to them, and they writhed round and round, faster and faster, till she told them to go. And they all went away directly, back to their holes, and on the lady's breast there would be a most curious, beautiful stone, shaped something like an egg, and colored dark blue and yellow, and red, and green, marked like a serpent's scales. It was called a glame stone, and with it one could do all sorts of wonderful things, and nurse said her great-grandmother had seen a glame stone with her own eyes, and it was for all the world shiny and scaly like a snake. And the lady could do a lot of other things as well, but she was quite fixed that she would not be married. And there were a great many gentlemen who wanted to marry her, but there were five of them who were chief, and their names were Sir Simon, Sir John, Sir Oliver, Sir Richard, and Sir Rowland. All the others believed she spoke the truth, and that she would choose one of them to be her man when a year and a day was done; it was only Sir Simon, who was very crafty, who thought she was deceiving them all, and he vowed he would watch and try if he could find out anything. And though he was very wise he was very young, and he had a smooth, soft face like a girl's, and he pretended, as the rest did, that he would not come to the castle for a year and a day, and he said he was going away beyond the sea to foreign parts. But he really only went a very little way, and came back dressed like a servant girl, and so he got a place in the castle to wash the dishes. And he waited and watched, and he listened and said nothing, and he hid in dark places, and woke up at night and looked out, and he heard things and he saw things that he thought were very strange. And he was so sly that he told the girl that waited on the lady that he was really a young man, and that he had dressed up as a girl because he loved her so very much and wanted to be in the same house with her, and the girl was so pleased that she told him many things, and he was more than ever certain that the Lady Avelin was deceiving him and the others. And he was so clever, and told the servant so many lies, that one night he managed to hide in the

Lady Avelin's room behind the curtains. And he stayed quite still and never moved, and at last the lady came. And she bent down under the bed, and raised up a stone, and there was a hollow place underneath, and out of it she took a waxen image, just like the clay one that I and nurse had made in the brake. And all the time her eyes were burning like rubies. And she took the little wax doll up in her arms and held it to her breast, and she whispered and she murmured, and she took it up and she laid it down again, and she held it high, and she held it low, and she laid it down again. And she said, "Happy is he that begat the bishop, that ordered the clerk, that married the man, that had the wife, that fashioned the hive, that harbored the bee, that gathered the wax that my own true love was made of." And she brought out of an aumbry a great golden bowl, and she brought out of a closet a great jar of wine, and she poured some of the wine into the bowl, and she laid her mannikin very gently in the wine, and washed it in the wine all over. Then she went to a cupboard and took a small round cake and laid it on the image's mouth, and then she bore it softly and covered it up. And Sir Simon, who was watching all the time, though he was terribly frightened, saw the lady bend down and stretch out her arms and whisper and sing, and then Sir Simon saw beside her a handsome young man, who kissed her on the lips. And they drank wine out of the golden bowl together, and they ate the cake together. But when the sun rose there was only the little wax doll, and the lady hid it again under the bed in the hollow place. So Sir Simon knew quite well what the lady was, and he waited and he watched, till the time she had said was nearly over, and in a week the year and a day would be done. And one night, when he was watching behind the curtains in her room, he saw her making more wax dolls. And she made five, and hid them away. And the next night she took one out, and held it up, and filled the golden bowl with water, and took the doll by the neck and held it under the water. Then she said—

Sir Dickon, Sir Dickon, your day is done,
You shall be drowned in the water wan.

And the next day news came to the castle that Sir Richard had been drowned at the ford. And at night she took another doll and tied a violet cord round its neck and hung it up on a nail. Then she said—

Sir Rowland, your life has ended its span,
High on a tree I see you hang.

And the next day news came to the castle that Sir Rowland had been hanged by robbers in the wood. And at night she took another doll, and drove her bodkin right into its heart. Then she said—

Sir Noll, Sir Noll, so cease your life,
Your heart piercèd with the knife.

And the next day news came to the castle that Sir Oliver had fought in a tavern, and a stranger had stabbed him to the heart. And at night she took another doll, and held it to a fire of charcoal till it was melted. Then she said —

    Sir John, return, and turn to clay
      In fire of fever you waste away.

And the next day news came to the castle that Sir John had died in a burning fever. So then Sir Simon went out of the castle and mounted his horse and rode away to the bishop and told him everything. And the bishop sent his men, and they took the Lady Avelin, and everything she had done was found out. So on the day after the year and a day, when she was to have been married, they carried her through the town in her smock, and they tied her to a great stake in the market-place, and burned her alive before the bishop with her wax image hung round her neck. And people said the wax man screamed in the burning of the flames. And I thought of this story again and again as I was lying awake in my bed, and I seemed to see the Lady Avelin in the market-place, with the yellow flames eating up her beautiful white body. And I thought of it so much that I seemed to get into the story myself, and I fancied I was the lady, and that they were coming to take me to be burnt with fire, with all the people in the town looking at me. And I wondered whether she cared, after all the strange things she had done, and whether it hurt very much to be burned at the stake. I tried again and again to forget nurse's stories, and to remember the secret I had seen that afternoon, and what was in the secret wood, but I could only see the dark and a glimmering in the dark, and then it went away, and I only saw myself running, and then a great moon came up white over a dark round hill. Then all the old stories came back again, and the queer rhymes that nurse used to sing to me; and there was one beginning "Halsy cumsy Helen musty," that she used to sing very softly when she wanted me to go to sleep. And I began to sing it to myself inside of my head, and I went to sleep.

The next morning I was very tired and sleepy, and could hardly do my lessons, and I was very glad when they were over and I had had my dinner, as I wanted to go out and be alone. It was a warm day, and I went to a nice turfy hill by the river, and sat down on my mother's old shawl that I had brought with me on purpose. The sky was grey, like the day before, but there was a kind of white gleam behind it, and from where I was sitting I could look down on the town, and it was all still and quiet and white, like a picture. I remembered that it was on that hill that nurse taught me to play an old game called "Troy Town," in which one had to dance, and wind in and out on a pattern in the grass, and then when one had danced and turned long enough the other person asks you questions, and you can't help answering whether you want to or not, and whatever you are told to do you feel you have to do it.

Nurse said there used to be a lot of games like that that some people knew of, and there was one by which people could be turned into anything you liked, and an old man her great-grandmother had seen had known a girl who had been turned into a large snake. And there was another very ancient game of dancing and winding and turning, by which you could take a person out of himself and hide him away as long as you liked, and his body went walking about quite empty, without any sense in it. But I came to that hill because I wanted to think of what had happened the day before, and of the secret of the wood. From the place where I was sitting I could see beyond the town, into the opening I had found, where a little brook had led me into an unknown country. And I pretended I was following the brook over again, and I went all the way in my mind, and at last I found the wood, and crept into it under the bushes, and then in the dusk I saw something that made me feel as if I were filled with fire, as if I wanted to dance and sing and fly up into the air, because I was changed and wonderful. But what I saw was not changed at all, and had not grown old, and I wondered again and again how such things could happen, and whether nurse's stories were really true, because in the daytime in the open air everything seemed quite different from what it was at night, when I was frightened, and thought I was to be burned alive. I once told my father one of her little tales, which was about a ghost, and asked him if it was true, and he told me it was not true at all, and that only common, ignorant people believed in such rubbish. He was very angry with nurse for telling me the story, and scolded her, and after that I promised her I would never whisper a word of what she told me, and if I did I should be bitten by the great black snake that lived in the pool in the wood. And all alone on the hill I wondered what was true. I had seen something very amazing and very lovely, and I knew a story, and if I had really seen it, and not made it up out of the dark, and the black bough, and the bright shining that was mounting up to the sky from over the great round hill, but had really seen it in truth, then there were all kinds of wonderful and lovely and terrible things to think of, so I longed and trembled, and I burned and got cold. And I looked down on the town, so quiet and still, like a little white picture, and I thought over and over if it could be true. I was a long time before I could make up my mind to anything; there was such a strange fluttering at my heart that seemed to whisper to me all the time that I had not made it up out of my head, and yet it seemed quite impossible, and I knew my father and everybody would say it was dreadful rubbish. I never dreamed of telling him or anybody else a word about it, because I knew it would be of no use, and I should only get laughed at or scolded, so for a long time I was very quiet, and went about thinking and wondering; and at night I used to dream of amazing things, and sometimes I woke up in the early morning and held out my arms with a cry. And I was frightened, too, because there were dangers, and some awful thing would happen to me, unless I took great care, if the story were true. These old tales were always in my head, night and morning, and I went over them and told them to myself over and over again, and went for walks in the places where nurse had told them to me; and when I sat in the nursery by the fire in the evenings I used to fancy nurse was sitting in the other chair, and telling me some wonderful story in a low voice, for fear anybody should be listening. But she used to like best to tell me about things when we were right out in the country, far from the house, because she said she was telling me such secrets, and walls have ears. And if it was something more than ever secret, we had to hide in brakes or woods; and I used to think it was such fun creeping along a hedge, and going very softly, and then we would get behind the bushes or run into the wood all of a sudden, when we were sure that none was watching us; so we knew that we had our secrets quite all to ourselves, and nobody else at all knew anything about them. Now and then, when we had hidden ourselves as I have described, she used to show me all sorts of odd things. One day, I remember, we were in a hazel brake, overlooking the brook, and we were so snug and warm, as though it was April; the sun was quite hot, and the leaves were just coming out. Nurse said she would show me something funny that would make me laugh, and then she showed me, as she said, how one could turn a whole house upside down, without anybody being able to find out, and the pots and pans would jump about, and the china would be broken, and the chairs would tumble over of themselves. I tried it one day in the kitchen, and I found I could do it quite well, and a whole row of plates on the dresser fell off it, and cook's little work-table tilted up and turned right over "before her eyes," as she said, but she was so frightened and turned so white that I didn't do it again, as I liked her. And afterwards, in the hazel copse, when she had shown me how to make things tumble about, she showed me how to make rapping noises, and I learnt how to do that, too. Then she taught me rhymes to say on certain occasions, and peculiar marks to make on other occasions, and other things that her great-grandmother had taught her when she was a little girl herself. And these were all the things I was thinking about in those days after the strange walk when I thought I had seen a great secret, and I wished nurse were there for me to ask her about it, but she had gone away more than two years before, and nobody seemed to know what had become of her, or where she had gone. But I shall always remember those days if I live to be quite old, because all the time I felt so strange, wondering and doubting, and feeling quite sure at one time, and making up my mind, and then I would feel quite sure that such things couldn't happen really, and it began all over again. But I took great care not to do certain things that might be very dangerous. So I waited and wondered for a long time, and though I was not sure at all, I never dared to try to find out. But one day I became sure that all that nurse said was quite true, and I was all alone when I found it out. I trembled all over with joy and terror, and as fast as I could I ran into one of the old brakes where we used to go—it was the one by the lane, where nurse made the little clay man—and I ran into it, and I crept into it; and when I came to the place where the elder was, I covered up my face with my hands and lay down flat on the grass, and I stayed there for two hours without moving, whispering to myself delicious, terrible things, and saying some words over and over again. It was all true and wonderful and splendid, and when I remembered the story I knew and thought of what I had really seen, I got hot and I got cold, and the air seemed full of scent, and flowers, and singing. And first I wanted to make a little clay man, like the one nurse had made so long ago, and I had to invent plans and stratagems, and to look about, and to think of things beforehand, because nobody must dream of anything that I was doing or going to do, and I was too old to carry clay about in a tin bucket. At last I thought of a plan, and I brought the wet clay to the brake, and did everything that nurse had done, only I made a much finer image than the one she had made; and when it was finished I did everything that I could imagine and much more than she did, because it was the likeness of something far better. And a few days later, when I had done my lessons early, I went for the second time by the way of the little brook that had led me into a strange country. And I followed the brook, and went through the bushes, and beneath the low branches of trees, and up thorny thickets on the hill, and by dark woods full of creeping thorns, a long, long way. Then I crept through the dark tunnel where the brook had been and the ground was stony, till at last I came to the thicket that climbed up the hill, and though the leaves were coming out upon the trees, everything looked almost as black as it was on the first day that I went there. And the thicket was just the same, and I went up slowly till I came out on the big bare hill, and began to walk among the wonderful rocks. I saw the terrible voor again on everything, for though the sky was brighter, the ring of wild hills all around was still dark, and the hanging woods looked dark and dreadful, and the strange rocks were as grey as ever; and when I looked down on them from the great mound, sitting on the stone, I saw all their amazing circles and rounds within rounds, and I had to sit quite still and watch them as they began to turn about me, and each stone danced in its place, and they seemed to go round and round in a great whirl, as if one were in the middle of all the stars and heard them rushing through the air. So I went down among the rocks to dance with them and to sing extraordinary songs; and I went down through the other thicket, and drank from the bright stream in the close and secret valley, putting my lips down to the bubbling water; and then I went on till I came to the deep, brimming well among the glittering moss, and I sat down. I looked before me into the secret darkness of the valley, and behind me was the great high wall of grass, and all around me there were the hanging woods that made the valley such a secret place. I knew there was nobody here at all besides myself, and that no one could see me. So I took off my boots and stockings, and let my feet down into the water, saying the words that I knew. And it was not cold at all, as I expected, but warm and very pleasant, and when my feet were in it I felt as if they were in silk, or as if the nymph were kissing them. So when I had done, I said the other words and made the signs, and then I dried my feet with a towel I had brought on purpose, and put on my stockings and boots. Then I climbed up the steep wall, and went into the place where there are the hollows, and the two beautiful mounds, and the round ridges of land, and all the strange shapes. I did not go down into the hollow this time, but I turned at the end, and made out the figures quite plainly, as it was lighter, and I had remembered the story I had quite forgotten before, and in the story the two figures are called Adam and Eve, and only those who know the story understand what they mean. So I went on and on till I came to the secret wood which must not be described, and I crept into it by the way I had found. And when I had gone about halfway I stopped, and turned round, and got ready, and I bound the handkerchief tightly round my eyes, and made quite sure that I could not see at all, not a twig, nor the end of a leaf, nor the light of the sky, as it was an old red silk handkerchief with large yellow spots, that went round twice and covered my eyes, so that I could see nothing. Then I began to go on, step by step, very slowly. My heart beat faster and faster, and something rose in my throat that choked me and made me want to cry out, but I shut my lips, and went on. Boughs caught in my hair as I went, and great thorns tore me; but I went on to the end of the path. Then I stopped, and held out my arms and bowed, and I went round the first time, feeling with my hands, and there was nothing. I went round the second time, feeling with my hands, and there was nothing. Then I went round the third time, feeling with my hands, and the story was all true, and I wished that the years were gone by, and that I had not so long a time to wait before I was happy for ever and ever.

Nurse must have been a prophet like those we read of in the Bible. Everything that she said began to come true, and since then other things that she told me of have happened. That was how I came to know that her stories were true and that I had not made up the secret myself out of my own head. But there was another thing that happened that day. I went a second time to the secret place. It was at the deep brimming well, and when I was standing on the moss I bent over and looked in, and then I knew who the white lady was that I had seen come out of the water in the wood long ago when I was quite little. And I trembled all over, because that told me other things. Then I remembered how sometime after I had seen the white people in the wood, nurse asked me more about them, and I told her all over again, and she listened, and said nothing for a long, long time, and at last she said, "You will see her again." So I understood what had happened and what was to happen. And I understood about the nymphs; how I might meet them in all kinds of places, and they would always help me, and I must always look for them, and find them in all sorts of strange shapes and appearances. And without the nymphs I could never have found the secret, and without them none of the other things could happen. Nurse had told me all about them long ago, but she called them by another name, and I did not know what she meant, or what her tales of them were about, only that they were very queer. And there were two kinds, the bright and the dark, and both were very lovely and very wonderful, and some people saw only one kind, and some only the other, but some saw them both. But usually the dark appeared first, and the bright ones came afterwards, and there were extraordinary tales about them. It was a day or two after I had come home from the secret place that I first really knew the nymphs. Nurse had shown me how to call them, and I had tried, but I did not know what she meant, and so I thought it was all nonsense. But I made up my mind I would try again, so I went to the wood where the pool was, where I saw the white people, and I tried again. The dark nymph, Alanna, came, and she turned the pool of water into a pool of fire....

EPILOGUE

"That's a very queer story," said Cotgrave, handing back the green book to the recluse, Ambrose. "I see the drift of a good deal, but there are many things that I do not grasp at all. On the last page, for example, what does she mean by 'nymphs'?"

"Well, I think there are references throughout the manuscript to certain 'processes' which have been handed down by tradition from age to age. Some of these processes are just beginning to come within the purview of science, which has arrived at them—or rather at the steps which lead to them—by quite different paths. I have interpreted the reference to 'nymphs' as a reference to one of these processes."

"And you believe that there are such things?"

"Oh, I think so. Yes, I believe I could give you convincing evidence on that point. I am afraid you have neglected the study of alchemy? It is a pity, for the symbolism, at all events, is very beautiful, and moreover if you were acquainted with certain books on the subject, I could recall to your mind phrases which might explain a good deal in the manuscript that you have been reading."

"Yes; but I want to know whether you seriously think that there is any foundation of fact beneath these fancies. Is it not all a department of poetry; a curious dream with which man has indulged himself?"

"I can only say that it is no doubt better for the great mass of people to dismiss it all as a dream. But if you ask my veritable belief—that goes quite the other way. No; I should not say belief, but rather knowledge. I may tell you that I have known cases in which men have stumbled quite by accident on certain of these 'processes,' and have been astonished by wholly unexpected results. In the cases I am thinking of there could have been no possibility of 'suggestion' or sub-conscious action of any kind. One might as well suppose a schoolboy 'suggesting' the existence of Æschylus to himself, while he plods mechanically through the declensions.

"But you have noticed the obscurity," Ambrose went on, "and in this particular case it must have been dictated by instinct, since the writer never thought that her manuscripts would fall into other hands. But the practice is universal, and for most excellent reasons. Powerful and sovereign medicines, which are, of necessity, virulent poisons also, are kept in a locked cabinet. The child may find the key by chance, and drink herself dead; but in most cases the search is educational, and the phials contain precious elixirs for him who has patiently fashioned the key for himself."

"You do not care to go into details?"

"No, frankly, I do not. No, you must remain unconvinced. But you saw how the manuscript illustrates the talk we had last week?"

"Is this girl still alive?"

"No. I was one of those who found her. I knew the father well; he was a lawyer, and had always left her very much to herself. He thought of nothing but deeds and leases, and the news came to him as an awful surprise. She was missing one morning; I suppose it was about a year after she had written what you have read. The servants were called, and they told things, and put the only natural interpretation on them—a perfectly erroneous one.

"They discovered that green book somewhere in her room, and I found her in the place that she described with so much dread, lying on the ground before the image."

"It was an image?"

"Yes, it was hidden by the thorns and the thick undergrowth that had surrounded it. It was a wild, lonely country; but you know what it was like by her description, though of course you will understand that the colors have been heightened. A child's imagination always makes the heights higher and the depths deeper than they really are; and she had, unfortunately for herself, something more than imagination. One might say, perhaps, that the picture in her mind which she succeeded in a measure in putting into words, was the scene as it would have appeared to an imaginative artist. But it is a strange, desolate land."

"And she was dead?"

"Yes. She had poisoned herself—in time. No; there was not a word to be said against her in the ordinary sense. You may recollect a story I told you the other night about a lady who saw her child's fingers crushed by a window?"

"And what was this statue?"

"Well, it was of Roman workmanship, of a stone that with the centuries had not blackened, but had become white and luminous. The thicket had grown up about it and concealed it, and in the Middle Ages the followers of a very old tradition had known how to use it for their own purposes. In fact it had been incorporated into the monstrous mythology of the Sabbath. You will have noted that those to whom a sight of that shining whiteness had been vouchsafed by chance, or rather, perhaps, by apparent chance, were required to blindfold themselves on their second approach. That is very significant."

"And is it there still?"

"I sent for tools, and we hammered it into dust and fragments."

"The persistence of tradition never surprises me," Ambrose went on after a pause. "I could name many an English parish where such traditions as that girl had listened to in her childhood are still existent in occult but unabated vigor. No, for me, it is the 'story' not the 'sequel,' which is strange and awful, for I have always believed that wonder is of the soul."

NORAH AND THE FAIRIES

Hume Nisbet

from *Stories Weird and Wonderful* (1900)

Over by the East, the pulsating stars resembled a Queensland opal, that most lovely of all gems to the color lover, full of light and fire, iridescent, yet rarely tender in its filmy softness. The sun was not yet over the misty ranges, but that it was near at hand that intense luminosity, which rendered one particular peak broader than the other peaks, showed. In another moment, that luminous whiteness would seem grey around the superior brightness of that dazzling orb. As yet, however, there was no glitter, but only cool radiance and melting tones.

Spring reigned over bush-land with its countless exquisite blossom and heath-bells. Varieties as the most delicate pinks, azures, and yellows blended amongst delicious grays, whites, and aesthetic greens. Young leaves vied the bloom of the peach and plum in their tints, with rose-red branches. There was not a shrub without its individual clustering of flowers, not a tree that was not festooned with loveliness, while over all trailed the silvery, dew-laden, gossamer webs of the bush-spider.

A chastened moment that was before the sun burst over the ranges. Opal-grey was the predominant tone, with subdued sparkles of prismatic colors. All the dark shadows of the night had fled, no deep spots broke the silken monotony. It was Australia's most ethereal month, and hour, when she might well compare with the ideal plains of Heaven, where there is no sun, neither is there shadow; but the glory of God fills it with purity.

A moment longer of this divine radiance and silent expectancy, while the little maid at the foot of the ivory-limbed gum tree, still sleeps on, dreaming about the fairies that have passed from the book under her head into her innocent brain. They have been with her all night, ever since the instant she had sunk, tired out with wanderings, until now. The Snow Queen had been with her, although she had never really seen snow in her life, also the little Sea Maid, although she had never yet seen the sea.

All night the elves, the fairies, the queer big-headed dwarfs and the sharp-nosed but benevolent old godmothers had been dancing over the young grasses and swinging amongst the spiders' webs. But they were creeping one by one back to their covers and taking their usual places inside the pages of her pillow book. She had seen them plain enough even while she slept, for the big moon had shone all night upon the frolics. The wild cats had watched also the funny beings, no bigger than themselves; therefore they were not the least afraid of these strange visitors to Australia any more than she was herself. The great bullfrog, with his wives and children, came out of the swamp and looked on also with his bulging eyes, grunting approval, while the others went all through the gamut of notes in their surprise.

She knew that she could see quite well, even though her wearied eyelids were fast shut, for didn't she see the laughing jackass sitting on the branch above her, looking down all night at the queer sight, with long beak nodding gravely in his wonderment, and the three feathers on his head standing up?15 So astonished was this laughing jackass that he hadn't laughed once all through the night, although there had been fun enough to make even a jackdaw tumble off a fence.

She had seen the flying foxes, head downwards, swing themselves backwards and forwards in their jubilation at the sights. The wombats also looked back and forgot to climb an inch higher in their stupid amazement. Only the bush-spiders spun on regardless of everything extraordinary, but they had some excuse for their industry, for there was such a crowd of fairy swingers that the poor spiders were kept busy all night making fresh swings for their little visitors.

Little Norah Westwood had been very hungry when she fell asleep the night before. Her pretty white pinafore and cotton dress were sadly torn also with prickly bushes through which she had brushed. All the day she had walked, not knowing where she was going, for it is so easy for the most experienced man or woman to get lost in the bush, far less a little girl of eight. Lured away by those wildflowers, she had gone on and on, without looking at first, and afterwards, when she wanted to get home to dinner, she had not been able to.

In Australia, if you walk on, thinking and without watching the direction you are taking in the bush, for half-an-hour, or even less time, and then look up, it is ten chances to one you will be lost. That is if you are not an experienced bushman. The landscape is as open, almost, as an English park. You can see a good way all round, for the gum-trees appear thinly clad. It seems easy enough to recover your way, and you begin to try it with perfect confidence.

The shape of a gum-tree in the distance strikes you as quite familiar. You go towards it, and when you have reached it you find you are wrong then you try once, twice, thrice, a dozen times in different directions, before the consciousness dawns on you that you are in a maze, out of which you cannot find a way.

The bright sun shines down upon you from a cloudless blue sky. You are in an open shadeless forest, with receding stretches of white-branched gum-

---

15 The laughing kookaburra, a member of the kingfisher bird family.

trees on every side, and a vast solitude of white-branched gum-trees on every side, and a vast solitude brooding over all.

This sunlit, bare solitude appalls you with a mighty fright all at once, and that horror never leaves you until you are discovered; or, failing that, perhaps until you fall down exhausted, athirst, and famishing, to yield up the ghost.

The white, bone-like trunks and branches of the gum-trees all round you remind you only now of the skeletons of men and women who have been lost in this weird solitude before. You run wildly at first, then madly, with shrieks of deadly fear, until your reason leaves you and you fall down and rise no more. Months afterwards perhaps a passing traveler may discover your skeleton, picked anatomically clean by the ants, and perhaps not half-a-dozen miles from where you started.

Little Norah had lost her way, but being a child, and fairy supported, she had none of the horrors that an adult might feel. She had all the faith and reliance of a child in her parents. They would be sure to miss her, they would be sure to look for her, and as they could do everything, they would be sure to find her. But being a healthy, beef-eating, colonial child, she had missed her dinner and supper dreadfully. That is until she fell asleep. Then the Fairy Godmother had come out of her book and fed her with grapes and watermelons and such delicious cakes, and all the other fairies had danced to amuse her while she ate the good things.

They were going away now, however, as fast as they could troop into their pictures. The second last to leave her was Cinderella in her ball dress. Now the Snow Queen with a wave of her white arm drifted away like a flash of fire and Norah awoke.

Awoke to find the sun streaming into her eyelids and almost blinding her; to get a glimpse of the laughing jackass as he shifted from the branch over her head, and flew away seriously and quietly to look after his daily business of catching snakes. There was nothing to laugh over at present, for the events of the night, and she being there all alone, were things for a jackass to think about sedately. By-and-by he might be able to laugh, when he forgot all about that night and watched his natural enemy, the black snake, fall through five hundred feet of air and break his back.

The frogs, wild cats, and flying foxes had also disappeared, and the dewdrops in which the elves had washed were being swiftly licked up by the hot morning sun. Worse than all, Norah's fairy feed seemed to have done her no good, for she was hungrier than ever.

She rose wearily and recommenced her walk of the preceding day through the bushes, picking plenty of lovely flowers until her arms were so full of blossoms that she was forced to drop them and gather a fresh lot.

The midday sun beat fiercely upon her face and shoulders until the heat felt like a heavy load. She wasn't walking fast now, indeed several times she fell and seemed to sleep. Then she would wake up, so hungry, so tired, so thirsty, and stagger on till she fell and slept again.

When the full moon rose that night, and the dew fell gently down and cooled the earth, she was sitting by the side of a water hole in a pretty dell. She was not at all hungry now, and although the water was there she didn't feel thirsty one bit. She was waiting for the fairies to come out of her book, and she had laid it down open before her so that they might have no trouble in getting free.

She had found a nice bed among the bracken ferns that clustered thickly round her. Over the ferns spread the heathbells and blossoms, amongst which already the spiders had begun to spin their swinging threads. Those were for the fairies she knew, so she waited patiently. with her dark eyes shining like stars.

The rabbits came out and sat round on their hind legs trimming their long ears with their forepaws. The little thick furred black-and-white spotted wild cats also came out and played round with each other while they waited for the coming fun.

She saw two wombats and a wallaby climb the tree behind—the tree that was before the silver moon. They climbed until they reached a high fork, and there they sat just under the swinging flying foxes, waiting like spectators in the gallery, for the performance to commence.

The laughing jackass came also after his day's work and sat on a branch, looking this way and that expectantly, and last of all the big and little frogs from the pool.

Then came her friends the fairies; straight out of the pages they all few, like a flock of cockatoos, and circled round her, Cinderella and her old Godmother, the Fairy Prince and the Sleeping Beauty, now wide-awake and happy; good dwarfs, mermaids, snow-maidens, and every one she had loved, without one wicked elf amongst them.

They fluttered about her on transparent wings, danced merrily over the ferns, and swung like happy children on the spider swings, while all the animals looked on solemnly. Norah watched them also. Watched them with eyes growing bigger and bigger with wonderment, and a strange rapture filling her heart.

Some transformation was taking place in her, she was sure, that would shortly enable her to fly as easily as those radiant creatures who moved around her on those glistening wings. Would she have wings like those pretty elves, all transparent and veined like crochet work, covered over with glitter? They were summer wings, Australian wings, the wings of the lady-bird, whom you pick off the gum-tree like a bit of brown shard and pitch away. Then it all opens up into the lovely tinted silk gauze. Or would she have wings of white feathers like the cockatoos and the angels? That was what she was thinking about as she watched the dancing with that curious fluttering at her heart.

Then the Snow Queen came over to her with the most lovely silver car, drawn by white horses, and invited her to enter and sit beside her.

This Norah did, and no sooner was she seated, then the magic car rose up, with all the fairy court attending, and flew away, past the moon—right on towards the stars.

LA BELLE DAME SANS MERCI

John Keats

(1819)

first published in its original version in *Life, Letters, and Literary Remains of John Keats* (1848)

O what can ail thee, knight-at-arms,
  Alone and palely loitering?
The sedge has withered from the lake,
  And no birds sing!

O what can ail thee, knight-at-arms,
  So haggard and so woe-begone?
The squirrel's granary is full,
  And the harvest's done.

I see a lily on thy brow,
  With anguish moist and fever-dew,
And on thy cheeks a fading rose
  Fast withereth too.

I met a lady in the meads,
  Full beautiful, a fairy's child;
Her hair was long, her foot was light,
  And her eyes were wild.

I made a garland for her head,
  And bracelets too, and fragrant zone;
She looked at me as she did love,
  And made sweet moan.

I set her on my pacing steed,
    And nothing else saw all day long,
For sidelong would she bend, and sing
    A faery's song.

She found me roots of relish sweet,
    And honey wild, and manna-dew,
And sure in language strange she said—
    "I love thee true."

She took me to her Elfin grot,
    And there she wept and sighed full sore,
And there I shut her wild, wild eyes
    With kisses four.

And there she lullèd me asleep,
    And there I dreamed—Ah! woe betide!—
The latest dream I ever dreamt
    On the cold hill side.

I saw pale kings and princes too,
    Pale warriors, death-pale were they all;
They cried—"La Belle Dame sans Merci
    Hath thee in thrall!"

I saw their starved lips in the gloam,
    With horrid warning gapèd wide,
And I awoke and found me here,
    On the cold hill's side.

And this is why I sojourn here,
    Alone and palely loitering,
Though the sedge is withered from the lake,
    And no birds sing.

A Night on the Enchanted Mountains

Charles Fenno Hoffman

first published in *Bentley's Miscellany* (1838)

It haunts me yet! that early dream
  Of first fond love:
Like the ice that floats on a summer stream
  From some frozen fount above:
Through my river of years twill drifting gleam,
  Where'er their waves may rove!

It flashes athwart each sunny hour,
With a strangely bright but chilling power,
    Ever and ever to mock their tide
        With its delusive glow;
    A fragment of hopes that were petrified
        Long, long ago!

YANKEE RHYMER

There are few parts of the United States which for beauty of scenery, amenity of climate, and I might add, the primitive character of the inhabitants, possess more peculiar attraction than the mountainous regions of eastern Tennessee.

It is a wild and romantic district composed of rocks and broken hills, where the primeval forests overhang valleys watered by limpid streams whose meadowy banks are grazed by innumerable herds of cattle. The various mountain ridges, which at one point traverse the country almost in parallel lines, while at another they sweep off in vast curves and describe a majestic amphitheater, are all more or less connected with the Appalachian chain, and share the peculiarities which elsewhere characterize those mountains. In some places the transition from valley to highland is so gradual, that you are hardly aware of the undulations of surface when passing over it. In others, the frowning heights rise in precipitous walls from the plains, while again the wood. ed and dome-like summits will heave upward from the broad meadows, like enormous tumuli heaped upon their bosom.

The hills also are frequently seamed with deep and dark ravines, whose sheer sides and dimly-descried bottom will make the eye swim as it tries to fathom them, while they are often pierced with cavernous galleries, which lead miles under ground, and branch off into grottos so spacious that an army might be marshaled within their yawning chambers.

Here too those remarkable conical cavities which are generally known by the name of "sink holes" in the western country are thickly scattered over the surface; and so perfect in shape are many of them, that it is difficult to persuade the ruder residents that they are not the work of art, nor fashioned out as drinking-bowls for the extinct monsters whose fossil remains are so abundant in this region. Indeed the singular formation of the earth's surface, with the entire seclusion in which they live amid their pastoral valleys, must account for and excuse many a less reasonable belief and superstition pre. vailing among those hospitable mountaineers. "The Enchanted Mountains," as one of the ranges I have been attempting to describe is called, are especially distinguished by the number of incredible traditions and wild superstitions connected with them. Those uncouth paintings along their cliffs, and the footprints of men and horses stamped on the solid rock upon the highest summits, as mentioned by Mr. Flint in his *Geography of the Western Country*, constitute but a small part of the material which they offer to an uneducated and imaginative people for the creation of strange fantasies. The singular echoes which tremble through these lonely glens and the shifting forms which, as the morning mist rises from the upland, may be seen stealing over the tops of the crags and hiding themselves within the crevices, are a like accounted for by supernatural causes.

Having always been imbued with a certain love of the marvelous, and being one of the pious few who in this enlightened age of reality nurse up a lingering superstition or two, I found myself while loitering through this romantic district and associating upon the most easy terms with its rural population, irresistibly imbibing a portion of the feeling and spirit which prevailed around me. The cavernous ravines and sounding aisles of all the tall forests had "airy tongues" for me, as well as those who are more familiar with their whisperings. But as for the freakish beings who were supposed to give them utterance as they pranked it away in the dim retreats around, I somehow or other could never obtain a fair sight of one of them. The forms that sometimes rose between my eyes and the mist breathing cascade, or flitted across the shadowy glade at some sudden turn of my forest-path, always managed to disappear behind some jutting rock, or make good their escape into some convenient thicket, before I could make out their lineaments or even swear to their existence at all. My repeated disappointments in this way had begun to put me quite out of conceit with my quickness and accuracy of vision, when a new opportunity was given me of testing them in the manner I am about to relate.

I happened one day to dine at a little inn situated at the mouth of a wooded gorge, where it lay tucked away so closely beneath the ponderous limbs of a huge tulip-tree, that the blue smoke from the kitchen fire alone betrayed its locality. My host proved to be one of those talkative worthies who being supplied with but little information to exercise his tongue upon, makes amends for the defects of education and circumstance, by dwelling with exaggeration upon every trivial incident around him. Such people in polished society become the scandal-mongers of the circle in which they move, while in more simple communities they are only the chroniclers of every thing marvelous that has occurred in the neighborhood "within the memory of the oldest inhabitant." I had hardly placed myself at the dinner-table, before my garrulous entertainer began to display his retentive faculties by giving me the exact year and day upon which every chicken with two heads, or calf with five legs, had been born through out the whole country round. Then followed the most minute particulars of a murder or two which had been perpetrated within the last twenty years; and after this I was drilled into the exact situations and bearings of a haunted house which I should probably see the next day, by pursuing the road I was then traveling; finally, I was inducted into all the arcana of a remarkable cavern in the vicinity,— where an "ouphe, gnome, moon-elf, or water-sprite" had taken up its residence, to the great annoyance ef every one except my landlord's buxom daughter who was said to be upon the most enviable terms with the freakish spirit of the grotto.[16]

The animated and almost eloquent description which mine host gave of that cavern made me readily overlook the puerile credulity with which he wound up his account of its peculiarities. It interested me so much indeed, that I determined to stable my horse for the night and proceed at once to explore the place. A fresh and blooming girl, with the laughing eye and free step of a mountaineer, volunteered to be my guide on the occasion; hinting at the same time, while she gave a mischievous look at her father. that I should find it difficult to procure a cicerone other than herself in the neighborhood. She then directed me how to find the principle entrance to the cave, where she promised to join me soon after.

A rough scramble in the hills soon brought me to the place of meeting, and entering the first chamber of the cavern which was large and well lighted from without, I stretched myself upon a rocky ledge which leaned over a brook that meandered through the place, and lulled by the dash of a distant waterfall surrendered myself to a thousand musing fancies.

Fatigue, from an early and long morning ride, or possibly too liberal a devotion to the good things which had been placed before me at table, caused me soon to be over taken by sleep. My slumbers however were broken and uneasy; and after repeatedly opening my eyes to look with some impatience at my watch, as I tossed upon my stony couch, I abandoned the idea of a nap

---

[16] An "ouphe" is a small, mischievous sprite.

entirely, momentarily expecting that my guide would make her appearance, and contented myself with gazing listlessly upon the streamlet which rippled over its pebbled bed beneath me. I must have remained for some time in this vacant mood, when my idle musings were interrupted by a new source of interest presenting itself.

A slight rustling near disturbed me, and turning round as I opened my eyes, a female figure in a drapery of snowy whiteness appeared to flit before them, and retire behind a tall cascade immediately in front of me. The uncertain light of the place, with the spray of the waterfall which partially impeded my view of the farther part of the cavern, made me at first doubt the evidence of my senses; but gradually a distinct form was perceptible amid the mist, apparently moving slowly from me, and beckoning the while to follow. The height of the figure struck me immediately as being about the same as that of the buxom daughter of my landlord; and though the proportions seemed more slender, I had no doubt, upon recalling her arch expression of countenance while her father was relating to me the wild superstitions of the cavern, that a ready solution of one of its mysteries at least was at hand. Some woman's whim. I had no doubt, prompted the girl to get up a little diversion at my expense, and sent her thither to put the freak in execution. I had been told that there were a dozen outlets to the cavern, and presumed that I was now to be involved in its labyrinths for the purpose of seeing in what part of the mountain I might subsequently make my exit. He is no true lover of a pair of bright eyes who will mar the jest of a pretty woman.

The lady beckoned and I followed.

I had some difficulty in scaling the precipice over which tumbled the water fall; but after slipping once or twice upon the wet ledges of rock, which supplied a treacherous foothold, I at last gained the summit and stood within a few yards of my whimsical conductor. She had paused upon the farthest side of the chamber into which the cavern here expanded. It was a vast and noble apartment. The lofty ceiling swelled almost into a perfect dome, save where a ragged aperture at the top admitted the noonday sun, whose rays as they fell through the vines and wild-flowers that embowered the orifice, were glinted back from a thousand sparry points and pillars around. The walls indeed were completely fretted with stalactites. In some places small and apparently freshly formed, they hung in fringed rows from the ceiling; in others they drooped so heavily as to knit the glistening roof to the marble floor beneath it, or rose in slender pyramids from the roof itself until they appeared to sustain the vault above.

The motion of the air created by the cascade gave a delightful coolness to this apartment, while the murmur of the falling water was echoed back from the vibrating columns with tones as rich and melodious as those which sweep from an Æolian harp.[17] Never methought had I seen a spot so alluring. And yet when I surveyed each charm of the grotto, I knew not whether I could be

---

[17] A wind harp.

contented in any one part of it. Nothing indeed could be more inviting to tranquil enjoyment than the place where I then stood; but the clustering columns, with their interlacing screen work of woven spar, allured my eye into a hundred romantic aisles which I longed to explore; while the pendant wild flowers which luxuriated in the sunlight around the opening above, prompted me to scale the dangerous height, and try what pinnacle of the mountain I might gain by emerging from the cavern through the lofty aperture.

These reflections were abruptly terminated by an impatient gesture from my guide, and for the first time I caught a glimpse of her countenance as she glided by a deep pool in which it was reflected.

That glance had a singular, almost a preternatural effect upon me; the features were different from those I had expected to behold. They were not those of the new acquaintance whom I thought I was following, but the expression they wore was one so familiar to me in bygone years, that I started as if I had seen an apparition.

It was the look of one who had been long since dead,—of one around whose name, when life was new, the whole tissue of my hopes and fears was woven,—for whom all my aspirations after worldly honors had been breathed,—in whom all my dreams of earthly happiness had been wound up. She had mingled in purer hours with all the fond and home-loving fancies of boyhood; she had been the queen of each romantic vision of my youth; and amid the worldly cares and selfish struggles of maturer life, the thought of her had lived separate and apart in my bosom, with no companion in its hallowed chamber save the religion learned at a mother's knee, save that hope of better things which once implanted by a mother's love survives amid the storms and conflicts of the world,—a beacon to warn us more often, alas! how far we have wandered from her teachings than to guide us to the haven whither they were meant to lead.

I had loved her and I had lost her: how, it matters not. Perchance disease had reft her from me by some sudden blow at the moment when possession made her dearest. Perchance I saw her fade in the arms of another, while I was banned and barred from ministering to a spirit that stole away to the grave with all I prized on earth. It boots not how I lost her; but he who has centered every thought and feeling in one only subject, whose morning hopes have for years gone forth to the same goal, whose evening reflections have for years come back to the same borne, whose waking visions and whose midnight dreams have for years been haunted by the same image, whose schemes of toil and advancement have all tended to the same end,—he knows what it is to have the pivot upon which every wheel of his heart hath turned wrenched from its centre,—to have the sun round which revolved every joy that lighted his bosom plucked from its system.

Well, it was her face. As I live, it was the soul-breathing features of Linda that now beamed before me, fresh as when in dawning womanhood they first caught my youthful fancy,—resistless as when in their noontide blaze of beauty I poured out my whole adoring soul before them. There was that same appealing look of the large lustrous eyes, the same sunny and soul-melting smile which, playing over a countenance thoughtful even to sadness, touched it with a beauty so radiant, that the charm seemed borrowed from heaven itself.

I could not but think it strange that such an image should be presented to my view in such a place; and yet if I now rightly recollect my emotions, surprise was the least active among them. I cared not why or whence the apparition came; I thought not whether it were reality or mocking semblance, the phantasy of my own brain, or the shadowy creation of some supernatural power around me. I knew only that it was there; I knew only that the eyes in whose perilous light my soul had bathed herself to madness beamed anew before me; that the lips whose lightest smile had often wrapt me in elysium; that the brow whose holy light—But why should I thus attempt to paint what pencil never yet hath reached?—why essay a portrait whose colors I have nowhere found, save in the heart where they are laid so deeply that death alone can dim them. Enough that the only human being to whom my spirit ever bowed in inferiority-enough that the idol to which it had knelt in adoration now stood palpably before it. An hour agone, and I would have crossed the threshold of the grave itself to stand one moment in that presence,—to gaze if but for an instant upon those features. What recked I now then, how or whence they were conjured up? Had The FIEND himself stood nigh, I would have pressed nearer and gazed and followed as I did.

The figure beckoned, and I went on.

The vaulted pathway was at first smooth and easily followed ; but after passing through several of the cavernous chambers into which it ever and anon expanded, the route became more and more difficult; loose masses of rock, encumbering the floor or drooping in pendant crags from the roof, rendered the defiles between them both toilsome and hazardous. The light which fell through the opening behind us soon disappeared entirely, and it gave me a singular sinking of the spirits, as we passed into deeper and deeper gloom, to hear the musical sounds which I have already noted in the grotto from which we first passed, dying away in the distance, and leaving the place at last in total silence. Long indeed after they had ceased to reach my ear with any distinctness, they would seem at times to swell along the winding vault, and break anew upon me at some turn in our devious route. So strangely too do the innumerable subtle echoes metamorphose each noise in these caverns, that I continually found myself mistaking the muttered reverberations for the sounds of a human voice. At one moment it seemed in gay tones to be calling me back to the sparry grotto and bright sunshine behind me, while the very next it appeared with sudden and harsh intonation to warn me against proceeding further. Anon it would die away with a mournful cadence, a melancholy wailing, like the requiem of one who was beyond the reach of all earthly counsel or assistance.

Again and again did I pause in my career to listen to this wild chanting, while my feelings would for the moment take their hue and complexion from the sources which thus bewildered my senses. I thought of my early dreams of fame and honor, of the singing hopes that lured me on my path, when one fatal image stepped between my soul and all its high endeavor. I thought of that buoyancy of spirit, once so irrepressible in its elasticity that it seemed proof alike against time and sorrow, now sapped, wasted, and destroyed by the frenzied pursuit of one object. I thought of the home which had so much to embellish and endear it, and which yet with all its heart-cheering joys had been neglected and left, like the sunlit grotto, to follow a shitting phantom through a heartless world. I thought of the reproachful voices around me, and the ceaseless upbraider in my own bosom, which told of time and talents wasted, of opportunities thrown away, of mental energies squandered, of heart, brain and soul consumed in a devotion deeper and more absorbing than Heaven itself exacts from its votaries. I thought, and I looked at the object for which I had lavished them all. I thought that my life must have been some hideous dream, some dread vision in which my fated soul was bound by imaginary ties to a being doomed to be its bane upon earth, and shut it out at last from heaven; and I laughed in scornful glee as I twisted my bodily frame in the hope that at length I might wake from that long. enduring sleep. I caught a smile from the lips; I saw a beckon from the hand of the phantom, and I wished still to dream, and to follow for ever. I plunged into the abyss of darkness to which it pointed; and reckless of everything I might leave behind followed wheresoever it might marshal me.

A damp and chilling atmosphere now pervaded the place, and the clammy moisture stood thick upon my brow as I groped my way through a labyrinth of winding galleries which intersected each other so often, both obliquely and transversely, that the whole mountain seemed honeycombed. At one moment the steep and broken pathway led up acclivities almost impossible to scale; at another the black edge of a precipice indicated our hazardous route along the brink of some unfathomed gulf; while again a savage torrent, roaring through the sinuous vault, left scarcely room enough for a foot-hold between the base of the wall and its furious tide.

And still my guide kept on and still I followed. Returning indeed, had the thought occurred to me, was now impossible; for the pale light which seemed to hang around her person, emanating as it were from her white raiment, was all that guided me through these shadowy realms. But not for a moment did I now think of retracing my steps, or pausing in that wild pursuit. Onward and still onward it led, while my spirit once set upon its purpose seemed to gather sterner determination from every difficulty it encountered, and to kindle once more with that indomitable buoyancy which was once the chief attribute of my nature.

At length the chase seemed ended, as we approached one of those abrupt and startling turns common in these caverns, where the passage, suddenly veering to the right or left, leads you, as if by design, to the sheer edge of some gulf that is impassable. My strange companion seemed pausing for a moment upon the brink of the abyss. It was a moment to me of delirious joy, mingled with more than mortal agony; the object of my wild pursuit seemed at length within my grasp. A single bound, and my outstretched arms would have encircled her person; a single bound—nay, the least movement towards her—might only have precipitated the destruction upon whose brink she hovered. Her form seemed to flutter upon the very edge of that horrid precipice, as gazing like one fascinated over it, she stretched her hand backward toward me. It was like inviting me to perdition. And yet, forgive me Heaven! to perish with her was my proudest hope, as I sprang to grasp it. But, oh God! what held I in that withering clasp? The ice of death seemed curdling in my veins as I touched those clammy and pulseless fingers. A strange and unhallowed light shot upward from the black abyss; and the features from which I could not take my eyes away were changed to those of a DEMON in that hideous glare. And now the hand that I had so longed to clasp closed with remorseless pressure round my own, and drew me toward the yawning gulf,—it tightened in its grasp, and I hovered still nearer to my horrid doom,—it clenched yet more closely, and the frenzied shriek I gave— AWOKE ME.

A soft palm was gently pressed against my own; a pair of laughing blue eyes were bent archly upon me; and the fair locks which floated over her blooming checks revealed the joyous and romping damsel who had promised to act as my guide through the cavern. She had been prevented by some household cares from keeping her appointment until the approach of evening made it too late, and she had taken it for granted that I had then returned to my lodgings at the inn. My absence from the breakfast table in the morning, however, had awakened some concern in the family, and induced her to seek me where we them met. The pressure of her hand in trying to awaken me will partially account for the latter part of my hideous dream; the general tenor of it is easily traceable to the impression made upon my mind by the prevalent superstition connected with the cavern; but no metaphysical ingenuity of which I am master can explain how one whose daily thoughts flow in so careless, if not gay a current as mine, even in a dream could have conjured up such a train of wild and bitter fancies; much less how the fearful tissue should have been so interwoven with the memory of an idle caprice of boyhood as to give new shape and reality to a phantom long—long since faded. And I could not but think that had a vision so strange and vivid swept athwart my brain at an earlier period of life, I should have regarded it as something more than an unmeaning phantasy! That mystical romance which is the religion of life's spring time would have interpreted my dream as a dark foreboding of the future, prophetic of hopes misplaced, of opportunities misapplied, of a joyless and barren youth, and a manhood whose best endeavor would be only a restless effort to lose in action the memory of the dreary past.

If half be true however that is told concerning them, still more extravagant sallies of the imagination overtake persons of quite as easy and indolent a disposition as my own, when venturing to pass a night upon the Enchanted Mountains.

The Women of the Wood

Abraham Merritt

first published in *Weird Tales* (August 1926)

McKay sat on the balcony of the little inn that squatted like a brown gnome among the pines on the eastern shore of the lake.

It was a small and lonely lake high up in the Vosges; and yet, lonely is not just the word with which to tag its spirit; rather was it aloof, withdrawn. The mountains came down on every side, making a great tree-lined bowl that seemed, when McKay first saw it, to be filled with the still wine of peace.

McKay had worn the wings in the world war with honor, flying first with the French and later with his own country's forces. And as a bird loves the trees, so did McKay love them. To him they were not merely trunks and roots, branches and leaves; to him they were personalities. He was acutely aware of differences in character even among the same species—that pine was benevolent and jolly; that one austere and monkish; there stood a swaggering bravo, and there dwelt a sage wrapped in green meditation; that birch was a wanton—the birch near her was virginal, still a dream.

The war had sapped him, nerve and brain and soul. Through all the years that had passed since then the wound had kept open. But now, as he slid his car down the vast green bowl, he felt its spirit reach out to him; reach out to him and caress and quiet him, promising him healing. He seemed to drift like a falling leaf through the clustered woods; to be cradled by gentle hands of the trees.

He had stopped at the little gnome of an inn, and there he had lingered, day after day, week after week.

The trees had nursed him; soft whisperings of leaves, slow chant of the needled pines, had first deadened, then driven from him the re-echoing clamor of the war and its sorrow. The open wound of his spirit had closed under their green healing; had closed and become scar; and even the scar had been covered and buried, as the scars on Earth's breast are covered and buried beneath the falling leaves of Autumn. The trees had laid green healing hands on his eyes, banishing the pictures of war. He had sucked strength from the green breasts of the hills.

Yet as strength flowed back to him and mind and spirit healed, McKay had grown steadily aware that the place was troubled; that its tranquillity was not perfect; that there was ferment of fear within it.

It was as though the trees had waited until he himself had become whole before they made their own unrest known to him. Now they were trying to tell him something; there was a shrillness as of apprehension, of anger, in the whispering of the leaves, the needled chanting of the pines.

And it was this that had kept McKay at the inn—a definite consciousness of appeal, consciousness of something wrong—something wrong that he was being asked to right. He strained his ears to catch words in the rustling branches, words that trembled on the brink of his human understanding.

Never did they cross that brink.

Gradually he had orientated himself, had focused himself, so he believed, to the point of the valley's unease.

On all the shores of the lake there were but two dwellings. One was the inn, and around the inn the trees clustered protectively, confiding; friendly. It was as though they had not only accepted it, but had made it part of themselves.

Not so was it of the other habitation. Once it had been the hunting lodge of long dead lords; now it was half ruined, forlorn. It stood across the lake almost exactly opposite the inn and back upon the slope a half mile from the shore. Once there had been fat fields around it and a fair orchard.

The forest had marched down upon them. Here and there in the fields, scattered pines and poplars stood like soldiers guarding some outpost; scouting parties of saplings lurked among the gaunt and broken fruit trees. But the forest had not had its way unchecked; ragged stumps showed where those who dwelt in the old lodge had cut down the invaders, blackened patches of the woodland showed where they had fired the woods.

Here was the conflict he had sensed. Here the green folk of the forest were both menaced and menacing; at war. The lodge was a fortress beleaguered by the woods, a fortress whose garrison sallied forth with axe and torch to take their toll of the besiegers.

Yet McKay sensed the inexorable pressing-in of the forest; he saw it as a green army ever filling the gaps in its enclosing ranks, shooting its seeds into the cleared places, sending its roots out to sap them; and armed always with a crushing patience, a patience drawn from the stone breasts of the eternal hills.

He had the impression of constant regard of watchfulness, as though night and day the forest kept its myriads of eyes upon the lodge; inexorably, not to be swerved from its purpose. He had spoken of this impression to the inn keeper and his wife, and they had looked at him oddly.

"Old Polleau does not love the trees, no," the old man had said. "No, nor do his two sons. They do not love the trees—and very certainly the trees do not love them."

Between the lodge and the shore, marching down to the verge of the lake was a singularly beautiful little coppice of silver birches and firs. The coppice stretched for perhaps a quarter of a mile, was not more than a hundred feet or two in depth, and it was not alone the beauty of its trees but their curious grouping that aroused McKay's interest so vividly. At each end of the coppice were a dozen or more of the glistening needled firs, not clustered but spread out as though in open marching order; at widely spaced intervals along its other two sides paced single firs. The birches, slender and delicate, grew within the guard of these sturdier trees, yet not so thickly as to crowd each other.

To McKay the silver birches were for all the world like some gay caravan of lovely demoiselles under the protection of debonair knights. With that odd other sense of his he saw the birches as delectable damsels, merry and laughing—the pines as lovers, troubadours in their green needled mail. And when the winds blew and the crests of the trees bent under them, it was as though dainty demoiselles picked up fluttering, leafy skirts, bent leafy hoods and danced while the knights of the firs drew closer round them, locked arms with theirs and danced with them to the roaring horns of the winds. At such times he almost heard sweet laughter from the birches, shoutings from the firs.

Of all the trees in that place McKay loved best this little wood; had rowed across and rested in its shade, had dreamed there and, dreaming, had heard again elfin echoes of the sweet laughter; eyes closed, had heard mysterious whisperings and the sound of dancing feet light as falling leaves; had taken dream draught of that gaiety which was the soul of the little wood.

And two days ago he had seen Polleau and his two sons. McKay had been dreaming in the coppice all that afternoon. As dusk began to fall he had reluctantly arisen and begun the row back to the inn. When he had been a few hundred feet from shore three men had come out from the trees and had stood watching him—three grim, powerful men taller than the average French peasant.

He had called a friendly greeting to them, but they had not answered it; stood there, scowling. Then as he bent again to his oars, one of the sons had raised a hatchet and had driven it savagely into the trunk of a slim birch beside him. He thought he heard a thin wailing cry from the stricken tree, a sigh from all the little wood.

McKay had felt as though the keen edge had bitten into his own flesh.

"Stop that!" he had cried, "Stop it, damn you!"

For answer the son had struck again—and never had McKay seen hate etched so deep as on his face as he struck. Cursing, a killing rage in heart, had swung the boat around, raced back to shore. He had heard the hatchet strike again and again and, close now to shore, had heard a crackling and over it once more the thin, high wailing. He had turned to look.

The birch was tottering, was falling. But as it had fallen he had seen a curious thing. Close beside it grew one of the firs, and, as the smaller tree crashed over, it dropped upon the fir like a fainting maid in the arms of a lover. And as it lay and trembled there, one of the great branches of the fir slipped from under it, whipped out and smote the hatchet wielder a crushing blow upon the head, sending him to earth.

It had been, of course, only the chance blow of a bough, bent by pressure of the fallen tree and then released as that tree slipped down. But there had been such suggestion of conscious action in the branch's recoil, so much of bitter anger in it, so much, in truth, had it been like the vengeful blow of a man that McKay had felt an eerie prickling of his scalp, his heart had missed its beat.

For a moment Polleau and the standing son had stared at the sturdy fir with the silvery birch lying on its green breast and folded in, shielded by, its needled boughs as though—again the swift impression came to McKay—as though it were a wounded maid stretched on breast, in arms, of knightly lover. For a long moment father and son had stared.

Then, still wordless but with that same bitter hatred on both their faces, they had stopped and picked up the other and with his arms around the neck of each had borne him limply away.

McKay, sitting on the balcony of the inn that morning, went over and over that scene; realized more and more clearly the human aspect of fallen birch and clasping fir, and the conscious deliberateness of the fir's blow. And during the two days that had elapsed since then, he had felt the unease of the trees increase, their whispering appeal became more urgent.

What were they trying to tell him? What did they want him to do?

Troubled, he stared across the lake, trying to pierce the mists that hung over it and hid the opposite shore. And suddenly it seemed that he heard the coppice calling him, felt it pull the point of his attention toward it irresistibly, as the lodestone swings and holds the compass needle.

The coppice called him, bade him come to it.

Instantly McKay obeyed the command; he arose and walked down to the boat landing; he stepped into his skiff and began to row across the lake. As his oars touched the water his trouble fell from him. In its place flowed peace and a curious exaltation.

The mist was thick upon the lake. There was no breath of wind, yet the mist billowed and drifted, shook and curtained under the touch of unfelt airy hands.

They were alive—the mists; they formed themselves into fantastic palaces past whose opalescent facades he flew; they built themselves into hills and valleys and circled plains whose floors were rippling silk. Tiny rainbows gleamed out among them, and upon the water prismatic patches shone and spread like spilled wine of opals. He had the illusion of vast distances—the hills of mist were real mountains, the valleys between them were not illusory. He was a colossus cleaving through some elfin world. A trout broke, and it was like leviathan leaping from the fathomless deep. Around the arc of its body rainbows interlaced and then dissolved into rain of softly gleaming gems—diamonds in dance with sapphires, flame hearted rubies and pearls with shimmering souls of rose. The fish vanished, diving cleanly without sound; the jeweled bows vanished with it; a tiny irised whirlpool swirled for an instant where trout and flashing arcs had been.

Nowhere was there sound. He let his oars drop and leaned forward, drifting. In the silence, before him and around him, he felt opening the gateways of an unknown world.

And suddenly he heard the sound of voices, many voices; faint at first and murmurous; louder they became, swiftly; women's voices sweet and lilting and mingled with them the deeper tones of men. Voices that lifted and fell in a wild, gay chanting through whose joyousness ran undertones both of sorrow and of rage—as though faery weavers threaded through silk spun of sunbeams sombre strands dipped in the black of graves and crimson strands stained in the red of wrathful sunsets.

He drifted on, scarce daring to breathe lest even that faint sound break the elfin song. Closer it rang and clearer; and now he became aware that the speed of his boat was increasing, that it was no longer drifting; that it was as though the little waves on each side were pushing him ahead with soft and noiseless palms. His boat grounded and as it rustled along over the smooth pebbles of the beach the song ceased.

McKay half arose and peered before him. The mists were thicker here but he could see the outlines of the coppice. It was like looking at it through many curtains of fine gauze; its trees seemed shifting, ethereal, unreal. And moving among the trees were figures that threaded the boles and flitted in rhythmic measures like the shadows of leafy boughs swaying to some cadenced wind.

He stepped ashore and made his way slowly toward them. The mists dropped behind him, shutting off all sight of shore.

The rhythmic flittings ceased; there was now no movement as there was no sound among the trees—yet he felt the little woods abrim with watching life. McKay tried to speak; there was a spell of silence on his mouth.

"You called me. I have come to listen to you—to help you if I can."

The words formed within his mind, but utter them he could not. Over and over he tried, desperately; the words seemed to die before his lips could give them life.

A pillar of mist whirled forward and halted, eddying half an arm length away. And suddenly out of it peered a woman's face, eyes level with his own. A woman's face—yes; but McKay, staring into those strange eyes probing his, knew that face though it seemed it was that of no woman of human breed. They were without pupils, the irises deer-like and of the soft green of deep forest dells; within them sparkled tiny star points of light like motes in a moon beam. The eyes were wide and set far apart beneath a broad, low brow over which was piled braid upon braid of hair of palest gold, braids that seemed spun of shining ashes of gold. Her nose was small and straight, her mouth scarlet and exquisite. The face was oval, tapering to a delicately pointed chin.

Beautiful was that face, but its beauty was an alien one; elfin. For long moments the strange eyes thrust their gaze deep into his. Then out of the mist two slender white arms stole, the hands long, fingers tapering. The tapering fingers touched his ears.

"He shall hear," whispered the red lips.

Immediately from all about him a cry arose; in it was the whispering and rustling of the leaves beneath the breath of the winds, the shrilling of the harp strings of the boughs, the laughter of hidden brooks, the shoutings of waters flinging themselves down to deep and rocky pools—the voices of the woods made articulate.

"He shall hear!" they cried.

The long white fingers rested on his lips, and their touch was cool as bark of birch on cheek after some long upward climb through forest; cool and subtly sweet.

"He shall speak," whispered the scarlet lips.

"He shall speak!" answered the wood voices again, as though in litany.

"He shall see," whispered the woman and the cool fingers touched his eyes.

"He shall see!" echoed the wood voices.

The mists that had hidden the coppice from McKay wavered, thinned and were gone. In their place was a limpid, translucent, palely green ether, faintly luminous—as though he stood within some clear wan emerald. His feet pressed a golden moss spangled with tiny starry bluets. Fully revealed before him was the woman of the strange eyes and the face of elfin beauty. He dwelt for a moment upon the slender shoulders, the firm small tip-tilted breasts, the willow litheness of her body. From neck to knees a smock covered her, sheer and silken and delicate as though spun of cobwebs; through it her body gleamed as though fire of the young Spring moon ran in her veins.

Beyond her, upon the golden moss were other women like her, many of them; they stared at him with the same wide set green eyes in which danced the clouds of sparkling moonbeam motes; like her they were crowned with glistening, pallidly golden hair; like hers too were their oval faces with the pointed chins and perilous elfin beauty. Only where she stared at him gravely, measuring him, weighing him—there were those of these her sisters whose eyes were mocking; and those whose eyes called to him with a weirdly tingling allure, their mouths athirst; those whose eyes looked upon him with curiosity alone and those whose great eyes pleaded with him, prayed to him.

Within that pellucid, greenly luminous air McKay was abruptly aware that the trees of the coppice still had a place. Only now they were spectral indeed; they were like white shadows cast athwart a glaucous screen; trunk and bough, twig and leaf they arose around him and they were as though etched in air by phantom craftsmen—thin, unsubstantial; they were ghost trees rooted in another space.

Suddenly he was aware that there were men among the women; men whose eyes were set wide apart as were theirs, as strange and pupilless as were theirs but with irises of brown and blue; men with pointed chins and oval faces, broad shouldered and clad in kirtles of darkest green; swarthy-skinned men muscular and strong, with that same lithe grace of the women—and like them of a beauty alien and elfin.

McKay heard a little wailing cry. He turned. Close beside him lay a girl clasped in the arms of one of the swarthy, green clad men. She lay upon his breast. His eyes were filled with a black flame of wrath, and hers were misted, anguished. For an instant McKay had a glimpse of the birch old Polleau's son had sent crashing down into the boughs of the fir. He saw birch and fir as immaterial outlines around the man and girl. For an instant girl and man and birch and fir seemed one and the same. The scarlet lipped woman touched his shoulder, and the confusion cleared.

"She withers," sighed the woman, and in her voice McKay heard a faint rustling as of mournful leaves. "Now is it not pitiful that she withers—our sister who was so young, so slender and so lovely?"

McKay looked again at the girl. The white skin seemed shrunken; the moon radiance that gleamed through the bodies of the others in hers was dim and pallid; her slim arms hung listlessly; her body drooped. The mouth too was wan and parched, the long and misted green eyes dull. The palely golden hair lusterless, and dry. He looked on slow death—a withering death.

"May the arm that struck her down wither!" the green clad man who held her shouted, and in his voice McKay heard a savage strumming as of winter winds through bleak boughs: "May his heart wither and the sun blast him! May the rain and the waters deny him and the winds scourge him!"

"I thirst," whispered the girl.

There was a stirring among the watching women. One came forward holding a chalice that was like thin leaves turned to green crystal. She paused beside the trunk of one of the spectral trees, reached up and drew down to her a branch. A slim girl with half-frightened, half-resentful eyes glided to her side and threw her arms around the ghostly bole. The woman with the chalice bent the branch and cut it deep with what seemed an arrow-shaped flake of jade. From the wound a faintly opalescent liquid slowly filled the cup. When it was filled the woman beside McKay stepped forward and pressed her own long hands around the bleeding branch. She stepped away and McKay saw that the stream had ceased to flow. She touched the trembling girl and unclasped her arms.

"It is healed," said the woman gently. "And it was your turn little sister. The wound is healed. Soon, you will have forgotten."

The woman with the chalice knelt and set it to the wan, dry lips of her who was—withering. She drank of it, thirstily, to the last drop. The misty eyes cleared, they sparkled; the lips that had been so parched and pale grew red, the white body gleamed as though the waning light had been fed with new.

"Sing, sisters," she cried, and shrilly. "Dance for me, sisters!"

Again burst out that chant McKay had heard as he had floated through the mists upon the lake. Now, as then, despite his opened ears, he could distinguish no words, but clearly he understood its mingled themes— the joy of Spring's awakening, rebirth, with the green life streaming singing up through every bough, swelling the buds, burgeoning with tender leaves the branches; the dance of the trees in the scented winds of Spring; the drums of the jubilant rain on leafy hoods; passion of Summer sun pouring its golden flood down upon the trees; the moon passing with stately step and slow and green hands stretching up to her and drawing from her breast milk of silver fire; riot of wild gay winds with their mad pipings and strummings;— soft interlacing of boughs, the kiss of amorous leaves—all these and more, much more that McKay could not understand since it dealt with hidden, secret things for which man has no images, were in that chanting.

And all these and more were in the measures, the rhythms of the dancing of those strange, green eyed women and brown skinned men; something incredibly ancient yet young as the speeding moment, something of a world before and beyond man.

McKay listened, McKay watched, lost in wonder; his own world more than half forgotten; his mind meshed in web of green sorcery.

The woman beside him touched his arm. She pointed to the girl.

"Yet she withers," she said. "And not all our life, if we poured it through her lips, could save her."

He looked; he saw that the red was draining slowly from the girl's lips, the luminous life tides waning; the eyes that had been so bright were misting and growing dull once more, suddenly a great pity and a great rage shook him. He knelt beside her, took her hands in his.

"Take them away! Take away your hands! They burn me!" she moaned.

"He tries to help you," whispered the green clad man, gently. But he reached over and drew McKay's hands away.

"Not so can you help her," said the woman.

"What can I do?" McKay arose, looked helplessly from one to the other. "What can I do to help?"

The chanting died, the dance stopped. A silence fell and he felt upon him the eyes of all. They were tense—waiting. The woman took his hands. Their touch was cool and sent a strange sweetness sweeping through his veins.

"There are three men yonder," she said. "They hate us. Soon we shall be as she is there—withering. They have sworn it, and as they have sworn so will they do. Unless—"

She paused; and McKay felt the stirrings of a curious unease. The moonbeam-dancing motes in her eyes had changed to tiny sparklings of red. In a way, deep down, they terrified him—those red sparklings.

"Three men?"—in his clouded mind was the memory of Polleau and his two strong sons. "Three men," he repeated, stupidly—"But what are three men to you who are so many? What could three men do against those stalwart gallants of yours?"

"No," she shook her head. "No—there is nothing our—men—can do; nothing that we can do. Once, night and day, we were gay. Now we fear—night and day. They mean to destroy us. Our kin have warned us. And our kin cannot help us. Those three are masters of blade and flame. Against blade and flame we are helpless."

"Blade and flame!" echoed the listeners. "Against blade and flame we are helpless."

"Surely will they destroy us," murmured the woman. "We shall wither all of us. Like her there, or burn—unless—"

Suddenly she threw white arms around McKay's neck. She pressed her lithe body close to him. Her scarlet mouth sought and found his lips and clung to them. Through all McKay's body ran swift, sweet flames, green fire of desire. His own arms went round her, crushed her to him.

"You shall not die!" he cried. "No—by God, you shall not!"

She drew back her head, looked deep into his eyes.

"They have sworn to destroy us," she said, "and soon. With blade and flame they will destroy us—these three—unless—"

"Unless?" he asked, fiercely.

"Unless you—slay them first!" she answered.

A cold shock ran through McKay, chilling the green sweet fires of his desire. He dropped his arm from around the woman; thrust her from him. For an instant she trembled before him.

"Slay!" he heard her whisper—and she was gone. The spectral trees wavered; their outlines thickened out of immateriality into substance. The green translucence darkened. He had a swift vertiginous moment as though he swung between two worlds. He closed his eyes. The vertigo passed and he opened them, looked around him.

McKay stood on the lakeward skirts of the little coppice. There were no shadows flitting, no sign of the white women and the swarthy, green clad men. His feet were on green moss; gone was the soft golden carpet with its blue starlets. Birches and firs clustered solidly before him. At his left was a sturdy fir in whose needled arms a broken birch tree lay withering. It was the birch that Polleau's men had so wantonly slashed down. For an instant he saw within the fir and birch the immaterial outlines of the green clad man and the slim girl who withered. For that instant birch and fir and girl and man seemed one and the same. He stepped back, and his hands touched the smooth, cool bark of another birch that rose close at his right.

Upon his hands the touch of that bark was like—was like?— yes, curiously was it like the touch of the long slim hands of the woman of the scarlet lips. But it gave him none of that alien rapture, that pulse of green life her touch had brought. Yet, now as then, the touch steadied him. The outlines of girl and man were gone.

He looked upon nothing but a sturdy fir with a withering birch fallen into its branches.

McKay stood there, staring, wondering, like a man who has but half awakened from dream. And suddenly a little wind stirred the leaves of the rounded birch beside him. The leaves murmured, sighed. The wind grew stronger and the leaves whispered.

"Slay!" he heard them whisper—and again: "Slay! Help us! Slay!"

And the whisper was the voice of the woman of the scarlet lips!

Rage, swift and unreasoning, sprang up in McKay. He began to run up through the coppice, up to where he knew was the old lodge in which dwelt Polleau and his sons. And as he ran the wind blew stronger, and louder and louder grew the whisperings of the trees.

"Slay!" they whispered. "Slay them! Save us! Slay!"

"I will slay! I will save you!" McKay, panting, hammer pulse beating in his ears, rushing through the woods heard himself answering that ever louder, ever more insistent command. And in his mind was but one desire—to clutch the throats of Polleau and his sons, to crack their necks; to stand by them then and watch them wither; wither like that slim girl in the arms of the green clad man.

So crying, he came to the edge of the coppice and burst from it out into a flood of sunshine. For a hundred feet he ran, and then he was aware that the whispering command was stilled; that he heard no more that maddening rustling of wrathful leaves. A spell seemed to have been loosed from him; it was as though he had broken through some web of sorcery. McKay stopped, dropped upon the ground, buried his face in the grasses.

He lay there, marshaling his thoughts into some order of sanity. What had he been about to do? To rush berserk upon those three who lived in the old lodge and—kill them! And for what? Because that elfin, scarlet lipped woman whose kisses he still could feel upon his mouth had bade him! Because the whispering trees of the little wood had maddened him with that same command!

And for this he had been about to kill three men!

What were that woman and her sisters and the green clad swarthy gallants of theirs? Illusions of some waking dream—phantoms born of the hypnosis of the swirling mists through which he had rowed and floated across the lake? Such things were not uncommon. McKay knew of those who by watching the shifting clouds could create and dwell for a time with wide open eyes within some similar land of fantasy; knew others who needed but to stare at smoothly falling water to set themselves within a world of waking dream; there were those who could summon dreams by gazing into a ball of crystal, others found their phantoms in saucers of shining ebon ink.

Might not the moving mists have laid those same hypnotic fingers upon his own mind—and his love for the trees the sense of appeal that he had felt so long and his memory of the wanton slaughter of the slim birch have all combined to paint upon his drugged consciousness the phantasms he had beheld?

Then in the flood of sunshine the spell had melted, his consciousness leaped awake?

McKay arose to his feet, shakily enough. He looked back at the coppice. There was no wind now, the leaves were silent, motionless. Again he saw it as the caravan of demoiselles with their marching knights and troubadours. But no longer was it gay. The words of the scarlet lipped woman came back to him—that gaiety had fled and fear had taken its place. Dream phantom or—dryad, whatever she was, half of that at least was truth.

He turned, a plan forming in his mind. Reason with himself as he might, something deep within him stubbornly asserted the reality of his experience. At any rate, he told himself, the little wood was far too beautiful to be despoiled. He would put aside the experience as dream—but he would save the little wood for the essence of beauty that it held in its green cup.

The old lodge was about a quarter of a mile away. A path led up to it through the ragged fields. McKay walked up the path, climbed rickety steps and paused, listening. He heard voices and knocked. The door was flung open and old Polleau stood there, peering at him through half shut, suspicious eyes. One of the sons stood close behind him. They stared at McKay with grim, hostile faces.

He thought he heard a faint, far off despairing whisper from the distant wood. And it was as though the pair in the doorway heard it too, for their gaze shifted from him to the coppice, and he saw hatred nicker swiftly across their grim faces; their gaze swept back to him.

"What do you want?" demanded Polleau, curtly.

"I am a neighbor of yours, stopping at the inn—" began McKay, courteously.

"I know who you are," Polleau interrupted brusquely, "But what is it that you want?"

"I find the air of this place good for me," McKay stifled a rising anger. "I am thinking of staying for a year or more until my health is fully recovered. I would like to buy some of your land and build me a lodge upon it."

"Yes, M'sieu?" there was acid politeness now in the powerful old man's voice. "But is it permitted to ask why you do not remain at the inn? Its fare is excellent and you are well liked there."

"I have desire to be alone," replied McKay. "I do not like people too close to me. I would have my own land, and sleep under my own roof."

"But why come to me?" asked Polleau. "There are many places upon the far side of the lake that you could secure. It is happy there, and this side is not happy, M'sieu. But tell me, what part of my land is it that you desire?"

"That little wood yonder," answered McKay, and pointed to the coppice.

"Ah! I thought so!" whispered Polleau, and between him and his sons passed a look of bitter understanding. He looked at McKay, somberly.

"That wood is not for sale, M'sieu," he said at last. "I can afford to pay well for what I want," said McKay. "Name your price."

"It is not for sale," repeated Polleau, stolidly, "at any price."

"Oh, come," laughed McKay, although his heart sank at the finality in that answer. "You have many acres and what is it but a few trees? I can afford to gratify my fancies. I will give you all the worth of your other land for it."

"You have asked what that place that you so desire is, and you have answered that it is but a few trees," said Polleau, slowly, and the tall son behind him laughed, abruptly, maliciously. "But it is more than that, M'sieu— Oh, much more than that. And you know it, else why would you pay such price? Yes, you know it—since you know also that we are ready to destroy it, and you would save it. And who told you all that, M'sieu?" he snarled.

There was such malignance in the face thrust suddenly close to McKay's, teeth bared by uplifted lip, that involuntarily he recoiled.

"But a few trees!" snarled old Polleau. "Then who told him what we mean to do—eh, Pierre?"

Again the son laughed. And at that laughter McKay felt within him resurgence of his own blind hatred as he had fled through the whispering wood. He mastered himself, turned away, there was nothing he could do— now. Polleau halted him.

"M'sieu," he said, "Wait. Enter. There is something I would tell you; something too I would show you. Something, perhaps, that I would ask you."

He stood aside, bowing with a rough courtesy. McKay walked through the doorway. Polleau with his son followed him. He entered a large, dim room whose ceiling was spanned with smoke blackened beams. From these beams hung onion strings and herbs and smoke cured meats. On one side was a wide fireplace. Huddled beside it sat Polleau's other son. He glanced up as they entered and McKay saw that a bandage covered one side of his head, hiding his left eye. McKay recognized him as the one who had cut down the slim birch. The blow of the fir, he reflected with a certain satisfaction, had been no futile one.

Old Polleau strode over to that son.

"Look, M'sieu," he said and lifted the bandage.

McKay with a faint tremor of horror, saw a gaping blackened socket, red rimmed and eyeless.

"Good God, Polleau!" he cried. "But this man needs medical attention. I know something of wounds. Let me go across the lake and bring back my kit. I will attend him."

Old Polleau shook his head, although his grim face for the first time softened. He drew the bandages back in place.

"It heals," he said. "We have some skill in such things. You saw what did it. You watched from your boat as the cursed tree struck him. The eye was crushed and lay upon his cheek. I cut it away. Now he heals. We do not need your aid, M'sieu."

"Yet he ought not have cut the birch," muttered McKay, more to himself than to be heard.

"Why not?" asked old Polleau, fiercely, "Since it hated him."

McKay stared at him. What did this old peasant know? The words strengthened that deep stubborn conviction that what he had seen and heard in the coppice had been actuality—no dream. And still more did Polleau's next words strengthen that conviction.

"M'sieu," he said, "you come here as ambassador—of a sort. The wood has spoken to you. Well, as ambassador I shall speak to you. Four centuries my people have lived in this place. A century we have owned this land. M'sieu, in all those years there has been no moment that the trees have not hated us—nor we the trees.

"For all those hundred years there have been hatred and battle between us and the forest. My father, M'sieu, was crushed by a tree; my elder brother crippled by another. My father's father, woodsman that he was, was lost in the forest—he came back to us with mind gone, raving of wood women who had bewitched and mocked him, luring him into swamp and fen and tangled thicket, tormenting him. In every generation the trees have taken their toll of us—women as well as men—maiming or killing us."

"Accidents," interrupted McKay. "This is childish, Polleau. You cannot blame the trees."

"In your heart you do not believe so," said Polleau. "Listen, the feud is an ancient one. Centuries ago it began when we were serfs, slaves of the nobles. To cook, to keep us warm in winter, they let us pick up the fagots, the dead branches and twigs that dropped from the trees. But if we cut down a tree to keep us warm, to keep our women and our children warm, yes, if we but tore down a branch—they hanged us, or they threw us into dungeons to rot, or whipped us till our backs were red lattices.

"They had their broad fields, the nobles—but we must raise our food in the patches where the trees disdained to grow. And if they did thrust themselves into our poor patches, then, M'sieu, we must let them have their way—or be flogged, or be thrown into the dungeons or be hanged.

"They pressed us in—the trees," the old man's voice grew sharp with fanatic hatred. "They stole our fields and they took the food from the mouths of our children; they dropped their fagots to us like dole to beggars; they tempted us to warmth when the cold struck our bones—and they bore us as fruit a-swing at the end of the foresters' ropes if we yielded to their tempting.

"Yes, M'sieu—we died of cold that they might live! Our children died of hunger that their young might find root space! They despised us—the trees! We died that they might live—and we were men!

"Then, M'sieu came the Revolution and the freedom. Ah, M'sieu, then we took our toll! Great logs roaring in the winter cold—no more huddling over the alms of fagots. Fields where the trees had been—no more starving of our children that theirs might live. Now the trees were the slaves and we the masters.

"And the trees knew and they hated us!

"But blow for blow, a hundred of their lives for each life of ours— we have returned their hatred. With axe and torch we have fought them—

"The trees!" shrieked Polleau, suddenly, eyes blazing red rage, face writhing, foam at the corners of his mouth and gray hair clutched in rigid hands—"The cursed trees! Armies of the trees creeping— creeping—closer, ever closer—crushing us in! Stealing our fields as they did of old! Building their dungeon round us as they built of old the dungeons of stone! Creeping—creeping! Armies of trees! Legions of trees! The trees! The cursed trees!"

McKay listened, appalled. Here was crimson heart of hate. Madness! But what was at the root of it? Some deep inherited instinct, coming down from forefathers who had hated the forest as the symbol of their masters. Forefathers whose tides of hatred had overflowed to the green life on which the nobles had laid their tabu—as one neglected child will hate the favorite on whom love and gifts are lavished? In such warped minds the crushing fall of a tree, the maiming sweep of a branch, might well appear as deliberate, the natural growth of the forest seem the implacable advance of an enemy.

And yet—the blow of the fir as the cut birch fell had been deliberate! and there had been those women of the wood—

"Patience," the standing son touched the old man's shoulder. "Patience! Soon we strike our blow."

Some of the frenzy died out of Polleau's face.

"Though we cut down a hundred," he whispered, "By the hundred they return! But one of us, when they strike—he does not return. No! They have numbers and they have—time. We are now but three, and we have little time. They watch us as we go through the forest, alert to trip, to strike, to crush!

"But M'sieu," he turned blood-shot eyes to McKay. "We strike our blow, even as Pierre has said. We strike at the coppice that you so desire. We strike there because it is the very heart of the forest. There the secret life of the forest runs at full tide. We know—and you know! Something that, destroyed, will take the heart out of the forest—will make it know us for its masters."

"The women!" the standing son's eyes glittered, "I have seen the women there! The fair women with the shining skins who invite—and mock and vanish before hands can seize them."

"The fair women who peer into our windows in the night—and mock us!" muttered the eyeless son.

"They shall mock no more!" shouted Polleau, the frenzy again taking him. "Soon they shall lie, dying! All of them—all of them! They die!"

He caught McKay by the shoulders, shook him like a child.

"Go tell them that!" he shouted. "Say to them that this very day we destroy them. Say to them it is we who will laugh when winter comes and we watch their round white bodies blaze in this hearth of ours and warm us! Go—tell them that!"

He spun McKay around, pushed him to the door, opened it and flung him staggering down the steps. He heard the tall son laugh, the door close. Blind with rage he rushed up the steps and hurled himself against the door. Again the tall son laughed. McKay beat at the door with clenched fists, cursing. The three within paid no heed. Despair began to dull his rage. Could the trees help him—counsel him? He turned and walked slowly down the field path to the little wood.

Slowly and ever more slowly he went as he neared it. He had failed. He was a messenger bearing a warrant of death. The birches were motionless; their leaves hung listlessly. It was as though they knew he had failed. He paused at the edge of the coppice. He looked at his watch, noted with faint surprise that already it was high noon. Short shrift enough had the little wood. The work of destruction would not be long delayed.

McKay squared his shoulders and passed in between the trees. It was strangely silent in the coppice. And it was mournful. He had a sense of life brooding around him, withdrawn into itself; sorrowing. He passed through the silent, mournful wood until he reached the spot where the rounded, gleaming barked tree stood close to the fir that held the withering birch. Still there was no sound, no movement. He laid his hands upon the cool bark of the rounded tree.

"Let me see again!" he whispered. "Let me hear! Speak to me!"

There was no answer. Again and again he called. The coppice was silent. He wandered through it, whispering, calling. The slim birches stood, passive with limbs and leaves adroop like listless arms and hands of captive maids awaiting with dull woe the will of conquerors. The firs seemed to crouch like hopeless men with heads in hands. His heart ached to the woe that filled the little wood, this hopeless submission of the trees.

When, he wondered, would Polleau strike. He looked at his watch again; an hour had gone by. How long would Polleau wait? He dropped to the moss, back against a smooth bole.

And suddenly it seemed to McKay that he was a madman—as mad as Polleau and his sons. Calmly, he went over the old peasant's indictment of the forest; recalled the face and eyes filled with the fanatic hate. Madness! After all, the trees were—only trees. Polleau and his sons—so he reasoned—had transferred to them the bitter hatred their forefathers had felt for those old lords who had enslaved them; had laid upon them too all the bitterness of their own struggle to exist in this high forest land. When they struck at the trees, it was the ghosts of these forefathers striking at the nobles who had oppressed them; it was themselves striking against their own destiny. The trees were but symbols. It was the warped minds of Polleau and his sons that clothed them in false semblance of conscious life in blind striving to wreak vengeance against the ancient masters and the destiny that had made their lives hard and unceasing battle against Nature. The nobles were long dead; destiny can be brought to grips by no man. But the trees were here and alive. Clothed in mirage, through them the driving lust for vengeance could be sated.

And he, McKay, was it not his own deep love and sympathy for the trees that similarly had clothed them in that false semblance of conscious life? Had he not built his own mirage? The trees did not really mourn, could not suffer, could not—know. It was his own sorrow that he had transferred to them; only his own sorrow that he felt echoing back to him from them.

The trees were—only trees.

Instantly, upon the heels of that thought, as though it were an answer, he was aware that the trunk against which he leaned was trembling; that the whole coppice was trembling; that all the little leaves were shaking, tremulously.

McKay, bewildered, leaped to his feet. Reason told him that it was the wind—yet there was no wind!

And as he stood there, a sighing arose as though a mournful breeze were blowing through the trees—and again there was no wind!

Louder grew the sighing and within it now faint wailings.

"They come! They come! Farewell sisters! Sisters—farewell!"

Clearly he heard the mournful whispers.

McKay began to run through the trees to the trail that led out to the fields of the old lodge. And as he ran the wood darkened as though clear shadows gathered in it, as though vast unseen wings hovered over it. The trembling of the coppice increased; bough touched bough, clung to each other; and louder became the sorrowful crying:

"Farewell sister! Sister—farewell!"

McKay burst out into the open. Halfway between him and the lodge were Polleau and his sons. They saw him; they pointed and lifted mockingly to him bright axes. He crouched, waiting for them to come, all fine spun theories gone and rising within him that same rage that hours before had sent him out to slay.

So crouching, he heard from the forested hills a roaring clamor. From every quarter it came, wrathful, menacing; like the voices of legions of great trees bellowing through the horns of tempest. The clamor maddened McKay; fanned the flame of rage to white heat.

If the three men heard it, they gave no sign. They came on steadily, jeering at him, waving their keen blades. He ran to meet them.

"Go back!" he shouted. "Go back, Polleau! I warn you!"

"He warns us!" jeered Polleau. "He—Pierre, Jean—he warns us!"

The old peasant's arm shot out and his hand caught McKay's shoulder with a grip that pinched to the bone. The arm flexed and hurled him against the unmaimed son. The son caught him, twisted him about and whirled him headlong a dozen yards, crashing him through the brush at the skirt of the wood.

McKay sprang to his feet howling like a wolf. The clamor of the forest had grown stronger.

"Kill!" it roared. "Kill!"

The unmaimed son had raised his axe. He brought it down upon the trunk of a birch, half splitting it with one blow. McKay heard a wail go up from the little wood. Before the axe could be withdrawn he had crashed a fist in the axe wielder's face. The head of Polleau's son rocked back; he yelped, and before McKay could strike again had wrapped strong arms around him, crushing breath from him. McKay relaxed, went limp, and the son loosened his grip. Instantly McKay slipped out of it and struck again, springing aside to avoid the rib breaking clasp. Polleau's son was quicker than he, the long arms caught him. But as the arms tightened, there was the sound of sharp splintering and the birch into which the axe had bitten toppled. It struck the ground directly behind the wrestling men. Its branches seemed to reach out and clutch at the feet of Polleau's son.

He tripped and fell backward, McKay upon him. The shock of the fall broke his grip and again McKay writhed free. Again he was upon his feet, and again Polleau's strong son, quick as he, faced him. Twice McKay's blows found their mark beneath his heart before once more the long arms trapped him. But their grip was weaker; McKay felt that now his strength was equal.

Round and round they rocked, McKay straining to break away. They fell, and over they rolled and over, arms and legs locked, each striving to free a hand to grip the other's throat. Around them ran Polleau and the one-eyed son, shouting encouragement to Pierre, yet neither daring to strike at McKay lest the blow miss and be taken by the other.

And all that time McKay heard the little wood shouting. Gone from it now was all mournfulness, all passive resignation. The wood was alive and raging. He saw the trees shake and bend as though torn by a tempest. Dimly he realized that the others must hear none of this, see none of it; as dimly wondered why this should be.

"Kill!" shouted the coppice—and over its tumult he heard the roar of the great forest:

"Kill! Kill!"

He became aware of two shadowy shapes, shadowy shapes of swarthy green clad men, that pressed close to him as he rolled and fought.

"Kill!" they whispered. "Let his blood flow! Kill! Let his blood flow!"

He tore a wrist free from the son's clutch. Instantly he felt within his hand the hilt of a knife.

"Kill!" whispered the shadowy men.

"Kill!" shrieked the coppice.

"Kill!" roared the forest.

McKay's free arm swept up and plunged the knife into the throat of Polleau's son! He heard a choking sob; heard Polleau shriek; felt the hot blood spurt in face and over hand; smelt its salt and faintly acrid odor. The encircling arms dropped from him; he reeled to his feet.

As though the blood had been a bridge, the shadowy men leaped from immateriality into substances. One threw himself upon the man McKay had stabbed; the other hurled upon old Polleau. The maimed son turned and fled, howling with terror. A white woman sprang out from the shadow, threw herself at his feet, clutched them and brought him down. Another woman and another dropped upon him. The note of his shrieking changed from fear to agony; then died abruptly into silence.

And now McKay could see none of the three, neither old Polleau or his sons, for the green clad men and the white women covered them!

McKay stood stupidly, staring at his red hands. The roar of the forest had changed to a deep triumphal chanting. The coppice was mad with joy. The trees had become thin phantoms etched in emerald translucent air as they had been when first the green sorcery had enmeshed him. And all around him wove and danced the slim, gleaming women of the wood.

They ringed him, their song bird-sweet and shrill; jubilant. Beyond them he saw gliding toward him the woman of the misty pillars whose kisses had poured the sweet green fire into his veins. Her arms were outstretched to him, her strange wide eyes were rapt on his, her white body gleamed with the moon radiance, her red lips were parted and smiling—a scarlet chalice filled with the promise of undreamed ecstasies. The dancing circle, chanting, broke to let her through.

Abruptly, a horror filled McKay. Not of this fair woman, not of her jubilant sisters—but of himself.

He had killed! And the wound the war had left in his soul, the wound he thought had healed, had opened.

He rushed through the broken circle, thrust the shining woman aside with his blood stained hands and ran, weeping, toward the lake shore. The singing ceased. He heard little cries, tender, appealing; little cries of pity; soft voices calling on him to stop, to return. Behind him was the sound of little racing feet, light as the fall of leaves upon the moss.

McKay ran on. The coppice lightened, the beach was before him. He heard the fair woman call him, felt the touch of her hand upon his shoulder. He did not heed her. He ran across the narrow strip of beach, thrust his boat out into the water and wading through the shallows threw himself into it.

He lay there for a moment, sobbing; then drew himself up, caught at the oars. He looked back at the shore now a score of feet away. At the edge of the coppice stood the woman, staring at him with pitying, wise eyes. Behind her clustered the white faces of her sisters, the swarthy faces of the green clad men.

"Come back!" the woman whispered, and held out to him slender arms.

McKay hesitated, his horror lessening in that clear, wise, pitying gaze. He half swung the boat around. His gaze dropped upon his blood-stained hands and again the hysteria gripped him. One thought only was in his mind— to get far away from where Polleau's son lay with his throat ripped open, to put the lake between that body and him.

Head bent low, McKay bowed to the oars, skimming swiftly outward. When he looked up a curtain of mist had fallen between him and the shore. It hid the coppice and from beyond it there came to him no sound. He glanced behind him, back toward the inn. The mists swung there, too, concealing it.

McKay gave silent thanks for these vaporous curtains that hid him from both the dead and the alive. He slipped limply under the thwarts. After a while he leaned over the side of the boat and, shuddering, washed the blood from his hands. He scrubbed the oar blades where his hands had left red patches. He ripped the lining out of his coat and drenching it in the lake he cleansed his face. He took off the stained coat, wrapped it with the lining round the anchor stone in the skiff and sunk it in the lake. There were other stains upon his shirt; but these he would have to let be.

For a time he rowed aimlessly, finding in the exertion a lessening of his soul sickness. His numbed mind began to function, analyzing his plight, planning how to meet the future—how to save him.

What ought he do? Confess that he had killed Polleau's son? What reason could he give? Only that he had killed because the man had been about to cut down some trees—trees that were his father's to do with as he willed!

And if he told of the wood woman, the wood women, the shadowy shapes of their green gallants who had helped him—who would believe?

They would think him mad—mad as he half believed himself to be.

No, none would believe him. None! Nor would confession bring back life to him he had slain. No; he would not confess.

But stay—another thought came! Might he not be—accused? What actually had happened to old Polleau and his other son? He had taken it for granted that they were dead; that they had died under those bodies white and swarthy. But had they? While the green sorcery had meshed him he had held no doubt of this—else why the jubilance of the little wood, the triumphant chanting of the forest?

Were they dead—Polleau and the one-eyed son? Clearly it came to him that they had not heard as he had, had not seen as he had. To them McKay and his enemy had been but two men battling, in a woodland glade; nothing more than that—until the last! Until the last? Had they seen more than that even then?

No, all that he could depend upon as real was that he had ripped out the throat of one of old Polleau's sons. That was the one unassailable verity. He had washed the blood of that man from his hands and his face.

All else might have been mirage—but one thing was true. He had murdered Polleau's son!

Remorse? He had thought that he had felt it. He knew now that he did not; that he had no shadow of remorse for what he had done. It had been panic that had shaken him, panic realization of the strangenesses, reaction from the battle lust, echoes of the war. He had been justified in that—execution. What right had those men to destroy the little wood; to wipe wantonly its beauty away?

None! He was glad that he had killed!

At that moment McKay would gladly have turned his boat and raced away to drink of the crimson chalice of the wood woman's lips. But the mists were raising, He saw that he was close to the landing of the inn.

There was no one about. Now was his time to remove the last of those accusing stains. After that—

Quickly he drew up, fastened the skiff, slipped unseen to his room. He locked the door, started to undress. Then sudden sleep swept over him like a wave, drew him helplessly down into ocean depths of sleep.

A knocking at the door awakened McKay, and the innkeeper's voice summoned him to dinner. Sleepily, he answered, and as the old man's footsteps died away, he roused himself. His eyes fell upon his shirt and the great stains now rusty brown. Puzzled, he stared at them for a moment, then full memory clicked back in place.

He walked to the window. It was dusk. A wind was blowing and the trees were singing, all the little leaves dancing; the forest hummed a cheerful vespers. Gone was all the unease, all the inarticulate trouble and the fear. The forest was tranquil and it was happy.

He sought the coppice through the gathering twilight. Its demoiselles were dancing lightly in the wind, leafy hoods dipping, leafy skirts ablow. Beside them marched the green troubadours, carefree, waving their needled arms. Gay was the little wood, gay as when its beauty had first drawn him to it.

McKay undressed, hid the stained shirt in his traveling trunk, bathed and put on a fresh outfit, sauntered down to dinner. He ate excellently. Wonder now and then crossed his mind that he felt no regret, no sorrow even, for the man he had killed. Half he was inclined to believe it all a dream—so little of any emotion did he feel. He had even ceased to think of what discovery might mean.

His mind was quiet; he heard the forest chanting to him that there was nothing he need fear; and when he sat for a time that night upon the balcony a peace that was half an ecstasy stole in upon him from the murmuring woods and enfolded him. Cradled by it he slept dreamlessly.

McKay did not go far from the inn that next day. The little wood danced gaily and beckoned him, but he paid no heed. Something whispered to wait, to keep the lake between him and it until word came of what lay or had lain there. And the peace still was on him.

Only the old innkeeper seemed to grow uneasy as the hours went by. He went often to the landing, scanning the further shore.

"It is strange," he said at last to McKay as the sun was dipping behind the summits. "Polleau was to see me here today. He never breaks his word. If he could not come he would have sent one of his sons."

McKay nodded, carelessly.

"There is another thing I do not understand," went on the old man. "I have seen no smoke from the lodge all day. It is as though they were not there."

"Where could they be?" asked McKay, indifferently.

"I do not know," the voice was more perturbed. "It all troubles me, M'sieu. Polleau is hard, yes; but he is my neighbor. Perhaps an accident—"

"They would let you know soon enough if there was anything wrong," McKay said.

"Perhaps, but—" the old man hesitated. "If he does not come tomorrow and again I see no smoke I will go to him," he ended.

McKay felt a little shock run through him—tomorrow then he would know, definitely know, what it was that had happened in the little wood.

"I would if I were you," he said. "I'd not wait too long either. After all—well, accidents do happen."

"Will you go with me, M'sieu," asked the old man.

"No!" whispered the warning voice within McKay. "No! Do not go!"

"Sorry," he said, aloud. "But I've some writing to do. If you should need me send back your man. I'll come."

And all that night he slept, again dreamlessly, while the crooning forest cradled him.

The morning passed without sign from the opposite shore. An hour after noon he watched the old innkeeper and his man row across the lake. And suddenly McKay's composure was shaken, his serene certainty wavered. He unstrapped his field glasses and kept them on the pair until they had beached the boat and entered the coppice. His heart was beating uncomfortably, his hands felt hot and his lips dry. He scanned the shore. How long had they been in the wood? It must have been an hour! What were they doing there? What had they found? He looked at his watch, incredulously. Less than fifteen minutes had passed.

Slowly the seconds ticked by. And it was all of an hour indeed before he saw them come out upon the shore and drag their boat into the water. McKay, throat curiously dry, a deafening pulse within his ears, steadied himself; forced himself to stroll leisurely down to the landing.

"Everything all right?" he called as they were near. They did not answer; but as the skiff warped against the landing they looked up at him and on their faces were stamped horror and a great wonder.

"They are dead, M'sieu," whispered the innkeeper. "Polleau and his two sons—all dead!"

McKay's heart gave a great leap, a swift faintness took him.

"Dead!" he cried. "What killed them?"

"What but the trees, M'sieu?" answered the old man, and McKay thought his gaze dwelt upon him strangely. "The trees killed them. See—we went up the little path through the wood, and close to its end we found it blocked by fallen trees. The flies buzzed round those trees, M'sieu, so we searched there. They were under them, Polleau and his sons. A fir had fallen upon Polleau and had crushed in his chest. Another son we found beneath a fir and upturned birches. They had broken his back, and an eye had been torn out—but that was no new wound, the latter." He paused.

"It must have been a sudden wind," said his man. "Yet I never knew of a wind like that must have been. There were no trees down except those that lay upon them. And of those it was as though they had leaped out of the ground! Yes, as though they had leaped out of the ground upon them. Or it was as though giants had torn them out for clubs. They were not broken—their roots were bare—"

"But the other son—Polleau had two?"—try as he might, McKay could not keep the tremor out of his voice.

"Pierre," said the old man, and again McKay felt that strange quality in his gaze. "He lay beneath a fir. His throat was torn out!"

"His throat torn out!" whispered McKay, His knife! The knife that had been slipped into his hand by the shadowy shapes!

"His throat was torn out," repeated the innkeeper. "And in it still was the broken branch that had done it. A broken branch, M'sieu, pointed as a knife. It must have caught Pierre as the fir fell and ripping through his throat—been broken off as the tree crashed."

McKay stood, mind whirling in wild conjecture. "You said—a broken branch?" McKay asked through lips gone white.

"A broken branch, M'sieu," the innkeeper's eyes searched him. "It was very plain—what it was that happened. Jacques," he turned to his man. "Go up to the house."

He watched until the man shuffled out of sight. "Yet not all plain, M'sieu," he spoke low to McKay. "For in Pierre's hand I found— this."

He reached into a pocket and drew out a button from which hung a strip of cloth. Cloth and button had once been part of that blood-stained coat which McKay had sunk within the lake; torn away no doubt when death had struck Polleau's son!

McKay strove to speak. The old man raised his hand. Button and cloth fell from it, into the water. A wave took it and floated it away; another and another. They watched it silently until it had vanished.

"Tell me nothing, M'sieu," the old innkeeper turned to him, "Polleau was hard and hard men, too, were his sons. The trees hated them. The trees killed them. And now the trees are happy. That is all. And the—souvenir—is gone. I have forgotten I saw it. Only M'sieu would better also—go."

That night McKay packed. When dawn had broken he stood at his window, looked long at the little wood. It was awakening, stirring sleepily like drowsy delicate demoiselles. He drank in its beauty—for the last time; waved it farewell.

McKay breakfasted well. He dropped into the driver's seat; set the engine humming. The old innkeeper and his wife, solicitous as ever for his welfare, bade him Godspeed. On both their faces was full friendliness—and in the old man's eyes somewhat of puzzled awe.

His road lay through the thick forest. Soon inn and lake were far behind him.

And singing went McKay, soft whisperings of leaves following him, glad chanting of needled pines; the voice of the forest tender, friendly, caressing—the forest pouring into him as farewell gift its peace, its happiness, its strength.

THE NYMPH OF THE WATERS

Anonymous

first published in *The New York Mirror and Ladies' Literary Gazette*
(July 1826)

In days of yore, there was occasionally to be seen, upon the Lurley, at sunset, in the twilight, and by moonlight, a maiden singing. Her beauty was of the most graceful and voluptuous kind, and her voice was the sweetest sound which had ever floated over the waters of the Rhine. Perhaps, both the scene and the hour entered for something into the extreme effects produced by her song. The Lurley is situated in the most beautiful part of the most beautiful of rivers. The rocks close in upon the stream, and overhang it on each side, and hence render it more rapid and tumultuous. The hour when she appeared was always in the calm of the summer evening, or the still deeper calm of the summer night, when the moon sheds her radiance of beauty and of peace upon the gliding river, and makes its waves appear as though they were formed of living light. At such times as these, the maid would be seen upon the rock, her long golden hair floating upon the evening breeze, or fantastically braided and twined with river-flowers. And, then, she would breathe forth sounds of such exquisite melody of such unmatched sweetness, and softness, and strength, that the boat-men, who were descending the Rbine, would become so enthralled in delight as totally to forget their boat—themselves—every thing but the music, which thus engrossed and charmed them. Hence would their boats, floating with the stream, no longer guided by their oar, become entangled among the currents and eddies which abound about this spot, and be dashed to pieces against the rocks.

At length, so many lives were lost, through the irresistible fascinations of this siren's song, that the people in the country round began, in the simple creed of those early times, to think that she was endued with magical power; and that she exerted it to the destruction of the human race. From time to time, however, she was known to do kindnesses to the boatmen on the Rhine. She would sometimes direct the young fishermen, who frequented the spot, where to cast their nets; and when they followed her directions, they were certain to make an immense draught. These fishers, who were the only persons who had ever seen the nymph closely, talked in raptures of her beauty, of her sweet voice, of her kind manner, of the real benefits which she conferred upon them. Thus it happened that, what with blame, and what with praise, the Nymph of the Lurley became the chief subject of which all persons spoke for many leagues around.

At length her fame reached the court of the Count Palatine, and shortly was the sole topic of discussion throughout its precincts. In bower, and in hall, by knight, and by lady, by baron and by squire, the Nymph of the Lurley was equally the subject of discourse. It was observed, however, that the matter was more favorite with the male than with the female courtiers. One young knight repeated what had been told to him concerning her beauty; another related the magical effects of her voice. The ladies, on the other hand, affected to disbelieve the more prominent points of these stories, and threw on them all, as much as they could, the coldness of doubt, and sneers, and utter disbelief.

At last, however, the son of the Count took up the cause of the Nymph of the Lurley; and it is astonishing how rapidly a change was operated in the opinions of the ladies of the court concerning her. It is even said that some of the foremost among them introduced the fashion of dressing their hair with water-lilies, brought from the Rhine; which was reported to be a favorite costume with the beautiful nymph. But of this there is, I think, not sufficient evidence.

It was not long before the young Count expressed his determination to make a journey to the Lurley, for the purpose of seeing its charming occupant. Many persons, however, adopted the darker theory concerning this mysterious being, and tried to dissuade the young Count from so perilous an adventure, representing her as a witch, who put on a beautiful semblance, and breathed sweet music, only to lure to their destruction all who came within the influence of her charms. But the Count was in the full flush of youth; and when was youth ever restrained by prudence, when beauty was in the case?

He set off, therefore, on his journey, accompanied by a brilliant suite of youthful knights, who burned to go upon so romantic an expedition. The Count made no secret of his intention of bringing the nymph away from the place which had been the scene of so many fatal mischiefs, and then judge impartially of the various stories in circulation respecting her. He embarked, therefore, upon the Rhine, in a splendidly ornamented bark, shining with gold, and streaming with his own banner, and the gay pennons of his various followers.

The sun had just set when they came within sight of the Lurley. A fine tint of deep rose-color still glowed in the western sky; while in the east, the cold, clear, blue of night gave distinctly to view the bright stars which shone amongst it. The boats glided rapidly with the stream; the current of which was already become quicker in proportion as they approached the Lake of St.

Goar. On the rock of the Lurley the nymph was seated, singing—her long hair was streaming upon the wind, and she held in her hands a girdle of river-coral. As they drew near, they began to distinguish the words of her song:

"Come, oh! come
To my wat'ry home—
The white shroud of lilies waits for thee!
The glistening wave
Is the mortal's grave—
But oh! 'tis a sweet, sweet home to me!
I float in the cool
And deep, dark pool;
They sink to the sand of the river bed—
And their dying wail
Is lost in the gale,
Which ripples the river above their head!

"The King of the Waters
Hath many daughters,
Some for the lake, and some for the sea;—
But, oh! it is mine
To watch o'er the Rhine—
The Rhine, in itself, is an ocean to me!
Its waves are as bright,
When in clear moonlight
They break, while the current onward rushes;
And the vines hang o'er
The craggy shore,
And adorn its face with their brilliant blushes!

"Oh! Father! hear me!
The bark draws near me,
To take me off to the dry, dry shore!
Where the waters flow not—
And the lilies glow not—
And the bubbling spring is heard no more!
Let thy car arise—
Let these mortals' eyes
See and shrink from thy matchless power—
Rhine, rise around me!
Let thy waters bound me
From these vain sons of a mortal hour!

It may be supposed that such a song as this would not be particularly prepossessing to the ears for which it was intended; but if any one formed such a supposition, he would be exceedingly mistaken. As in some more modern instances, the sound was so exquisite that the sense was wholly unheeded. The Count and his companions were entranced; they scarcely breathed, lest the slightest particle of sound should be lost to them. The rowers, even, though composed of old boatmen, who regarded the nymph as an evil-doing witch, paused upon their stroke, and remained with uplifted oars, wholly inthralled by such sweet music. Nay, it is said that one of the oldest of them, who had been deaf for years, regained his hearing on this occasion: but this needs confirmation.

The boats floated towards the rock, drifting with the current. The boatmen utterly neglected to attend to their charge. At length, of a sudden, when the nymph began the last of the above stanzas, and invoked the King of the Waters to show his might, the persons on board the boats were, in some degree, roused from their torpor, by the violent heaving and swelling of the river, which began to rise on all sides, as though under the impulse of a vast but invisible convulsion. There was no wind. The banners drooped along their staves, and the calm sky was unobscured by a single cloud. But the Rhine showed every mark of a violent storm, which reigned in the waters, though it in no degree extended to the air. The waves rose in tumultuous agitation— rushing and foaming as though the winds of equinox swept over them.

"It is the work of that hell-born witch!" exclaimed one of the attendants; and he leveled his crossbow at her as he spoke. The Count called to him to stay his hand, but he was too late. The man let fly his bolt; but a huge wave reared its crest before it, and the arrow fell harmless into the water. The river rose more and more rapidly; and at last, three enormous waves, which reached the part of the Lurley where the nymph was sitting, assumed the appearance of a glittering car, drawn by two foaming horses; though some of the spectators thought that this appearance was only the addition of fancy to a casual formation.

Be this as it may, into the largest of the three waves the nymph threw herself, and as she disappeared from the astonished sight of the Count and his party, they heard her exquisite voice breathing the following words:

> *"I go, I go*
> *To my home below—*
> *'Tis sweet and fair with the river flowers:*
> *Coral and amber*
> *Bedeck my chamber,*
> *And gems shine bright in my liquid bowers.*
> *Go, Prince. in peace,*
> *The storm shall cease;*
> *A kind heart beats within thy breast;*
> *But yon churlish groom*

> *Shall meet his doom:*
> *In the wave, tonight, shall he take his rest!*
>
> *"The river shall side,*
> *To the distant tide,*
> *And shine as it hath always shone;*
> *But I no more*
> *Shall behold this shore,*
> *I go, and am forever gone!*
> *But a spot so dear*
> *Still will keep me near—*
> *My spirit will float in this river-lake;*
> *And strangers will come*
> *To my Lurley-home*
> *Ages hence, for that spirit's sake!"*

There was now no longer doubt of the nature of this fascinating being. She was an Ondine, or Water-spirit. Over these the human race have no power.

Her parting prophecy was fulfilled in every particular. The only person who suffered from this expedition, was the man who leveled his crossbow at her. His foot slipped as he was stepping on shore, and the wave, having once closed over him, did not loose its hold again.

The Ondine has never since been seen on the Lurley; nor has her song been heard there. But the fishermen say, that she still amuses herself by imitating and repeating their voices; and, to hear these remarkable sounds, strangers still flock to the abode of "the Nymph of the Waters."

Seppi, the Goatherd:
A Fairy Tale of Switzerland

C. B. Burckhardt

from *Fairy Tales and Legends of Many Nations* (1847)

The mezereon and the mountain lilies bloomed upon the hills and the wall-wort on the edge of the forest, or among the hedges which enclosed fields and gardens; and the Senners, that is, the cowherds and the goatherds, of the Poster-valley prepared for departure with their flocks to the beautiful pasture among the Alps. For miles, even before the droves of cattle came in sight, could the bells of the herds and the merry lowing of the cows be heard, for Peter Saibel, the big senner, alone, drove more than one hundred cows to the Alps. Slowly, and with solemn mien, he headed the procession. In his hand he carried the long staff, and his hat and shoes were adorned with loops and rosettes of many-colored ribbons.

Close behind him, and, as it were, imitating him in grandeur and pride, followed the beauty of the herd, the queen cow, the victress of the cow fights which frequently take place in the Alps. As a diadem she wore an immense wreath of mountain flowers, and her large bell was suspended from her neck by an embroidered collar. Behind her came the other cows, all adorned with variegated ribbons, with wreaths, bouquets and merry bells; following these, came the keeper of the young cattle, with the calves and oxen; and lastly came Seppi, the goatherd, with his numberless flock of goats, a handsome and good boy of about fourteen years, with long blonde curls, a tall, well-formed figure, and so kind an expression of face that every child in the valley was fond of him.

No one, at all the farm-houses which the imposing procession passed, paid much attention to the vain and stylish senner, who proudly strutted in front of his herd; but young and old had a smile and a friendly nod for Seppi, who looked extremely well in his red vest and clear white shirt collar, and even the boys said to each other: "Just look, what a fine fellow our Seppi is! He will be the smartest man in the valley when he once gets along in the world, and earns money to dress himself better. But just look at the senner: he looks like St. Stephen in a cabbage garden!" and all laughed and agreed with the speaker.

When the droves had reached the plains among the Alps, and the cattle quietly sought pasture, the herds divided, and Seppi with his goats came wear a pretty large pond. The goatherd was tired of his long walks and stretched himself among the high grass by the water's edge, and, although the sun still stood very high, it was cool by the water's side, and a gentle air rippled the waves, and the blue sky reflected its image back on the surface of the clear water. Seppi always was happy at heart, though he was the poorest lad in the whole Puster-valley, but today he was especially happy, because spring had returned upon the beautiful green Alps, and our boy could again take his herds to pasture upon the rich blooming meadows. And for this reason he sang one merry song after the other, for the world and all around him delighted him.

Suddenly, as he lay quietly in the high grass, he saw a light fog arise on the top of the waters, and the fog became thicker and thicker every moment. He closely watched this phenomenon, and observed a most lovely figure gradually emerging from the fog as from a close veil. She wore a wreath of water lilies around her long black hair, a golden crown rested upon that, and in the midst of the crown sparkled a large diamond. She was more beautiful than the picture of the Madonna in the forest chapel, which was the most beautiful thing Seppi had ever seen.

"I wonder if that is like a fairy!" Seppi thought to himself, and had a great inclination to run away. But the beautiful lady beckoned him, and said, "Sing that beautiful song again, my boy, for that has called me hither, and I will richly reward you for it."

"Well,' said Seppi to himself, as he lost all fear, "she speaks so kind and so friendly, and I think she is too beautiful to do me any harm, as stupid people say that mermaids are apt to do." And he sung his song again and again, until the fairy signified that she was obliged to him and had heard enough.

"I will now give you a cup full of gold sand; with that you can buy land, hire people, and have as big a herd as your senner," she said. "Or perhaps you have another wish, which you want me to fulfill?"

"If you are a water fairy," replied Seppi, confidently, "I would rather that you showed me your sub-marine dominions; it must be very cool and beautiful beneath the blue waters."

"Give me your hand, then," said the fairy, who guided him across the waters, and Seppi found to his astonishment that his feet remained perfectly dry; in the middle of the pond she stopped and touched the surface of the water with a small wand of whalebone; and the waves opened, and a large staircase appeared, the steps of which were of pure crystal; the fairy conducted Seppi down the stairs, who wondered whether down below there he would find such beautiful green mats, and such handsome flowers as above, where the bright sun shone; and gladly would he have jumped down three or four steps at a time, in order to be quickly there. But this was not so easily done, for he seemed to have walked more than an hour already, and still the stairs appeared to have no end. But every moment the fairy seemed to him more beautiful; he loved her more and more, and it appeared as if all that shone around him only came from her eyes, which were as blue as the horizon he loved to look upon. Her hand was as white as snow, and her nails looked like painted rose-leaves; her small foot scarcely touched the ground, and lay like a lily in its sandal. Seppi could not cease looking at her, and he felt, of a sudden, as if it would be the greatest misfortune that could happen to him, if he were compelled again to separate from her; for in all the world, as far as he had seen it, he had never seen anything as beautiful as the water fairy, and he required no other gift from her than the permission to remain near her as long as he should live. And this he told her in all confidence, and even before they had reached her domains; but though she listened to those words with a kindly smile, and gently smoothed his golden hair, she made no reply.

Then Seppi took courage and said: "Did you not promise me, in payment for my song, to fulfill my dearest wish? Now there will never be anything so dear to me as yourself, and therefore you must go with me to the beautiful green Alps, and always remain there with me."

"I dare not live by the light, or among men," answered the fairy sadly; "and cannot therefore grant you that wish, as much as I might desire to do so. But come first down to my dwelling, and you will find many other things worthy of your wish."

"If you dare not return to the light with me, no one shall prevent me from staying down below here with you. And that you may see that I am in earnest in my request, just have the stairs destroyed as soon as we are down; for, without you, I do not wish to return to the world."

"Only once every hundred years, and then only for one day, I may rise above the surface of the waters," said the fairy, "and no one but myself can conduct you back to your home. Therefore consider well what you desire; for I either lead you up this day before the sun goes down, or you must remain a hundred years here in the depths of the water. And if I even conduct you back, if afterwards you should change your mind, I should lose my life, as many of my sisters have done before me. When the first ray of the sun touches me before the century is past, I shall undergo a fearful transformation, which the greatest magician in the world cannot release me from. Therefore, I pray you, abandon your wish, which you may easily rue afterwards."

But Seppi only became more anxious and excited by this reply, and swore, by all he held holy and dear, that he would remain with her as long as he lived. Then suddenly a high portal opened before him, which led to a large saloon, where many elves were playing. A chandelier with more than a hundred branches was suspended from the ceiling, and burned blue, red, green, white, and yellow flames; these made the saloon look as bright as if the sun shone into it, and spread a delicious odor all around. Here, little lake elves were dancing yonder, small fairies were seated around a little table, eating diminutive sea-snails, which were most deliciously prepared.

Another set were amusing themselves by playing at feather-ball with a ball no bigger than a pea, and adorned with the most beautiful plumes of the humming-bird. Seppi would gladly have joined this play, but wherever he stepped, he drove the little people away, for he might have buried ten of them beneath his foot. And then his figure cast such a large shadow that the company always sat in the dark when he approached within a few steps of them, and they begged the fairy to protect them from that fearful giant, of whose thundering voice they were so much afraid.

Now Seppi was very much annoyed that he could not play and gamble with the silly little folks, and that he should appear such a fright to them. The fairy, who observed that he was annoyed, conducted him to a sofa in the corner, and by a wink commanded her servants to bring all sorts of refreshments to her guest. And in large crystal bowls they brought sweet watermelons and all sorts of beautifully prepared fishes and crabs; in short, everything they had handy—and Seppi did full justice to the excellent fare, for he had eaten nothing all day. His master, moreover, was a very close and stingy man, and did not give his servants enough to eat. But although Seppi was very hungry, and had never enjoyed so splendid a table before, yet there was something wanting which even the fairy could not provide for him. There was no bread beneath the water; and although all the viands were excellent, they did not taste right to Seppi, since he had not the "staff of life," to which he had always been used.

"Now you see," said the beautiful fairy, sadly, "that you will miss many things below here, to which you were accustomed in the world above, and which, with all my power, I cannot provide for you. Why, why, would you stay here with me, when you like it so well among mankind, and in your pure Alpine air?"

But Seppi consoled her, and said that he would willingly miss all terrestrial enjoyments, to be allowed to remain with her, and even now he would again leave his home to follow her, if she were to bring him back to the upper world. Then her face beamed with joy and happiness.

She now showed the boy her beautiful garden. There, on high espaliers, grew rare flowers, of wonderful color, and fruits so large and beautiful, as Seppi had never seen them before. He asked the fairy whether she would permit him to pluck some of these beautiful things, and she replied that everything in her whole kingdom was his as well as her own. Then Seppi wanted to pull a beautiful rose which hung heavy upon the stem, but when he took it into his hand, he found that it was only a work of art, cut from a red jewel, and that the green leaves were made of chrysoprase. It was the same case with the fruits: the great plums which invited Seppi, were made of sapphire, and the apples of rubies, the pears of agate and emerald; in short, all were made of jewels: but though they were beautiful and looked inviting, Seppi could not eat them. Then a shade of discontent passed over his face, for there he had seen happy children at play, and could not join them, or share their joys. He found the rarest fruits, but could not eat them; and, with the exception of the fairy, no one understood his language, or would reply to him. True she was always near him, as Seppi had desired, and studied constantly to make him happy; but she could not succeed in it; nay, Seppi even began to be afraid of the wonderful things he saw everywhere around him, and the mysterious power of the fairy filled him with awe.

"I pray you," he said one day to her, "conduct me from the artificial garden, and from the splendid saloon, to some green meadow, where plain simple grass is growing, such as my goats eat; there I will again sing all my songs to you, all those songs you love so well."

Then the fairy sighed, for her kingdom consisted only of the great magic garden, and the beautiful saloon, and she could easily perceive that these two places did not suit her favorite. For not once since had he sung so happily as at the time when he sat last by the side of the lake: and when he now, at the request of the fairy, sang one of his old melodies, it had no longer the happy, merry sound as of yore, for Seppi's heart was no more happy; on the contrary, he was sad and languishing. And yet now he was so much better off than at the time when he was but a poor goatherd, and had to starve in the employ of the avaricious senner. What then ailed him?—As he had wished, he was always daily and hourly by the beautiful fairy, who nursed and cherished him like a child. He dined every day off five courses, and from golden dishes; slept on a soft, luxurious bed, and beneath a silken cover. And here, in the realms of fairy land, reigned an everlasting spring, and it never became night: but the flowers and fruits were only artificial, and the light was not that of the sun, but of thousands of lamps which bung upon the ceiling of the saloon, and against the crystal walls, and burned always. In the world above, no one had cared for poor Seppi, who had no parents or relatives, and his goats, at the utmost, used at times to lick his hands with their small lips. Now, the beautiful fairy kissed his forehead. played with his locks, and brought him new and beautiful presents every day. And with all this Seppi became more sorrowful, day after day, and his merry eyes looked dim and sad; he would have almost given his life to pass another hour by the pond, where the fairy had met him, and he was constantly thinking of the clear bright sun, the blue ether, and the high grass, that grew so merrily upon earth, and so fast that he used to see, each morning, the progress it had made during the night. In the fairy's empire everything was beautiful beyond description, but he never could feel at home; he wanted so many things that he had been used to in the world above—his brown bread, the berries he used to pluck in the forest, even his goats, which were wont to come at his call.

"I really wish," he said to himself, "the fairy would leave me alone for a moment. I would, just for fun, see whether I could find the crystal stairs by which I came down here. Only for curiosity—I would not ascend—for I am very well here, and the fairy is so kind to me, and loves me so much."

And just as if the fairy could read his thoughts, she said, on the following morning, "Seppi, I must leave you for a few hours! Try and pass your time as best you can. When I come back I expect to give you a joyful surprise." It was her intention to swim as nearly as possible to the surface of the water, and see whether no child approached its neighborhood; then she would coax it to the edge of the lake, and quickly draw it down with her, so that her dear Seppi might have a human being near him to cheer him up again.

Whilst she was thus waiting and hiding herself beneath the water lilies and large leaves that floated upon the pond, so that no rays of the sun could reach her, Seppi was walking about, torn by restlessness and discontent. He wanted to know whether that staircase was still standing, and secretly, like an evil conscience, he stole from the saloon. And behold, he found the crystal steps, which he had descended with the fairy about a month ago, as he thought, and his heart beat with joy.

"Why did not the good fairy have these stairs torn down, as I begged of her? then these tempting thoughts would not have entered my head. But I will ascend a little way, to see whether I cannot discover the blue sky through the water," he said, as he ascended higher and higher.

But had not the fairy told him that he could not leave the place alone,— that she must herself conduct him back to the light? True, but perhaps she only meant to frighten him from the attempt; he could not easily convince himself; he wanted to see whether he really could not emerge into the open air, and then he would quietly return to his place, and the fairy should never know anything of this attempt. No, he would never endanger the life of this beautiful and kind friend, as little as he would leave her; for he knew how much she loved him; and that she would weep her clear blue eyes blind if he were to desert her.

But as he thought so, he had already gained the last steps; and now all his good intentions suddenly were forgotten, he would and must again behold the beautiful green earth and the blue sky—and with all his strength he pressed against the crystal ceiling, through which he had entered with the fairy as through a door.

The fairy, who, as I have above related, was watching close behind, for a child, now suddenly perceived her faithless favorite; she saw his danger; he would immediately die, if he had left her domains (whither he had gone of his own free will) alone: she saw that the door began to move, by the heavy pushes of Seppi, and forgot her own safely, in her anxiety to save him. Quick as lightning she flew to his side, took him by the hand, and she herself opened the portal, so that Seppi in an instant was above the waters.

Greedily he breathed the fresh mountain air that wafted across the Alps— but alas!—a broad ray of the sun fell like melted gold through the portal upon the poor fairy, and with a dying voice she sighed aloud. Frightened, Seppi looked around towards her, and he saw how the folds of the green veil she wore turned into green leaves, her feet and golden sandals changed into yellow roots, and her tall beautiful figure appeared as a reed shrub above the water. And then the waves took Seppi, and carried him playfully to the shore; he rubbed his eyes, stretched out his arms towards the reed, which a few moments before had stood by his side, but which now raised its head in the middle of the pond, and reached its thin, trembling arms languishingly towards the shore. A soft wail and a sigh passed through the reeds, and cut, like a bitter reproach, through poor Seppi's soul. He covered his face with his hands, and ran away, so as not to see the sad reed shrub any more. Thus he finally reached the senner's cottage, which belonged to his master, Peter Saibel. There he found an old man, of whom he inquired for the senner.

"I am the senner," replied the other.

"But what has become of Peder Saibel?" asked Seppi in astonishment.

"Why, youngster, you must have been drinking," replied the old man; "the Saibel owned this senner's hut long before me, and has been dead these eighty years. My father used to tell me the story about him, and about a young lad, and that both of them had disappeared on the very same day, and that it was just on the day when the cattle were driven out for the first time in spring—Peter's body was found by some of the mountaineers; but he had always been a loose character, and stayed, perhaps, too late at the tavern; then he probably crossed a Harach (frozen snow-drift between the mountains) and was lost. But the young lad, the goatherd, never was heard of again."

At first Seppi thought that the old man was crazy, but a young maiden came in, who seemed to assert all that her father had said. Eighty years then had passed, and this long time had seemed to him, whilst in the fairy's dominions, scarcely as many days. If he only had had a little more patience, a century would have been passed, and the beautiful fairy might have brought him back to the Alps without losing her life in the attempt!

And now all joy for him was at an end, for he could indeed no longer look upon the clear blue sky, with a pure heart and a clear conscience; for had he not become stained with guilt—did not the death of the beautiful fairy rest upon his mind! He no longer found joy in contemplating the mounttains, and the valleys, or in the bright sunshine; all the day long he lay by the side of the lake, and listened to the sad sighing of the reeds. Nay, he even once passed a night there, in order that he might be as near as possible to the fairy. He then dreamed that he saw her again floating upon the water, as he had first beheld her, wrapped in a thin green veil of fog, and that she again, in all her beauty and loveliness, offered him her hand to conduct him down to her submarine palace. And he hastily arose to walk towards her, but no kind hand now held him above the water; he sank—and the cool waves closed over him. For a moment the mirror of the lake trembled and shook, and then it again became quiet and calm as before.

Seppi never again rose from the waters; and to this day a soft sighing and murmuring is heard through the reeds that grow in solitary lakes and ponds; and that is the endless sorrow of the poor transformed fairy, for her lost favorite.

THE ENCHANTED LAKE

Anonymous

first published in *The New York Mirror and Ladies' Literary Gazette*
(May 1828)

The enthusiasm of the poet has owned an excitement which it never till then knew, and he has felt the inequality of language to feeling, in bis first view of the lake of Geneva. On her broad and ample bosom, the Alps meet with the only mirror capable of reflecting their towering grandeur, while the mighty objects themselves, in whose dim perspective the power of vision seems lost, appear to isolate the beautiful scene from the remainder of the world. It was, in former times, the favorite recreation of the Genevese, when the heat of the day was over, to sail across the lovely surface of the lake; and upon a vernal night, when the blue arch of heaven, studded with its innumerable stars, was reflected on the bosom of its waters, might be seen the barks of the careless citizens bounding from shore to shore, their slender sails silvered by the moon-beams, and in the distance resembling fallen luminaries over the vast space. The tinkling of the guitar, and the wild melodies of the Pays de Vaud, occasionally arose, even when the skiffs they proceeded from were out of the hearer's sight, for the stillness of the scene seemed to echo the sound, and give the wild notes of the musician the attributes of an enchanter's spell.

One passage, however, is shunned by the fair adventurers, who, as they pass the boundary, cross themselves with devout fervor; and neither inducement nor irony will prevail even on the hardier and more fearless sex to suffer their boats to approach the current, between the village of Clâse and Geneva, when night has cast its shadows over the lake. It need scarcely be said, in explanation, that there is some romantic legend associated with this part which has the power of exciting their terrors. The popular superstition appears to be, that a spirit, in the form of a beautiful woman, after a certain hour of night, roves along in a small skiff the forbidden passage, enchanting those who have the misfortune of hearing her, with strains more divine than any which ever issued from lips mortal or immaterial, for the unhallowed purpose of causing their instant destruction. The spectre is said to have once inhabited the form of a daughter of a patriot of Geneva, and to have fallen enamored with a young Savoyard, who, after gaining her affections, attempted to instill into her mind notions of treason against her country, which she consequently was near betraying. Indignant at the ungenerous use which he had made of her love, and of his subsequent desertion, she died, and, after her death, the popular story declares her to have been seen making the voyage between the city and that part of the coast where she had first beheld her lover, whose perfidy she revenges by alluring the rest of his sex, by the melody of her voice, to a whirlpool, which was within the enchanted course, and in the vortex of which her victims met with immediate destruction.

The tale was currently believed by the generality of the citizens of Geneva; many affected to despise and turn it into ridicule, but even the greatest skeptics never gave so effectual a proof of their courage as to venture near the current in which the beautiful siren was said to harbor. One high. spirited youth alone, the son of the governor of Geneva, is said to have dared to explore the mysterious course. In despite of a solemn oath, which, in an hour of filial affection, his mother had wrung from him, pledging that he would never attempt the forbidden voyage, after being irritated by the taunting jeers of his companions, he swore to sail his skiff from Geneva to Clâse, along the haunt. ed current, and to tear a lock of hair from the head of the spectre lady, should fortune so far favor him as to bring him within the sphere of her fascination. Carelessly laughing at the consequences, amidst the boisterous shouts of his companions, and the silent fears of many of them, the gallant victor unmoored his light bark, and soon her white sail became a speck in the horizon.

The evening, at the time when he left the shore, was beautiful; the queen of the skies was careering in her chariot above his head, shedding a favorable light over his course; and, as he bounded over the waters, his little skiff seemed to cut her way through a sheet of silver. Ere he was out of sight, the face of the heavens changed, the moon was overshadowed by giant storm-clouds, and a hoarse muttering wind traveled over the surface of the lake, which appeared to be convulsed by an unusual sensation.

The storm continued incessantly, and, as the red flashes of the lightning illumined the dark surface of the water, there appeared a distant object resembling a vessel, tossed to and fro by the violence of the waves; upon its disappearance, all hope ceased in the breasts of the anxious watchers, of ever again beholding the daring explorer of the mysterious waters. The morning, however, arrived, and with it, to their astonishment, came Victor, who was at the manège where the young nobles of Geneva were accustomed to meet, and he upbraided them, in terms not over courteous, for so cowardly breaking their promise. Although a deriding laugh burst from his lips, his companions perceived they were colorless and shriveled, and his hitherto blooming countenance had a shade of darkness spread over it, as if it had been recently paralyzed either by horror or excessive emotion. As his companions viewed this marked and awful alteration, in a countenance and form which had so often excited their jealousy, they eagerly pressed around him, to be informed of the events of the preceding night. He at first evaded the question, by asking their right to inquire, which he haughtily affirmed they had forfeited, by not fulfilling their own part of the pledge: he, however, before he left the mange, declared that he had made the voyage without meeting the object of his curiosity, and explained the disorder of his appearance from the violent effects of the storm.

It was the evident intention of Victor to appear careless and indifferent, but his efforts were unavailing; his manner was abstracted; some deep and intense feeling seemed buried in his heart; and his abrupt start, and vacant stare, whenever he was addressed, were sufficient evidence that, whatever might have been the events of the night, they had made a deep and absorbing impression on his mind.

Not many hours had elapsed after Victor's return, before various tales were circulated over the city of his bold and presumptuous voyage. The governor determined to set at rest the floating rumors which, unwilling as he was to confess it, caused considerable disquiet in his own mind, and exercise his paternal, and, if it were necessary, his judicial authority, to ascertain the truth from the lips of his son himself. Upon inquiry, he found that Victor had, although it was then but the middle of the day, retired to rest, under the plea of indisposition and excessive fatigue. His mother went, a short time afterwards, into his apartment, and, as he appeared sunk in the deepest repose, she retired, with her mind considerably alleviated. About midnight, however, as her son had been, as she supposed, asleep for many hours, her maternal feelings became again excited, and she left her own sleeping-room to quiet them, when, to her unsuppressed horror, she found his chamber empty. The castle was immediately alarmed, and instant inquiries were made within its walls, but with no effect, till messengers were despatched to the different gates of the city, from one of which it was discovered that the young count had passed, in his way to the borders of the lake; from which it was further found, that he had set sail about an hour after midnight, in the direction of the mysterious current. The city, before daybreak, was in a tumult, till it was proclaimed that the count had returned safe and uninjured.

On the eventful night of the idle boast, which induced Victor to brave the threats and taunts of his companions, he set sail in the manner before described. Highly excited by wine, and jarred with their boisterous revelry, the soft wind that was blowing over the lake, though hardly sufficient to ruffle its surface, cooled the warm temperature of his blood, which gradually became softened by the beautiful scene around him. As the borders of the lake lost themselves in the receding distance, and as the last faint sound of the voices of his friends on the shore died away, the stars above him appeared of a brilliancy he never before witnessed. The gentle breeze that wafted him from the shore had completely expired, yet his bark, to his surprise, made way at a considerable rate, although neither swayed by tide nor current. Moved by some strange impulse, she cut through the lake, whose waters appeared more wonderfully transparent than ever; the stars reflected were like so many balls of fire glowing in the deep, and he appeared riding on a nether heaven. All traces of the shore became invisible from a storm which was raging in its neighborhood, and the farther he proceeded the greater became the surpassing glory of the scene. Thousands of stars were shooting from the heavens, and illumining the mid-air with a light far surpassing in brilliancy the rays of the sun; the moon was surrounded with a halo of amazing grandeur, and the water sparkled like a huge sea of liquid crystal, with the reflection of the stars which appeared continually falling on its surface, and glancing from its depths. The bark continued to proceed as if propelled by an irresistible impulse, till it veered round, and all the skill he possessed as a steersman was not sufficient to put her on a right tack. At this moment all the fearful tales that be had heard of the viewless siren, that was said to haunt this spot, rushed on his mind with quick and pauseless array. The scene around him was magnificent—it was no longer night, nor was it the open glare of day that made every object brilliant around him. The sky was of a light blue, but so bright as to cause a painful sensation in beholding it; the lake looked like a sea of molten diamonds, and the middle regions of air were occupied by revolving bodies of light, of a magnitude which the highest flights of imagination had never pictured. The bark continued to wheel round, till the efforts of Victor to urge her forward were interrupted, by what he had long ardently anticipated, but mysteriously dreaded. It was a strain of music —if that word can convey sounds which were never heard before in a terrene world. No mortal language can convey the softly-swelling notes which alternately rose and died away—it was not like the gust of the feathered minstrels, nor the exquisite touches produced by the finger of art—nor the full deep tones of woman's voice; but it had all the sweetness of each, without a resemblance to either. They rose and inflated his heart, and he sank powerless in his skiff, exhausted with the excitement of his feeling. Ere he recovered himself, a voice met his ears, yet more beautiful than woman's, and in a tone and language which, although he had never heard it before, seemed familiar to him, conveyed feelings to his soul, of whose existence he had till then been ignorant.

Yet the master-spring of his feelings was yet to be aroused, when, as he looked to see whence the music proceeded, he found a skiff by the side of his own. It was made of a huge pearl, scooped out by fingers which could never have been mortal. The sail was like the silver wing of an insect fluttering in the breeze; but the figure which stood at the helm, and from which the music evidently proceeded, completed the enchantment. Was it an angel or a woman?—too voluptuous for the one, too celestial for mortality! He gazed as if he would gaze his soul away in those eyes which seemed a heaven of their own; lips, that if they wooed to destruction, threw flowers in the path; and a form too bright for reality, too glorious to belong to the world.

While under the delusion of the sweet spell that kept his reason prisoner, she flung her white arms round the prow of the vessel, which had slightly the appearance of a stringed instrument, thrilled in a strain which, though unknown, fell consciously with a heavenly cadence on his fluctuating soul:

The Song of the Siren

"I know thee I know thee—thou fair-haired boy!
Thou art come to the home of light and joy,
To the home of each fair and each lovely thing,
Where the bright flowers blow, and the sweet birds sing!
Where the founts are clear as the skies above,
And the soft wind speaks like whispered love!
Where the violet breathes on the dawn-lit air
Of a spring which never dies;
And the asphodel shines as marble fair,
And the stars like woman's eyes.
Where the sunrise is bright as the sunset is calm,
And the silent midnight, from her couch of balm,
Hearth naught but the far-stream's careless hum—
To this home of delight hath thy light bark come.

"I love thee—I love thee—thou fair-haired boy!
My home shall be thine in this land of joy;—
I knew thou wert born, and thy couch have made
Of violet wreaths, near the musk-rose shade,
Where the citrons' scent, and the sound of the spring,
Are borne on the faint wind's fitful wing.
And oh! far other delights than these!—
Heaven's music to lull thee to rest,
When thy form shall be lapped on a maiden's knees,
And thy head on her warm white breast;
Bright glances to meet, soft kisses to close
Thine eyes, when a moment they break their repose;
With none to disturb, and naught to alloy,
Mine arms are thy home, thou fair-haired boy."

Twice he shunned the sorceress; but on the third day there was weeping in the streets of Geneva, and the citizens spoke not, but stood whispering in groups, as if each was fearful of the solitude of his own thoughts.

When the night came, its fearful darkness brought fresh terror with it, and they shuddered as they heard the lake growling in the distance—the morning brought its sun to dissipate their terrors, but Victor never saw its light again.

THE MOORLAND STREAM

Arthur L. Salmon

first published in *The Outlook* (January 1919)

The water-nymph by the beautiful riverside was lonely; she was tired of its loveliness, because the ache of solitude had stolen into the secret places of her heart. Her eyes, that had the very light and color of the clear amber pools into which she gazed, held an appeal to which these could not respond; they could only reply to her gaze with her own image, so that their only answer was the wistful look that was her own. It was not enough to bathe herself in the cool reaches where the water lingered calmly, or to sit on stained lichened boulders, her feet lifted and borne forward by the swift current; it was not enough to plunge into the rainbow-hued spray of the greater cascades, beneath which the sunlit air quivered with motion and humidity. And when the setting light came richly through the roof of interlacing boughs, flooding warmly to the ferns and tangle of the banks, though her own body might be transfigured with its kisses, the cry of her longing rose more insistently than ever, and the song upon her lips died as though it had been an idle mockery. Among other things that Hesperus brings home is this craving for companionship.

It was not always that she felt thus; and, in-deed, an impetuous moorland stream with its perpetual pulsing of life is never so solitary as the depths of a forest, or a vast open downland or the bank of a still lake. The stream itself is like a living companion, with many varying moods, with moments of quick passion and spaces of lingering repose; it has the compulsion of a permanent motive, and even in its apparent languors there is always movement. Changeful feature and whim are yet consistent with an abiding purpose. But there were times when the nearness of intense moorland solitudes asserted itself, when a chilling sense of present desolation, a daunting memory of past prehistoric activities quenched forever, stole to the waterside, bringing to it a spirit of mystery and doom. The stream, after all, was the child of these sad fastnesses, and could not escape wholly from their broodings, the prevalent atmosphere of their bygone. There were grim secrets buried, yet not quite forgot-ten, on the exquisite yet mystical moorside, and from these the sparkling limpid river was not quite free; strange unseen presences seemed at times to come to its borders and whisper to it. Out there in the grand lonely places were stones of ancient unknown significance; there were relics of low wild wood-land, whose trees appeared to contort with the throes of some horrible secret; there were boulders, blue-grey and cold, that in moments of gathering dusk seemed to move and beckon, or behind which half-seen figures appeared to lurk threateningly, with some private disconcerting meaning. And the nymph, with dim ancestral memories of a sunnier clime, with dreams that came from Greece, or perhaps from that Mysian river in which Hylas dipped his pitcher, felt sometimes in this land of equal loveliness a disquieting homesickness, a fear, the chill of the unfriended.

And now once more this feeling was surging to its height within her, so that the beauty of the evening hour seemed more of a mockery than a consolation. Some old primeval instinct rose with strange dominating power, and pointed her to a resource which she had tried before, though always disappointingly. She knew that she held a secret of calling which must ever bring its response; a gift had been bestowed upon her which, at least once yearly, would bring her desire, though the answer proved never to be actually the thing desired. Is there ever a wish strongly passioned that does not thus bring its rewarding and its defeating? Do not the gods often speak our doom by the granting of our prayers? So, sitting there with that beauty of the elder world which was hers in face and limb, that beauty which has been taken from our sight because man mistook the symbol for the reality, she sang that song which was her call, which no mortal ear could hear and not respond. It stole across the wonderful expanse of turf and gorse and heather, it lingered around grey tors and low half-hidden boulders, but it did not reach the homes of men—they were too distant, wrapped in their bowers of woodbine and roses, with quiet wisps of smoke above that caught the deepening flush of sunset. Few ever came from them to this remoter solitude; there was no highway near, the dim tracks of the old people were deserted or only trodden at night by processions of the long dead.

But there was one abroad on the moors who heard, though he did not know that he heard. He was a growing lad of thick-coming fancies and dreams, now passing homeward within hail of the river. In his heart as in hers was some primitive impulse of desire, so that he, himself longing, felt the call, and he, himself seeking, was willing to be found. To him it was only the voice of the stream that came over the bushy hillocks to him, bringing a wish to lave his tired feet in its waters and to drink from its clear flowing. And so he hastened down into the hollow of the river-valley, to a spot where its crags, though wet and slippery, might yet serve in some sort as stepping-stones for reaching the other side. The spell of the stream was upon him; he must cross to that fair margin which he saw before him. It was there that she was sitting, with her tenderness of beauty still more etherealized by that soft light which was growing hazy beneath the branches. Did he see her? Did his ears truly catch that low compelling melody? He took off his shoes and placed his white feet confidently on the smoothened rocks round which the powerful water was swirling. It was treacherous footing, but he knew no fear. Midway of the stream was a sunken, sloping rock over which the water flowed unbroken, with calm appearance that belied its secret power. At that moment, the lad needed all his watchfulness, all his strength, to hold his balance, he raised his eyes, saw the entrancing loveliness, gave a cry, and was swept from his feet, striking his head against a sharp crag as he fell. He had heard the call and had answered. She sought him, in that mystical twilight of rapid waters; she brought him to the surface, she laid him on the soft grassy bank. With water in her palm she washed the blood that welled from his forehead; she drew back his wet, clinging hair from his closed eyes; she kissed the lips and cheek and hands. Must it be now as so often before, that she had won her desire only to lose it? Was it fated that she should lure this fair lad to his death? Death!—It was what she had never understood; it was the malady of these mortals to whom she yearned, whom she would fain have loved and lived with for ever; it was a curse that came from her longing, the dire mystery that was always the response of her lonely call. Could not her own lips give life, and her clinging arms bring a replying warmth? Shadows began to steal around; from the great moor came only a sense of remote and mocking desolation. And the boy did not awaken.

I

THE NYMPH OF THE FOUNTAIN

Johann Karl August Musäus
TRANSLATED BY ADOLF ZYTOGORSKI

from *Select Popular Tales from the German of Musaeus* (1845)

first published as "Die Nymphe des Brunnens" in
Volksmärchen der Deutschen (1783)

Three miles beyond Dinkelsbuhl, in Swabia, there stood in former times an old castle, which belonged to a powerful knight called Wackerman Uhlfinger, the flower of fist and club ruling knighthood, the terror of the Swabian confederated states, as well as of all travelers and merchants, who had no letter of protection from him. Whenever Wackerman put on his cuirass and helmet, girded his sword on his loins, and buckled his golden spurs on his heels, he was, after the manner of his contemporaries, a rude hard-hearted man, who considered robbery and plunder the prerogative of nobility; he made war against the weak; and, because he himself was lusty and stout, he recognized no other law than the right of the strong. When it was rumored, "Uhlfinger is approaching—Wackerman comes," terror spread throughout Swabia; the people fled into the fortified cities, and the watchmen from the battlements of the walls blew their horns, and made known the approach of danger. In that rude age, however, this barbarous heroism did not make his fame so abhorred throughout the land, as would have been the case in our more civilized age.

But this dreaded man, when he had laid aside his armor at home, was as quiet as a lamb, hospitable as an Arabian, a good-tempered head of the family and a tender husband. His wife was a tender and loving woman, well-bred and virtuous; like whom there are very few, even in this day. She loved her husband with inviolable constancy, and attended industriously to her household concerns, never looked out of the lattice in search of unlawful adventures when her husband was away, but covered her distaff with flax as fine as silk, turned her spindle with an active hand, and wove a thread which the Lydian Arachne would have claimed as her own. She was the mother of two daughters, whom she brought up with the greatest care, in virtue and frugality. In this cloister-like seclusion nothing disturbed her happiness but the freebooties of her husband, who enriched himself with unrighteous wealth. In her heart she disapproved of these privileged robberies, and it gave her no joy when he presented her with lordly stuffs, embroidered with gold and silver for rich clothes. "What good is plunder to me," she often said to herself, "on which hang sobs and tears?" She threw these gifts with secret aversion into her chests, and thought them worthy of no further notice, compassionated the unfortunate ones who fell into Wackerman's custody, and, through her intercession, often set them at liberty, and provided them with money for their journey.

At the foot of the castled mountain, a plentiful spring, concealed among deep bushes, gushed out of a natural grotto, and, according to an old tradition, it was inhabited by a water nymph called Nixa, and the saying went that she sometimes, on particular occasions, showed herself in the castle. The noble lady often wandered alone to this spring, when, in the absence of her husband, she wished to breathe fresh air, outside the thick walls of the castle, or to perform some charitable deeds in retirement without attracting notice. She met there the poor whom the porters would not admit, and distributed, on certain days, not only the best things from her table, but carried her humble good-nature sometimes as far as the holy Landgravine Elizabeth, who, with stoical contempt of all repugnant feelings, with her royal hand, at St. Elizabeth's well, washed the beggars' linen.

Once Wackerman had gone with his followers to encamp and to waylay the merchants who came from Augsburg market; and stayed away longer than was his wont. This made the tender wife anxious; she fancied that her lord had met with some misfortune; that he might be slain, or have fallen into the enemy's power. Her heart was so heavy that she could neither sleep nor rest; already many days had she fretted, wavering between fear and hope, and often she cried out to the dwarf who held watch on the tower, "Kleinhansel, look out! what rustles through the wood? What sound of trampling in the valley? In what direction does the dust blow? Does Wackerman approach?" But Kleinhansel answered very sorrowfully, "Nothing stirs in the wood. Nothing rides in the valley; no dust is blown, and no plume of feathers waves." This went on till night, when the evening star rose, and the light of the fall moon shone over the eastern mountains. Then she could not contain herself between the four walls of her chamber; she threw on her mantle, stole through the gates into the beech-grove, and wandered to her beloved spot, the crystal spring, in order to indulge undisturbed her sorrowful thoughts. Her eyes flowed with tears, and her mouth uttered melodious wailings which mingled with the rushing of the stream, as it murmured from the spring through the grass. While she approached the grotto, it appeared as if a light shadow hovered at its entrance; but her heart was so much troubled that she recked very little of it, and, at first sight, she thought that the quivering moonlight had presented to her this ideal figure. When she came nearer, the white figure seemed to move and to motion her with the hand. Then a shuddering came over her, yet she did not retreat, but stood to see what it really was. The tradition of the spring of Nixa, which was believed in the country round, was not unknown to her. She now recognized in the white lady, the nymph of the spring, and this appearance seemed to her to foretell some important event in the family. What thought could now be nearer to her than that of her husband? She tore her black locks, and raised a loud cry. "Oh unhappy day! Wackerman! Wackerman! thou art fallen, cold and dead! Thou hast made me a widow, and thy children orphans." Whilst she thus lamented and wrung her hands, a soft voice proceeded from the grotto: "Matilda, fear not, I announce no misfortune to thee. Approach nearer, I am thy friend and desire to converse with thee." The noble lady saw so little cause of alarm in the figure and speech of Nixa, that she took courage to accept the invitation. She entered the grotto; the inhabitant took her hand friendlily, kissed her forehead, sat down cordially beside her, and began;—"Welcome to my dwelling, beloved mortal; thy heart is pure and clear as the water of my spring, therefore are the invisible powers favorable to thee. I will disclose to thee the fate of thy life, the only token of favor which I can grant thee. Thy husband lives, and before morning dawns he will again be in thy arms. Do not fear nor mourn for him; the spring of thy life will earlier fade than his; but before that, thou shalt kiss another daughter, who, born in an eventful hour, shall derive thereby, in a changeful uncertain manner, both good and bad fate. The stars are not unpropitious to her; but a hateful counter influence shall rob the orphan of the happiness of a mother's care." It grieved the noble lady very much, when she heard that her little daughter should be deprived of a mother's care, and she burst into loud weeping. The Nymph was much moved: "Weep not," said she, "I will take the place of a mother to thy child, when thou canst not guide her; but with this condition, that thou choose me as godmother to the tender child, that I may have an interest in her. Then remember, that if thou wilt intrust this child to my care she must bring back to me the sponsor's gift that I will give her at her christening." The lady Matilda acquiesced in this desire; thereupon the Nixa picked up a smooth pebble, and gave it her, saying, further, that she was to send it by a trusty maiden to throw it into the spring as a mark of invitation to the sponsorship. The lady Matilda promised faithfully to perform all, kept these words in her heart, and returned to the castle; but the nymph went back again into the spring and disappeared.

Not long after, the dwarf blew the trumpet joyfully from the tower, and Wackerman, with his followers, rode into the court laden with rich booty. After the course of a year, the lady perceived that the prophecy was about to be fulfilled; but it gave her great anxiety how she should manage about the sponsorship; her thoughts were all taken up how she should disclose to her husband her adventure at Nixa's spring. It came to pass that Wackerman received a challenge from a knight whom he had offended, and they resolved upon a combat for life or death. He hastily prepared for his journey, and when he was on the point of setting out, and, according to custom, took leave of his wife, she inquired carefully about his designs, pressed him, contrary to her usual habit, to tell her against whom he was marching; and, when he kindly reproved her unusual curiosity, she covered her face and wept bitterly. This touched the knight to the heart, though he would not show it, but set off and hastened to the place of action, attacked his adversary, slew him after a spirited contest, and returned home triumphantly. His affectionate wife received him with open arms, conversed with him cheerfully, and left nothing untried to sound him, with smooth words and womanly arts, as to what adventure he had undertaken; but he carefully locked up his heart, fastened all its approaches with the bars of insensibility, and revealed nothing to her; nay, much more, he jested at her curiosity, and said laughingly, "Oh! mother Eve, thy daughters are not yet degenerate; curiosity and inquisitiveness are still woman's heritage to this day; any one of these would have desired to pluck from the forbidden tree, or to lift up the lid of the prohibited dish, and would thereby have let out the little mouse that lay therein."—"Pardon me, beloved husband," answered the prudent lady, "men have also received their appointed share of mother Eve's heritage; the only difference is, that a worthy woman dares keep no secret from her husband. I lay a wager that, if my heart could conceal anything from you, you would not sleep nor rest till I had disclosed to you my secret."—"And I," answered he, "give you my word that your secret would not concern me at all: I allow you to make the trial."

This was the point to which the lady Matilda wanted to bring her husband. "Well," said she, "my dear lord, it is permitted me to choose one of the sponsors who shall stand godmother to my child. Now, I have a friend in my mind unknown to you, and my request is that you never press me to tell you who she is, how she comes, nor where she dwells. When you have promised me this on your knightly honor, and kept your promise, I shall have lost my wager, and will freely acknowledge that manly spirit triumphs over womanly weakness." Wackerman unhesitatingly gave his wife this promise, and she rejoiced at the happy success of her stratagem. In a few days a little girl was born. Although the father would rather have embraced a son, he rode very cheerfully to his neighbors and friends, to invite them to the christening.

The company assembled on the appointed day; and, when the mother heard the noise of carriages, the neighing of horses, and the bustle in the courtyard, she called a trusty servant to her, and said, "Take this pebble, throw it silently behind thee, into the Nixa's spring." The servant did as the lady had enjoined, and, before he returned, an unknown lady entered the room where the company were assembled, bowed courteously to the lords and ladies present, and, as the child was brought in, and the priest approached the font, she took her place among the godmothers. Every one gave place to her as a stranger, and she held the child first in her arms over the font. All eyes were fixed on her, as she was so beautiful, so well-bred, and so sumptuously clothed. She had a flowing robe of sky-blue silk, open up the front, and white satin underneath; over this she was adorned with jewels and pearl ornaments as richly as our Lady at Loretto on a gala day. A glittering sapphire clasped her transparent veil, which fell in thin folds from the crown of her head over her beautifully-arranged hair, across her shoulders, and down to her feet; but the veil was wet, as if it had been dipped in water. The unexpected appearance of the strange lady had so much interrupted the assembled godmothers in their devotions, that they forgot to give the child a name; so the priest baptized it Matilda, after its mother. When the christening was over, the little Matilda was carried back to her mother, and the godfathers crowded around to wish the child happiness, and the godmothers to offer their presents. The lady Matilda seemed somewhat embarrassed at the aspect of Nixa; perhaps also surprised that she had so faithfully kept her word. She cast a stolen glance at her husband, who answered with a smile, in which she could read nothing; and, for the rest, he seemed to take no further notice of the stranger. The godmothers' presents now gave them other occupation; a shower of gold streamed, from liberal hands, over the child. The unknown at last approached with her present, and disappointed the expectations of all the sponsors. They anticipated, from the splendidly-attired lady, a jewel or other memorial of great worth, particularly as she produced a silken pocket, which she drew out of another with great care; but my lady godmother had nothing wrapped up in it but a musk-apple, turned in wood. She laid this solemnly in the child's cradle, kissed the mother friendlily on the forehead, and left the room. At this pitiful present, a secret whisper arose among those present, which soon broke out into a scornful laugh. There failed not to arise many malicious remarks and speculations as to how she came into the room; but, as the knight and his lady observed a profound silence, there remained nothing for the curious chatterers but to entertain their own idle conjectures. The unknown appeared no more, and none knew whither she had vanished.

Wackerman was secretly tormented with the desire to ask who the stranger might be, as nobody knew the name by which the lady with the wet veil was called; only his dislike, as a knight, to show himself guilty of woman's weakness, and the inviolability of his plighted word, bound his tongue, when, in the hours of matrimonial intimacy, the question would rise, as it often did, to his lips, "Tell me, my dear, who was the godmother with the wet veil?" He thought, however, to gain the secret from her in time, and reckoned on the qualities of woman's heart, which possesses in as small a degree the gift of secrecy, as a sieve the property of retaining fluid. But this time he was out in his reckoning; the Lady Matilda knew how to keep silence, and preserve the mysterious riddle as carefully in her heart, as she did the musk-apple in her jewel-box.

Before the little girl had escaped from leading-strings, the prophecy of the nymph was fulfilled on her good mother; she fell suddenly ill, and died, without having time to think of the musk-apple, or with it, according to the arrangement of Nixa, to commend the little Matilda to her care. Her husband was then present at a tournament at Augsburg, and, honored with the approbation of the Emperor Frederic, returned home. When the dwarf, from the tower, saw his lord riding in the distance, he blew his horn, according to custom; but he did not produce from it a cheerful note, but, on the contrary, blew a mournful strain. This went through the knight's heart, and pierced his very soul. "What sound," said he, "strikes on my ear? Do you hear, squires, is it not a dissonant croak, a death-song? Kleinhansel announces nothing good to us." The squires, too, were confounded; they saw their lord mournful, and said to one another, "That is the note of the bird 'kreideweiss.' May God avert misfortune—there is a corpse in the castle!" Wackerman spurred on his steed, and rode over the plain so swiftly, that the sparks flew from his horse's heels. The drawbridge fell, he looked into the courtyard, and, alas! the sign of death was placed before the castle-gate—a lantern, without a light, adorned with waving crape, while all the window-shutters were closed. Then he perceived, by the sobs and lamentations of the servants, that the Lady Matilda was no more! At the head of the coffin he saw the two eldest daughters, clothed in black, who wept over their deceased mother with many tears. At the foot of the coffin sat the youngest daughter; as yet unable to comprehend her loss, pulling to pieces, with childish glee, and playing with, the flowers with which the bier was adorned. This melancholy sight overpowered Wackerman's manly firmness; he wept and wailed aloud, threw himself on the cold body, bedewed the pale cheeks with his tears, pressed with trembling mouth the white lips, and gave way, without restraint, to all the bitter feelings of his heart. Then he hung up his weapons in the armory, sat by the coffin in a flapped hat and black mourning cloak, bewailed his departed wife, and bestowed upon her the last honors, in a magnificent funeral.

According to the observation of a great man, the most violent grief is always the shortest; and so this distressed widower soon forgot his sorrow, and thought seriously of repairing his loss by taking a second wife. His choice fell on an impetuous active woman, quite the reverse of the gentle Matilda. The government of the house took immediately another form; the new mistress behaved proudly and imperiously to the servants; she loved splendor and extravagance; and there was no end to the feasts and banquets which she gave. The house was soon peopled with numerous descendants of the new stock; and the daughters by the first marriage were no longer thought of. When the elder daughters grew up, the stepmother sought to rid herself of them, and sent them to board in a convent, at Dünkelsbühl; the little Matilda was placed under the care of a nurse, and was transferred to a little remote chamber, where she was out of sight of the vain lady, who did not meddle much with the cares of the family. Her extravagant expenditure increased also; so that the profits of the *fist and club* rights, though the knight did not slacken his former activity, were no longer sufficient; and she often saw herself compelled to make use of the property left by her predecessor, or to borrow gold from the Jews. Once she found herself in a particularly distressing position. She sought through drawers and chests for something valuable, and at last discovered a secret compartment, and a concealed press, in which, to her great joy, she found the Lady Matilda's jewel-case. The sparkling jewels, diamond rings, earrings, bracelets, girdles, and other trinkets, delighted her charmed eyes. She examined all accurately, counted piece by piece, and calculated in her mind what profit this splendid discovery would bring her. Among these valuables the wooden musk-apple met her eyes. For a long time she did not know what to make of it; she tried to unscrew it, but it was swollen by the damp. She shook it in her hand, and found it as light as an empty nut; so she took it for an empty ring-case, and supposing it contained nothing valuable, she threw it at once out of the window. At this moment, the little Matilda was sitting in her narrow garden, playing with her doll. When she saw the wooden ball roll down on the ground, she threw the doll out of her hand, seized her new plaything with childish eagerness, and was as much delighted with her discovery as her mamma with hers. She amused herself many days with this toy, and would not let it out of her hands. One beautiful summer's day, the nurse desired to enjoy, with her foster daughter, the fresh breeze by the rock spring; at evening-tide the child asked for her honey-roll, which her nurse had forgotten to bring. She did not wish to go back again; and to keep the child in good humor she went into the thicket to pluck for her a handful of raspberries. The child, in the meantime, played with the musk-apple, threw it here and there, like a catch-ball, till, in one of the throws, the child's plaything fell into the spring. Immediately there stood before her a young lady, as beautiful as an angel, and as mild as one of the Graces. The child, alarmed at the sudden appearance, thought she saw her stepmother before her, who always thrust her rudely about, and beat her whenever she came under her eye. But the Nymph caressed her with soft words: "Fear not, dear little one," said she, "I am thy godmother, come to me. See, here is thy plaything which fell into the spring." And with these words, she took up the little Matilda in her lap, pressed her tenderly to her bosom, embraced and kissed her, and moistened her with tears. "Poor orphan," said she, "I have promised to take a mother's place to thee, and I will fulfill it. Visit me often, thou wilt always find me in this grotto, if thou wilt throw a stone into the spring. Examine this musk-apple carefully, and do not play with it, for fear of losing it; it will grant thee three wishes. When thou art grown up I will tell thee more; now thou canst not comprehend." She then gave her many good admonitions, suited to the child's age, and enjoined perfect silence as to what had happened. The nurse came back, and the Nymph disappeared.

The proverb says, "Now-a-days, no child is prudent; in olden times it was different." The little Matilda, at least, was a wise and cautious child; she had discretion enough not to mention her lady godmother to her nurse, but, on her return home, asked for a needle and thread, and sewed up the musk-apple carefully in the lining of her dress. Her wishes and thoughts were now all directed to the Nixa's spring; as often as the weather allowed, she obliged her nurse to take a walk; and because she could not refuse anything to the coaxing child, and this desire seemed natural to her, (for the grotto had been her mother's favorite resting-place,) she the more willingly agreed to the wish of the little one. The child always knew how to find a pretext to send her nurse away; and as soon as she had turned her back, the stone fell into the water, and procured for her the society of the charming godmother. After a few years the little orphan bloomed into maidenhood, and her beauty opened like a bud of the hundred-blossoming rose, which, transplanted among a crowd of variegated flowers, shone forth in modest dignity. She bloomed, it is true, only in a narrow garden; she lived retired among the servants, and when her luxurious mother feasted, she was never brought in, but sat in her chamber, occupied with household work; and in the evening, after accomplishing her day's task, she found ample compensation for the noisy joys from which she was excluded, in the society of the Nymph of the Fountain; she was not only her companion and friend, but also her teacher; she instructed the maiden in all the arts of womanly skill, and formed her mind and habits after the example of her virtuous mother. One day the Nymph seemed to redouble her tenderness towards the charming Matilda, she clasped her in her arms, drooped her head on her shoulders, and was so melancholy and sorrowful, that the maiden, too, was infected by it, and could not refrain from letting some tears fall on her godmother's hand, as she silently kissed her. At this mutual feeling the Nymph was still more sorrowful: "Child," said she, with a mournful voice, "thou weepest and knowest not why, but thy tears are a presentiment of thy fate. A great change menaces thy house on the mountain; before the reaper handles the scythe, and the wind blows over the stubble of the wheat-fields, it will be deserted and waste. When the servants of the castle go out in the evening twilight to draw water from my spring, and return with empty pails, then know that misfortune is at hand. Take care of thy musk-apple, which will grant thee three wishes, and be not prodigal of them. Farewell, in this place we meet not again." She then taught the maiden the mysterious properties of the apple, that she might make use of it in case of necessity, wept and sobbed at parting, and as soon as the maiden was fully instructed in the mystic words, she finally disappeared.

At the time of the wheat harvest, the drawers of water returned one evening with empty pitchers, pale and terrified, trembling in all their limbs, as if shaking with the cold of an intermittent fever; and they related that the White Lady had been seen sitting by the spring, with mournful gestures, wringing her hands and loudly wailing, a sign which foreboded no good. This the warriors and armor-bearers mocked at; they thought it delusion, and mere woman's prattle. Curiosity impelled some to investigate the affair; they saw the apparition, but recovering their presence of mind, went forward to the spring. When they came there, the White Lady had disappeared, and many were the comments and discussions on the matter; nobody could understand the omen, Matilda alone knew, but she would not divulge it, because the Nymph had enjoined silence. She sat alone and sad in her chamber, in fear and expectation of the things that should happen.

Wackerman could not satisfy his extravagant wife by robbery and plunder, and when he did not go out on these predatory expeditions, she prepared for him daily a life of pleasure, called his topers together, encouraged his love of wine, and never allowed him to wake from his sleep of intoxication, and to perceive the decay of his house. When money or food were wanting, fresh supplies were always procured by the robbery of Jacob Fugger's heavy wagon, or by the seizure of rich parcels from Venice. Tired of these extortions, the general congress of the Suabian alliance at last resolved on Uhlfinger's destruction, since dissuasions and warnings had been tried in vain. Before he even thought it was seriously intended, the soldiers of the allied cities stood before the gate of his mountain fortress, and hemmed him in; and there remained nothing for him now but to sell his life as dearly as possible. The bombs and pieces of artillery shook the bastions, and the cross-bow men, on both sides, did their best; bolts and arrows showered thick, and one of them, in an unlucky hour, pierced the visor of Wackerman's helmet, sunk deep into his brain, and in a few moments he lay in the cold sleep of death. At the fall of their lord, his men-at-arms fell into confusion; some of the faint-hearted ones showed the white feather, while the braver warriors rushed down again from the tower. The enemy now observed that disorder and confusion reigned within the tower, the besiegers assailed it more violently, climbed the walls, won the gate, let down the drawbridge, and put all they met with to the sword. Even the cause of all the mischief, the extravagant wife, was slain with all her children by the furious warriors, who were as furious against the plundering nobility as afterwards were the rebels in the Suabian peasants' war. The castle was entirely pillaged, set on fire, and, at last, leveled with the ground. During the tumult of the battle, Matilda kept quite quiet in the Patmos of her little attic, locked the door, and bolted it fast inside. But as she observed that all without was confusion, and that castle and bars could give her no further security, she threw her veil over her, turned her musk-apple three times in her hand, caught it skillfully while she repeated the little sentence which the Nymph taught her: "Night behind me, day before me, so that nobody may see me." And thus she walked unseen through the enemy's host, and out of the paternal citadel, although with a deeply sorrowful heart, and without knowing which way to take. As long as her tender feet did not refuse her their wonted service, she hastened on from the theatre of cruelty and devastation, until, overcome by night and weariness, she resolved to lodge under a wild pear-tree in the open field. She sat down on the cool turf and gave free vent to her tears. Once more she looked round the country, and wished to bless the spot, where she had passed the years of childhood; as she raised her eyes, she saw a blood-red sign of fire rise to heaven, by which she judged that the mansion of her ancestors would soon be a prey to the flames. She turned her eyes away from this miserable spectacle, and earnestly desired that the twinkling stars might grow pale, and the morning dawn appear in the east. Before it grew light, and while the morning dew lay in drops on the grass, the uncertain pilgrim set off, and soon reached a village, where she was received by a good-natured peasant woman, and refreshed with a morsel of bread and a cup of milk. With this woman she exchanged her own dress for a peasant's clothing, and joined a caravan of merchants, who escorted her to Augsburg. In this woful and deserted condition, no other choice remained for her than to hire herself as a servant; but, because it was out of the season, for a long time she could not find a situation.

Count Conrad of Schwabeck, a German knight of the cross, and also governor and protector of the bishopric of Augsburg, possessed there a sort of court, where he was accustomed to spend the winter. In his absence a housekeeper dwelt there, called Dame Gertrude, who conducted the domestic affairs. This woman was considered a perfect Zantippe, by the whole city; no servant could remain with her, for she brawled and blustered about the house like a noisy ghost. The servants feared the rattle of her keys as children do the bugbear Rupert; the least neglect, or even only her own wicked tempers, cups and pots must compensate for; or she would arm her robust hands with a bunch of keys, and beat the servants on the back and loins black and blue; in short, if anybody wanted to describe a wicked woman, he said, she is as mischievous as Dame Trube at the county court. One day she had carried her punishments to such a violent height, that all her servants ran away; and just at this time the gentle Matilda arrived and offered herself for service. To conceal her elegant shape, she had padded one shoulder as if she were deformed; a broad headcloth concealed her beautiful silken hair, and she had spread over her hands and face with soot, to affect the skin of the Romani. When she rang the door-bell, and announced herself, Dame Gertrude put her head out of the window, and perceiving this odd figure, she thought it was a beggar, and called out, "This is no almonry, go to Jacob Fugger's almshouses, there farthings are distributed," and then she hastily shut the window. Miss Matilda would not let this deter her; she rang long, till the housekeeper again appeared, intending to requite her importunity with a torrent of scoldings. But before she could open her toothless mouth, the maiden made known to her her wishes. "Who art thou," asked Dame Gertrude, "and what canst thou do?" The pretended servant answered,—

> "A poor young orphan maid am I,
>   Matilda named in infancy.
> I can iron, crimp, and sew,
>   Spin and weave each varied hue,
> Knit and net, and cut, and pound,
>   Roast and boil, and salt the round;
> A skillful hand in every art,
>   Alert and active as a hart."

When the housekeeper heard these words, and perceived that the nut-brown maiden possessed so many useful talents, she opened the door, gave her the fee penny, and led her into the kitchen. She managed her employments so well that Dame Gertrude quite lost her habit of throwing pots at her servants. Although she always continued severe and sulky, and would blame everything, and wish it better done; still she never met with opposition or retort from the maiden, who defended herself only by meekness and patience against her bitterness. She was better and more bearable than she had been for many years;—a proof that good servants and good management, as well as good weather, make good and well-conducted governors. At the time of the first snow, the housekeeper had the house cleaned and swept, the windows washed, the curtains put up, and everything prepared for the reception of her lord, who arrived with a numerous train of servants, and a multitude of horses and hunting hounds, at the beginning of the winter.

It happened one morning when Matilda drew water in the court, that the Count met her, and his appearance produced feelings in her heart, quite new and strange to her; the most beautiful young man she had ever seen stood before her; the cheerful fire of his sparkling eyes, his waving light hair, half concealed under the shadow of the ostrich feather in his hat, and his firm walk and noble manner, operated so powerfully on the maiden, that her heart beat quicker, and her blood rushed faster through her veins. She now perceived, for the first time, the great difference of her present station from that in which she was born, and this feeling oppressed her more than the heavy bucket; very sorrowful she went back into the kitchen, and for the first time failed in her functions, and spoiled the soup, which procured for her, from the housekeeper, a sharp reproof. By night and day the handsome knight hovered before her eyes, it pleased her to see him often, and when he went across the courtyard, and she heard his spurs jingle, she always perceived a want of water in the kitchen, and hastened with a pail to the spring; if only she might obtain a sight of the handsome young nobleman.

Count Conrad seemed to live only for enjoyment, he missed no kind of diversion and no festivity in the rich city, which intercourse with Venice had made luxurious. When Shrove-Tuesday's mummeries began, the intoxication of joy seemed at its height. Matilda had no share in any of the sports, but sat in the smoky kitchen, and wept her languishing eyes almost sore, mourned over the caprice of fortune, which overwhelmed her favorites with the joys of life, and cast away from her despised devotees every happy moment. Her heart was sorrowful, without her properly knowing why; she was quite ignorant that love had nestled in her heart. This troublesome guest, who makes confusion in every house where he takes shelter, in the daytime whispered to her a thousand romantic thoughts, and entertained her at night with waggish dreams. Soon she wandered with the lord in a flower-garden— soon she was confined between the holy walls of a cloister, and the Count stood outside the grating, desiring to converse with her, and the strict Abbess would not allow it; soon again she was dancing with him at a ball. This delightful dream was often destroyed suddenly by the sound of Gertrude's bunch of keys, with which in the morning she summoned the servants to their work. Still the ideas which this fantasy had excited during the night-season proved a source of enjoyment to her by day. Love shuns no danger, climbs mountains and rocks, jumps down precipices, finds ways and paths through the Libyan desert, and swims on the back of the white bull over the stormy sea. The loving Matilda mourned and philosophized long till she found a means to realize her most beautiful dream. She had the musk-apple of her godmother Nixa, which would procure her the fulfillment of three wishes. It had not occurred to her hitherto to open it and prove its properties; and now she wished to make the first trial.

The citizens of Augsburg, on the birth of Prince Marcus, prepared a magnificent banquet in honor of the Emperor Frederic, and this feasting was to last three days, and many Prelates, Counts, and Lords were invited from the neighborhood. Every day was set apart for a prize, and every evening the most beautiful maidens were invited to the town-hall, to dance with the noble knights, and this was to last till morning. Knight Conrad did not fail to be present at these festivities, and in the dance was the great hero and favorite of all the ladies and young maidens. Matilda had resolved on this occasion to undertake an adventure. After she had arranged the kitchen, and all was quiet in the house, she went to her chamber, washed with fine soap the sooty paint from her skin, and let the natural lilies and roses shine forth. Then she took the musk-apple in her hand, and wished for a box with a new dress, as beautiful and splendid as possible, with proper trimmings. She opened the lid, and drew forth a piece of silk, which lengthened and widened itself, rushed like a stream of water down to her lap, and became a perfect dress, with all the little ornaments pertaining to it, and it fitted her body as if it had been poured on it. She now delayed not to put her design into execution;—she turned the apple three times in her hand and said,—

> "Let all eyes close,
> And all repose."

Immediately a deep sleep fell on all the servants, from the vigilant housekeeper to the porter. Miss Matilda was quickly outside the gate, wandered invisible through the streets, and entered with the demeanor of a goddess into the dancing-hall. Each and all wondered at the charming form of the maiden, and in the balcony which ran round the hall arose a whispering noise, as when the preacher says "Amen" from the pulpit. Some wondered at the beauty of the form of the unknown, others at the taste of her dress, whilst some desired to know who she was, and from whence she came, although no neighbor could give another a satisfactory answer. Among the knights and nobles who pressed around to view the stranger maiden, the Count was not the last; he thought he had never seen a more happy physiognomy, nor a more charming form. He approached her, and asked her to dance; she modestly offered her hand, and danced beautifully to the admiration of all. Her light foot seemed scarcely to touch the ground; but the movements of her body were so noble and easy, that she charmed every eye. Knight Conrad enjoyed the dance with all his heart; he was quite smitten with his beautiful partner, and never left her side,—said all the fine things he could think of to her, and pressed his love-suit with earnestness and passion. Miss Matilda was as little mistress of her heart; she conquered and was conquered; her first essay in love flattered her with agreeable consequences, and it was impossible to her to conceal her feelings under the veil of womanly reserve, so that the knight might not remark that he was not a hopeless lover. It only remained for him now to know who the beautiful unknown was, and where she dwelt, that he might pursue his fortune. All inquiries were in vain; she evaded every question, and with much trouble he obtained from her the promise to attend the dance on the following evening. He intended to outwit her, lest perchance she should not keep her word; and he despatched all his servants to lie in wait, in order to discover her dwelling when she should go home.

The morning was scarcely dawned ere Matilda found an opportunity to escape from the knight and to leave the dancing-hall. As soon as she was out of the hall, she turned her musk-apple three times in her hand, and repeated the little charm,—"Night behind me, day before me, so that nobody may see me,"—and so she reached her chamber without the Count's twilight birds, who were fluttering up and down every street, being able to perceive her. With her usual skill, she locked up her silken clothes in her chest, put on again her dirty kitchen-dress; set about her business; was earlier up than the rest of the servants, whom Dame Gertrude roused from their beds by the bunch of keys, and thus Miss Matilda earned a little praise from the housekeeper. Never had a day appeared so long to the knight as that after the ball; every hour seemed to him a year; the earnest desire and longing, the annoying doubts and cares, lest the inscrutable beauty should disappoint him, all disquieted his heart: suspicion is a consequence of love, and this now ran through his head as fast as the greyhounds through the court. In the evening he prepared for the ball, dressed himself more carefully than the previous day, and the three golden rings, the high distinction of nobility, set with diamonds, sparkled now on the edge of his ruff. He was the first at the place of the joyous meeting, examined every comer with the keen glance of his noble eyes, and awaited with impatience the appearance of the queen of the ball. The evening star had risen high above the horizon before the maiden found time to go to her chamber, and to think of what she would do; whether she should ask the second wish of the musk-apple, or reserve it for a more important event in her life. The faithful counsellor Reason advised her to adopt the latter course; but Love demanded the first with such impetuosity, that Dame Reason could not get in a word, and at last was not at all listened to. Matilda wished for another dress of rose-colored satin, with a set of jewels as beautiful and splendid as a king's daughter was accustomed to wear. The good-natured musk-apple gave her what was in its power, and the dress excelled her expectation. Cheerfully she made her toilet, and, by the help of the talisman, arrived, unperceived by any mortal eyes, where she was so anxiously expected. She was much more charming than the preceding day, and when the knight perceived her, his heart leaped for joy, and a power as irresistible as the gravitation of the earth impelled him towards her, through the vortex of dancers, there to stammer out his feelings. His heart beat, and his limbs shook; for he had already given up all hopes of again seeing the maiden. To recover himself again, and to hide his confusion, he asked her to dance, and all parties drew aside to look at this noble pair. The beautiful unknown floated delightfully round on the arm of the agile knight, as the goddess of flowers in spring, borne on the wings of the zephyr.

At the conclusion of the dance Count Conrad at last led the tired dancer, under pretext of seeking refreshment, into a side apartment; told her, in the language of a fine courtier, how charming he had found the previous day; but imperceptibly the cold court language changed into the language of the heart, and he ended with a declaration of love, as tender and sincere as a wooer is accustomed to use who seeks a bride. The maiden listened to the knight with bashful joy, and after her beating heart and glowing cheeks had plainly manifested her feelings, and a declaration of her sentiments was demanded, she said very modestly, "What you have told me, noble knight, both yesterday and today, of your tender love, pleases me well, for I cannot believe that you are talking to me with deceitful words; but how am I to share your married love, since you are a knight of Malta and have taken a vow to remain in singleness all your life? If your meaning were only mischief and gallantry, you have spoken all your smooth words to the winds; therefore, explain the riddle, and tell me how you can arrange it so that we may be wedded according to the rules of holy Church, and our union be indissoluble before God and man?" The knight answered earnestly and honorably, "You speak like a prudent and virtuous maiden, and I will, therefore, to your honest question give a candid answer, and free you from your doubts. At the time when I was admitted into the order of the Cross, my brother William, the heir of the family, was still alive; but since his death, I have obtained a dispensation, as the last of my race, to be married, and to renounce the order, when it pleases me. But love for woman had never fettered my heart until the day I saw you. From that moment I was convinced that you, and no other, was destined by Heaven to become my wife. If you refuse me not your hand, nothing but death shall ever sever us."—"Reflect well," answered Matilda, "that you do not afterwards repent; acting first and reflecting afterwards has brought much mischief into the world. You know not whether I am worthy of you, nor of what station and rank I am; whether I am your equal in birth and fortune, or whether only a borrowed glitter dazzles before your eyes. It becomes not a man of your station to promise anything thoughtlessly; but sacredly to fulfill his promise according to the usage of noble hearts."

Knight Conrad seized her quickly by the hand, pressed her to his bosom, and fondly exclaimed, "That I promise you, upon my honor and salvation! If you," continued he, "were the child of the lowest man; only a pure and innocent maiden; I will honorably make you my wife, and promote you to wealth and honor." Then he took a diamond ring, of great worth, from his finger, gave it into her hand as a pledge of fidelity, took the first kiss from her pure lips, and said, "That you may not mistrust my promise, I invite you to my house in three days, where I will appoint my friends, the prelates and lords, and other noblemen, to witness our marriage." Matilda, however, resolutely declined this, because the quick current of the knight's love did not altogether satisfy her, and she wished first to prove the constancy of his affection. He did not cease to press her for her consent; but she would neither say yes nor no. As on the previous day, the company separated at morning dawn; Matilda disappeared; and the knight, from whose eyes sleep had fled, called his housekeeper very early, and gave her orders to prepare a splendid feast. As death, that dreaded skeleton, wanders with its scythe through palaces and thatched cottages, and unrelentingly mows down and kills all it meets; so Dame Gertrude, the evening before the feast, armed her inexorable hand with the slaughtering knife, to the destruction of chickens and ducks, and bore in her hand, like the fates, the life or death of the tenantry of the poultry-yard. By her polished and murderous steel, the careless inhabitants fell by dozens; for the last time their wings fluttered mournfully, and chickens, and pigeons, and foolish capons, and even turkey-cocks yielded up their lives. Miss Matilda had so many to pick, to scald, and to cook, that she was obliged to be up the whole night; still she cared not for the trouble, for she knew that the grand banquet was all on her account.

The feast began; the host moved quickly about to every comer in the hall, and, whenever the bell rang, he expected his unknown beloved to enter the door; but, when it was opened, only a prelate entered, or a solemn matron, or a venerable bailiff. The guests had been long assembled, and the server had not yet served up the meats. Knight Conrad still tarried for his beautiful bride; but as she delayed so long, with secret vexation he directed the server to arrange the table. They sat down and found one extra dish; but nobody could guess who it was that had slighted the invitation of their host. Every moment the knight's cheerfulness diminished, he could no longer banish the look of dejection from his forehead, although he exerted himself by a forced serenity to keep up the good humor of his guests. This moody temper of their host soon soured the sweetness of social joy among the guests, and the feasting chamber became as still and quiet as a funeral assembly. The instruments which should have played to the expected dances were sent away; and thus ended the feast at Count Conrad's house, once the abode of mirth. The dejected guests disappeared earlier than usual, and the knight longed for the solitude of his own chamber, to give himself up to his melancholy grief, and to reflect, undisturbed, on the disappointments of love. He tossed impatiently in his bed, and knew not what interpretation to put on his deceived hopes. His blood boiled in his veins; morning came before he had closed his eyes, the servants entered and found their lord struggling with wild fantasies, and, to all appearance, in a high fever. Then the whole house was thrown into confusion, physicians ran up and down stairs, wrote prescriptions a yard long, and in the apothecaries' shops all the mortars were at work, as if they were sounding for matins. But the little herb, Eyebright, which alone softens the longings of love, no physician had prescribed; therefore, the sick man abused the restorative balsam, and pearl tincture, refused to subject himself to any regimen, and desired the physicians no longer to trouble him with their follies, but to let the sand gradually cease to flow in his hour-glass, without shaking it with their helping hands.

Seven days had Count Conrad wasted away in secret sorrow, so that the rose faded from his cheeks, the fire of his eyes disappeared, and life and breath only hovered between his lips, like a light morning fog in the valley, which only needs the least breath of wind to dissipate it entirely. Miss Matilda had accurate knowledge of all that passed in the house; it was not caprice nor prudish affectation, that she had not accepted the invitation; it cost her a hard struggle between head and heart, between reason and passion, before she could resolve not to listen to the voice of her beloved. Partly she wished to prove the constancy of his vehement protestations, partly she felt some hesitation in employing the third wish of the musk-apple; for though she thought that, as a bride, a new dress would become her, yet her godmother had enjoined her to use her three wishes prudently. But on the day of the feast her heart was very heavy: she sat in a corner and wept bitterly. The illness of the knight, of which she easily divined the cause, troubled her still more, and when she heard the danger he was in she was inconsolable. On the seventh day, according to the prognostications of the physicians, life or death was to be determined. It is easy to judge that Matilda voted for the life of her beloved; and that she could most probably effect this recovery was not unknown to her; only she found great difficulty as to the manner in which she should behave. Still, among the thousand faculties which love awakens and discloses, one is always that of *invention*. When Matilda went, according to custom, early in the morning, to the housekeeper, to take counsel with her about the affairs of the kitchen, Dame Gertrude was so unnerved that she could not fix her thoughts on common things, nor attend to the choice of meats; great tears, like droppings from a roof, rolled down her leathern cheeks. "Alas, Matilda!" sobbed she, "I shall soon cease to be housekeeper here; our poor master cannot live out the day." This was very mournful news! The maiden thought she should sink with terror; but she recovered courage, and said, "Do not despair for the life of our lord, he will not die, but will recover: last night I had a good dream." The old woman was a living dream-book; hunted up every dream of the servants, whenever she could catch one; always explained it so that the fulfillment came to her liking—for the most agreeable dreams with her always alluded to quarrels, contentions, and scoldings. "Tell thy dream," said she, "that I may explain it."—"It seemed to me," began Matilda, "as if I were at home with my dear mother, who took me aside, and taught me to cook a broth from nine different kinds of herbs, which would cure any sickness, if only three spoonfuls of it are swallowed. 'Prepare this for thy lord,' said she, 'and he will recover from that hour.'" Dame Gertrude was much astonished at this dream, and abstained this time from her customary interpretations. "Thy dream is wonderful," said she, "and not accidental. Prepare thy broth at once, for breakfast; I will see if I can prevail on our lord to taste it."

Count Conrad lay in silent meditation, faint and powerless; he felt that he was on his last journey, and wished to receive the last consolations of the Church; when Dame Gertrude went in to him, drew him away by her voluble tongue from his meditations, and tormented him with well-intentioned talkativeness, so that he, to get rid of her, promised what she desired. In the mean while Matilda prepared her broth, put into it different kitchen herbs, and costly spices, and laid in it the diamond ring which the knight had given her as a pledge of fidelity, and called the servants to take it in. The sick man feared the loud eloquence of the housekeeper, which still rang in his ears so loudly, that he compelled himself to take a spoonful of the soup. As he touched the bottom, he observed a strange substance, which he fished up, and found it, to his astonishment, a diamond ring. His eye immediately shone full of life and youthful fire, the sickliness of his appearance was gone, and he emptied the whole cup with a decided appetite, to the great joy of Dame Gertrude and the expecting servants. All ascribed the extraordinary recovery to the soup, for the knight had not let any of them perceive the ring. Then he turned to Dame Gertrude, and said, "Who prepared this food which has done me so much good, restored my strength, and recalled me to life?" The careful old woman wished that the invalid would keep quiet, and not talk so much; she therefore said, "Do not distress yourself, my lord, as to who prepared the broth; it is well for you and for us that it has worked the healthful effect which we hoped from it." But the knight was not to be put off with this answer; he demanded a reply to his question, to which the housekeeper at last responded;—that there was a servant in the kitchen, called the little gipsy, who was skillful in the knowledge of all herbs and plants, and that it was she who had prepared the broth that had made the knight so well. "Bring her to me," said the knight, "that I may thank her for this panacea of life."—"Hold," answered the housekeeper, "her look would disgust you: in form she is like a hooded owl, she has a hump on her back, is dressed in dirty clothes, and her face and hands are smeared with dirt and soot."—"Do my commands," said the Count, "and without a moment's delay." Dame Gertrude obeyed, called Matilda quickly out of the kitchen, threw a cloak over her which she was accustomed to wear at church, and led her, thus adorned, to the sick-chamber. The knight commanded her to retire, and when he had closed the door he said, "Little girl, confess to me freely, how didst thou become possessed of the ring which I found in the bowl in which you prepared my breakfast?"—"Noble knight," answered the maiden, modestly and respectfully, "I had the ring from you; you adorned me with it on the second evening of the dance, when you swore your love to me; see now, if my form and origin deserve that you should pine away and sink into the grave. Your condition grieved me, therefore I have no longer delayed to show you your error." Count Conrad had not expected such an antidote to love; for a moment he was confounded and silent. But the form of the charming dancer soon hovered before his eyes, and he could not make it agree with the antitype now before him. He thought, that perhaps his passion had been discovered, and that they wished to cure him by an innocent deceit; still the true ring which he had received back, made him think that the beautiful unknown was in some manner connected with the scheme; then he thought he would question the servant, and try to entangle her in her talk. "If you are that gentle maiden," said he, "who pleased me so much, and to whom I plighted my troth, do not doubt that I will truly keep my promise; but beware of deceiving me. Can you again take the form which appeared to me two successive nights in the dancing-hall? can you make your body as slender and even as a young fir-tree? can you change your dingy skin like a snake, and show different colors like a chameleon; so shall the word that I spoke when I gave away the ring, be 'yea and amen.' But if you cannot perform the conditions of this stipulation, I will have you scourged as a mischievous deceiver, till you tell me how you became possessed of this ring." Matilda sighed; "Ah, is it only the glitter of the form, noble knight, that pleased your eyes? Woe is me! if time or circumstances should destroy these fleeting charms; if old age bends my slender shape and crooks my back; if my roses and lilies fade, my fine skin wrinkles and dries; if my deceitful figure, in which I now stand before you, really belonged to me, what would become of your plighted faith?" Knight Conrad wondered at this discourse, which seemed too wise and reflecting for a kitchen-maid. "Know," was his answer, "beauty commands a man's love, but virtue knows how to keep fast the soft bands of love."—"Well," answered she, "I go to fulfill your conditions, prepare your heart to decide my fate."

The Knight still wavered between hope and fear of a new deception; he rang for the housekeeper, and commanded her to "escort the maiden to her chamber, that she may clothe herself neatly; remain at the door till she comes out—I await you in the reception-room." Dame Gertrude took her prisoner with strict care, not knowing what her lord's command might mean. In going up she said, "Hast thou clothes to adorn thyself? why hast thou concealed them from me? If thou wantest any, follow me to my chamber, I will lend thee as many as thou needest." Hereupon she described her old-fashioned wardrobe (in which she had dressed herself for half a century) piece by piece, with eager remembrance of former times. Matilda had little need of any, she only desired a small piece of soap, and a handful of bran, took a washing-basin full of water, went into her chamber and fastened the bolt, while Dame Gertrude stood outside the door with great anxiety, expecting what would happen. The knight, full of expectation as to the issue of his love adventure, forsook his couch, clothed himself in elegant attire, and went into his state room, pacing the room with quick, uneven strides. Just as the clock on the Augsburg town-hall, and eighteen other clocks, told the hour of noon, a train of a silken robe rustled through the antechamber, and Miss Matilda entered, with hesitation and dignity, adorned as a bride, and beautiful as the Goddess of Love when she returned to Paphos from the council of the Gods on Mount Olympus. With the rapture of a delighted lover, the knight Conrad cried, "Goddess or mortal, whoever you may be, behold me here at your feet, ready to renew the vow that I have made you, if you will accept my heart and hand." The maiden modestly raised the knight: "Softly, noble knight," said she, "do not be in a hurry with your vow; you see me here in my proper form, though still unknown to you: a smooth face has betrayed many men. The ring is still in your hands." Immediately the knight took it from his finger; the maiden relinquished her hand to the charming knight, and he placed the ring upon her finger. "You are now my chosen," said she; "I can no longer conceal myself; I am the daughter of Wackerman Uhlfinger, the stout old knight, whose unhappy fate is, without doubt, not unknown to you; sorrowfully, I escaped from the ruin of my father's house, and have in your dwelling, though in a mean condition, found shelter and security." Then she related to him her history, and did not conceal from him the secret of the musk-apple.

Count Conrad no more remembered that he had been at the point of death, but on the following day again invited the guests, whom his dejection had previously scared away so easily, and when the server served up, and counted around, no extra cover was found. Then the knight quitted the order, left the court, and solemnized his marriage with great splendor. The newly-married couple passed the first year of their union at Augsburg, in joy and innocent mirth. Impressed with feelings of delightful emotion, the youthful wife, leaning on the bosom of her wedded lord, confided to him the happy feelings of her heart, which overflowed with joy. "My heart, beloved lord," said she once, "in possessing you is at rest; no other wish remains to me; I give up the third wish of my musk-apple; if you have any concealed desire in your heart, make it known to me; I will make it mine, and from that hour it shall be accomplished." Count Conrad pressed his beloved wife heartily in his arms, and protested that no wish remained to him on earth but the continuance of their happiness. The musk-apple thus lost all its value in the eyes of its possessor, and she only preserved it in thankful remembrance of her godmother Nixa. Count Conrad had still a mother alive, who lived on her jointure at Schwabeck, whose hand the innocent daughter-in-law had a great desire to kiss, and to thank her for her valiant son; still the Count, under various pretenses, declined the journey to his mother; but showed an inclination to visit a fief which had fallen to him, and which was not far from Wackerman's ruined castle. Matilda was very willing to visit once more the land where she had passed the days of her first youth. She sought out the ruins of her father's house, wept over the ashes of her parents, went to the Nixa's spring, and hoped that her presence would again invite the Nymph to make herself visible. Many stones dropped into the spring without the hoped-for effect, even the musk-apple swam like a bubble on the water, and she had the trouble of fishing it out for herself. The Nymph no more appeared, although another sponsorship was impending, for Lady Matilda was on the point of presenting her husband with a marriage blessing. She gave birth to a son as beautiful as Cupid, and the joy of the parents was so great that they nearly hugged him to death; the mother would not put him out of her arms, and watched every breath of the innocent little angel, although the Count had hired a cunning nurse to take care of the little child. But on the third night, when all in the castle lay buried in sleep, after the noise and bustle of a feast, the mother awoke from a sweet slumber, and when she awoke the baby was gone from her arms! Astonished, the terrified Countess cried out, "Nurse, where have you laid my baby?" The nurse answered, "Noble lady, the dear little boy is in your arms." Bed and chamber were anxiously searched, but nothing was found except some drops of blood on the floor of the chamber. When the nurse perceived this, she raised a loud cry, "Oh, God and the Saints have pity on us! the man-wolf has been here and carried the child away!" The mother wept herself pale and thin for the loss of her noble boy, and the father was inconsolable. Although the knight had not, in reality, a mustard-grain of belief in the man-wolf, but treated it as woman's prattle, yet he could in no way clear up the mystery. He consoled his sorrowful wife as he best could; and she, to please him, compelled herself to assume a more cheerful mien. That anodyne of pain, beneficent time, at last healed the mother's heart-wound, and the loss was repaired by a second son. Boundless was the joy in the palace over the beautiful heir; the Count feasted with great mirth with all his neighbors within a day's journey round, the cup of joy passed unceasingly from hand to hand, from the host and guests to the door-keeper; all drank to the health of the new-born. The apprehensive mother would not have the child out of her sight, and watched its sweet sleep as long as her strength permitted; but when at last the demands of nature must be obeyed, she took the golden chain from her neck, passed it round the baby's body, and fastened the other end to her arm, signed herself and the child with the cross, that the man-wolf might have no power nor influence over it, and she soon fell into an irresistible slumber. When she awoke with the first dawn of morning, oh misery! the sweet boy had disappeared from her arms. In the utmost alarm she cried as before, "Nurse, where have you laid my baby?" and the nurse answered likewise, "Noble lady, the dear little boy is in your arms." Immediately she looked for the golden chain which she had fastened to her arm, and found that a link had been cut through by a sharp steel instrument, and she fainted away with terror. The nurse alarmed the house, the servants hastened in, full of consternation, and when Count Conrad heard what had happened, his heart burned with anger and indignation, he drew his knightly sword, intending to cleave the nurse's head. "Wicked woman!" thundered he with furious voice, "did I not give you strict orders to remain awake all night, that, if this monster came to rob the sleeping mother, you, by your screams, might alarm the house? Sleep now, indolent one, the sleep of death!" The woman fell on her knees before him: "Worshipful lord," said she, "by God's mercy, I conjure you to grant me some moments, that I may not take the crime which mine eyes have seen into the grave with me, and which should not have been extorted from me if it were not for the torture." The Count was astonished. "What crime," asked he. "have your eyes seen, so black that your tongue refuses to mention it? Freely declare to me, without torture, what is known to you, like a true maiden."— "My lord," sobbed the servant, "what moves you to hear your misfortune? It is better that the frightful secret should be buried with my corpse in the cold grave."

But Count Conrad only became more desirous to know the secret; he took the woman aside into a private room, and, overcome by threats and promises, she disclosed to him what he had been so very desirous to know:—"Your wife," said she, "you must know, my lord, is an enchantress; but she loves you above measure, and her love goes so far, that she spares not her own children, thereby to procure the means of preserving your favor, and her beauty unchangeable. In the night, when all were asleep in great security, she placed herself as if she also slumbered. I did the same, I know not why. Soon she called me by my name, but I answered not, but pretended to snore and make a rattling in my throat. As she thought that I was fast asleep, she sat up in bed, took the baby, pressed it to her bosom, kissed it heartily, and whispered these words, which I clearly heard:—'Son of my love, be a means to preserve to me thy father's love; go now to thy little brother, thou innocent, that I may prepare with nine different herbs and thy little bones a strengthening drink, which shall preserve my beauty and thy father's favor.' When she had thus said, she drew forth a diamond needle, as sharp as a dagger, out of her hair, and pierced the baby to the heart, let it bleed a few drops, and, when it no longer struggled, she laid it before her, took the musk-apple, muttered some words, and when she lifted the lid, a light flame of fire blazed from it, as from a pitch-barrel, which consumed the corpse in a few moments; the ashes and little bones she collected carefully into a little box, and pushed it under the bedstead. Then she cried with an anxious voice, as if she had suddenly awoke from sleep—'Nurse, where have you laid my baby?' and I answered, with fear and trembling, in dread of her enchantments, 'Noble lady, the dear little lord is in your arms.' Then she began to behave as if she were very sorrowful, and I ran out of the chamber for the purpose of calling help. Behold, worshipful lord, these are the details of the shameful deed which you have obliged me to disclose to you; I am ready to prove the truth of my report by a red-hot iron bar, which I will carry with my naked hands three times up and down the castle-yard."

Count Conrad stood as if petrified; for a long time he could not utter a word. When he had collected himself, he said, "What need is there of the fiery ordeal? your words bear the impress of truth; I feel and believe that all is as you have said: keep this frightful secret fast in your heart; tell it to no man, not even to the priest when you make confession. I will procure for you a letter of pardon from the Bishop of Augsburg, that this sin shall not be imputed to you either in this world or in the next. I will now go with a dissembling visage to this viper; take care that you, when I embrace her, and pretend to console her grief, draw forth the box of bones from under the bed unperceived, this will be more than proof to me. With a slightly clouded forehead, and a somewhat sorrowful look, but still like a determined man, he entered his wife's apartment, who received her lord with innocent eyes, but with a silent, mournful soul. Her face was like an angel's, and this extinguished the rage and fury with which his heart burned. The spirit of revenge softened into compassion and pity, he pressed the unfortunate lady tenderly to his bosom, and she poured tears of heartfelt anguish over his garments. He comforted her, talked kindly to her, and hastened soon to leave the theatre of cruelty and horror. The nurse had in the mean time prepared what she had been ordered; and delivered to the Count, in secret, the horrible receptacle of bones. It cost him a severe struggle in his heart before he could resolve what he should do with the supposed enchantress. At last he was of opinion that he would get rid of her without creating noise and wonder. He set off, and rode to Augsburg, and gave the steward these orders:—"When the Countess goes out of her chamber, after nine days, to bathe as usual, have the bath-room well heated, and bolt firmly the doors, that she may faint in the bath from the great heat, and may at last expire." The steward received this command with heartfelt sorrow, for all the servants loved the Countess Matilda, as a gentle and amiable mistress; still he did not dare open his mouth against his lord, because he perceived his great earnestness and impatience.

On the ninth day Matilda ordered the bath to be heated; she thought her husband would not remain long in Augsburg, and she wished that, on his return, all traces of their misfortune should be wiped away. When she entered the bath-room the air around her was greatly heated. She wished to draw back, but a strong hand pushed her violently into the chamber, and immediately all the doors were bolted and locked. She cried in vain for help; nobody listened; the fire was only stirred up hotter, so that the stove glowed red-hot, like a potter's oven. At this circumstance, the Countess easily guessed what was to happen; she resigned herself to her fate; only the shameful suspicion for which she was being punished tormented her soul more than this ignominious death. She employed the last moments of recollection in taking a silver needle out of her hair, and writing these words on the white wall of the room: "Farewell, Conrad; I die willingly at thy command; but I die innocent." Then she threw herself on a little couch, to begin her death-struggle, but nature involuntarily strove, for a little moment of time, to prevent her destruction.

In the anguish of the stifling heat, the unhappy dying one threw herself here and there; the musk-apple, which she always carried about with her, fell to the ground, she picked it up immediately, and cried, "Oh! Godmother Nixa, if it be in your power, free me from an ignominious death, and make my innocence clear."

She hastily took the lid off, there arose from the musk-apple a thick mist, which spread itself through the whole chamber, and the Countess immediately perceived that there arose a coolness, so that she felt no more anguish and heat. The cloud of vapor at last collected into a tall figure, and the lady Matilda, who now no longer thought of dying, saw, with unspeakable delight, the lovely Nymph before her, the dear little baby in her arms, wrapped up in a little chrism-cloth, and in her hand the other little boy, in white robes, with rose-colored borders.

"Welcome, beloved Matilda," said the Nymph. "Well for thee that thou didst not use the third wish of the musk-apple so thoughtlessly as thou didst the two first. Here are two living witnesses of thine innocence, with which thou wilt triumph over the black calumny under which thou wast almost slain. The evil star of thy life has now declined to its fall, henceforth the musk-apple will not grant any more wishes, because nothing now remains for thee to wish more; but I will explain to thee the riddle of thy mournful lot. Know that the mother of thy husband is the author of all thy misfortunes. To this proud woman her son's marriage was as a poniard stab in her heart; she believed that Count Conrad had disgraced the nobility of his house by marrying a kitchen-maid; she immediately uttered curses and execrations against him, and would no longer acknowledge him as her son. All her thoughts and meditations were directed to destroy thee, although the vigilance of thy husband always prevented this wicked design. Still she contrived at last to deceive him by the hypocritical nurse. By great promises, she prevailed on this woman to take thy firstborn son in sleep from thy arms, and to throw it, like a dog, into the water. Luckily she selected the spring from my grotto for this crime; I received the boy with loving arms, and watched over him as a mother. Thus too she confided to me the second son of my beloved Matilda. This deceitful nurse was thy accuser; she persuaded the Count that thou wert a magician; that a salamander flame came out of the musk-apple (whose secret thou shouldst have carefully preserved) and destroyed the boy, whose ashes thou preparedst into a love-drink. She showed thy husband a small vessel, filled with pigeon and chicken bones, which he believed to be the remains of his child, and he gave orders to smother thee in the bath during his absence. In a few hours thou wilt again lean upon his friendly bosom."

When the Nymph had thus spoken, she bent over the Countess's face, kissed her forehead, and, without waiting for an answer, wrapped herself in her thick veil of vapor, and vanished away.

The servants of the Count were in the meanwhile busy, to kindle again the extinguished fire; it seemed to them as if they heard human voices inside, whence they supposed that the Countess was still alive. But all their trouble was in vain; the wood caught as little fire as if the stove had been heated with snow-balls. Soon Count Conrad rode home, and anxiously asked how it was with his wife. The servants informed him, how they had well heated the bath, but that the fire was suddenly extinguished; and that they believed the Countess was still alive. This very much rejoiced his heart; he went to the door, and cried through the keyhole, "Dost thou live, Matilda?" and the Countess recognized her husband's voice, and answered, "Beloved lord, I live and my children live also." Enraptured at this speech, the impatient Count had the door broken open, because the key was not ready at hand, rushed into the bathroom to the feet of his innocent wife, bedewed her pure hands with a thousand tears of repentance, brought her and her pledges of love, to the joy and delight of the whole house, out of the frightful death-chamber back into her apartment, and heard from her mouth the whole particulars of the shameful slander, and the robbery of the children. Immediately he gave the command to seize the malicious nurse, and to shut her up in the bathroom. The fire in the stove began to burn merrily, the flames ascended on high, and speedily this devilish woman died a miserable and deserved death.

CARNABY'S FISH

Carl Jacobi

first published in *Weird Tales* (July 1945)

Mr. Jason Carnaby was a man of medium height, medium features, and medium habits. At forty-six he was one of those bachelors who, having passed from youth well into middle age, would have attracted no comment other than a casual query as to why he had never married. He operated a small real-estate business with rather shabby offices in the town of La Plante and, with the exception of a stenographer who came in two days a week, he worked quite alone.

Inasmuch as La Plante was located near the Atlantic coast, much of his business had to do with shore property, summer homes and cottages. These holdings moved fairly fast, but occasionally he acquired a home which refused to attract a buyer.

Of all these, the Dumont place was undoubtedly the most difficult to move. While it was listed as "shore property," it was actually on Philip's Lake, a short distance inland. It was part of an estate which had passed through probate, old Captain Du-mont having died more than five years ago. Since that time it had had but one occupant, a Dr. Septimus Levasear, who had lived there almost a year and a half before his death, which had come about suddenly and somewhat obscurely.

The death of the doctor, who had been an amiable fellow, if somewhat distant and hazy at times, had given rise to some of the rumors which had become attached to the Dumont place and made it so difficult to sell or rent.

Dr. Levaseur had died of a heart attack, apparently brought on by overexertion. He had been found on the East road the night of a big storm half-clad, a crucifix clutched in his hand. Mr. Carnaby, who was the soul of the conventional, had always regarded the doctor as somewhat queer, but, in final analysis, Mr. Carnaby's judgment was circumscribed by the question of rent, and Dr. Levaseur had always paid his rent promptly.

Nevertheless, his strange death had doubtless been the basis for the rumors that there was something odd about the house, that the whole property was damned, and that finally, Philip's Lake was "queer." Mr. Carnaby was admittedly at a loss as to how these stories had got started; the circumstance of Dr. Levaseur's having been found clasping a crucifix and but half-clad on the East road might have excited the superstitious, but Mr. Carnaby failed to discover how the lake came to be implicated. Since other property in Mr. Carnaby's hands adjoined the lake, he was irritated, lest some stigma similar to that attaching to the Dumont place should likewise become attached to other properties. He made some effort to isolate rumors concerning Philip's Lake, and finally got down to two basic tales.

Three cottage residents on the opposite shore from the Dumont place said that a small area of water far out toward the center of Philip's Lake was frequently rough and white-capped, when not a breath of wind was stirring. Mr. Carnaby's very reasonable suggestion that the lake might be connected to the ocean by underground channels opening off from the vicinity of the disturbed area was brushed aside. The cottagers countered with an additional tale to the effect of a pale light or a shimmering radiance which sometimes wafted over the lake like a will-o'-the-wisp. And finally, old John Bailey told of hearing on several occasions a melodious singing far out from shore, singing which was so wonderfully lovely he wanted to swim out to it, though he hadn't been in the water "for nigh unto sixty years." Whatever the source of these old wives tales, they played their part in the failure of the Dumont house to attract a renter.

After repeated efforts to dispose of the property, all of which came to nothing, Mr. Carnaby decided one morning in July that something final should be done about the Dumont place. Accordingly, he gave the keys of his office to his stenographer, hitched his horse to the buckboard, and headed down the East road. In due time he reached Gail's Corners, where he rested the horse and refreshed himself with a soft drink at the settlement's only store, through the display windows of which he could see across the summer landscape to the circle of drab gray water which was Philip's Lake. He knew that this body of water was only by courtesy called a lake, for it was merely a small quay from which on occasion a neck of water afforded an outlet to the Atlantic.

As he stood there, gazing out at its surface, it occurred to him that he had never, after all, actually examined the lake; that is, he had not gone out on it, though he handled property touching upon it on all sides. There was something strangely melancholy and at the same time somberly attractive about Philip's Lake, and it might well be worth while to row out on to it, provided the flat-bottomed rowboat which had always laid along the shore of the Dumont place was still there. At the same time, it might not be amiss to idle away a little time in fishing, a recreation for which Mr. Carnaby had found all too little time. Acting on this impulse, he bought a cane pole, a spool of line, and several varieties of artificial bait, and resumed his journey.

He reached the property at length: an old style Cape Cod house, rectangular in shape, with a narrow veranda and an acre of surrounding ground. It seemed, as he stood in the weed-grown yard, that the house had a detached look, as if in some way it did not belong there. Gazing at the lake again, he had the rather uncomfortable impression that it too had been superimposed upon the landscape like a double exposure photograph. He entered the house and went through the building room by room, making notes on the back of an old envelope as to repairs that should be made, their approximate cost and other items.

Finished, he locked the door and passed down the path toward the lake. A dozen yards from the house stood a stone well with a pagoda roof over it. At the shore he mused for some time over an old harpoon which Captain Dumont apparently had cast there in an idle moment. The weapon reminded him that Captain Dumont had served on a whaler in his younger days.

The flat-bottomed rowboat was still there. Mr. Carnaby bailed out the rain water with some effort, threw his new fishing tackle across the thwart and pushed out on to the lake. On the water the impression that the closely-wooded shores were somehow out of proportion came again, and he took off his spectacles and rubbed them with a polishing cloth. He began to feel that he had come here not of his own will but in response to an indefinable and growing attraction emanating from the depths of the green waves.

What a queer creature man is, Mr. Carnaby thought, to create a fascination for the unpleasant. He thrust away a desire to leap overboard and, with an effort, began to arrange his tackle.

For an hour he fished. Having no leader, he fastened the plug directly to the line and proceeded to throw the bait as far out as he could with the aid of the pole, and then jerk it gently along through the water.

Tiring of his fruitless efforts at length, and wanting to rest his eyes from the glare of the sunlight on the water, Mr. Carnaby leaned back and lowered his lids. The day was drowsy, and so, too, was he. When he awoke, the sun had gone down and the gloom of late twilight was dropping upon the lake. In his boat, Mr. Carnaby was far out from shore, drifting aimlessly.

Indeed, he was approximately in the center of the lake, and a little wind was rippling the water there. Suddenly conscious of the time, Mr. Carnaby took up the oars and began to row hard. It did not occur to him that his fish-pole was propped under one thwart with the line trailing behind the boat in the water until in the half-darkness he saw the pole abruptly bend almost double. He barely had time to grab it and pull with all his strength.

The fish came through the water slowly, heavily. As it drew closer, Carnaby could sense rather than see it weaving to and fro in the black water, not so much struggling to free itself as reluctant to come with the line, though his catch did not seem to come willingly. It was somewhat awkward to handle the cane-pole in his cramped quarters, but at last Carnaby got his catch alongside, and reached down to complete his capture.

His first impression was that he had caught a catfish. His second was of something so infinitely more horrible that an involuntary exclamation of horror escaped him.

But the twilight, surely, played his eyes tricks. He had now laid his pole down, and, still holding the line, though with uncertain eyes averted from his catch, he slipped a small flashlight from his pocket, switched it on, and turned the comparatively feeble ray on to his catch.

A woman's head drifted there, looking up at him—an exquisite feminine face with long blond hair trailing in the water, which, rippling over the countenance white in that darkness, revealed teeth bared in an expression of unutterable malignance. The barbs of one of the gang hooks had bitten deep into the red mouth, and from it flowed a thin stream of blood.

It was a live, a perfectly moulded human head—but the body was that of a fish, with tail and fins!

For several seconds Mr. Barnaby sat frozen to immobility. Then the flashlight slipped from his hands; he dropped the line and began to row wildly for shore.

He beached the boat and staggered unsteadily up the path. When he reached the house he halted breathlessly, overcome by nervous reaction. The shadow of his patiently waiting horse and buckboard loomed beyond the gate, but in spite of this bewildering horror, he did not feel up to driving the lonely road back just yet. He climbed the stoop, inserted his key into the lock with trembling hands, and re-entered the house, The stillness of the long-closed interior closer about him like a cloak, soothing his troubled nerves. He lit a lamp, carried it into the living room and placed it on the table. Then he got out his pipe and began to smoke slowly and deliberately.

Was he mad, he wondered, or was the thing he had seen only the after-effect of a latent dream? Had he witnessed some phantasmagoria, created by water and darkness which his numbed senses had reformed into a vagary of the subconscious? One thing was certain. Tell his experience to the townsfolk of La Plante, and he might as well write a no-sale ticket for the property. Once such a story got around, no amount of advertising would be able to overcome the superstitious aura that had already begun to gather around the Damont place.

It came to him that certain rumors concerning Dr. Levaseur and his strange death had been bruited about with raised eyebrows—vague, formless whisperings. Certainly the man had been odd, and the oddity of his character was brought home to Carnaby now as he looked upon the room in which he stood.

The walls had been done over in a shade of bluish green that was dark and cheerless. The rug was a light brown, and the border design resembled thick layers of pebbles interlaced with sand. On one wall was an old print of Heinrich Heine; near it hung a faded etching of a sailing vessel in a storm; and in one corner stood a bookcase filled with large and obviously heavy volumes.

Still smoking and somewhat calmer now, Mr. Carnaby crossed to the books. *Loreleysage in Dichtang und Musik. Mysteries of the Sea*, by Cornelius Van de Mar. *The History of Ailantis*, by Lewis Spence. As he stood looking at these titles, Carnaby became aware again, by a process of idea-association, of the nature of Dr. Levaseur's curious obsession. He was instantly apprehensive again, and curiously disturbed, for his memory brought back vividly that strange and horrible experience on the lake.

Dr. Levaseur had claimed to be an authority on loreleis, on marine lures of legend and mythology, and he had written several papers on these old beliefs. Surely these were somewhere available, thought Carnaby. Yet he was briefly reluctant to look for them, a little afraid of what he might find. However, after but a few moments of hesitation, he set about searching for Dr. Levaseur's papers among the publications in the bookcase, and in a short time found a thick sheaf of dusty foolscap, closely written in a fine, precise hand.

This he carried to a chair and read.

At first, in his nervous haste, he found it difficult to keep his attention to the pages, but gradually the brooding silence of the house drifted out of his consciousness. He read for an hour, and at the end of that time he sat back in silent amazement. Dr. Levaseur had apparently been not only an authority on loreleis and ancient allied folklore, but he had also been versed in a myriad of psychic phenomena which had any kind of marine background. And, incredible as it seemed, the doctor apparently had accepted many of these tales as factual accounts.

He had written at some length the account of the Tsiang Lora siren which hardened Dutch sailors had reported dwelt near an islet off the southeast coast of Java. Seen only at night, cloaked in bluish-white radiance, this siren, like her many mythological counterparts, took the form of a woman, lovely and ethereal, whose whispered plea for help drifted across the water with all the power of a lodestone. Dr. Levaseur had added to this narrative the factual results of several geodetic surveys made by the Netherlands East Indies Hydrographical Department, pointing out that the sea floor at this point of latitude and longitude sloped sharply upward and formed a shallow reef or submerged tableland. In addition, the doctor recounted the foundering of a Dutch brigantine near this location in the early sixties. This ship had carried a passenger, a rich Malay woman, who was suspected of being a priestess of the *dularna* sect.

He had carefully chronicled the tale of Dabra Khan in the Arabian Gulf, a masculine lorcles who supposedly shouted false commands in the helmsman's ears during a storm; of McClannon's Folly, a needle spire of sock off the Cornish coast which changed to a voluptuous maiden clinging to a spar when viewed through a lane of fog, each case described with scholarly directness.

But toward the end of the manuscript there was an underlined paragraph that Mr. Carnaby read several times.

It is now four months since I have come here. Yesterday I went out upon Philip's Lake for the first time, and I know now that I was not wrong in my judgment. It is there, it called out to me, and for a moment I thought I saw it in all its malevolent beauty.

I cannot wait until I have seen it again. Tomorrow, taking full precautions, and using all the powers at my disposal, I shall strive to entice is from its lair. The desire is almost overwhelming.

Mr. Carnaby sat looking off into space for a long time. At length he put his pipe into his pocket and returned the manuscript to the bookcase. He blew out the lamp and made his way out of the house to the buck-board. He was in deep, perturbed thought as he drove slowly home.

Thereafter, Mr. Carnaby made no further attempt to find a renter for the Dumont place. He filed the deed and abstract away in an old shoe-box, marked: *Miscellaneous N.G.*, and he went about his business, saying nothing to anyone about his experience on the lake.

In this manner fail passed into winter, and the town of La Plante went about its routine in its usual fashion. It was the following spring, a balmy day in early May, that Mr. Carnaby chanced to meet his old friend, Lawyer Herrick, as the latter was emerging from the courthouse.

"Well, how's business?" Herrick inquired politely, accepting Mr. Carnaby's cigar. "Should be a run on shore property this summer, what with that new pike cut through from Kenleyville."

"Yes, there should," Mr. Carnaby agreed.

"I see you've got the Dumont place rented again," Herrick continued. "I thought you would in time. It's a nice place."

Mr. Carnaby looked at the lawyer sharply. "Why no, it's not rented. What ever made you think it was?"

Herrick flicked his cigar ash into the wind and frowned slightly. "I drove by there yesterday, and I thought I saw a woman sitting on the shore, sunning herself. A woman with blond hair."

"Is that so?" said the real estate man. "That's odd."

It was so odd that he decided to visit the property the next day. He could, he told himself, kill two birds with one stone. A tenant farther down the East road had complained of a bad roof, and Mr. Carnaby had put off for some time the task of inspecting it.

When he turned into the lane leading to the Dumont house, Mr. Carnaby cast a quick glance at the shore. The westering sun was in his eyes, and the fire-like reflection from one of the windows blinded him, but for a moment he fancied he saw a woman sitting on the shore. But at second glance, somewhat out of range of the sun's reflection, he saw nothing; the place bore the unmistakable appearance of desertion—not alone the house, in its aloof desolation, but all the land belonging to it.

Mr. Carnaby opened the house and went into the living room. With all his experience in entering long-closed houses, he could never repress the initial spell of depression which swept over him as his nostrils caught the smell of dust and stale air. Nothing was changed from his visit of six months before.

Yet he had, however, curiously, expected change; the casual suggestion inherent in Herrick's brief conversation had affected him most disagreeably; it had caused him to think again of that horrible experience on the lake, of Dr. Levaseur's pursuits and death, of the tales concerning the Dumont place.

He lit the lamp, for daylight was fading outside, and already the room was hazed with early twilight. He lit his pipe, too, and, as usual, the tobacco smoke soothed him somewhat. Now that he was here, his thoughts returned again to Dr. Levaseur's manuscript; he took it from the bookcase where he had left it, and sat down to glance through it again. This time, however, he could find no attraction in the written words—the paragraphs seemed stilted, disconnected, even absurd. Nevertheless, cold as he remained to Dr. Levaseur's thesis of the reality of loreleis and similar creatures, he was most unpleasantly impressed by the scholarly, almost dryly erudite weight of evidence which the doctor had adduced to sustain certain half-hinted beliefs. And there was that curious reference to "something" in Philip's Lake.

Something like an hour passed before he heard the singing. Even then he was hardly aware of it, so soft was the voice and so far off. But presently he looked up from the manuscript and listened. Almost at the limit of his hearing range it sounded, the overtones blending into the sighing of the wind.

Definitely it was a woman's voice, singing a strange lilting melody. It grew louder, and, despite an apprehensive hesitation, Carnaby strode to the window and opened it. It was a song such as he had never heard before, sung in a contralto, wandering up and down the octaves in an aimless yet appealing way. Through the window he could see no living person, only the shadowy lombardies that matched down the slope to the shore of the lake.

The singing grew louder until it seemed to resound from the walls of the room. And now as he listened, Mr. Carnaby experienced a strange sensation, It was as if every nerve and fiber of his body responded to that voice and urged him to go to its source. It was a lure, and with his bucolic matter-of-factness the real estate man unconsciously fought it with all his will.

He might as well have been fastened to a steel cable. Step by step he found himself drawn across the room to the door and out on to the veranda. There he halted again, all but overcome by that voice.

On feet that were dead things Mr. Carnaby strode down the steps and down the path. He passed the well and continued to the shore of the lake. Black water rippled at his feet.

And then he saw her. She was twenty yards from shore, waist deep in the water, moving slowly toward him. In the moonlight he could see her carmine lips as she sang her golden song. He could see her dripping tresses coiling about her nude shoulders. On she came, and still he stood there transfixed, held by some alien power.

Suddenly the singing ceased. Mr. Carnaby felt something snap in his consciousness like a clipped wire. The woman was directly before him now, and as she advanced, the lower portion of her body came clear of the water. A greenish scaled body edged with white. The body of a fish! The head and breasts were those of a woman, but even as he watched, he saw that head bloat and swell, lose its features, change to a horrible reptilian mass that gazed upon him with diabolic fury!

He turned, the spell broken, and the thing lunged toward him, seeming to move through the air. Down the beach Mr. Carnaby ran, a mighty horror assailing him, but his steps were turned to lead. Then, even as he faltered, he caught the glint of moonlight on a shaft in the sand. Old Captain Dumont's harpoon.

Driven by the wild impulse to save himself, he bent down, seized it and turned to face the monster. His heart stood still. There it was directly before him, a horrendous, loathsome beast with slavering lips and blazing, hyalescent eyes. It closed in, and as it did, Mr. Carnaby drove the harpoon before him with every ounce of strength he possessed. He felt the stinging recoil, but whether it was merely his arm reaching the limit of its range he did not know. Things became vague and indistinct for Mr. Carnaby then. A piercing scream seared into his ears. The monster wavered and sank backward, Then, uttering low, mewling cries, it turned and scrambled down the beach.

Simultaneously the surface of the black lake seemed to rear upward and boil in a great cauldron of lashing waves and foam.

The thing reeled into the water. Twenty yards from shore it fell forward like a spent juggernaut. For a moment it lay there, body awash, heaving up and down. Then slowly it sank from sight.

Mr. Carnaby spent eleven days in the La Plante hospital under close surveillance of his physician. Upon his release, he forced himself, however reluctantly, to return to the Dumont place and make a thorough investigation, He found the harpoon on the beach, where he had left it; he found also the indentations of his footprints.

He found nothing more. Moreover, the house seemed exceedingly pleasant, even inviting. He could discover but one somewhat odd fact, and this mattered hardly at all—the report of the governmental meteorological station at the county seat nine miles east stated that, from May seventh to May sixteenth inclusive, wind velocities in the La Plante district were at the lowest point they had been for the entire year. Yet, during that time Philip's Lake remained in a turbulent state, white-capped and sullen with angry waves.

The effect of all this was to inspire Mr. Carnaby with the conviction that, in time, the Dumont place might after all be made to pay. He paid it another visit and found nothing altered; he took time to make a few repairs and had the house cleaned up a little. In a fortnight he managed to find a young couple who wanted the house, and rented it forthwith.

He waited uneasily for several weeks for any word of trouble, but nothing came from the Damont place but the rent, with pleasant regularity, and presently Mr. Carnaby began to look back upon his experience as a kind of neurotic condition which had given him unhealthy hallucinations.

It was ten months before he visited Gail's Corners again. On that occasion he had to pay a visit to the village doctor concerning a property he was handling for him. He found the doctor just back from the country, offered him a cigar, and lit one for himself.

"It's a coincidence seeing you, Carnaby," said Dr. Holmes. "I've just come from one of your tenants and I need a drink, bad. Just get that bottle and the glasses from that cupboard, will you?"

Carnaby did so, his eyebrows raised.

"Which tenants?"

"The Plaisiers. They're on the Dumont place."

A ball of alarm exploded inside Carnaby; he sat down, feeling his mouth going dry. "Nothing wrong, is there?"

"Wrong? God knows what you'd call it, Carnaby." He shook his head and poured himself a drink. "I delivered her baby all right—usually have trouble with the first, you know—but I didn't have any trouble with the delivery. But the baby! My God, Carnaby!—I never saw a baby that looked so much like a fish in all my life!"

He poured a drink for Carnaby and looked up to hand it to him. He was not across the desk from him where but a moment before he had been. Quietly, without a sound, Mr. Carnaby had fainted.

BELLS OF OCEANA

Arthur J. Burks

first published in *Weird Tales* (December 1927)

It was on a heavily laden troopship, westward heading. Hours before, the sun had gone down toward China, trailing ebon night behind her. For a full week, since dropping the California coast behind us, there had been nothing in all the wild waste of waters for us to see except ourselves. No ship's funnels broke the lowering horizon, no sign of land, for our skipper had chosen a passage lying somewhere in between the usual steamer lanes. The nearest land, save that which stretched in eternal darkness some three miles below us, was more than a thousand miles beyond the southern horizon. We were just a single ship, burdened with a precious freight of souls, upon an ocean that seemed endless. The first day out had been squally, and everyone had been sick, save those of us who had gone down to the sea in ships before. But with the dawning of the second morning the sea had calmed down, and our vessel rode through the blue, toward the horizon bowl which ever crept before us, in the golden wake of the setting sun. The voyage, if the old salts spoke truly, would be uneventful; but with that strange premonitory feeling which comes to all of us at times, I did not believe them.

Something, from the very first, warned me that our voyage was ill-fated. I couldn't explain my feeling. It wasn't a feeling of dread, exactly, nor of fear. Just a strange feeling of unease, much like that which comes to people on their voyage, when a ship is rolling slightly under their feet, and everything, until they get their sea-legs, seems strangely out of focus. That doesn't explain it, I know; but it is as near as I can put my feeling into words.

I knew, when the sun went down ahead of us, with the hundred and eightieth meridian less than twenty-four hours ahead, that we were on the eve of strange, momentous happenings. To add to my feeling of unease, and as though it had been all planned out by some invisible something or somebody, in the vague beginning, the officer who should have had the watch that night fell suddenly ill, and I was called upon to take his place. I knew, as I donned my belt, holster and pistol, that I but obeyed the will of some invisible prompter—a prompter without a name.

We had seven sentries out at various important places about the ship, and I made the routine inspections before turning in, less than an hour before midnight. When I entered my stateroom and turned on the light, that feeling of unease was more pronounced than it had been at any time previously. I had the feeling, though I had locked my door when I had last quitted my stateroom, that I had entered again immediately after someone had left it. Yet that was impossible. I had carried the key in my pocket all the time, and my cabin-boy was not provided with one. There was no way that anyone, or anything, could have entered my stateroom in my absence, save—

Still as though my every move had been ordered by some invisible prompter, my eyes darted to the porthole beside my bed. It was quite too small for the passage of a human body, and even to think of such a thing were the utmost folly. If anyone had gone out through the porthole, that one had fallen, or plunged into the sea; for had the porthole been ever so big, there was absolutely no way one could have left my stateroom by that way and still remained upon the ship—unless that one had gone out and were even now hanging by his hands along the ship's side. So strongly had the feeling of an alien presence obtruded itself upon me that, in spite of knowing myself an utter fool for entertaining any doubt whatsoever, I strode to the porthole and looked out. There was nothing, of course, save water, now black and forbidding, stretching away to the south, to a horizon that, since night had fallen, seemed to have crept quite close to us to watch our passing.

Still unsatisfied, in spite of arguing with myself, condemning myself for a fool, I deliberately closed the glass which masked the port, took my seat in a chair beside the bunk, facing the round glass—which resembled, to an imagination suddenly fevered, the eye of a huge one-eyed giant—of the porthole, and began to undress. Mechanically I lifted first one foot and then the other, removing shoes and stockings.

But I kept my eyes upon the closed porthole—and that feeling of an unseen presence in the room was stronger as the moments fled. My undressing completed, I stood erect to turn out the lights, and paused in the very act, a cry of terror smothered in my throat by a sheer act of will.

For the most fleeting of seconds, I had seen a dead-white face outside the glass which covered the porthole! It was the face of a person who had drowned, I told myself wildly, and the dripping hair wore a coronet of fluttering seaweed. The eyes of this strange outsider stared straight into mine, devoid of expression, totally unwinking, and the lips, which seemed blue as though with icy cold long endured, smiled a thin and ironic smile. It took all the courage I possessed, which is little enough in the face of the unknown, to hurl myself across the bed, right hand extended toward the heavy screw which held the circular piece of glass in place. In the instant my hand would have touched the glass, the ship rode into the edge of the storm that was to fill the remainder of the night, and the stem of the steamer rose dizzily on the crest of a mighty wave, dragging all the vessel with it; and the face slid slowly out of sight below the porthole, the bluish lips still smiling ironically.

I admit that I was trembling, that my fingers were unsteady as I fumbled with the screw to unloose the glass. When the porthole was open once more, and the cold breeze of this latitude came in to fan my fevered face, I thrust my head out of the port and gazed right and left, and up and down, along the curving side of the ship. But there was nothing, except straight ahead, on our portside. And even there, there was nothing but black water, huge mountainous waves, touched with whitecaps at their crests, like flying shrouds, or like lacy streamers created as a fringe for the mantle of night.

I watched several of the waves sweep under the vessel, which rose and fell sluggishly. The waves seemed to be traveling in no certain direction, but broke into a veritable welter of warring forces, roaring as they came together with the roaring of maddened, deep-throated bulls; valleys with darkness on their floors, mountain-tops touched with snow that shifted eerily in the breeze.

I was about to close the port when, many yards away from the ship, as though born of the womb of old ocean, I heard the bells!

Like the tiny bells which the bellwether wears to signal the ewes and the lambs, was the tinkling of the bells—like those bells, yet not like them, totally out of place in mid-ocean, and I felt a strange prickling of the scalp as I listened. Hurriedly, driven by a fear I could not have explained then, nor can I now explain, I closed the porthole again—and whirled about with another scream, which this time came forth from my quivering lips in spite of all I could do to prevent.

Just inside my stateroom door stood my sergeant of the guard, and his lips were trembling more wildly than my own, his eyes protruded, his face was chalk-white, and he was striving with all his power to speak. As I watched his manful struggle, I dreaded for him to speak—for I knew that what he had come to tell me would be something strange and terrible, something hitherto entirely outside my experience.

"Sir," he managed at last, when I stiffly nodded permission for him to speak, "I just made the rounds of the sentries."

Here the poor fellow stopped, unable to go on, and his knees knocked together audibly.

"Yes, sergeant," I managed to mutter, "you went the usual rounds of the sentries, and then?"

"The sentry who should be on duty on the main deck, forward of the bridge, is missing."

Of course I knew on the instant that there might be many reasons for the failure of the sergeant of the guard to find the sentry—many logical reasons. The sentry might have quitted his post (a violation of regulations, true) for a quiet cigarette in the lee of a lifeboat; he might have been walking his post in the direction taken by the sergeant, so that the latter had not overtaken him, even with a complete circling of the main deck; he might—oh, there were many logical explanations; but I guessed intuitively that none of these reasons fitted the case. For one thing, the sergeant of the guard was an old-timer, had spent many years of his life at sea—yet he was frightened half out of his wits, and I knew he held as many decorations for bravery as any other officer or man in the marine corps. There was something terrible, something—if you will—uncanny, behind this disappearance of the sentry.

I muttered an oath, more to prod my own flagging courage than for any other reason, and started toward the door, motioning the sergeant to precede me. But he shook his head stubbornly and barred my way. I halted, for it was evident that he had not completed his report.

"You'll maybe think me daft," he said; "but I couldn't let you go out there, sir, without telling you everything. The corporal on watch at the head of the promenade gangway told me a strange story just before I made my rounds. He had opened the door leading onto the starboard promenade, for a look at the weather outside, and just as he was about to close it again, the ship lifted on the crest of a huge wave—and out beyond the wave, many yards away from the ship, he heard something which he likened to the tinkling of little bells!"

"Good God!" I exclaimed.

"And," the sergeant continued, "all the time I was looking for the missing sentry, I had the idea there was someone behind me, following me every step of the way; yet when I whirled to look, the deck behind me was empty."

"And you found no sign of the sentry?" I said stupidly.

The sergeant shook his head.

"Nothing," he said, "except—except—well, sir, you'll maybe think me daft, as I said before; but on the spot where the sentry had stood to wait for me on my last round, I found wet marks on the deck floor—the marks, as near as I could tell with my flashlight, of bare feet!"

Mechanically, as the sergeant spoke, I had done donning my clothes, leaving my shoes, however, unlaced. I felt an icy chill along my spine as the sergeant continued, and I dreaded, as I had never dreaded anything before, to ask him further about those wet footprints on the deck.

"The wet footprints," he went on, and he was talking wildly now, his words tripping over one another, so rapidly were they uttered, as though he wished to finish his report before I could interrupt again, "led away where the sentry should have been standing, straight to the starboard rail. Right at the rail I stooped to examine the prints more closely. They were the footprints of a human being, I was sure, and the marks of the toes were blurred, and very wide, as though whoever—or to hat ever—had made them, had been carrying a burden in his arms!"

"Good God, sergeant!" I said again; "what are you driving at?"

"Just this, sir. There's something terribly wrong with this ship. *Something took that sentry bodily over the side!*"

I believe that putting a name, however meaningless, to what was in my own mind, caused a little of my courage to return, for I did not find it difficult now to leave the stateroom. The sergeant almost trod on my heels as I hurried to the main deck, starboard side, where the wind wrapped icy fingers around me, chilling me to the bone on the instant.

As I hurried forward I looked over the side, into the welter of waters—and stopped short.

Behind me the sergeant groaned—hollowly, like a man who has been mortally wounded. For out of the waters, away to starboard, came the sound of tinkling bells! I darted to the rail and leaned far outboard, striving to pierce the gloom. But there was nothing save the watery wastes, mountains and valleys—and two spots of greenish phosphorescence, far out, like serpent's eyes which watched the passing ship. But when I looked at them closely, straining my eyes, seeking the form below the eyes, the twin balls of eery flame vanished, a wall of water obtruding itself between.

Well, we found the sentry, sprawled on his face, where the sergeant should have found him on his rounds. I turned the body over. It was dripping wet, entirely nude, and the lips and cheeks as coldly blue as though the corpse had been dragged for hours on a line in the wake of the ship.

No matter how secluded one's life may have been, no matter how carefully one may have been guarded during one's lifetime, there come into the lives of most of us certain inexplicable happenings which may never be forgotten. This matter of the dead sentry was one of these for me, and I shall go to my grave with the memory of his cold cheeks and bluish lips limned upon the retina of my very soul. So many strange circumstances—thank God that, at the moment, I could not look into the two hours or more of terror which even then stretched before me, else I should most surely have gone entirely mad—were there connected with this matter that, taken altogether, it is little wonder that I have been unable to forget, or ever shall forget. The roaring of the wind which was lashing all the ocean into fury, a maelstrom in mid-ocean, ghostly whitecaps stretching away into darkness, into seeming infinity; the frightened sergeant behind me, his teeth chattering with fear; the dead sentry at my feet, his body blue with cold, entirely nude as I have said; the marks on the deck of huge bare feet, wet as though the feet had come up out of the sea; the eery sound of bells between our vessel and the lowering horizon—and that dead-white face which I had seen beyond the porthole of my own cabin a half-hour before.

What was the explanation of it all? What was the cause of the bells, if bells there were? What had come up out of the sea to stride barefooted across the promenade deck of the slumbering troopship? Had my sentry seen whatever had come for him before he had been taken?

Add to all these circumstances the fact that all hell was loose in the watery wastes, that it was now after midnight, and you will understand a little of my feelings. Never before or since have I been so frightened as I was then. I don't regard myself as a coward, nor am I ordinarily superstitious; but show me the man who is without fear in the presence of the unknown, the utterly uncanny, and I will show you a man who has no soul.

I whirled, bumping into the sergeant, who manfully muffled a scream at my unexpected movement, and started, almost blindly, toward the stern of the troopship. As I strode along, with the sergeant at my heels once more, strange images fled across my mind. I remembered the tale of *Die Lorelei*, the maiden who lured sailors to their death with her eery singing, and strained my eyes through the gloom, seeking shapes I feared to see. Then my mind went farther back, to the years before I could read, years in which, thirsty for knowledge, I studied pictures out of old histories to satisfy my longings for wisdom. One of these pictures came back to my mind as I hurried aft: a picture of a hideous monster of unbelievable proportions, who had come up from behind the ocean's horizon, blotting out the sunlight, long arms extended into the picture's foreground, the right hand holding aloft a mediaeval sailing-vessel which had been lifted bodily from the ocean. A fantastic picture, I knew now, drawn to prove the existence of terrible monsters beyond the horizon to which, as yet, no caravel or galleon had dared travel. I wondered, as I strode aft, why this old picture should return to my mind at this time, and fear was at my throat again as I walked.

"I am coming, oh, my beloved!"

The words, high-pitched with ecstasy, came from straight ahead of me, and out of the heavy shadow cast by a huge funnel stepped one of my sentries. Just for a second, as he strode toward the starboard rail, I could see his face—and the face was transfigured, as though the man gazed into the very soul of the Perfect Sweetheart somewhere beyond the rail. Slowly, step by step, as though he would prolong the joy of anticipation, the sentry, who had hurled his rifle aside, approached the rail, still with his eyes fixed on the welter of waters overside, while I halted spellbound to watch what he would do. From out of the waters there came once more the tinkling of bells! And with the sound, as though the sound had been a signal, a huge shadow detached itself from the shadow whence the sentry had stepped but a moment ago, and loomed high above the luckless youth. At the same time the ship climbed high upon a monster wave, so that her starboard side went down, down, until white water came over the side—and when she straightened again, shuddering through all of her, the sentry had vanished. From well rearward of where the man had disappeared, from out of the smother of waters, there came a single long-drawn cry—and it was not a cry of terror, not a cry of pain, but a scream of ecstasy!

"He's gone, sergeant," I said stupidly, "but what took him? Not the wave: he had but to seize the rail to save himself."

"Did you see the shadow, lieutenant?" tire sergeant replied.

I did not answer. He knew I had seen it.

We strode on again, heading toward the stem of the ship; and all about us now, over the ship, on either side of her—but never on her—there tinkled the eery, unexplainable bells!

W e stood at last in the very stem of the troopship, gazing into the ghostly wake far below our coign of vantage, and with certain care I followed the wake rearward with my eyes. But one could not follow it far.

That was the circumstance which impressed itself upon me almost at once. The wake died away, short off, within less than a dozen yards of the ship's stern—as though, at the very moment of birth, it had been ignominiously smothered.

In a trice I understood the reason, and thought I understood many things besides. For, like a monster raft, stretching away rearward as far as I could see, and into the darkness beyond my vision to right and left, there followed us, close to, an undulating mass of odorless seaweed. Acres and acres of it there were, rising and falling sluggishly, but keeping pace with the troopship through the night and the storm! Again there came that sound of bells, and my hair stiffened at the base of my skull when I saw, watching the seaweed, the result of the tinkling of the bells. The seaweed, when the bells sounded, seemed imbued suddenly with life that was utterly and completely rampant. Long tendrils of the stuff drew away to right and left below us, as though endowed with will of their own, and these tendrils, countless thousands of them, collided with other tendrils in the mass, and slithered over them so that all the mass of the seaweed writhed as though in torment, resembling countless hordes of serpents gathered together from all the evil places of the earth—and where the tendrils had drawn aside I could see black water in the rift as though the tendrils had drawn aside so that I might see. Some terrible fascination held me, my eyes fixed on that space of black water, for several moments after the tendrils of seaweed had drawn away to right and left—and up from the depths, into the opening, came two who filled all my being with abject terror—and something else.

One of the two was dead, I knew on the instant, for I could see his face, all white and drawn, yet with the blue lips smiling, of the ill-fated sentry who had gone over the side before my very eyes. And he had been brought up from the depths in the arms of—I hesitate to give the creature a name. A woman? I scarcely know; yet this I do know: in the instant I looked into her eyes, raised to mine for a full minute, I understood the ecstasy which I had read in the face of the sentry whom she now held in her arms. Her breasts, nude and unashamed, were the breasts of a buxom woman, her lips as red as full-blown roses, her hair as black as the wings of a crow, a mantle of loveliness all about her wondrous body, whipping this way and that in the storm.

Her eyes swerved away from mine, and one arm, shapely and snowy, raised aloft from the water—and to my ears came again the sound of tinkling bells. Once more the seaweed writhed and twisted, pressed forward about the ship; but a single mass of it detached itself from the larger mass, pressed close to the—should I call her "woman"?—and swerved away again; and the arms of the beautiful creature were empty. Instinctively I whirled about, knowing somehow that I must move my head before I met this creature's eyes again, and stared forward to the shadowy portion of the promenade whence the sentry had emerged before his plunge over the side. Up the starboard side of the ship crept a veritable wall of seaweed; up to the rail, pausing there for a moment, then to the deck, where it writhed for a moment or two, taking a weird distorted shape that made me think of a man, yet which I knew was not a man, before it strode into the center of the promenade. From out of the heart of this monstrosity there dropped soggily a white, cold figure. The second sentry had returned, as the first had done!

Why? Why? Why? What did all this unbelievable terror mean?

I knew, as I searched through all my experience, seeking the key to this uncanny enigma, that we were heading westward outside the usually traveled sea-lanes; that ships seldom, if ever, came this way; that in seven days we had seen not one vessel, nor even the smoke of one upon the horizon. Why did not vessels come this way?

But I could not answer my many questions. I could only ask them, and hope within me that they be not answered, ever. Nauseated by the return of the dead sentry, nude as the first had been, I closed my eyes for a moment, and when I opened them again, there was no seaweed, no monstrous shape, upon the promenade; but even from where I stood I could see the wet footprints—and wondered whom next the creature of the deep would claim from aboard our ill-fated vessel.

Resolutely I drew my pistol and returned once more toward the stem of the vessel. This creature of the depths, whatever it was, had taken life—twice. Whatever it was, it was mortal, and whatever is mortal a bullet will slay. But, in the very act of whirling, I stopped short—for between me and the stern of the vessel, smiling dreamily, water rippling over her nude and glorious body to splash upon the deck, stood the creature who had come from the depths in the wake of the ship, bearing the dead man in her arms. My arm fell to my side, my weapon clattered to the deck, and as I moved forward once more, slowly, a step at a time as the sentry had done, the wondrous creature held out her dripping arms, and my eyes drank in all the glorious wonder of her, from head to—*but she had no feet!*

Where the feet should have been, and the legs, there were neither legs nor feet, but a scaly column, wet and dripping, like a serpent with a woman's body. I screamed in terror and unbelief, but it was too late, and her arms were about me, preventing all escape. But, with the touch of those arms, I did not wish to struggle. I knew what had happened to the two sentries, knew the same was in prospect for me; yet at the moment there seemed nothing in all the world more worth-while than to slip over the side, into the depths, with the arms of this wondrous creature about me.

"Lieutenant! Lieutenant! For the love of God, what is happening to you?"

It was the voice of the sergeant of the guard, freighted with abysmal terror; but I did not care. The shapely, strangely warm arms of the sea-creature were about me, and the sound of the bells, unbelievably sweet now, was in my ears. For me the world had ceased to exist, save for knowledge that these two things were true. I was carried to the rail, and sent over slowly, without commotion, as comfortable as though I had been riding on a couch of eiderdown—and came to myself to know myself lost indeed.

I was deep down, whirling over and over behind the whirling screws of the ship, holding my breath until my lungs were nigh to bursting, swimming with all my might, striving to reach the surface, and life-giving air, when I hadn't the slightest idea which way was upward. With all my power I fought toward the surface, but my progress was slow and dragging, for there was a weight about my knees, as though arms were clasped about them, striving to hold me down. A wordless voice was in my ears, begging, beseeching, and there was something in the voice which made my struggles seem foolish and unnecessary, so that I desired never to reach the air I needed. I closed my eyes, which I had opened instinctively upon striking the water, and two lips pressed firmly against my own—and those lips saved my life, and my reason; for they were the cold lips of a corpse, with neither love nor challenge in them. I flailed out once more, and my hand caught in the line which the steamer dragged over her stern to measure the knots she traveled. All about me as I was hurled forward, now under water, now with nostrils out for a brief breathing-space, the mass of seaweed rose and fell on the heavy seas.

God knows how I ever got back aboard the troopship; but I awoke at mess-call in the morning, and sent immediately for the sergeant of the guard.

"What happened after I came back aboard last night, sergeant?" I asked abruptly.

The sergeant of the guard stared at me as though he thought me insane.

"I don't understand you," he managed finally.

"Have we finally passed through the area of seaweed?"

"Seaweed? Is the lieutenant making sport of me? We're two thousand miles from any land, except the ocean bottom, and there ain't any seaweed anywhere! I don't understand you!"

"Let it pass," I said. "When did you last visit the sentries last night?"

"Just before midnight, sir."

"And were all of them at their post of duty?"

"Yes, sir."

"And what about the bells?"

Again the sergeant's puzzlement was so genuine that I knew he did not understand my meaning. How much of my experience had been real, how much fantasy? I tried another tack.

"Did you make a round of the sentries after midnight?"

The sergeant shook his head sheepishly—it is one of the rules of guard duty that one visit to all sentries must take place between midnight and morning.

"Then the guard hasn't been mustered this morning? Is everyone present? You don't know? Then go at once and find out."

Ten minutes later the sergeant returned, chalk-white of face, to report that two of the guard were missing, and could not be found anywhere aboard. He told me their names, and instantly my mind went back to the night of uncanny happenings just past, and the two nude bodies brought back from the deep in the arms of—whom? Or what?

I never knew, and to this day the questions I have propounded have never been answered.

But this I know: there are strange things, and sounds, in the sea near the hundred and eightieth meridian, a thousand miles north of Honolulu—and this is the strangest incident in my night of terror: the clothing which I donned next morning was entirely dry; but my hair was stiff with salt water, and there was the tang of seaweed in my room when I awoke.

I looked, too, at the glass which covered the porthole beside my bed: outside that glass were the smudged prints of thin lips, the blur above them which told of a face pressed against the glass from outside—as though somebody, or something, had tried to peer in, between nightfall and morning!

And the bells? I still can hear them, in memory, when sometimes I waken at sea after midnight, and the rolling and the plunging of the ship tell me that a storm is making.

THE DEVIL OF THE MARSH

H. B. Marriott Watson

from *Diogenes of London, and Other Fantasies and Sketches* (1893)

It was nigh upon dusk when I drew close to the Great Marsh, and already the white vapors were about, riding across the sunken levels like ghosts in a churchyard. Though I had set forth in a mood of wild delight, I had sobered in the lonely ride across the moor and was now uneasily alert. As my horse jerked down the grassy slopes that fell away to the jaws of the swamp I could see thin streams of mist rise slowly, hover like wraiths above the long rushes, and then, turning gradually more material, go blowing heavily away across the flat. The appearance of the place at this desolate hour, so remote from human society and so darkly significant of evil presences, struck me with a certain wonder that she should have chosen this spot for our meeting. She was a familiar of the moors, where I had invariably encountered her; but it was like her arrogant caprice to test my devotion by some such dreary assignation. The wide and horrid prospect depressed me beyond reason, but the fact of her neighborhood drew me on, and my spirits mounted at the thought that at last she was to put me in possession of herself. Tethering my horse upon the verge of the swamp, I soon discovered the path that crossed it, and entering struck out boldly for the heart. The track could have been little used, for the reeds, which stood high above the level of my eyes upon either side, straggled everywhere across in low arches, through which I dodged, and broke my way with some inconvenience and much impatience. A full half hour I was solitary in that wilderness, and when at last a sound other than my own footsteps broke the silence the dusk had fallen.

I was moving very slowly at the time, with a mind half disposed to turn from the melancholy expedition, which it seemed to me now must surely be a cruel jest she had played upon me. While some such reluctance held me, I was suddenly arrested by a hoarse croaking which broke out upon my left, sounding somewhere from the reeds in the black mire. A little further it came again from close at hand, and when I had passed on a few more steps in wonder and perplexity, I heard it for the third time. I stopped and listened, but the marsh was as a grave, and so taking the noise for the signal of some raucous frog, I resumed my way. But in a little the croaking was repeated, and coming quickly to a stand I pushed the reeds aside and peered into the darkness. I could see nothing, but at the immediate moment of my pause I thought I detected the sound of some body trailing through the rushes. My distaste for the adventure grew with this suspicion, and had it not been for my delirious infatuation I had assuredly turned back and ridden home. The ghastly sound pursued me at intervals along the track, until at last, irritated beyond endurance by the sense of this persistent and invisible company, I broke into a sort of run. This, it seemed, the creature (whatever it was) could not achieve, for I heard no more of it, and continued my way in peace. My path at length ran out from among the reeds upon the smooth flat of which she had spoken, and here my heart quickened, and the gloom of the dreadful place lifted. The flat lay in the very centre of the marsh, and here and there in it a gaunt bush or withered tree rose like a spectre against the white mists. At the further end I fancied some kind of building loomed up; but the fog which had been gathering ever since my entrance upon the passage sailed down upon me at that moment and the prospect went out with suddenness. As I stood waiting for the clouds to pass, a voice cried to me out of its centre, and I saw her next second with bands of mist swirling about her body, come rushing to me from the darkness. She put her long arms about me, and, drawing her close, I looked into her deep eyes. Far down in them, it seemed to me, I could discern a mystic laughter dancing in the wells of light, and I had that ecstatic sense of nearness to some spirit of fire which was wont to possess me at her contact.

"At last," she said, "at last, my beloved!" I caressed her.

"Why," said I, tingling at the nerves, "why have you put this dolorous journey between us? And what mad freak is your presence in this swamp?" She uttered her silver laugh, and nestled to me again.

"I am the creature of this place," she answered. "This is my home. I have sworn you should behold me in my native sin ere you ravished me away."

"Come, then," said I; "I have seen; let there be an end of this. I know you, what you are. This marsh chokes up my heart. God forbid you should spend more of your days here. Come."

"You are in haste," she cried. "There is yet much to learn. Look, my friend," she said, "you who know me, what I am. This is my prison, and I have inherited its properties. Have you no fear?"

For answer I pulled her to me, and her warm lips drove out the horrid humors of the night; but the swift passage of a flickering mockery over her eyes struck me as a flash of lightning, and I grew chill again.

"I have the marsh in my blood," she whispered: "the marsh and the fog of it. Think ere you vow to me, for I am the cloud in a starry night."

A lithe and lovely creature, palpable of warm flesh, she lifted her magic face to mine and besought me plaintively with these words. The dews of the nightfall hung on her lashes, and seemed to plead with me for her forlorn and solitary plight.

"Behold!" I cried, "witch or devil of the marsh, you shall come with me! I have known you on the moors, a roving apparition of beauty; nothing more I know, nothing more I ask. I care not what this dismal haunt means; not what these strange and mystic eyes. You have powers and senses above me; your sphere and habits are as mysterious and incomprehensible as your beauty. But that," I said, "is mine, and the world that is mine shall be yours also."

She moved her head nearer to me with an antic gesture, and her gleaming eyes glanced up at me with a sudden flash, the similitude (great heavens!) of a hooded snake. Starting, I fell away, but at that moment she turned her face and set it fast towards the fog that came rolling in thick volumes over the flat. Noiselessly the great cloud crept down upon us, and all dazed and troubled I watched her watching it in silence. It was as if she awaited some omen of horror, and I too trembled in the fear of its coming.

Then suddenly out of the night issued the hoarse and hideous croaking I had heard upon my passage. I reached out my arm to take her hand, but in an instant the mists broke over us, and I was groping in the vacancy. Something like panic took hold of me, and, beating through the blind obscurity, I rushed over the flat, calling upon her. In a little the swirl went by, and I perceived her upon the margin of the swamp, her arm raised as in imperious command. I ran to her, but stopped, amazed and shaken by a fearful sight. Low by the dripping reeds crouched a small squat thing, in the likeness of a monstrous frog, coughing and choking in its throat. As I stared, the creature rose upon its legs and disclosed a horrid human resemblance. Its face was white and thin, with long black hair; its body gnarled and twisted as with the ague of a thousand years. Shaking, it whined in a breathless voice, pointing a skeleton finger at the woman by my side.

"Your eyes were my guide," it quavered. "Do you think that after all these years I have no knowledge of your eyes? Lo, is there aught of evil in you I am not instructed in? This is the Hell you designed for me, and now you would leave me to a greater."

The wretch paused, and panting leaned upon a bush, while she stood silent, mocking him with her eyes, and soothing my terror with her soft touch.

"Hear!" he cried, turning to me, "hear the tale of this woman that you may know her as she is. She is the Presence of the marshes. Woman or Devil I know not, but only that the accursed marsh has crept into her soul and she herself is become its Evil Spirit; she herself, that lives and grows young and beautiful by it, has its full power to blight and chill and slay. I, who was once as you are, have this knowledge. What bones lie deep in this black swamp who can say but she? She has drained of health, she has drained of mind and of soul; what is between her and her desire that she should not drain also of life? She has made me a devil in her Hell, and now she would leave me to my solitary pain, and go search for another victim. But she shall not!" he screamed through his chattering teeth; "she shall not! My Hell is also hers! She shall not!"

Her smiling untroubled eyes left his face and turned to me: she put out her arms, swaying towards me, and so fervid and so great a light glowed in her face that, as one distraught of superhuman means, I took her into my embrace. And then the madness seized me.

"Woman or devil," I said, "I will go with you! Of what account this pitiful past? Blight me even as that wretch, so be only you are with me."

She laughed, and, disengaging herself, leaned, half-clinging to me, towards the coughing creature by the mire.

"Come," I cried, catching her by the waist. "Come!" She laughed again a silver-ringing laugh. She moved with me slowly across the flat to where the track started for the portals of the marsh. She laughed and clung to me.

But at the edge of the track I was startled by a shrill, hoarse screaming; and behold, from my very feet, that loathsome creature rose up and wound his long black arms about her shrieking and crying in his pain. Stooping I pushed him from her skirts, and with one sweep of my arm drew her across the pathway; as her face passed mine her eyes were wide and smiling. Then of a sudden the still mist enveloped us once more; but ere it descended I had a glimpse of that contorted figure trembling on the margin, the white face drawn and full of desolate pain. At the sight an icy shiver ran through me. And then through the yellow gloom the shadow of her darted past me to the further side. I heard the hoarse cough, the dim noise of a struggle, a swishing sound, a thin cry, and then the sucking of the slime over something in the rushes. I leapt forward: and once again the fog thinned, and I beheld her, woman or devil, standing upon the verge, and peering with smiling eyes into the foul and sickly bog. With a sharp cry wrung from my nerveless soul, I turned and fled down the narrow way from that accursed spot; and as I ran the thickening fog closed round me, and I heard far off and lessening still the silver sound of her mocking laughter.

The Kelpie

Manly Wade Wellman

first published in *Weird Tales* (July 1936)

No sooner had Cannon closed and latched the door than Lu was in his arms, and they were kissing with the hungry fierceness of lovers who doubt their own good fortune. Thus for a delirious, heart-battering moment; then Lu pulled nervously away.

"We're being watched," she whispered breathlessly.

The big, dark man laughed down at her worried blue eyes, her shining wealth of ale-brown hair, her face like an ivory heart, the apprehensive tautness of her slender figure.

"That's guilty conscience, Lu," he teased. "You know I wouldn't have invited you to my apartment without giving my man the night off. And even if someone did see us, why be afraid? Don't we love each other?"

She allowed him to bring her into the parlor and draw her down beside him on a divan, but she still mused apprehensively.

"I could swear there were eyes upon us," she insisted, half apologetically. "Hostile eyes."

"Maybe they're spirits," Cannon cried gayly, his own twinkling gaze sweeping around to view in turn the paintings on the walls, the hooded lamps, the bookshelves, the rich, comfortable furniture, the big box-shaped aquarium in the darkest corner. Again he chuckled. "Spirits—that's a pun, you know. The lowest form of wit."

From a taboret at his elbow he lifted a decanter of brandy, and poured two drinks with a humorous flourish. Lu, forgetting her uneasiness of a moment be fore, lifted her glass.

"To us," she toasted.

But Cannon set his own drink down untasted and peered around a second time, this time without gayety. "You've got me thinking it now," he muttered.

"Thinking what?"

"That something is watching and not liking what it sees." He glanced quickly over his shoulder, then continued, as if seeking to reassure them both. "Nothing in that corner, of course, except the aquarium."

"What's the latest tenantry there?" La asked, glad to change the disquieting subject.

"Some Scotch water plants—new laboratory project." Cannon was at ease the moment his hobby came into the conversation. "They arrived this afternoon in a sealed tin box. Doctor MacKenzie's letter says they were gathered from the Pool Kelp, wherever that is in his highland wildernesses. I'm letting them soak and wash overnight. In the morning I'll begin experimenting.

Lu sipped more brandy, her eyes interested. "Pool Kelp," she repeated. "It sounds seaweedy."

"But these are fresh-water growths. As I say, I never heard of the pool before." Cannon broke off. "Here, though, why talk botany when we can—"

His lips abruptly smothered hers, his arms gathered her so close as to bruise her. But even as she yielded happily to his embrace the telephone rang loudly in the front entry, Cannon released her with a muttered curse of impatience, rose and hurried out to answer. He closed the door behind him, and his voice, muffled and indistinct, sounded aggrieved as he spoke into the transmitter.

Lu, finishing her brandy alone, picked up the drink Cannon had set down. As she lifted it to her lips she glanced idly over the rim of the glass at the moist tangle in the aquarium. In the dim light it seemed to fall into all manner of rich greens darkest emerald, beryl, malachite, olive, grass, lettuce. Something moved, too, filliped and swerved in the heart of the little submerged grove.

Cannon was still talking. Lu rose, drink in hand, to stroll curiously toward the big glass box. As she did so the moving trifle seemed to glide upward toward the surface. Coming closer yet, Lu paused to peer in the half-light.

A fish? If so, a very green fish and a very small one—perhaps a tadpole. A bubble broke audibly on top of the water.

Lu, genuinely interested, bent closer, just as something rose through the little ripples and hooked its tip on the rim of the aquarium.

It was a tiny, spinach-colored hand.

Half a second later another fringe of tiny fingers appeared, clutching the rim in turn. Lu, woodenly motionless, stared in her effort to rationalize. She could see the tiny digits, each tapering and flexible, each armed with a jet-colored claw. Through the glass, under and behind the fingers, she made out thumbs deft, opposable thumbs and smooth, wet palms of a dead, oystery gray. Her breath caught in mute, helpless astonishment. A blunt head rose slowly into view behind and between the fists, something with flat brow, broad lump of nose and wide mouth, like a grotesque Mayan mask—and it was *growing*.

Lu told herself, a little stupidly, that she must not have seen clearly at first. She had thought the creature a little green minnow, but it was as big as a squirrel. No, as big as a baby! Its bright eyes, white-ringed, fixed hers, projecting a wave of malignant challenge that staggered her like a blow. The full, lead-hued lips parted loosely and the forked tip of a purple tongue quivered out for a moment. A snaky odor steamed up to Lu's nostrils, making her dizzy and weak. Wet, scabby-green shoulders had heaved into view by now, and after them the twin mounds of a grotesquely feminine bosom. The thing was climbing out at her, and as it did so it swelled and grew, grew...

The brandy-glass fell from her hand and loudly exploded into splinters upon the floor. The sound of the breaking gave Lu back her voice, and she screamed tremulously, then managed to move back and away, half stumbling and half staggering. The monster, all damp and green and stinking, was writhing a leg into view. Lu noted that, and then everything went into a whirling white blur and she began to collapse.

Faintly she heard the rush of Cannon's feet, felt the clutch of his strong arms as though many thicknesses of fabric separated them from her. He almost shouted her name in panic. After a moment her sight and mind cleared, and she looked up into his concerned face. With all her shaken strength she clung to him.

"That thing," she chattered, "that horrid female thing in the aquarium—"

Cannon managed a comforting tone. "But there's nothing, dearest, nothing at all. Those two brandies you took mine, too, you shameless glutton —went to your head."

"Look at it!" She pointed an unsteady finger. "Deep down there in the weeds."

He looked. "Oh, that?" he laughed. "I noticed it, too, just before you came. It's a little frog or toad must have been gathered with the weeds and shipped all the way from Scotland."

Lu caressed her throbbing forehead with her slender white hand and mumbled something about "seeing things." Already she believed that she had somehow dreamed of the green water-monster. Still, it was a distinct effort to walk with Cannon to the aquarium and look in. Through the thick tangle of stems and fronds that made a dank stew in the water she could make out a tiny something that wriggled and glided. It was only minnow-size after all, and seemed smooth and innocuous. Funny what notions two quick drinks will give you...

She lowered a cupped palm toward the surface, as if to scoop down and seize the little creature, but the chilly touch of the topmost weed-tips repelled her, and she drew back her arm.

"You'd never catch it." Cannon told her. "It won't wait for you to grab. I had a try when I first saw it, and got a wet sleeve—and this."

He held out his left hand. For the first time that evening Lu saw the gold band that he wore on his third finger.

"A ring," her lover explained. "It was lying on the bottom. Apparently it came with the weeds, too."

"You put it on your wedding finger!" Lu wailed.

"That was the only one it would fit," Cannon defended as she caught his hand and tugged with all her might at the ring. It did not budge.

"Please," she begged, "get rid of it."

"Why, Lu, what's the trouble? Are you being jealous because a present was given me by that mess of weed—or maybe by the little lady frog?"

The tiny swimmer in the tank splashed water, as if in punctuation of his joke, and Cannon, falling abruptly silent, suddenly began wrenching at the gold circlet. But not even his strength, twice that of Lu, could bring it over the joint.

"Here, I don't like this," he announced, his voice steady but a little tight. "I'm going to put soap on my finger. That will make the thing slip off."

Lu made no reply, but her eyes encouraged him. Cannon kissed her pale forehead, strode across the room and into a little corridor beyond. After a moment Lu could hear the spurt of a water-jet in a bowl, then the sound of industrious scrubbing with lather,

In command of herself once again but still a trifle faint and shaky, Lu leaned her hand lightly upon the thick, smooth edge of the aquarium glass. A fond little smile came to her lips as she pondered on Cannon's eagerness to please her whim. Not even in a silly little matter like this one did he cross her will or offer argument that might embarrass or hurt her. The shedding of that ring would be a symbol between them, of understanding and faith.

Her eyes dropped to the table that stood against the aquarium, with its litter of papers and notebooks. At the edge nearest Lu lay a thick volume bound in gray—a dictionary. What was the term she had puzzled over? Oh, yes... Still lounging with one hand on the glass, she flipped the book open with the other and turned the pages to the K's:

Kelp: Any one of various large brown seaweeds of the families *Laminariaceae* and *Fucaceae*.

Her hazy memory had been right, then, about the word. But why should a body of fresh water be called Pool Kelp? Glancing back at the page, her eyes caught the next definition.

It answered her question.

Kelpie: (*Gael. Myth.*) A malicious water spirit or demon believed to haunt streams or marshes. Sometimes it falls in love with human beings, striving jealously against mortal rivals...

The words swam before her vision, for the snake-smell had risen sickeningly around her. And something was gripping the hand that rested on the rim of the tank.

Lu's mouth opened, but, as before, terror throttled her. Like a sleeper in the throes of nightmare, she struggled half-heartedly. She dared not look, yet some power forced her head around.

The grip had shifted to her wrist. Long, claw-tipped fingers were clamped there—fingers as large as her own, scrofulous green and of a swampy chill.

Lu's eyes slid in fascinated horror along the scale-ridged, corded arm to the moldy-looking body, stuck and festooned over with weed-fronds, that was rising from the water. Another foul hand stole swiftly out, fastened on Lu's shoulder, and jerked her close. The flat, grotesque face, grown to human size, was level with hers, its eyes triumphant within their dead white rings, its dark tongue quivering between gaping lips.

Yet again Lu tried to find her voice. All she could achieve was a wordless moan, no louder than a sigh.

"Did you call, sweetheart?" came Cannon's cheery response from his washing.

"I'll be with you in a minute now; this thing is still hanging on like a poor relation!"

The reptilian jaw dropped suddenly, like the lid of a box turned upside down. Lu stared into the slate-gray cave that was the yawning mouth. Teeth, sharp teeth, gleamed there—not one row, but many.

Lu's hands lifted feebly in an effort at defense, then dropped wearily to her sides. The monster crinkled its humid features in something like a triumphant grin. Then its blunt head shot forward with incredible swiftness, nuzzling Lu at the juncture of neck and shoulder.

For a moment she felt exquisite pain, as of many piercing needles. After that she neither felt, heard nor saw anything.

The medical examines was drawing a sheet over the still, agony-distorted body of the dead girl. The police sergeant, scribbling his final notes, addressed Cannon with official sternness.

"Sorry," he said, "but you haven't explained this business at all satisfactorily. You come down to headquarters with me."

Cannon glanced wanly up from his senseless wrestling with the ring that would not quit his wedding finger. "I didn't do it," he reiterated dully.

The medical examiner was also speaking, more to himself than anyone: "An autopsy might clear up some points, Those inflamed, suppurated wounds on the neck might have been made by a big water-snake. Or," he added, with a canny glance at the sergeant, "by a poisoned weapon constructed to simulate such a creature's bite."

Cannon's last vestige of control went. "I tell you," he snarled desperately, "that she and I were the only living things here tonight—the only living things." He broke off, becoming aware of movement in the aquarium. "Except, of course, that little frog in there."

The creature among the weeds, a tiny sliver of agile greenness, cavorted for a moment on the surface of the water as if in exultation, then, before any of the three watchers could get a fair look at it, dived deep into the heart of the floating mess.

THE WATER LADY:
A LEGEND

Anonymous

first published in *The Port Folio* (June 1822)

There is a mystery in these sombre shades,
A secret horror in this dark, deep flood:
'T seems as if beings of another race
Here lurk invisible, except what time
Eve's dusky hour, and night's congenial gloom,
Permit them show themselves in human guise.—
Men say that fays, and elves, and water spirits,
Affect such haunts—and this is surely one.

On the banks of one of the streams falling into the Inn, are the remains of an old castle, not far from a narrow defile or glen where the waters, being hemmed in, rush with impetuosity through fragments of rock impeding their course. Of these the following legend is related. The last possessor of the castle, which had not been inhabited for several centuries, was Count Albert, a youthful nobleman, descended from an illustrious ancestry: daring, enthusiastic, and addicted to study; but his studies were of such a nature that they incurred for him, among his credulous dependents, the imputation of holding un-hallowed intercourse with supernatural beings. Independently however, of the censures his conduct occasioned in this respect, he was admired by all for possessing, in an eminent degree, personal courage and prowess, qualities so necessary, and therefore so highly prized, in those ages. Yet even those who were most forward to commend his undauntedness could not forbear blaming the indiscretions of his curiosity, which led him to venture into scenes that would, by the fancied horror attached to them have appalled the bravest of his followers. During the most stormy weather, when the spirits of the air were supposed to be wreaking their fury on the elements—in the depth of night, at what hour the departed were supposed to revisit the earth, and forms obscure and terrific to appear to the unfortunate traveler who should be bewildered on his way,— even at such seasons would Albert venture into the recesses of the woods, enjoy the conflict of nature on the blasted heath, and explore the wildest solitudes around his domain.

Such practices occasioned much conjecture and rumor—and many prophesied, that some terrible visitation would overtake the man, who, if not actually leagued with the powers of dark-ness, delighted in all that was terrific and appalling; nor did the less scrupulous or the more imaginative hesitate to relate with particular circumstance and detail, the dreadful mysteries he was reported, at such times, to have witnessed.

In the defile, which, as has been stated, was in the immediate vicinity of the castle, it was said that a fairy, or spirit, named by the peasantry the Water Lady, had been heard by night singing within a cave hollowed in the rock, just above the most dangerous part of the current.

Albert was determined to ascertain the truth, and, if possible obtain an interview with the supernatural inhabitant of the *Black Water Vault*. Such a daring project excited the horror of all who heard it: since many were the tales respecting persons having been enticed to listen to the strains of the spirit, and afterwards perishing in the foaming waters: for she was said to delight in attracting the unwary, and the curious. But though the design of the young Count appeared so fraught with danger and obstinate temerity, nothing could induce him to abandon the enterprise; neither the entreaties of his friends, nor those to Bertha, his betrothed bride, whom he was shortly to conduct of the altar; it rather seemed as if all obstacles and dissuasives did but irritate his unhallowed curiosity. One evening, the third of the new moon the Count, attended by two companions, whom he had prevailed upon to assist him in rowing his boat, and steering it among the eddies of the torrent, departed for the scene of research.—They proceeded in silence, for Albert was buried in thought, the others were mute from apprehension. No sooner did they approach the narrow pass where the foaming and congregated waters dash furiously through the contracted channel than was heard the voice of one within the cavern.

The music was so strangely sweet and fascinating, that, although struck with awe at the supernatural sounds, they were induced to advance. A form was soon dimly descried: It was that of a female arrayed in floating drapery, but her features they might not discern, as she wore a thick veil. They continued to approach the spot so as to be able to catch distinctly the following words, which were chanted in a tone of solemn adjuration.

> By the treasures of my cave,
> More than avarice could crave,
> More than Fortune vet e'er gave,
> I charge thee, youth, appear.
>
> Here I wait thy will and best,
> Here with me thou'lt safely rest,

Thou art he, my chosen guest;—
   Then enter thou, nor fear.

   Mortal, now, in dead of night,
   Magic spell of friendly sprite,
   To favor thee, hath bound aright
   Aught that would thee harm.

   Hither, hasten, youthful rower:
   In my secret, inmost bower,
   "Thou shalt find a worthy dower;—
   Defy not, then, my charm.

By this time they had arrived opposite to the cave: Albert motioned to his companions to stay the bark, and scarcely had they obeyed, when having leapt into the flood, he was soon descried by them climbing up the jutting crags below the cavern—he entered beneath its low-browed opening, and disappeared. Gazing upon each other with looks of dread, and fearing to speak, lest there should be horror in the tones of their own voices, they retired to some distance, waiting in the hope that the adventurer might reappear: at length, they returned to the castle, in the same silence of terror as they had hitherto observed. "Where was their companion, the Count—had he perished?—How had they lost him—what had they beheld?" These and similar questions were put to them by the terrified inmates: their replies were brief, vague, incoherent, but all of dreadful import: and no doubt remained as to the youth's having become the victim of his own temerity.

The following morning when the family was assembled, and preparing to commence their matin repast, Lord Albert advanced into the hall, and took his wonted station at the table, with the usual salutations. All started as if a spectre had stood before them—yet, strange to say, no one dared to address him as to his absence, or his mysterious return—for he had apparently but just quitted his chamber, clad in his wonted morning apparel: every one was as spellbound, since no sooner did any attempt to question the Count, than he felt the words die away upon his lips. There sat a wondrous paleness on his brow, yet was it not sad; there was, too, a more than common fire in the expression of his eye; he was thoughtful—at times abstracted, but instantly roused himself, and essayed to animate the conversation. If the silence of the others was singular, that of Albert himself was equally so, for he took no notice whatever of the occurrences of the preceding evening.

No sooner had he quitted the hall, than every one began to enquire of his neighbor, if he knew when, or how the Count had returned—to wonder at their own silence on this topic, and impute it to some magic charm. Day after day did they continue to express to each other their astonishment, their surmises, their apprehensions; but even his most familiar friends did not venture ever to speak a syllable to him on the subject of their curiosity:

among other circumstances, which were whispered about, it had been remarked, that instead of the ring the Count used to wear, which was of great value and family antiquity, he now had one, of which the circlet itself, and not the ornament, was apparently cut out of a single piece of emerald, and, as some averred, who had taken the opportunity of examining it, unperceived by its wearer, inscribed with mystic characters.

In time, however, these circumstances ceased to be the theme of conversation, and even appeared forgotten during the preparations for the approaching nuptials between the Count and the Lady Bertha; and were never mentioned during the gaieties attendant upon their solemnization. On the evening after the bridal day, while the Count was conversing apart with one of his guests, in the recess of an oriel window, the faint beam of the new moon fell upon his face—he looked up aghast as if struck by some sudden, dreadful recollection, and, dashing his hand against his forehead, rushed wildly out of the apartment. Consternation seized all who witnessed this dreadful burst of dismay, of which none could tell the cause.

Retired from his guests, the Count was hastily pacing to and fro, in a long gallery leading to his private apartments, when Bertha broke in upon him. She did not notice his extreme disorder, being herself hardly less agitated; but informed him, that on the preceding night, a figure veiled in long flowing drapery, had been seen standing at their chamber door, and the next morning a ring picked up by her attendants on the very spot where this mysterious appearance had been observed. She then gave the ring to her Lord—it was that which he had formerly won.

"Fatal, fatal night! Listen, Bertha!" exclaimed he, in a tone of anguish. "Impelled by curiosity, I visited the cave of the 'Water-Lady;' it was on the third of the moon. She compelled me to an interchange of rings: from her it was that I received this fatal one, which you observe on my finger, and which I am bound by a solemn vow never to lay aside. I vowed also,"—he shuddered as he spoke—"to consent to receive a visit from her on the third of the moon —this I was obliged to do, or incur all the consequences of her wrath, while yet in her power: from that fatal period, I have been obliged to submit to these intercourses with a strange being—the consequence of my unhallowed curiosity. Last night was due to her!"

Bertha listened in horror—the Count looked on his finger, the circlet of emerald was gone; how he knew not, but he hoped that he was now released from his terrible vow, yet felt a strange presentiment of impending misfortune. Bertha notwithstanding her own distress, endeavored to cheer him, but became alarmed herself at the ashy paleness of his countenance: he tried to persuade her he was not so disturbed as she imagined, and turned to a mirror, for the purpose of seeing whether his features wore the deadly aspect she fancied—but a cry of horror issued from his lips; the mirror had reflected his dress, but neither his hands nor his face. He felt that he was under the bann of that mysterious being, with whom his fate was so strangely linked.[18]

A deadly chill darted through his heart; he rushed to his chamber, but no sooner had he laid his fingers upon the bolt of the door, that he felt them grasped by a cold icy hand.

"Albert," cried a voice, "thou hast broken the compact so solemnly ratified between us. Last night was the third of the moon: know that spirits may not be trifled with."

Bertha had followed her bridegroom: she had heard the awful voice—she felt that some strange visitation was at hand, yet was not therefore deterred from entering the apartment.

The next day no traces of either Albert or Bertha could be discovered, they were never seen again; and all agreed that they had perished by the revenge of the "Water Lady." The castle was deserted: became a ruin—and the peasantry used ever afterwards to point out with dismay the fatal cavern of the Black Water Vault, and to relate to the traveler the legend of the Water-Lady.

---

[18] A "bann" is an announcement of intended marriage.

THE SORCERESS OF THE SEA

W.

first published in *The Memorial* (1826)

The Summer's sun looks down
  Upon the glassy deep;
And quietly the busy waves
  Are cradled to their sleep.

Fanned by the gentle airs
  That skim the waters blue,
A youthful Mariner is seen
  To steer his white canoe.

Alone his barque he steers—
  A wayward wight is he;
Fast by the helm all day he sits
  Communing with the sea.

From common men, he seems
  To live, for aye, apart;
Some hidden thing of guilt, appears
  To weigh upon his heart.—

At witching hour of night,
  Beneath the moonlight sheen,
To ply the oar, or spread the sail,
  That Mariner is seen.—

What tempts that wanderer
  The deep-sea waves to woo?
Why sits he there, the live-long day,
  Steering his white canoe?

At midnight's witching hour.
  Along the water dark,
Why hurries on this Mariner
  His solitary barque?—

The demons of the deep—
  The phantoms of the air—
Above,—below,—around,—appear
  To haunt him everywhere.—

Behold that form of light!
  What may the vision be
Whose image looks so fairy-like,
  Emerging from the sea?—

Her hand transparent seems
  With which she calls away;
And in her eye of melting blue,
  A thousand cupids play:—

The music of her breath
  Falls like the evening dews;—
Behold, with what a look of love,
  The Mariner she woos!

Her pensive downcast eyes,
  Now seem to chide delay;
And now, with her enticing tongue
  She summons him away!—

"Come to me Mariner,—
  Enter my coral grove;
A bower for thee I have prepared,
  Come, come and be my love:—

"The beauties of the deep,—
  The treasures of the sea,—
From mortal eye that lie concealed
  " Shall be revealed to thee:—

"On sands of gold I tread,—
  On beds of pearl I lie,—

The diamond rock I sit upon,
    The ocean queen am I.—

"Pleasant my mansion is;
    There sportive sea-nymphs play;
And happily, my Mariner,
    We 'Il pass our hours away:—

"For thee the banquet waits;
    Come hither and partake;
The flowers my mossy couch that deck,
    Were gathered for thy sake:—

"Music all sorrow steeps
    In sweet oblivion, there;
Then live with me my Mariner,
    With me these pleasures share:—

"Pillowed thy head shall be
    On this devoted breast;
And when the feast of love is o'er,
    I'll sing thee to thy rest."

With many an amorous glance—
    —Waving her locks of green—
So sings the sorceress of the sea,—
    So sings the ocean queen.—

Stay thee, enamored youth.—
    Death is the proffered bliss;
Dash from thy lip the charmed bowl!
    Avoid the adder's kiss!

Hag of the mist is she,
    That dwells beneath the flood;
That lures the shipwrecked mariner,
    And drinks the seaman's blood.

Her potent spells prevail,
    Like snake the bird that charms,—
Behold, she lures him to the brink,
    And clasps him in her arms.

That barque is seen no more—
    And o'er the black domains

Of that lone melancholy deep—
    A horrid stillness reigns.—

Another image now,
    The wily sorceress takes;
A monster is her nether shape,
    Her hair a coil of snakes:

Wrinkled, her visage seems
    With envy pale and lean;
The scaly serpent, fed by her,
    At either breast is seen:

Her bloated rolling eyes
    The fires of anguish dart;
Disease feeds on her creeping flesh,
    The vulture on her heart!

"Welcome!" the Harpy cries—
    "Mariner thou art mine!"—
And from the precipice of rock
    She plunges in the brine.

Hark! from the whelming waves
    Comes laughter loud and hoarse!
Whilst, dimly through the mist is seen,
    The haggard fiend Remorse.—

Red rolls the troubled tide,—
    The water-spectre shrieks,—
The birds of darkness flap their wings,
    And whet their ravenous beaks.

What ghastly corse is that
    Borne on the foaming flood?
His breast with gashes cover'd o'er,
    His visage black with blood?—

"The Mariner!"—replies
    The Sorceress of the sea;
"I give his body to the winds,
    His spirit dwells with me."

BY THE YELLOW MOONROCK

William Sharp
(WRITING AS FIONA MACLEOD)

from *The Hills of Ruel, and Other Stories* (1921)

first published in longer form in *The Dominion of Dreams* (1899)

Rory MacAlpine the piper had come down the Strath on St. Bride's Eve, for the great wedding at the farm of his kinsman Donald Macalister. Every man and woman, every boy and girl, who could by hook or by crook get to the big dance at the barns was to be seen there: but no one that danced till he or she could dance no more had a wearier joy than Rory with the pipes. Reels and strathspeys that every one knew gave way at last to wilder strathspeys that no one had ever heard before…and why should they, since it was the hill-wind and the mountain-torrent and the roar of pines that had got loose in Rory's mind, and he not knowing it any more than a leaf that sails on the yellow wind?

He played with magic and pleasure, and had never looked handsomer, in his new grandeur of clothes, and with his ruddy hair aflame in the torchlight, and his big blue eyes shining as with a lifting, shifting fire. But those who knew him best saw that he was strangely subdued for Rory MacAlpine, or at least, that he laughed and shouted (in the rare intervals when he was not playing, and there were two other pipers present to help the Master) more by custom than from the heart.

"What is't, Rory?" said Dalibrog to him, after a heavy reel wherein he had nearly killed a man by swinging upon and nigh flattening him against the wall.

"Nothing, foster-brother dear; it's just nothing at all. Fling away, Dalibrog; you're doing fine."

Later old Dionaid took him aside to bid him refresh himself from a brew of rum and lemons she had made, with spice and a flavor of old brandy— "Barra Punch" she called it—and then asked him if he had any sorrow at the back of his heart.

"Just this," he said in a whisper, "that Rory MacAlpine's fëy."

"Fëy, my lad, an' for why that? For sure, I'm thinking it's fëy with the good drink you have had all day, an' now here am I spoiling ye with more."

"Hush, woman; I'm not speaking of what comes wi' a drop to the bad. But I had a dream, I had; a powerful strange dream, for sure. I had it a month ago; I had it the night before I left Strathandra; and I had it this very day of the days, as I lay sleepin' off the kindness I had since I came into Strathraonull."

"An' what will that dream be, now? "

"Sure, it's a strange dream, Dionaid Macalister. You know the great yellow stone that rises out of the heather on the big moor of Dalmonadh, a mile or more beyond Tom-na-shee?"

"Ay, the Moonrock they call it: it that fell out o' the skies, they say."

"The Yellow Moonrock. Ay, the Yellow Moonrock; that's its name, for sure. Well, the first time I dreamed of it I saw it standing fair yellow in the moonshine. There was a moorfowl sitting on it, and it flew away. When it flew away I saw it was a ptarmigan, but she was as clean brown as though it were summer and not midwinter, and I thought that strange."

"How did you know it was a ptarmigan? It might have been a moorhen or a—"

"Hoots, woman, how do I know when it's wet or fine, when it's day or night? Well, as I was saying, I thought it strange; but I hadn't turned over that thought on its back before it was gone like the shadow o' a peewit, and I saw standing before me the beautifulest woman I ever saw in all my life. I've had sweethearts here and sweethearts there, Dionaid-nic-Tormod, and long ago I loved a lass who died, Sine MacNeil; but not one o' these, not sweet Sine herself, was like the woman I saw in my dream, who had more beauty upon her than them altogether, or than all the women in Strathraonull and Strathandra."

"Have some more Barra punch, Rory," said Miss Macalister drily.

"Whist, ye old fule, begging your pardon for that same. She was as white as new milk, an' her eyes were as dark as the two black pools below Annora Linn, an' her hair was as long an' wavy as the shadows o' a willow in the wind; an' she sat an' she sang, an' if I could be remembering that song now it's my fortune I'd be making, an' that quick too."

"And where was she?"

"Why, on the Moonrock, for sure. An' if I hadn't been a good Christian I'd have bowed down before her, because o'—because—well, because o' that big stare out of her eyes she had, an' the beauty of her, an' all. An' what's more, by the Black Stone of Iona, if I hadn't been a God-fearin' man I'd have run to her, an' put my arms round her, an' kissed the honey lips of her till she cried out, • For the Lord's sake, Rory MacAlpine, leave off!'"

"It's well seen you were only in a dream, Rory MacAlpine."

At another time Rory would have smiled at that, but now he just stared.

"She said no word," he added, "but lifted a bit of hollow wood or thick reed. An' then all at once she whispered, 'I'm bonnie St. Bride of the Mantle,' an' wi' that she began to play, an' it was the finest, sweet, gentle, little music in the world. But a big fear was on me, an' I just turned an' ran."

"No man'll ever call ye a fool again to my face, Rory MacAlpine. I never had the thought you had so much sense.

"She didna let me run so easy, for a grey bitch went yapping and yowling at my heels; an' just as I tripped an' felt the bad hot breath of the beast at my throat, I woke, an' was wet wi' sweat."

"An' you've had that dream three times?"

"I've had it three times, and this very day, to the Stones be it said. Now, you're a wise woman, Dionaid Macalister, but can you tell me what that dream means? "

"If you're really fey, I'm thinking I can, Rory MacAlpine."

"It's a true thing: Himself knows it."

"And what are you fey of?"

"I'm fey with the beauty o' that woman."

"There's good women wi' the fair looks on them in plenty, Rory; an' if you prefer them bad, you needna wear out new shoon before you'll find them."

"I'm fey wi' the beauty o' that woman. I'm fey wi the beauty o' that woman that had the name o' Bride to her."

Dionaid Macalister looked at him with troubled eyes.

"When she took up the reed, did you see anything that frighted you?"

"Ay. I had a bit fright when I saw a big black adder slip about the Moonrock as the ptarmigan flew off; an' I had the other half o' that fright when I thought the woman lifted the adder, but it was only wood or a reed, for amn't I for telling you about the gentle, sweet music I heard?" Old Dionaid hesitated; then, looking about her to see that no one was listening, she spoke in a whisper:

"An' you've been fey since that hour because o' the beauty o' that woman?"

"Because o' the sore beauty o' that woman."

"An' it's not the drink? "

"No, no, Dionaid Macalister. You women are always for hurting the feelin's o' the drink. It is not the innycent drink, I am telling you; for sure, no; no, no, it is not the drink."

"Then I'll tell you what it means, Rory MacAlpine. It wasn't Holy St. Bride—"

"I know that, ye old—, I mean, Miss Macalister."

"It was the face of the *Bhean-Nimhir* you saw, the face of *Nighean-Imhir*, an' this is St. Bride's Night, an' it is on this night of the nights she can be seen, an' beware o' that seeing, Rory MacAlpine."

"The *Bhean-Nimhir*, the *Nighean-Imhir*...the Serpent Woman, the Daughter of Ivor—" muttered Rory; "where now have I heard tell o' the Daughter of Ivor?"

Then he remembered an old tale of the isles, and his heart sank, because the tale was of a woman of the underworld who could suck the soul out of a man through his lips, and send it to slavery among the people of ill-will, whom there is no call to speak of by name; and if she had any spite, or any hidden wish that is not for our knowing, she could put the littleness of a fly's bite on the hollow of his throat, and take his life out of his body, and nip it and sting it till it was no longer a life, and till that went away on the wind that she chased with screams and laughter.

"Some say she's the wife of the *Amadan-Dhu*, the Dark Fool," murmured Dionaid, crossing herself furtively, for even at Dalibrog it was all Protestantry now.

But Rory was not listening. He sat intent, for he heard music—a strange music.

Dionaid shook him by the shoulder.

"Wake up, Rory, man; you'll be having sleep on you in another minute."

Just then a loud calling for the piper was heard, and Rory went back to the dancers. Soon his pipes were heard, and the reels swung to that good glad music, and his face lighted up as he strode to and fro, or stopped and tap-tapped away with his right foot, while drone and chanter all but burst with the throng of sound in them.

But suddenly he began to play a reel that nigh maddened him, and his own face was wrought so that Dalibrog came up and signed to stop, and then asked him what in the name o' Black Donald he was playing.

Rory laughed foolishly.

"Oh, for sure, it's just a new reel o' my own. I call it 'The Reel of Ivor's Daughter.' An' a good reel it is too, although it's Rory MacAlpine says it."

"Who is she, an' what Ivor will you be speaking of ?"

"Oh, ask the Amadan-Dhu; it's he will be knowing that. No, no, now, I will not be naming it that name; sure, I will call it instead the Serpent-Reel."

"Come now, Rory, you've played enough, an' if your wrist's not tired wi' the chanter, sure, it must be wi' lifting the drink to your lips. An' it's time, too, these lads an' lasses were off."

" No, no, they're waiting to bring in the greying of the day—St. Bride's Day. They'll be singing the hymn for that greying, 'Bride bhoidheach muime Chriosda.'"

"Not they, if Dalibrog has a say in it! Come, now, have a drink with me, your own foster-brother, an' then lie down an' sleep it off, an' God's blessing be on you."

Whether it was Dalibrog's urgency, or the thought of the good drink he would have, and he with a terrible thirst on him after that lung-bursting reel of his, Rory went quietly away with the host, and was on a mattress on the floor of a big, empty room, and snoring hard, long before the other pipers had ceased piping, or the last dancers flung their panting breaths against the frosty night.

An hour after midnight Rory woke with a start. He had "a spate of a headache on," he muttered, as he half rose and struck a match against the floor. When he saw that he was still in his brave gear, and had lain down "just as he was," and also remembered all that had happened and the place he was in, he wondered what had waked him.

Now that he thought of it, he had heard music: yes, for sure, music—for all that it was so late, and after every one had gone home. What was it? It was not any song of his own, nor any air he had. He must have dreamed that it came across great lonely moors, and had a laugh and a moan and a sudden cry in it.

He was cold. The window was open. That was a stupid, careless thing of Donald Macalister to do, and he sober, as he always was, though he could drink deep; on a night of frost like this Death could slip in on the back of a shadow and get his whisper in your ear before you could rise for the stranger.

He stumbled to his feet and closed the window. Then he laid down again, and was nearly asleep, and was confused between an old prayer that rose in his mind like a sunken spar above a wave; and whether to take Widow Sheen a packet of great thick Sabbath peppermints, or a good heavy twist of tobacco; and a strange delightsome memory of Dionaid Macalister's brew of rum and lemons with a touch of old brandy in it; when again he heard that little, wailing, fantastic air, and sat up with the sweat on his brow.

The sweat was not there only because of the little thin music he heard, and it the same, too, as he had heard before; but because the window was wide open again, though the room was so heavy with silence that the pulse of his heart made a noise like a jumping rat.

Rory sat, as still as though he were dead, staring at the window. He could not make out whether the music was faint because it was so far away, or because it was played feebly, like a child's playing, just under the sill.

He was a big, strong man, but he leaned and wavered like the flame of a guttering candle in that slow journey of his from the mattress to the window. He could hear the playing now quite well. It was like the beautiful, sweet song of « Bride bhoidheach muime Chriosda," but with the holy peace out of it, and with a little, evil, hidden laugh flapping like a wing against the blessed name of Christ's foster-mother. But when it sounded under the window, it suddenly was far; and when it was far, the last circling peewit-lilt would be at his ear like a skiffing bat.

When he looked out, and felt the cold night lie on his skin, he could not see because he saw too well. He saw the shores of the sky filled with dancing lights, and the great lighthouse of the moon sending a foam-white stream across the delicate hazes of frost which were too thin to be seen, and only took the sharp edges off the stars, or sometimes splintered them into sudden dazzle. He was like a man in a sail-less, rudderless boat, looking at the skies because he lay face upward and dared not stoop and look into the dark, slipping water alongside.

He saw, too, the hornlike curve of Tom-na-shee black against the blueness, and the inky line of Dalmonadh Moor beyond the plumy mass of Dalibrog woods, and the near meadows where a leveret jumped squealing, and then the bare garden with ragged gooseberry-bushes like scraggy, hunched sheep, and at last the white gravel-walk bordered with the withered roots of pinks and southernwood.

Then he looked from all these great things and these little things to the ground beneath the window. There was nothing there. There was no sound. Not even far away could he hear any faint, devilish music. At least—

Rory shut the window, and went back to his mattress and lay down.

"By the sun an' wind," he exclaimed, "a man gets fear on him nowadays, like a cold in the head when a thaw comes." Then he lay and whistled a blithe catch. For sure, he thought, he would rise at dawn and drown that thirst of his in whatever came first to hand.

Suddenly he stopped whistling, and on the uplift of a lilting turn. In a moment the room was full of old silence again.

Rory turned his head slowly. The window was wide open.

A sob died in his throat. He put his hands to his dry mouth; the back of it was wet with the sweat on his face.

White and shaking, he rose and walked steadily to the window. He looked out and down: there was no one, nothing.

He pulled the ragged cane chair to the sill, and sat there, silent and hopeless.

Soon big tears fell one by one, slowly, down his face.

He understood now. His heart filled with sad, bitter grief and brimmed over, and that was why the tears fell.

It was his hour that had come and opened the window.

He was cold, and as faint with hunger and heavy with thirst as though he had not put a glass to his lips or a bit to his mouth for days instead of for hours; but for all that, he did not feel ill, and he wondered and wondered why he was to die so soon, and he so well-made and handsome, and unmarried too, and now with girls as eager to have him as trouts for a May fly.

And after a time Rory began to dream of that great beauty that had troubled his dreams; and while he thought of it, and the beautiful, sweet wonder of the woman who had it, she whom he had seen sitting in the moonshine on the yellow rock, he heard again the laughing, crying, fall and lilt of that near and far song. But now it troubled him no more.

He stooped, and swung himself out of the window, and at the noise of his feet on the gravel a dog barked. He saw a white hound running swiftly across the pasture beyond him. It was gone in a moment, so swiftly did it run. He heard a second bark, and knew that it came from the old deerhound in the kennel. He wondered where that white hound he had seen came from, and where it was going, and it silent and white and swift as a moonbeam, with head low and in full sleuth.

He put his hand on the sill, and climbed into the room again; lifted the pipes which he or Donald Macalister had thrown down beside the mattress; and again, but stealthily, slipped out of the window.

Rory walked to the deerhound and spoke to it. The dog whimpered, but barked no more. When the piper walked on, and had gone about a score yards, the old hound threw back his head and gave howl upon howl, long and mournful. The cry went from stead to stead; miles and miles away the farm-dogs answered.

Perhaps it was to drown their noise that Rory began to finger his pipes, and at last let a long drone go out like a great humming cockchafer on the blue frosty stillness of the night. The crofters at Moor Edge heard his pibroch as he walked swiftly along the road that leads to Dalmonadh Moor. Some thought it was uncanny; some that one of the pipers had lost his way, or made an early start; one or two wondered if Rory MacAlpine were already on the move, like a hare that could not be long in one form.

The last house was the gamekeeper's, at Dalmonadh Toll, as it was still called. Duncan Grant related next day that he was wakened by the skreigh of the pipes, and knew them for Rory MacAlpine's by the noble, masterly fashion in which drone and chanter gave out their music, and also because that music was the strong, wild, fearsome reel that Rory had played last in the byres, that which he had called "The Reel of the Daughter of Ivor."

"At that," he added, each time he told the tale, "I rose and opened the window, and called to MacAlpine. 'Rory,' I cried, 'is that you?'

"'Ay,' he said, stopping short, an' giving the pipes a lilt.

"'Ay, it's me an' no other, Duncan Grant.'

"'I thought ye would be sleeping sound at Dalibrog?'

"But Rory made no answer to that, and walked on. I called to him in the English: 'Dinna go out on the moor, Rory! Come in, man, an' have a sup o' hot porridge an' a mouthful with them.' But he never turned his head; an' as it was cold an' dark, I said to myself that doited fools must gang their ain gait, an' so turned an' went to my bed again, though I hadn't a wink so long as I could hear Rory playing."

But Duncan Grant was not the last man who heard "The Reel of the Daughter of Ivor."

A mile or more across Dalmonadh Moor the heather-set road forks. One way is a cart-way to Balnaree; the other is the drover's way to Tom-na-shee and the hill countries beyond. It is up this, a mile from the fork, that the Yellow Moonrock rises like a great fang out of purple lips. Some say it is of granite, and some marble, and that it is an old cromlech of the forgotten days; others that it is an unknown substance, a meteoric stone believed to have fallen from the moon.

Not near the Moonrock itself, but five score yards or more away, and perhaps more ancient still, there is a group of three lesser fang-shaped boulders of trap, one with illegible runic writing or signs. These are familiar to some as the Stannin' Stanes; to others, who have the Gaelic, as the Stone Men, or simply as the Stones, or the Stones of Dalmonadh. None knows anything certain of this ancient cromlech, though it is held by scholars to be of Pictish times.

Here a man known as Peter Lamont, though commonly as Peter the Tinker, an idle, homeless vagrant, had taken shelter from the hill-wind which had blown earlier in the night, and had heaped a bed of dry bracken. He was asleep when he heard the wail and hum of the pipes.

He sat up in the shadow of one of the Stones. By the stars he saw that it was still the black of the night, and that dawn would not be astir for three hours or more. Who could be playing the pipes in that lonely place at that hour?

The man was superstitious, and his fears were heightened by his ignorance of what the unseen piper played (and Peter the Tinker prided himself on his knowledge of pipe music) and by the strangeness of it. He remembered, too, where he was. There was not one in a hundred who would lie by night among the Stannin' Stanes, and he had himself been driven to it only by heavy weariness and fear of death from the unsheltered cold. But not even that would have made him lie near the Moonrock. He shivered as memories of wild stories rose ghastly one after the other.

The music came nearer. The tinker crawled forward, and hid behind the Stone next the path, and cautiously, under a tuft of bracken, stared in the direction whence the sound came.

He saw a tall man striding along in full Highland gear, with his face death-white in the moonshine, and his eyes glazed like those of a leistered salmon. It was not till the piper was close that Lamont recognised him as Rory MacAlpine.

He would have spoken—and gladly, in that lonely place, to say nothing of the curiosity that was on him—had it not been for those glazed eyes and that set, death-white face.

The man was fey. He could see that. It was all he could do not to keep away like a rabbit.

Rory MacAlpine passed him, and played till he was close on the Moonrock. Then he stopped, and listened, leaning forward as though straining his eyes to see into the shadow.

He heard nothing, saw nothing, apparently. Slowly he waved a hand across the heather.

Then suddenly the piper began a rapid talking. Peter the Tinker could not hear what he said, perhaps because his own teeth chattered with the fear that was on him.

Once or twice Rory stretched his arms, as though he were asking something, as though he were pleading.

Suddenly he took a step or two forward, and in a loud, shrill voice cried:

"By Holy St. Bride, let there be peace between us, white woman!

"I do not fear you, white woman, because I too am of the race of Ivor:

"My father's father was the son of Ivor mhic Alpein, the son of Ivor the Dark, the son of Ivor Honeymouth, the son of Ruaridh, the son of Ruaridh the Red, of the straight, unbroken line of Ivor the King:

"I will do you no harm, and you will do me no harm, white woman:

"This is the Day of Bride, the day for the daughter of Ivor. It is Rory MacAlpine who is here, of the race of Ivor. I will do you no harm, and you will do me no harm:

"Sure, now, it was you who sang. It was you who sang. It was you who played. It was you who opened my window:

"It was you who came to me in a dream, daughter of Ivor. It was you who put your beauty upon me. Sure, it is that beauty that is my death, and I am hungering and thirsting for it."

Having cried thus, Rory stood, listening, like a crow on a furrow when it sees the wind coming.

The tinker, trembling, crept a little nearer. There was nothing, no one.

Suddenly Rory began singing in a loud, chanting, monotonous voice:

> *"An diugh La' Bride,*
> *Thig nighean Imhir as a choc,*
>   *Cha bean mise do nighean Imhir,*
> *'S cha bhean Imhir dhomh."*

>   *(Today, the day of Bride,*
>   *The daughter of Ivor shall come from the knoll:*
>   *I will not touch the daughter of Ivor,*
>   *Nor shall the daughter of Ivor touch me.)*

Then, bowing low, with fantastic gestures, and with the sweep of his plaid making a shadow like a flying cloud, he sang again:

> *"La' Bride nam brig ban*
> *Thig an rigen ran a tom*
>   *Cha bhoin mise fis an rigen ran,*
> *'S cha bhoin an rigen ran rim."*

>   *(On the day of Bride of the fair locks,*
>   *The noble queen will come from the hill;*
>   *I will not molest the noble queen,*
>   *Nor will the noble queen molest me.)*

"An' I, too, Nighean Imhir," he cried in a voice more loud, more shrill, more plaintive yet, "will be doing now what our own great forbear did, when he made *tabhartas agus twis* to you, so that neither he nor his seed for ever should die of you ; an' I, too, Ruaridh MacDhonuill mhic Alpein, will make offering and incense." And with that Rory stepped back, and lifted the pipes, and flung them at the base of the Yellow Moonrock, where they caught on a jagged spar and burst with a great wailing screech that made the hair rise on the head of Peter the Tinker, where he crouched sick with the white fear.

"That for my *tabhartas*," Rory cried again, as though he were calling to a multitude; "an' as I've no tuts, an' the only incense I have is the smoke out of my pipe, take the pipe an' the tobacco too, an' it's all the smoke I have or am ever like to have now, an' as good incense too as any other, daughter of Ivor."

Suddenly Peter Lamont heard a thin, strange, curling, twisting bit of music, so sweet for all its wildness that cold and hunger went below his heart. It grew louder, and he shook with fear. But when he looked at Rory MacAlpine, and saw him springing to and fro in a dreadful reel, and snapping his fingers and flinging his arms up and down like fails, he could stand no more, but with a screech rose and turned across the heather, and fluttered and fell and fell and fluttered like a wounded snipe.

He lay still once, after a bad fall, for his breath was like a thistledown blown this way and that above his head. It was on a heathery knoll, and he could see the Moonrock yellow-white in the moonshine. The savage lilt of that jigging wild air still rang in his ears, with never a sweetness in it now, though when he listened it grew fair and light-some, and put a spell of joy and longing in him. But he could see nothing of Rory.

He stumbled to his knees and stared. There was something on the road.

He heard a noise as of men struggling. But all he saw was Rory MacAlpine swaying and swinging, now up and now down; and then at last the piper was on his back in the road and tossing like a man in a fit, and screeching with a dreadful voice, "Let me go ! let me go! Take your lips off my mouth! take your lips off my mouth!"

Then, abruptly, there was no sound, but only a dreadful silence; till he heard a rush of feet, and heard the heather-sprigs break and crack, and something went past him like a flash of light.

With a scream he flung himself down the heather knoll, and ran like a driven hare till he came to the white road beyond the moor; and just as dawn was breaking, he fell in a heap at the byre-edge at Dalmonadh Toll, and there Duncan Grant found him an hour later, white and senseless still.

Neither Duncan Grant nor any one else believed Peter Lamont's tale, but at noon the tinker led a reluctant few to the Yellow Moonrock.

The broken pipes still hung on the jagged spar at the base. Half on the path and half on the heather was the body of Rory MacAlpine. He was all but naked to the waist, and his plaid and jacket were as torn and ragged as Lamont's own, and the bits were scattered far and wide.

His lips were blue and swelled. In the hollow of his hairy, twisted throat was a single drop of black blood.

"It's an adder's bite," said Duncan Grant.

None spoke.

THE MOON-SLAVE

Barry Pain

from *Stories in the Dark* (1901)

The Princess Viola had, even in her childhood, an inevitable submission to the dance; a rhythmical madness in her blood answered hotly to the dance music, swaying her, as the wind sways trees, to movements of perfect sympathy and grace.

For the rest, she had her beauty and her long hair, that reached to her knees, and was thought lovable; but she was never very fervent and vivid unless she was dancing; at other times there almost seemed to be a touch of lethargy upon her. Now, when she was sixteen years old, she was betrothed to the Prince Hugo. With others the betrothal was merely a question of state. With her it was merely a question of obedience to the wishes of authority; it had been arranged; Hugo was *comme ci, comme ça*—no god in her eyes; it did not matter. But with Hugo it was quite different—he loved her.

The betrothal was celebrated by a banquet, and afterwards by a dance in the great hall of the palace. From this dance the Princess soon made her escape, quite discontented, and went to the furthest part of the palace gardens, where she could no longer hear the music calling her.

"They are all right," she said to herself as she thought of the men she had left, "but they cannot dance. Mechanically they are all right; they have learned it and don't make childish mistakes; but they are only one-two-three machines. They haven't the inspiration of dancing. It is so different when I dance alone."

She wandered on until she reached an old forsaken maze. It had been planned by a former king. All round it was a high crumbling wall with foxgloves growing on it. The maze itself had all its paths bordered with high opaque hedges; in the very centre was a circular open space with tall pine-trees growing round it. Many years ago the clue to the maze had been lost; it was but rarely now that anyone entered it. Its gravel paths were green with weeds, and in some places the hedges, spreading beyond their borders, had made the way almost impassable.

For a moment or two Viola stood peering in at the gate—a narrow gate with curiously twisted bars of wrought iron surmounted by a heraldic device.

Then the whim seized her to enter the maze and try to find the space in the centre. She opened the gate and went in.

Outside everything was uncannily visible in the light of the full moon, but here in the dark shaded alleys the night was conscious of itself. She soon forgot her purpose, and wandered about quite aimlessly, sometimes forcing her way where the brambles had flung a laced barrier across her path, and a dragging mass of convolvulus struck wet and cool upon her cheek. As chance would have it she suddenly found herself standing under the tall pines, and looking at the open space that formed the goal of the maze. She was pleased that she had got there. Here the ground was carpeted with sand, fine and, as it seemed, beaten hard. From the summer night sky immediately above, the moonlight, unobstructed here, streamed straight down upon the scene.

Viola began to think about dancing. Over the dry, smooth sand her little satin shoes moved easily, stepping and gliding, circling and stepping, as she hummed the tune to which they moved. In the centre of the space she paused, looked at the wall of dark trees all round, at the shining stretches of silvery sand and at the moon above.

"My beautiful, moonlit, lonely, old dancing-room, why did I never find you before?" she cried; "but," she added, "you need music—there must be music here."

In her fantastic mood she stretched her soft, clasped hands upwards towards the moon.

"Sweet moon," she said in a kind of mock prayer, "make your white light come down in music into my dancing-room here, and I will dance most deliciously for you to see." She flung her head backward and let her hands fall; her eyes were half closed, and her mouth was a kissing mouth. "Ah! sweet moon," she whispered, "do this for me, and I will be your slave; I will be what you will."

Quite suddenly the air was filled with the sound of a grand invisible orchestra. Viola did not stop to wonder. To the music of a slow saraband she swayed and postured. In the music there was the regular beat of small drums and a perpetual drone. The air seemed to be filled with the perfume of some bitter spice. Viola could fancy almost that she saw a smoldering camp-fire and heard far off the roar of some desolate wild beast. She let her long hair fall, raising the heavy strands of it in either hand as she moved slowly to the laden music. Slowly her body swayed with drowsy grace, slowly her satin shoes slid over the silver sand.

The music ceased with a clash of cymbals. Viola rubbed her eyes. She fastened her hair up carefully again. Suddenly she looked up, almost imperiously.

"Music! more music!" she cried.

Once more the music came. This time it was a dance of caprice, pelting along over the violin-strings, leaping, laughing, wanton. Again an illusion seemed to cross her eyes. An old king was watching her, a king with the sordid history of the exhaustion of pleasure written on his flaccid face. A hook-nosed courtier by his side settled the ruffles at his wrists and mumbled, "*Ravissant! Quel malheur que la vieillesse!*"[19] It was a strange illusion. Faster and faster she sped to the music, stepping, spinning, pirouetting; the dance was light as thistle-down, fierce as fire, smooth as a rapid stream.

The moment that the music ceased Viola became horribly afraid. She turned and fled away from the moonlit space, through the trees, down the dark alleys of the maze, not heeding in the least which turn she took, and yet she found herself soon at the outside iron gate. From thence she ran through the palace garden, hardly ever pausing to take breath, until she reached the palace itself. In the eastern sky the first signs of dawn were showing; in the palace the festivities were drawing to an end. As she stood alone in the outer hall Prince Hugo came towards her.

"Where have you been, Viola?" he said sternly. "What have you been doing?"

She stamped her little foot.

"I will not be questioned," she replied angrily.

"I have some right to question," he said.

She laughed a little.

"For the first time in my life," she said, "I have been dancing."

He turned away in hopeless silence.

The months passed away. Slowly a great fear came over Viola, a fear that would hardly ever leave her. For every month at the full moon, whether she would or no, she found herself driven to the maze, through its mysterious walks into that strange dancing-room. And when she was there the music began once more, and once more she danced most deliciously for the moon to see. The second time that this happened she had merely thought that it was a recurrence of her own whim, and that the music was but a trick that the imagination had chosen to repeat. The third time frightened her, and she knew that the force that sways the tides had strange power over her. The fear grew as the year fell, for each month the music went on for a longer time— each month some of the pleasure had gone from the dance. On bitter nights in winter the moon called her and she came, when the breath was vapor, and the trees that circled her dancing-room were black bare skeletons, and the frost was cruel. She dared not tell anyone, and yet it was with difficulty that she kept her secret. Somehow chance seemed to favor her, and she always found a way to return from her midnight dance to her own room without being observed. Each month the summons seemed to be more imperious and urgent. Once when she was alone on her knees before the lighted altar in the private chapel of the palace she suddenly felt that the words of the familiar Latin prayer had gone from her memory. She rose to her feet, she sobbed bitterly, but the call had come and she could not resist it. She passed out of the chapel and down the palace-gardens. How madly she danced that night!

[19] "Ravishing! What a misfortune old age is!"

She was to be married in the spring. She began to be more gentle with Hugo now. She had a blind hope that when they were married she might be able to tell him about it, and he might be able to protect her, for she had always known him to be fearless. She could not love him, but she tried to be good to him. One day he mentioned to her that he had tried to find his way to the centre of the maze, and had failed. She smiled faintly. If only she could fail! But she never did.

On the night before the wedding, day she had gone to bed and slept peacefully, thinking with her last waking moments of Hugo. Overhead the full moon came up the sky. Quite suddenly Viola was wakened with the impulse to fly to the dancing-room. It seemed to bid her hasten with breathless speed. She flung a cloak around her, slipped her naked feet into her dancing-shoes, and hurried forth. No one saw her or heard her—on the marble staircase of the palace, on down the terraces of the garden, she ran as fast as she could. A thorn-plant caught in her cloak, but she sped on, tearing it free; a sharp stone cut through the satin of one shoe, and her foot was wounded and bleeding, but she sped on. As the pebble that is flung from the cliff must fall until it reaches the sea, as the white ghost-moth must come in from cool hedges and scented darkness to a burning death in the lamp by which you sit so late—so Viola had no choice. The moon called her. The moon drew her to that circle of hard, bright sand and the pitiless music.

It was brilliant, rapid music tonight. Viola threw off her cloak and danced. As she did so, she saw that a shadow lay over a fragment of the moon's edge. It was the night of a total eclipse. She heeded it not. The intoxication of the dance was on her. She was all in white; even her face was pale in the moonlight. Every movement was full of poetry and grace.

The music would not stop. She had grown deathly weary. It seemed to her that she had been dancing for hours, and the shadow had nearly covered the moon's face, so that it was almost dark. She could hardly see the trees around her. She went on dancing, stepping, spinning, pirouetting, held by the merciless music.

It stopped at last, just when the shadow had quite covered the moon's face, and all was dark. But it stopped only for a moment, and then began again. This time it was a slow, passionate waltz. It was useless to resist; she began to dance once more. As she did so she uttered a sudden shrill scream of horror, for in the dead darkness a hot hand had caught her own and whirled her round, *and she was no longer dancing alone.*

The search for the missing Princess lasted during the whole of the following day. In the evening Prince Hugo, his face anxious and firmly set, passed in his search the iron gate of the maze, and noticed on the stones beside it the stain of a drop of blood. Within the gate was another stain. He followed this clue, which had been left by Viola's wounded foot, until he reached that open space in the centre that had served Viola for her dancing-room. It was quite empty. He noticed that the sand round the edges was all worn down, as though someone had danced there, round and round, for a long time. But no separate footprint was distinguishable there. Just outside this track, however, he saw two footprints clearly defined close together: one was the print of a tiny satin shoe; the other was the print of a large naked foot—a cloven foot.

MAY DAY EVE

Algernon Blackwood

from *The Listener and Other Stories* (1907)

I.

It was in the spring when I at last found time from the hospital work to visit my friend, the old folklorist, in his country isolation, and I rather chuckled to myself, because in my bag I was taking down a book that utterly refuted all his tiresome pet theories of magic and the powers of the soul.

These theories were many and various, and had often troubled me. In the first place, I scorned them for professional reasons, and, in the second, because I had never been able to argue quite well enough to convince or to shake his faith, in even the smallest details, and any scientific knowledge I brought to bear only fed him with confirmatory data. To find such a book, therefore, and to know that it was safely in my bag, wrapped up in brown paper and addressed to him, was a deep and satisfactory joy, and I speculated a good deal during the journey how he would deal with the overwhelming arguments it contained against the existence of any important region outside the world of sensory perceptions.

Speculative, too, I was whether his visionary habits and absorbing experiments would permit him to remember my arrival at all, and I was accordingly relieved to hear from the solitary porter that the "professor" had sent a "veeckle" to meet me, and that I was thus free to send my bag and walk the four miles to the house across the hills.

It was a calm, windless evening, just after sunset, the air warm and scented, and delightfully still. The train, already sinking into distance, carried away with it the noise of crowds and cities and the last suggestions of the stressful life behind me, and from the little station on the moorland I stepped at once into the world of silent, growing things, tinkling sheep-bells, shepherds, and wild, desolate spaces.

My path lay diagonally across the turfy hills. It slanted a mile or so to the summit, wandered vaguely another two miles among gorse-bushes along the crest, passed Tom Bassett's cottage by the pines, and then dropped sharply down on the other side through rather thin woods to the ancient house where the old folklorist lived and dreamed himself into his impossible world of theory and fantasy. I fell to thinking busily about him during the first part of the ascent, and convinced myself, as usual, that, but for his generosity to the poor, and his benign aspect, the peasantry must undoubtedly have regarded him as a wizard who speculated in souls and had dark dealings with the world of faery.

The path I knew tolerably well. I had already walked it once before—a winter's day some years ago—and from the cottage onward felt sure of my way; but for the first mile or so there were so many cross cattle-tracks, and the light had become so dim that I felt it wise to inquire more particularly. And this I was fortunately able to do of a man who with astonishing suddenness rose from the grass where he had been lying behind a clump of bushes, and passed a few yards in front of me at a high pace downhill toward the darkening valley.

He was in such a state of hurry that I called out loudly to him, fearing to be too late, but on hearing my voice he turned sharply, and seemed to arrive almost at once beside me. In a single instant he was standing there, quite close, looking, with a smile and a certain expression of curiosity, I thought, into my face. I remember thinking that his features, pale and wholly untanned, were rather wonderful for a countryman, and that the eyes were those of a foreigner; his great swiftness, too, gave me a distinct sensation—something almost of a start—though I knew my vision was at fault at the best of times, and of course especially so in the deceptive twilight of the open hillside.

Moreover—as the way often is with such instructions—the words did not stay in my mind very clearly after he had uttered them, and the rapid, panther-like movements of the man as he quickly vanished down the hill again left me with little more than a sweeping gesture indicating the line I was to follow. No doubt his sudden rising from behind the gorse-bush, his curious swiftness, and the way he peered into my face, and even touched me on the shoulder, all combined to distract my attention somewhat from the actual words he used; and the fact that I was traveling at a wrong angle, and should have come out a mile too far to the right, helped to complete my feeling that his gesture, pointing the way, was sufficient.

On the crest of the ridge, panting a little with the unwonted exertion, I lay down to rest a moment on the grass beside a flaming yellow gorse-bush. There was still a good hour before I should be looked for at the house; the grass was very soft, the peace and silence soothing. I lingered, and lit a cigarette. And it was just then, I think, that my subconscious memory gave back the words, the actual words, the man had spoken, and the heavy significance of the personal pronoun, as he had emphasized it in his odd foreign voice, touched me with a sense of vague amusement: "The safest way for you now," he had said, as though I was so obviously a townsman and might be in danger on the lonely hills after dark. And the quick way he had reached my side, and then slipped off again like a shadow down the steep slope, completed a definite little picture in my mind. Then other thoughts and memories rose up and formed a series of pictures, following each other in rapid succession, and forming a chain of reflections undirected by the will and without purpose or meaning. I fell, that is, into a pleasant reverie.

Below me, and infinitely far away, it seemed, the valley lay silent under a veil of blue evening haze, the lower end losing itself among darkening hills whose peaks rose here and there like giant plumes that would surely nod their great heads and call to one another once the final shadows were down. The village lay, a misty patch, in which lights already twinkled. A sound of rooks faintly cawing, of sea-gulls crying far up in the sky, and of dogs barking at a great distance rose up out of the general murmur of evening voices. Odors of farm and field and open spaces stole to my nostrils, and everything contributed to the feeling that I lay on the top of the world, nothing between me and the stars, and that all the huge, free things of the earth—hills, valleys, woods, and sloping fields— lay breathing deeply about me.

A few sea-gulls—in daytime hereabouts they fill the air—still circled and wheeled within range of sight, uttering from time to time sharp, petulant cries; and far in the distance there was just visible a shadowy line that showed where the sea lay.

Then, as I lay gazing dreamily into this still pool of shadows at my feet, something rose up, something sheet-like, vast, imponderable, off the whole surface of the mapped-out country, moved with incredible swiftness down the valley, and in a single instant climbed the hill where I lay and swept by me, yet without hurry, and in a sense without speed. Veils in this way rose one after another, filling the cups between the hills, shrouding alike fields, village, and hillside as they passed, and settled down somewhere into the gloom behind me over the ridge, or slipped off like vapor into the sky.

Whether it was actually mist rising from the surface of the fast-cooling ground, or merely the earth

giving up her heat to the night, I could not determine. The coming of the darkness is ever a series of mysteries. I only know that this indescribable vast stirring of the landscape seemed to me as though the earth were unfolding immense sable wings from her sides, and lifting them for silent, gigantic strokes so that she might fly more swiftly from the sun into the night. The darkness, at any rate, did drop down over everything very soon afterward, and I rose up hastily to follow my pathway, realizing with a degree of wonder strangely new to me the magic of twilight, the blue open depths into the valley below, and the pale yellow heights of the watery sky above.

I walked rapidly, a sense of chilliness about me, and soon lost sight of the valley altogether as I got upon the ridge proper of these lonely and desolate hills.

It could not have been more than fifteen minutes that I lay there in reverie, yet the weather, I at once noticed, had changed very abruptly, for mist was seething here and there about me, rising somewhere from smaller valleys in the hills beyond, and obscuring the path, while overhead there was plainly a sound of wind tearing past, far up, with a sound of high shouting. A moment before it had been the stillness of a warm spring night, yet now everything had changed; wet mist coated me, raindrops smartly stung my face, and a gusty wind, descending out of cool heights, began to strike and buffet me, so that I buttoned my coat and pressed my hat more firmly upon my head.

The change was really this—and it came to me for the first time in my life with the power of a real conviction—that everything about me seemed to have become suddenly alive.

It came oddly upon me—prosaic, matter-of-fact, materialistic doctor that I was—this realization that the world about me had somehow stirred into life; oddly, I say, because Nature to me had always been merely a more or less definite arrangement of measurement, weight, and color, and this new presentation of it was utterly foreign to my temperament. A valley to me was always a valley; a hill, merely a hill; a field, so many acres of flat surface, grass or ploughed, drained well or drained ill; whereas now, with startling vividness, came the strange, haunting idea that after all they could be something more than valley, hill, and field; that what I had hitherto perceived by these names were only the veils of something that lay concealed within, something alive. In a word, that the poetic sense I had always rather sneered at, in others, or explained away with some shallow physiological label, had apparently suddenly opened up in myself without any obvious cause.

And, the more I puzzled over it, the more I began to realize that its genesis dated from those few minutes of reverie lying under the gorse-bush (reverie, a thing I had never before in all my life indulged in!), or, now that I came to reflect more accurately, from my brief interview with that wild-eyed, swift-moving, shadowy man of whom I had first inquired the way.

I recalled my singular fancy that veils were lifting off the surface of the hills and fields, and a tremor of excitement accompanied the memory. Such a thing had never before been possible to my practical intelligence, and it made me feel suspicious—suspicious about myself. I stood still a moment—I looked about me into the gathering mist, above me to the vanishing stars, below me to the hidden valley, and then sent an urgent summons to my individuality, as I had always known it, to arrest and chase these undesirable fancies.

But I called in vain. No answer came. Anxiously, hurriedly, confusedly, too, I searched for my normal self, but could not find it; and this failure to respond induced in me a sense of uneasiness that touched very nearly upon the borders of alarm.

I pushed on faster and faster along the turfy track among the gorse-bushes with a dread that I might lose the way altogether, and a sudden desire to reach home as soon as might be. Then, without warning, I emerged unexpectedly into clear air again, and the vapor swept past me in a rushing wall and rose into the sky. Anew I saw the lights of the village behind me in the depths, here and there a line of smoke rising against the pale yellow sky, and stars overhead peering down through thin wispy clouds that stretched their wind-signs across the night.

After all, it had been nothing but a stray bit of sea-fog driving up from the coast, for the other side of the hills, I remembered, dipped their chalk cliffs straight into the sea, and strange lost winds must often come a-wandering this way with the sharp changes of temperature about sunset. None the less, it was disconcerting to know that mist and storm lay hiding within possible reach, and I walked on smartly for a sight of Tom Bassett's cottage and the lights of the Manor House in the valley a short mile beyond.

The clearing of the air, however, lasted but a very brief while, and vapor was soon rising about me as before, hiding the path and making bushes and stone

walls look like running shadows. It came, driven apparently, by little independent winds up the many side gullies, and it was very cold, touching my skin like a wet sheet. Curious great shapes, too, it assumed as the wind worked to and fro through it: forms of men and animals; grotesque, giant outlines; ever shifting and running along the ground with silent feet, or leaping into the air with sharp cries as the gusts twisted them inwardly and lent them voice. More and more I pushed my pace, and more and more darkness and vapor obliterated the landscape. The going was not otherwise difficult, and here and there cowslips glimmered in patches of dancing yellow, while the springy turf made it easy to keep up speed; yet in the gloom I frequently tripped and plunged into prickly gorse near the ground, so that from shin to knee was soon a-tingle with sharp pain. Odd puffs and spits of rain stung my face, and the periods of utter stillness were always followed by little shouting gusts of wind, each time from a new direction. Troubled is perhaps too strong a word, but flustered I certainly was; and though I recognized that it was due to my being in an environment so remote from the town life I was accustomed to, I found it impossible to stifle altogether the feeling of malaise that had crept into my heart, and I looked about with increasing eagerness for the lighted windows of Bassett's cottage.

More and more, little pin-pricks of distress and confusion accumulated, adding to my realization of being away from streets and shop-windows, and things I could classify and deal with. The mist, too, distorted as well as concealed, played tricks with sounds as well as with sights. And, once or twice, when I stumbled upon some crouching sheep, they got up without the customary alarm and hurry of sheep, and moved off slowly into the darkness, but in such a singular way that I could almost have sworn they were not sheep at all, but human beings crawling on all-fours, looking back and grimacing at me over their shoulders as they went. On these occasions—for there were more than one—I never could get close enough to feel their woolly wet backs, as I should have liked to do; and the sound of their tinkling bells came faintly through the mist, sometimes from one direction, sometimes from another, sometimes all round me as though a whole flock surrounded me; and I found it impossible to analyse or explain the idea I received that they were not sheep-bells at all, but something quite different.

But mist and darkness, and a certain confusion of the senses caused by the excitement of an utterly strange environment, can account for a great deal. I pushed on quickly. The conviction that I had strayed from the route grew, nevertheless, for occasionally there was a great commotion of seagulls about me, as though I had disturbed them in their sleeping-places. The air filled with their plaintive cries, and I heard the rushing of multitudinous wings, sometimes very close to my head, but always invisible owing to the mist. And once, above the swishing of the wet wind through the gorse-bushes, I was sure I caught the faint thunder of the sea and the distant crashing of waves rolling up some steep-throated gully in the cliffs. I went cautiously after this, and altered my course a little away from the direction of the sound.

Yet, increasingly all the time, it came to me how the cries of the sea-birds sounded like laughter, and how the everlasting wind blew and drove about me with a purpose, and how the low bushes persistently took the shape of stooping people, moving stealthily past me, and how the mist more and more resembled huge protean figures escorting me across the desolate hills, silently, with immense footsteps. For the inanimate world now touched my awakened poetic sense in a manner hitherto unguided, and became fraught with the pregnant messages of a dimly concealed life. I readily understood, for the first time, how easily a superstitious peasantry might people their world, and how even an educated mind might favor an atmosphere of legend. I stumbled along, looking anxiously for the lights of the cottage.

Suddenly, as a shape of writhing mist whirled past, I received so direct a stroke of wind that it was palpably a blow in the face. Something swept by with a shrill cry into the darkness. It was impossible to prevent jumping to one side and raising an arm by way of protection, and I was only just quick enough to catch a glimpse of the sea-gull as it raced past, with suddenly altered flight, beating its powerful wings over my head. Its white body looked enormous as the mist swallowed it. At the same moment a gust tore my hat from my head and flung the flap of my coat across my eyes. But I was well-trained by this time, and made a quick dash after the retreating black object, only to find on overtaking it that I held a prickly branch of gorse. The wind combed my hair viciously. Then, out of a corner of my eye, I saw my hat still rolling, and grabbed swiftly at it; but just as I closed on it, the real hat passed in front of me, turning over in the wind like a ball, and I instantly released my first capture to chase it. Before it was within reach, another one shot between my feet so that I stepped on it. The grass

seemed covered with moving hats, yet each one, when I seized it, turned into a piece of wood, or a tiny gorse-bush, or a black rabbit hole, till my hands were scored with prickles and running blood. In the darkness, I reflected, all objects looked alike, as though by general conspiracy.

I straightened up and took a long breath, mopping the blood with my handkerchief. Then something tapped at my feet, and on looking down, there was the hat within easy reach, and I stooped down and put it on my head again. Of course, there were a dozen ways of explaining my confusion and stupidity, and I walked along wondering which to select. My eyesight, for one thing—and under such conditions why seek further? It was nothing, after all, and the dizziness was a momentary effect caused by the effort and stooping.

But for all that, I shouted aloud, on the chance that a wandering shepherd might hear me; and of course no answer came, for it was like calling in a padded room, and the mist suffocated my voice and killed its resonance.

It was really very discouraging: I was cold and wet and hungry; my legs and clothes torn by the gorse, my hands scratched and bleeding; the wind brought water to my eyes by its constant buffeting, and my skin was numb from contact with the chill mist. Fortunately I had matches, and after some difficulty, by crouching under a wall, I caught a swift glimpse of my watch, and saw that it was but little after eight o'clock. Supper I knew was at nine, and I was surely over halfway by this time. But here again was another instance of the way everything seemed in a conspiracy against me to appear otherwise than ordinary, for in the gleam of the match my watch-glass showed as the face of a little old gray man, uncommonly like the folklorist himself, peering up at me with an expression of whimsical laughter. My own reflection it could not possibly have been, for I am clean-shaven, and this face looked up at me through a running tangle of gray hair. Yet a second and third match revealed only the white surface with the thin black hands moving across it.

II.

And it was at this point, I well remember, that I reached what was for me the true heart of the adventure, the little fragment of real experience I learned from it and took back with me to my doctor's life in London, and that has remained with me ever since, and helped me to a new sympathetic insight into the intricacies of certain curious mental cases I had never before really understood.

For it was sufficiently obvious by now that a curious change had been going forward in me for some time, dating, so far as I could focus my thoughts sufficiently to analyze, from the moment of my speech with that hurrying man of shadow on the hillside. And the first deliberate manifestation of the change, now that I looked back, was surely the awakening in my prosaic being of the "poetic thrill"; my sudden amazing appreciation of the world around me as something alive. From that moment the change in me had worked ahead subtly, swiftly. Yet, so natural had been the beginning of it, that although it was a radically new departure for my temperament, I was hardly aware at first of what had actually come about;

and it was only now, after so many encounters, that I was forced at length to acknowledge it.

It came the more forcibly too, because my very commonplace ideas of beauty had hitherto always been associated with sunshine and crude effects; yet here this new revelation leaped to me out of wind and mist and desolation on a lonely hillside, out of night, darkness, and discomfort. New values rushed upon me from all sides. Everything had changed, and the very simplicity with which the new values presented themselves proved to me how profound the change, the readjustment, had been. In such trivial things the evidence had come that I was not aware of it until repetition forced my attention: the veils rising from valley and hill; the mountain tops as personalities that shout or murmur in the darkness; the crying of the sea birds and of the living, purposeful wind; above all, the feeling that Nature about me was instinct with a life differing from my own in degree rather than in kind; everything, from the conspiracy of the gorse-bushes to the disappearing hat, showed that a fundamental attitude of mind in me had changed—and changed, too, without my knowledge or consent.

Moreover, at the same time the deep sadness of beauty had entered my heart like a stroke; for all this mystery and loveliness, I realized poignantly was utterly independent and careless of me, as me; and that while I must pass, decay, grow old, these manifestations would remain for ever young and unalterably potent. And thus gradually had I become permeated with the recognition of a region hitherto unknown to me, and that I had always depreciated in others and especially, it now occurred to me, in my friend the old folklorist.

Here surely, I thought, was the beginning of conditions which, carried a little further, must become pathogenic. That the change was real and pregnant I had no doubt whatever. My consciousness was expanding and I had caught it in the very act. I had of course read much concerning the changes of personality, swift, kaleidoscopic—had come across something of it in my practice—and had listened to the folklorist holding forth like a man inspired upon ways and means of reaching concealed regions of the human consciousness, and opening it to the knowledge of things called magical, so that one became free of a larger universe. But it was only now for the first time, on these bare hills, in touch with the wind and the rain, that I realized in how simple a fashion the frontiers of consciousness could shift this way and that, or with what touch of genuine awe the certainty might come that one stood on the borderland of new, untried, perhaps dangerous, experiences.

At any rate, it did now come to me that my consciousness had shifted its frontiers very considerably, and that whatever might happen must seem not abnormal, but quite simple and inevitable, and of course utterly true. This very simplicity, however, doing no violence to my being, brought with it none the less a sense of dread and discomfort; and my dim awareness that unknown possibilities were about me in the night puzzled and distressed me perhaps more than I cared to admit.

III.

All this that takes so long to describe became apparent to me in a few seconds. What I had always despised ascended the throne.

But with the finding of Bassett's cottage, as a signpost close to home, my former sang-froid, my stupidity, would doubtless return, and my relief was therefore considerable when at length a faint gleam of light appeared through the mist, against which the square dark shadow of the chimney-line pointed upwards. After all, I had not strayed so very far out of the way. Now I could definitely ascertain where I was wrong.

Quickening my pace, I scrambled over a broken stone wall, and almost ran across the open bit of grass to the door. One moment the black outline of the cottage was there in front of me, and the next, when I stood actually against it—there was nothing! I laughed to think how utterly I had been deceived. Yet not utterly, for as I groped back again over the wall, the cottage loomed up a little to the left, with its windows lighted and friendly, and I had only been mistaken in my angle of approach after all. Yet again, as I hurried to the door, the mist drove past and thickened a second time—and the cottage was not where I had seen it!

My confusion increased a lot after that. I scrambled about in all directions, rather foolishly hurried, and over countless stone walls it seemed, and completely dazed as to the true points of the compass. Then suddenly, just when a kind of despair came over me, the cottage stood there solidly before my eyes, and I found myself not two feet from the door. Was ever mist before so deceptive? And there, just behind it, I made out the row of pines like a dark wave breaking through the night. I sniffed the wet resinous odor with joy, and a genuine thrill ran through me as I saw the unmistakable yellow light of the windows. At last I was near home and my troubles would soon be over.

A cloud of birds rose with shrill cries off the roof and whirled into the darkness when I knocked with my stick on the door, and human voices, I was almost certain, mingled somewhere with them, though it was impossible to tell whether they were within the cottage or outside. It all sounded confusedly with a rush of air like a little whirlwind, and I stood there rather alarmed at the clamor of my knocking. By way, too, of further proof that my imagination had awakened, the significance of that knocking at the door set something vibrating within me that most surely had never vibrated before, so that I suddenly realized with what atmosphere of mystical suggestion is the mere act of knocking surrounded—knocking at a door— both for him who knocks, wondering what shall be revealed on opening, and for him who stands within, waiting for the summons of the knocker. I only know that I hesitated a lot before making up my mind to knock a second time.

And, anyhow, what happened subsequently came in a sort of haze. Words and memory both failed me when I try to record it truthfully, so that even the faces are difficult to visualize again, the words almost impossible to hear.

Before I knew it the door was open and before I could frame the words of my first brief question, I was within the threshold, and the door was shut behind me.

I had expected the little dark and narrow hallway of a cottage, oppressive of air and odor, but instead I came straight into a room that was full of light and full of—people. And the air tasted like the air about a mountain-top.

To the end I never saw what produced the light, nor understood how so many men and women found space to move comfortably to and fro, and pass each other as they did, within the confines of those four walls. An uncomfortable sense of having intruded upon some private gathering was, I think, my first emotion; though how the poverty-stricken countryside could have produced such an assemblage puzzled me beyond belief. And my second emotion—if there was any division at all in the wave of wonder that fairly drenched me—was feeling a sort of glory in the presence of such an atmosphere of splendid and vital youth. Everything vibrated, quivered, shook about me, and I almost felt myself as an aged and decrepit man by comparison.

I know my heart gave a great fiery leap as I saw them, for the faces that met me were fine, vigorous, and comely, while burning everywhere through their ripe maturity shone the arduous of youth and a kind of deathless enthusiasm. Old, yet eternally young they were, as rivers and mountains count their years by thousands, yet remain ever youthful; and the first effect of all those pairs of eyes lifted to meet my own was to send a whirlwind of unknown thrills about my heart and make me catch my breath with mingled terror and delight. A fear of death, and at the same time a sensation of touching something vast and eternal that could never die, surged through me.

A deep hush followed my entrance as all turned to look at me. They stood, men and women, grouped about a table, and something about them—not their size alone—conveyed the impression of being gigantic, giving me strangely novel realizations of freedom, power, and immense existence more or less than human.

I can only record my thoughts and impressions as they came to me and as I dimly now remember them. I had expected to see old Tom Bassett crouching half asleep over a peat fire, a dim lamp on the table beside him, and instead this assembly of tall and splendid men and women stood there to greet me, and stood in silence. It was little wonder that at first the ready question died upon my lips, and I almost forgot the words of my own language.

"I thought this was Tom Bassett's cottage!" I managed to ask at length, and looked straight at the man nearest me across the table. He had wild hair falling about his shoulders and a face of clear beauty. His eyes, too, like all the rest, seemed shrouded by something veil-like that reminded me of the shadowy man of whom I had first inquired the way. They were shaded—and for some reason I was glad they were.

At the sound of my voice, unreal and thin, there was a general movement throughout the room, as though everyone changed places, passing each other like those shapes of fluid sort I had seen outside in the mist. But no answer came. It seemed to me that the mist even penetrated into the room about me and spread inwardly over my thoughts.

"Is this the way to the Manor House?" I asked again, louder, fighting my inward confusion and weakness. "Can no one tell me?"

Then apparently everyone began to answer at once, or rather, not to answer directly, but to speak to each other in such a way that I could easily overhear. The voices of the men were deep, and of the women wonderfully musical, with a slow rhythm like that of the sea, or of the wind through the pine-trees outside. But the unsatisfactory nature of what they said only helped to increase my sense of confusion and dismay.

"Yes," said one; "Tom Bassett was here for a while with the sheep, but his home was not here."

"He asks the way to a house when he does not even know the way to his own mind!" another voice said, sounding overhead it seemed.

"And could he recognize the signs if we told him?" came in the singing tones of a woman's voice close behind me.

And then, with a noise more like running water, or wind in the wings of birds, than anything else I could liken it to, came several voices together:

"And what sort of way does he seek? The splendid way, or merely the easy?"

"Or the short way of fools!"

"But he must have some credentials, or he never could have got as far as this," came from another.

A laugh ran round the room at this, though what there was to laugh at I could not imagine. It sounded like wind rushing about the hills. I got the impression too that the roof was somehow open to the sky, for their laughter had such a spacious quality in it, and the air was so cool and fresh, and moving about in currents and waves.

"It was I who showed him the way," cried a voice belonging to someone who was looking straight into my face over the table. "It was the safest way for him once he had got so far—"

I looked up and met his eye, and the sentence remained unfinished. It was the hurrying, shadowy man of the hillside. He had the same shifting outline as the others now, and the same veiled and shaded eyes, and as I looked the sense of terror stirred and grew in me. I had come in to ask for help, but now I was only anxious to be free of them all and out again in the rain and darkness on the moor. Thoughts of escape filled my brain, and I searched quickly for the door through which I had entered. But nowhere could I discover it again. The walls were bare; not even the windows were visible. And the room seemed to fill and empty of these figures as the waves of the sea fill and empty a cavern, crowding one upon another, yet never occupying more space, or less. So the coming and going of these men and women always evaded me.

And my terror became simply a terror that the veils of their eyes might lift, and that they would look at me with their clear, naked sight. I became horribly aware of their eyes. It was not that I felt them evil, but that I feared the new depths in me their merciless and terrible insight would stir into life. My consciousness had expanded quite enough for one night! I must escape at all costs and claim my own self again, however limited. I must have sanity, even if with limitations, but sanity at any price.

But meanwhile, though I tried hard to find my voice again, there came nothing but a thin piping sound that was like reeds whistling where winds meet about a corner. My throat was contracted, and I could only produce the smallest and most ridiculous of noises. The power of movement, too, was far less than when I first came in, and every moment it became more difficult to use my muscles, so that I stood there, stiff and awkward, face to face with this assemblage of shifting, wonderful people.

"And now," continued the voice of the man who had last spoken, "and now the safest way for him will be through the other door, where he shall see that which he may more easily understand."

With a great effort I regained the power of movement, while at the same time a burst of anger and a determination to be done with it all and to overcome my dreadful confusion drove me forward.

He saw me coming, of course, and the others indeed opened up and made a way for me, shifting to one side or the other whenever I came too near them, and never allowing me to touch them. But at last, when I was close in front of the man, ready both to speak and act, he was no longer there. I never saw the actual change—but instead of a man it was a woman! And when I turned with amazement, I saw that the other occupants walking like figures in some ancient ceremony, were moving slowly toward the far end of the room. One by one, as they filed past, they raised their calm, passionless faces to mine, immensely vital, proud, austere, and then, without further word or gesture, they opened the door I had lost and disappeared through it one by one into the darkness of the night beyond. And as they went it seemed that the mist swallowed them up and a gust of wind caught them away, and the light also went with them, leaving me alone with the figure who had last spoken.

Moreover it was just here that a most disquieting thought flashed through my brain with unreasoning conviction, shaking my personality, as it were, to the foundations: viz., that I had hitherto been spending my life in the pursuit of false knowledge, in the mere classifying and labelling of effects, the analysis of results, scientific so called; whereas it was the folklorist, and such like, who with their dreams and prayers were all the time on the path of real knowledge, the trail of causes; that the one was merely adding to the mechanical comfort and safety of the body, ultimately degrading the highest part of man, and never advancing the type, while the other—but then I had never yet believed in a soul—and now was no time to begin, terror or no terror. Clearly, my thoughts were wandering.

IV.

It was at this moment the sound of the purring first reached me—deep, guttural purring—that made me think at once of some large concealed animal. It was precisely what I had heard many a time at the Zoological Gardens, and I had visions of cows chewing the cud, or horses munching hay in a stall outside the cottage. It was certainly an animal sound, and one of pleasure and contentment.

Semi-darkness filled the room. Only a very faint moonlight, struggling through the mist, came through the window, and I moved back instinctively toward the support of the wall against my back. Somewhere, through openings, came the sound of the night driving over the roof, and far above I had visions of those everlasting winds streaming by with clouds as large as continents on their wings. Something in me wanted to sing and shout, but something else in me at the same time was in a very vivid state of unreasoning terror. I felt immense, yet tiny, confident, yet timid; a part of huge, universal forces, yet an utterly small, personal, and very limited being.

In the corner of the room on my right stood the woman. Her face was hid by a mass of tumbling hair,

that made me think of living grasses on a field in June. Thus her head was partially turned from me, and the moonlight, catching her outline, just revealed it against the wall like an impressionist picture. Strange hidden memories stirred in the depths of me, and for a moment I felt that I knew all about her. I stared about me quickly, nervously, trying to take in everything at once. Then the purring sound grew much louder and closer, and I forgot my notion that this woman was no stranger to me and that I knew her as well as I knew myself. That purring thing was in the room close beside me. Between us two, indeed, it was, for I now saw that her arm nearest to me was raised, and that she was pointing to the wall in front of us.

Following the direction of her hand, I saw that the wall was transparent, and that I could see through a portion of it into a small square space beyond, as though I was looking through gauze instead of bricks. This small inner space was lighted, and on stooping down I saw that it was a sort of cupboard or cell-like cage let into the wall. The thing that purred was there in the centre of it.

I looked closer. It was a being, apparently a human being, crouched down in its narrow cage, feeding. I saw the body stooping over a quantity of coarse-looking, piled-up substance that was evidently food. It was like a man huddled up. There it squatted, happy and contented, with the minimum of air, light, and space, dully satisfied with its prisoned cage behind the bars, utterly unconscious of the vast world about it, grunting with pleasure, purring like a great cat, scornfully ignorant of what might lie beyond. The cell, moreover, I saw was a perfect masterpiece of mechanical contrivance and inventive ingenuity—the very last word in comfort, safety and scientific skill. I was in the act of trying to fit in my memory some of the details of its construction and arrangement, when I made a chance noise, and at once became too agitated to note carefully what I saw. For at the noise the creature turned, and I saw that it was a human being—a man. I was aware of a face close against my own as it pressed forward, but a face with embryonic features impossible to describe and utterly loathsome, with eyes, ears, nose and skin, only just sufficiently alive and developed to transfer the minimum of gross sensation to the brain. The mouth, however, was large and thick-lipped, and the jaws were still moving in the act of slow mastication.

I shrank back, shuddering with mingled pity and disgust, and at the same moment the woman beside me called me softly by my own name. She had moved forward a little so that she stood quite close to me, full in the thin stream of moonlight that fell across the floor, and I was conscious of a swift transition from hell to heaven as my gaze passed from that embryonic visage to a countenance so refined, so majestic, so divinely sensitive in its strength, that it was like turning from the face of a devil to look upon the features of a goddess.

At the same instant I was aware that both beings—the creature and the woman—were moving rapidly toward me.

A pain like a sharp sword dived deep down into me and twisted horribly through my heart, for as I saw them coming I realized in one swift moment of terrible intuition that they had their life in me, that they were born of my own being, and were indeed projections of myself. They were portions of my consciousness projected outwardly into objectivity, and their degree of reality was just as great as that of any other part of me.

With a dreadful swiftness they rushed toward me, and in a single second had merged themselves into my own being; and I understood in some marvelous manner beyond the possibility of doubt that they were symbolic of my own soul: the dull animal part of me that had hitherto acknowledged nothing beyond its cage of minute sensations, and the higher part, almost out of reach, and in touch with the stars, that for the first time had feebly awakened into life during my journey over the hill.

V.

I forget altogether how it was that I escaped, whether by the window or the door. I only know I found myself a moment later making great speed over the moor, followed by screaming birds and shouting winds, straight on the track downhill toward the Manor House. Something must have guided me, for I went with the instinct of an animal, having no uncertainties as to turnings, and saw the welcome lights of windows before I had covered another mile. And all the way I felt as though a great sluice gate had been opened to let a flood of new perceptions rush like a sea over my inner being, so that I was half ashamed and half delighted, partly angry, yet partly happy.

Servants met me at the door, several of them, and I was aware at once of an atmosphere of commotion in the house. I arrived breathless and hatless, wet to the skin, my hands scratched and my boots caked with mud.

"We made sure you were lost, sir," I heard the old butler say, and I heard my own reply, faintly, like the voice of someone else:

"I thought so too."

A minute later I found myself in the study, with the old folklorist standing opposite. In his hands he held the book I had brought down for him in my bag, ready addressed. There was a curious smile on his face.

"It never occurred to me that you would dare to walk—tonight of all nights," he was saying.

I stared without a word. I was bursting with the desire to tell him something of what had happened and try to be patient with his explanations, but when I sought for words and sentences my story seemed suddenly flat and pointless, and the details of my adventure began to evaporate and melt away, and seemed hard to remember.

"I had an exciting walk," I stammered, still a little breathless from running. "The weather was all right when I started from the station."

"The weather is all right still," he said, "though you may have found some evening mist on the top of the hills. But it's not that I meant."

"What then?"

"I meant," he said, still laughing quizzically, "that you were a very brave man to walk tonight over the enchanted hills, because this is May Day eve, and on May Day eve, you know, They have power over the minds of men, and can put glamour upon the imagination—"

"Who—'they?' What do you mean?"

He put my book down on the table beside him and looked quietly for a moment into my eyes, and as he did so the memory of my adventure began to revive in detail, and I thought quickly of the shadowy man who had shown me the way first. What could it have been in the face of the old folklorist that made me think of this man? A dozen things ran like flashes through my excited mind, and while I attempted to seize them I heard the old man's voice continue. He seemed to be talking to himself as much as to me.

"The elemental beings you have always scoffed at, of course; they who operate ceaselessly behind the screen of appearances, and who fashion and mould the moods of the mind. And an extremist like you— for extremes are always dangerously weak—is their legitimate prey."

"Pshaw!" I interrupted him, knowing that my manner betrayed me hopelessly, and that he had guessed much. "Any man may have subjective experiences, I suppose—"

Then I broke off suddenly. The change in his face made me start; it had taken on for the moment so exactly the look of the man on the hillside. The eyes gazing so steadily into mine had shadows in them, I thought.

"Glamour!" he was saying, "all glamour! One of them must have come very close to you, or perhaps touched you." Then he asked sharply, "Did you meet anyone? Did you speak with anyone?"

"I came by Tom Bassett's cottage," I said. "I didn't feel quite sure of my way and I went in and asked." "All glamour," he repeated to himself, and then

aloud to me, "and as for Bassett's cottage, it was burnt down three years ago, and nothing stands there now but broken, roofless walls—"

He stopped because I had seized him by the arm. In the shadows of the lamp-lit room behind him I thought I caught sight of dim forms moving past the book-shelves. But when my eye tried to focus them they faded and slipped away again into ceiling and walls. The details of the hill-top cottage, however, started into life again at the sight, and I seized my friend's arm to tell him. But instantly, when I tried, it all faded away again as though it had been a dream, and I could recall nothing intelligible to repeat to him.

He looked at me and laughed.

"They always obliterate the memory afterwards," he said gently, "so that little remains beyond a mood, or an emotion, to show how profoundly deep their touch has been. Though sometimes part of the change remains and becomes permanent—as I hope in your case it may."

Then, before I had time to answer, to swear, or to remonstrate, he stepped briskly past me and closed the door into the hall, and then drew me aside farther into the room. The change that I could not understand was still working in his face and eyes.

"If you have courage enough left to come with me," he said, speaking very seriously, "we will go out again and see more. Up till midnight, you know, there is still the opportunity, and with me perhaps you won't feel so—so—"

It was impossible somehow to refuse; everything combined to make me go. We had a little food and then went out into the hall, and he clapped a wide-awake on his gray hairs. I took a cloak and seized a walking-stick from the stand. I really hardly knew what I was doing. The new world I had awakened to seemed still a-quiver about me.

As we passed out on to the gravel drive the light from the hall windows fell upon his face, and I saw that the change I had been so long observing was nearing its completeness, for there breathed about him that keen, wonderful atmosphere of eternal youth I had felt upon the inmates of the cottage. He seemed to have gone back forty years; a veil was gathering over his eyes; and I could have sworn that somehow his stature had increased, and that he moved beside me with a vigor and power I had never seen in him before.

And as we began to climb the hill together in silence I saw that the stars were clear overhead and there was no mist, that the trees stood motionless without wind, and that beyond us on the summit of the hills there were lights dancing to and fro, appearing and disappearing like the inflection of stars in water.

The Man Who Went Too Far

E. F. Benson

first published in *Pall Mall Magazine* (June 1904)

The little village of St. Faith's nestles in a hollow of wooded till up on the north bank of the river Fawn in the country of Hampshire, huddling close round its grey Norman church as if for spiritual protection against the fays and fairies, the trolls and "little people," who might be supposed still to linger in the vast empty spaces of the New Forest, and to come after dusk and do their doubtful businesses. Once outside the hamlet you may walk in any direction (so long as you avoid the high road which leads to Brockenhurst) for the length of a summer afternoon without seeing sign of human habitation, or possibly even catching sight of another human being.

Shaggy wild ponies may stop their feeding for a moment as you pass, the white scuts of rabbits will vanish into their burrows, a brown viper perhaps will glide from your path into a clump of heather, and unseen birds will chuckle in the bushes, but it may easily happen that for a long day you will see nothing human. But you will not feel in the least lonely; in summer, at any rate, the sunlight will be gay with butterflies, and the air thick with all those woodland sounds which like instruments in an orchestra combine to play the great symphony of the yearly festival of June.

Winds whisper in the birches, and sigh among the firs; bees are busy with their redolent labour among the heather, a myriad birds chirp in the green temples of the forest trees, and the voice of the river prattling over stony places, bubbling into pools, chuckling and gulping round corners, gives you the sense that many presences and companions are near at hand.

Yet, oddly enough, though one would have thought that these benign and cheerful influences of wholesome air and spaciousness of forest were very healthful comrades for a man, in so far as Nature can really influence this wonderful human genus which has in these centuries learned to defy her most violent storms in its well-established houses, to bridle her torrents and make them light its streets, to tunnel her mountains and plough her seas, the inhabitants of St. Faith's will not willingly venture into the forest after dark. For in spite of the silence and loneliness of the hooded night it seems that a man is not sure in what company he may suddenly find himself, and though it is difficult to get from these villagers any very clear story of occult appearances, the feeling is widespread. One story indeed I have heard with some definiteness, the tale of a monstrous goat that has been seen to skip with hellish glee about the woods and shady places, and this perhaps is connected with the story which I have here attempted to piece together. It too is well-known to them; for all remember the young artist who died here not long ago, a young man, or so he struck the beholder, of great personal beauty, with something about him that made men's faces to smile and brighten when they looked on him. His ghost they will tell you "walks" constantly by the stream and through the woods which he loved so, and in especial it haunts a certain house, the last of the village, where he lived, and its garden in which he was done to death. For my part I am inclined to think that the terror of the forest dates chiefly from that day.

So, such as the story is, I have set it forth in connected form. It is based partly on the accounts of the villagers, but mainly on that of Darcy, a friend of mine and a friend of the man with whom these events were chiefly concerned.

The day had been one of untarnished midsummer splendor, and as the sun drew near to its setting, the glory of the evening grew every moment more crystalline, more miraculous.

Westward from St. Faith's the beechwood which stretched for some miles toward the heathery upland beyond already cast its veil of clear shadow over the red roofs of the village, but the spire of the grey church, over-topping all, still pointed a flaming orange finger into the sky. The river Fawn, which runs below, lay in sheets of sky-reflected blue, and wound its dreamy devious course round the edge of this wood, where a rough two-planked bridge crossed from the bottom of the garden of the last house in the village, and communicated by means of a little wicker gate with the wood itself. Then once out of the shadow of the wood the stream lay in flaming pools of the molten crimson of the sunset, and lost itself in the haze of woodland distances.

This house at the end of the village stood outside the shadow, and the lawn which sloped down to the river was still flecked with sunlight. Garden-beds of dazzling color lined its gravel walks, and down the middle of it ran a brick pergola, half-hidden in clusters of rambler-rose and purple with starry clematis. At the bottom end of it, between two of its pillars, was slung a hammock containing a shirtsleeved figure.

The house itself lay somewhat remote from the rest of the village, and a footpath leading across two fields, now tall and fragrant with hay, was its only communication with the high road.

It was low-built, only two stories in height, and like the garden, its walls were a mass of flowering roses. A narrow stone terrace ran along the garden front, over which was stretched an awning, and on the terrace a young silent-footed man-servant was busied with the laying of the table for dinner. He was neat-handed and quick with his job, and having finished it he went back into the house, and reappeared again with a large rough bath-towel on his arm. With this he went to the hammock in the pergola.

"Nearly eight, sir," he said.

"Has Mr. Darcy come yet?" asked a voice from the hammock.

"No, sir."

"If I'm not back when he comes, tell him that I'm just having a bathe before dinner."

The servant went back to the house, and after a moment or two Frank Halton struggled to a sitting posture, and slipped out on to the grass. He was of medium height and rather slender in build, but the supple ease and grace of his movements gave the impression of great physical strength: even his descent from the hammock was not an awkward performance. His face and hands were of very dark complexion, either from constant exposure to wind and sun, or, as his black hair and dark eyes tended to show, from some strain of southern blood. His head was small, his face of an exquisite beauty of modeling, while the smoothness of its contour would have led you to believe that he was a beardless lad still in his teens. But something, some look which living and experience alone can give, seemed to contradict that, and finding yourself completely puzzled as to his age, you would next moment probably cease to think about that, and only look at this glorious specimen of young manhood with wondering satisfaction.

He was dressed as became the season and the heat, and wore only a shirt open at the neck, and a pair of flannel trousers. His head, covered very thickly with a somewhat rebellious crop of short curly hair, was bare as he strolled across the lawn to the bathing-place that lay below. Then for a moment there was silence, then the sound of splashed and divided waters, and presently after, a great shout of ecstatic joy, as he swam up-stream with the foamed water standing in a frill round his neck. Then after some five minutes of limb-stretching struggle with the flood, he turned over on his back, and with arms thrown wide, floated down-stream, ripple-cradled and inert. His eyes were shut, and between half-parted lips he talked gently to himself.

"I am one with it," he said to himself, "the river and I, I and the river. The coolness and splash of it is I, and the water-herbs that wave in it are I also. And my strength and my limbs are not mine but the river's. It is all one, all one, dear Fawn." A quarter of an hour later he appeared again at the bottom of the lawn, dressed as before, his wet hair already drying into its crisp short curls again. There he paused a moment, looking back at the stream with the smile with which men look on the face of a friend, then turned towards the house. Simultaneously his servant came to the door leading on to the terrace, followed by a man who appeared to be some half-way through the fourth decade of his years. Frank and he saw each other across the bushes and garden-beds, and each quickening his step, they met suddenly face to face round an angle of the garden walk, in the fragrance of syringa.

"My dear Darcy," cried Frank, "I am charmed to see you." But the other stared at him in amazement.

"Frank!" he exclaimed.

"Yes, that is my name," he said, laughing; "what is the matter?" Darcy took his hand.

"What have you done to yourself?" he asked.

"You are a boy again."

"Ah, I have a lot to tell you," said Frank.

"Lots that you will hardly believe, but I shall convince you—"

He broke off suddenly, and held up his hand.

"Hush, there is my nightingale," he said.

The smile of recognition and welcome with which he had greeted his friend faded from his face, and a look of rapt wonder took its place, as of a lover listening to the voice of his beloved.

His mouth parted slightly, showing the white line of teeth, and his eyes looked out and out till they seemed to Darcy to be focussed on things beyond the vision of man. Then something perhaps startled the bird, for the song ceased.

"Yes, lots to tell you," he said. "Really I am delighted to see you. But you look rather white and pulled down; no wonder after that fever. And there is to be no nonsense about this visit. It is June now, you stop here till you are fit to begin work again. Two months at least."

"Ah, I can't trespass quite to that extent."

Frank took his arm and walked him down the grass.

"Trespass? Who talks of trespass? I shall tell you quite openly when I am tired of you, but you know when we had the studio together, we used not to bore each other. However, it is ill talking of going away on the moment of your arrival. Just a stroll to the river, and then it will be dinner-time."

Darcy took out his cigarette case, and offered it to the other.

Frank laughed.

"No, not for me. Dear me, I suppose I used to smoke once. How very odd!"

"Given it up?"

"I don't know. I suppose I must have. Anyhow I don't do it now. I would as soon think of eating meat."

"Another victim on the smoking altar of vegetarianism?"

"Victim?" asked Frank. "Do I strike you as such?"

He paused on the margin of the stream and whistled softly. Next moment a moor-hen made its splashing flight across the river, and ran up the bank. Frank took it very gently in his hands and stroked its head, as the creature lay against his shirt.

"And is the house among the reeds still secure?" he half-crooned to it. "And is the missus quite well, and are the neighbors flourishing? There, dear, home with you," and he flung it into the air.

"That bird's very tame," said Darcy, slightly bewildered.

"It is rather," said Frank, following its flight.

During dinner Frank chiefly occupied himself in bringing himself up-to-date in the movements and achievements of this old friend whom he had not seen for six years. Those six years, it now appeared, had been full of incident and success for Darcy; he had made a name for himself as a portrait painter which bade fair to outlast the vogue of a couple of seasons, and his leisure time had been brief. Then some four months previously he had been through a severe attack of typhoid, the result of which as concerns this story was that he had come down to this sequestered place to recruit.

"Yes, you've got on," said Frank at the end. "I always knew you would. A.R.A. with more in prospect. Money? You roll in it, I suppose, and, O Darcy, how much happiness have you had all these years? That is the only imperishable possession. And how much have you learned? Oh, I don't mean in Art. Even I could have done well in that."

Darcy laughed.

"Done well? My dear fellow, all I have learned in these six years you knew, so to speak, in your cradle. Your old pictures fetch huge prices. Do you never paint now?"

Frank shook his head.

"No, I'm too busy," he said.

"Doing what? Please tell me. That is what everyone is for ever asking me."

"Doing? I suppose you would say I do nothing."

Darcy glanced up at the brilliant young face opposite him.

"It seems to suit you, that way of being busy," he said. "Now, it's your turn. Do you read? Do you study? I remember you saying that it would do us all—all us artists, I mean—a great deal of good if we would study any one human face carefully for a year, without recording a line."

"Have you been doing that?"

Frank shook his head again.

"I mean exactly what I say," he said. "I have been doing nothing. And I have never been so occupied. Look at me; have I not done something to myself to begin with?"

"You are two years younger than I," said Darcy, "at least you used to be. You therefore are thirty-five. But had I never seen you before I should say you were just twenty. But was it worth while to spend six years of greatly-occupied life in order to look twenty? Seems rather like a woman of fashion."

Frank laughed boisterously.

"First time I've ever been compared to that particular bird of prey," he said. "No, that has not been my occupation—in fact I am only very rarely conscious that one effect of my occupation has been that. Of course, it must have been if one comes to think of it. It is not very important."

"Quite true my body has become young. But that is very little; I have become young."

Darcy pushed back his chair and sat sideways to the table looking at the other.

"Has that been your occupation then?" he asked.

"Yes, that anyhow is one aspect of it. Think what youth means! It is the capacity for growth, mind, body, spirit, all grow, all get stronger, all have a fuller, firmer life every day. That is something, considering that every day that passes after the ordinary man reaches the full-blown flower of his strength, weakens his hold on life. A man reaches his prime, and remains, we say, in his prime for ten years, or perhaps twenty. But after his primest prime is reached, he slowly, insensibly weakens. These are the signs of age in you, in your body, in your art probably, in your mind. You are less electric than you were. But I, when I reach my prime—I am nearing it—ah, you shall see." The stars had begun to appear in the blue velvet of the sky, and to the east the horizon seen above the black silhouette of the village was growing dove-colored with the approach of moon-rise.

White moths hovered dimly over the garden-beds, and the footsteps of night tip-toed through the bushes. Suddenly Frank rose.

"Ah, it is the supreme moment," he said softly. "Now more than at any other time the current of life, the eternal imperishable current runs so close to me that I am almost enveloped in it. Be silent a minute."

He advanced to the edge of the terrace and looked out, standing stretched with arms outspread. Darcy heard him draw a long breath into his lungs, and after many seconds expel it again. Six or eight times he did this, then turned back into the lamplight.

"It will sound to you quite mad, I expect," he said, "but if you want to hear the soberest truth I have ever spoken and shall ever speak, I will tell you about myself. But come into the garden if it is not damp for you. I have never told anyone yet, but I shall like to tell you. It is long, in fact, since I have even tried to classify what I have learned."

They wandered into the fragrant dimness of the pergola, and sat down. Then Frank began:

"Years ago, do you remember," he said, "we used often to talk about the decay of joy in the world. Many impulses, we settled, had contributed to this decay, some of which were good in themselves, others that were quite completely bad. Among the good things, I put what we may call certain Christian virtues, renunciation, resignation, sympathy with suffering, and the desire to relieve sufferers, but out of those things spring very bad ones, useless renunciation, asceticism for its own sake, mortification of the flesh with nothing to follow, no corresponding gain that is, and that awful and terrible disease which devastated England some centuries ago, and from which by heredity of spirit we suffer now, Puritanism. That was a dreadful plague, the brutes held and taught that joy and laughter and merriment were evil: it was a doctrine the most profane and wicked. Why, what is the commonest crime one sees? A sullen face. That is the truth of the matter. Now all my life I have believed that we are intended to be happy, that joy is of all gifts the most divine. And when I left London, abandoned my career, such as it was, I did so because I intended to devote my life to the cultivation of joy, and, by continuous and unsparing effort to be happy. Among people, and in constant intercourse with others, I did not find it possible; there were too many distractions in towns and work-rooms, and also too much suffering. So I took one step backwards or forwards, as you may choose to put it, and went straight to Nature, to trees, birds, animals, to all those things which quite clearly pursue one aim only, which blindly follow the great native instinct to be happy without any care at all for morality, or human law or divine law. I wanted, you understand, to get all joy first-hand and unadulterated, and I think it scarcely exists among men; it is obsolete."

Darcy turned in his chair.

"Ah, but what makes birds and animals happy?" he asked. "Food, food and mating."

Frank laughed gently in the stillness.

"Do not think I became a sensualist," he said. "I did not make that mistake. For the sensualist carries his miseries pick-a-back, and round his feet is wound the shroud that shall soon enwrap him. I may be mad, it is true, but I am not so stupid anyhow as to have tried that. No, what is it that makes puppies play with their own tails, that sends cats on their prowling ecstatic errands at night?"

He paused a moment.

"So I went to Nature," he said. "I sat down here in this New Forest, sat down fair and square, and looked. That was my first difficulty, to sit here quiet without being bored, to wait without being impatient, to be receptive and very alert, though for a long time nothing particular happened. The change in fact was slow in those early stages."

"Nothing happened?" asked Darcy, rather impatiently, with the sturdy revolt against any new idea which to the English mind is synonymous with nonsense. "Why, what in the world should happen?"

Now Frank as he had known him was the most generous but most quick-tempered of mortal men; in other words his anger would flare to a prodigious beacon, under almost no provocation, only to be quenched again under a gust of no less impulsive kindliness. Thus the moment Darcy had spoken, an apology for his hasty question was half-way up his tongue. But there was no need for it to have traveled even so far, for Frank laughed again with kindly, genuine mirth.

"Oh, how I should have resented that a few years ago," he said. "Thank goodness that resentment is one of the things I have got rid of. I certainly wish that you should believe my story—in fact, you are going to—but that you at this moment should imply that you do not does not concern me."

"Ah, your solitary sojournings have made you inhuman," said Darcy, still very English.

"No, human," said Frank. "Rather more human, at least rather less of an ape."

"Well, that was my first quest," he continued, after a moment, "the deliberate and unswerving pursuit of joy, and my method, the eager contemplation of Nature. As far as motive went, I daresay it was purely selfish, but as far as effect goes, it seems to me about the best thing one can do for one's follow-creatures, for happiness is more infectious than small-pox. So, as I said, I sat down and waited; I looked at happy things, zealously avoided the sight of anything unhappy, and by degrees a little trickle of the happiness of this blissful world began to filter into me. The trickle grew more abundant, and now, my dear fellow, if I could for a moment divert from me into you one half of the torrent of joy that pours through me day and night, you would throw the world, art, everything aside, and just live, exist. When a man's body dies, it passes into trees and flowers. Well, that is what I have been trying to do with my soul before death."

The servant had brought into the pergola a table with syphons and spirits, and had set a lamp upon it. As Frank spoke he leaned forward towards the other, and Darcy for all his matter-of-fact common sense could have sworn that his companion's face shone, was luminous in itself. His dark brown eyes glowed from within, the unconscious smile of a child irradiated and transformed his face. Darcy felt suddenly excited, exhilarated.

"Go on," he said. "Go on. I can feel you are somehow telling me sober truth. I daresay you are mad; but I don't see that matters."

Frank laughed again.

"Mad?" he said. "Yes, certainly, if you wish. But I prefer to call it sane. However, nothing matters less than what anybody chooses to call things. God never labels his gifts; He just puts them into our hands; just as he put animals in the garden of Eden, for Adam to name if he felt disposed.

"So by the continual observance and study of things that were happy," continued he, "I got happiness, I got joy. But seeking it, as I did, from Nature, I got much more which I did not seek, but stumbled upon originally by accident. It is difficult to explain, but I will try.

"About three years ago I was sitting one morning in a place I will show you tomorrow. It is down by the river brink, very green, dappled with shade and sun, and the river passes there through some little clumps of reeds. Well, as I sat there, doing nothing, but just looking and listening, I heard the sound quite distinctly of some flute-like instrument playing a strange unending melody. I thought at first it was some musical yokel on the highway and did not pay much attention. But before long the strangeness and indescribable beauty of the tune struck me.

"It never repeated itself, but it never came to an end, phrase after phrase ran its sweet course, it worked gradually and inevitably up to a climax, and having attained it, it went on; another climax was reached and another and another. Then with a sudden gasp of wonder I localized where it came from. It came from the reeds and from the sky and from the trees. It was everywhere, it was the sound of life. It was, my dear Darcy, as the Greeks would have said, it was Pan playing on his pipes, the voice of Nature. It was the life-melody, the world-melody."

Darcy was far too interested to interrupt, though there was a question he would have liked to ask, and Frank went on:

"Well, for the moment I was terrified, terrified with the impotent horror of nightmare, and I stopped my ears and just ran from the place and got back to the house panting, trembling, literally in a panic. Unknowingly, for at that time I only pursued joy, I had begun, since I drew my joy from Nature, to get in touch with Nature. Nature, force, God, call it what you will, had drawn across my face a little gossamer web of essential life. I saw that when I emerged from my terror, and I went very humbly back to where I had heard the Pan-pipes. But it was nearly six months before I heard them again."

"Why was that?" asked Darcy.

"Surely because I had revolted, rebelled, and worst of all been frightened. For I believe that just as there is nothing in the world which so injures one's body as fear, so there is nothing that so much shuts up the soul. I was afraid, you see, of the one thing in the world which has real existence. No wonder its manifestation was withdrawn."

"And after six months?"

"After six months one blessed morning I heard the piping again. I wasn't afraid that time."

"And since then it has grown louder, it has become more constant. I now hear it often, and I can put myself into such an attitude towards Nature that the pipes will almost certainly sound. And never yet have they played the same tune, it is always something new, something fuller, richer, more complete than before."

"What do you mean by 'such an attitude towards Nature'?" asked Darcy.

"I can't explain that; but by translating it into a bodily attitude it is this."

Frank sat up for a moment quite straight in his chair, then slowly sunk back with arms outspread and head drooped.

"That;" he said, "an effortless attitude, but open, resting, receptive. It is just that which you must do with your soul."

Then he sat up again.

"One word more," he said, "and I will bore you no further. Nor unless you ask me questions shall I talk about it again. You will find me, in fact, quite sane in my mode of life. Birds and beasts you will see behaving somewhat intimately to me, like that moor-hen, but that is all. I will walk with you, ride with you, play golf with you, and talk with you on any subject you like. But I wanted you on the threshold to know what has happened to me. And one thing more will happen."

He paused again, and a slight look of fear crossed his eyes.

"There will be a final revelation," he said, "a complete and blinding stroke which will throw open to me, once and for all, the full knowledge, the full realization and comprehension that I am one, just as you are, with life. In reality there is no 'me,' no 'you,' no 'it.' Everything is part of the one and only thing which is life. I know that that is so, but the realisation of it is not yet mine.

"But it will be, and on that day, so I take it, I shall see Pan. It may mean death, the death of my body, that is, but I don't care. It may mean immortal, eternal life lived here and now and for ever.

"Then having gained that, ah, my dear Darcy, I shall preach such a gospel of joy, showing myself as the living proof of the truth, that Puritanism, the dismal religion of sour faces, shall vanish like a breath of smoke, and be dispersed and disappear in the sunlit air. But first the full knowledge must be mine."

Darcy watched his face narrowly.

"You are afraid of that moment," he said. Frank smiled at him.

"Quite true; you are quick to have seen that. But when it comes I hope I shall not be afraid."

For some little time there was silence; then Darcy rose. "You have bewitched me, you extraordinary boy," he said. "You have been telling me a fairy-story, and I find myself saying, 'Promise me it is true.'"

"I promise you that," said the other.

"And I know I shan't sleep," added Darcy.

Frank looked at him with a sort of mild wonder as if he scarcely understood.

"Well, what does that matter?" he said.

"I assure you it does. I am wretched unless I sleep."

"Of course I can make you sleep if I want," said Frank in a rather bored voice.

"Well, do."

"Very good: go to bed. I'll come upstairs in ten minutes."

Frank busied himself for a little after the other had gone, moving the table back under the awning of the verandah and quenching the lamp. Then he went with his quick silent tread upstairs and into Darcy's room. The latter was already in bed, but very wide-eyed and wakeful, and Frank with an amused smile of indulgence, as for a fretful child, sat down on the edge of the bed.

"Look at me," he said, and Darcy looked.

"The birds are sleeping in the brake," said Frank softly, "and the winds are asleep. The sea sleeps, and the tides are but the heaving of its breast. The stars swing slow, rocked in the great cradle of the Heavens, and—"

He stopped suddenly, gently blew out Darcy's candle, and left him sleeping.

Morning brought to Darcy a flood of hard common sense, as clear and crisp as the sunshine that filled his room. Slowly as he woke he gathered together the broken threads of the memories of the evening which had ended, so he told himself, in a trick of common hypnotism. That accounted for it all; the whole strange talk he had had was under a spell of suggestion from the extraordinary vivid boy who had once been a man; all his own excitement, his acceptance of the incredible had been merely the effect of a stronger, more potent will imposed on his own. How strong that will was, he guessed from his own instantaneous obedience to Frank's suggestion of sleep. And armed with impenetrable common sense he came down to breakfast. Frank had already begun, and was consuming a large plateful of porridge and milk with the most prosaic and healthy appetite.

"Slept well?" he asked.

"Yes, of course. Where did you learn hypnotism?"

"By the side of the river."

"You talked an amazing quantity of nonsense last night," remarked Darcy, in a voice prickly with reason.

"Rather. I felt quite giddy. Look, I remembered to order a dreadful daily paper for you. You can read about money markets or politics or cricket matches." Darcy looked at him closely. In the morning light Frank looked even fresher, younger, more vital than he had done the night before, and the sight of him somehow dinted Darcy's armor of common sense.

"You are the most extraordinary fellow I ever saw," he said. "I want to ask you some more questions."

"Ask away," said Frank.

For the next day or two Darcy plied his friend with many questions, objections and criticisms on the theory of life, and gradually got out of him a coherent and complete account of his experience. In brief, then, Frank believed that "by lying naked," as he put it, to the force which controls the passage of the stars, the breaking of a wave, the budding of a tree, the love of a youth and maiden, he had succeeded in a way hitherto undreamed of in possessing himself of the essential principle of life. Day by day, so he thought, he was getting nearer to, and in closer union with, the great power itself which caused all life to be, the spirit of nature, of force, or the spirit of God. For himself, he confessed to what others would call paganism; it was sufficient for him that there existed a principle of life. He did not worship it, he did not pray to it, he did not praise it. Some of it existed in all human beings, just as it existed in trees and animals; to realize and make living to himself the fact that it was all one, was his sole aim and object.

Here perhaps Darcy would put in a word of warning.

"Take care," he said. "To see Pan meant death, did it not."

Frank's eyebrows would rise at this.

"What does that matter?" he said. "True, the Greeks were always right, and they said so, but there is another possibility. For the nearer I get to it, the more living, the more vital and young I become."

"What then do you expect the final revelation will do for you?"

"I have told you," said he. "It will make me immortal."

But it was not so much from speech and argument that Darcy grew to grasp his friend's conception, as from the ordinary conduct of his life. They were passing, for instance, one morning down the village street, when an old woman, very bent and decrepit, but with an extraordinary cheerfulness of face, hobbled out from her cottage. Frank instantly stopped when he saw her.

"You old darling! How goes it all?" he said.

But she did not answer, her dim old eyes were riveted on his face; she seemed to drink in like a thirsty creature the beautiful radiance which shone there. Suddenly she put her two withered old hands on his shoulders.

"You're just the sunshine itself," she said, and he kissed her and passed on.

But scarcely a hundred yards further a strange contradiction of such tenderness occurred. A child running along the path towards them fell on its face and set up a dismal cry of fright and pain. A look of horror came into Frank's eyes, and, putting his fingers in his ears, he fled at full speed down the street, and did not pause till he was out of hearing. Darcy, having ascertained that the child was not really hurt, followed him in bewilderment.

"Are you without pity then?" he asked. Frank shook his head impatiently.

"Can't you see?" he asked. "Can't you understand that that sort of thing, pain, anger, anything unlovely, throws me back, retards the coming of the great hour! Perhaps when it comes I shall be able to piece that side of life on to the other, on to the true religion of joy. At present I can't."

"But the old woman. Was she not ugly?"

Frank's radiance gradually returned.

"Ah, no. She was like me. She longed for joy, and knew it when she saw it, the old darling."

Another question suggested itself.

"Then what about Christianity?" asked Darcy.

"I can't accept it. I can't believe in any creed of which the central doctrine is that God who is Joy should have had to suffer. Perhaps it was so; in some inscrutable way I believe it may have been so, but I don't understand how it was possible. So I leave it alone; my affair is joy."

They had come to the weir above the village, and the thunder of riotous cool water was heavy in the air. Trees dipped into the translucent stream with slender trailing branches, and the meadow where they stood was starred with midsummer blossomings. Larks shot up caroling into the crystal dome of blue, and a thousand voices of June sang round them. Frank, bare-headed as was his wont, with his coat slung over his arm and his shirt sleeves rolled up above the elbow, stood there like some beautiful wild animal with eyes half-shut and mouth half-open, drinking in the scented warmth of the air. Then suddenly he flung himself face downwards on the grass at the edge of the stream, burying his face in the daisies and cowslips, and lay stretched there in wide-armed ecstasy, with his long fingers pressing and stroking the dewy herbs of the field. Never before had Darcy seen him thus fully possessed by his idea; his caressing fingers, his half-buried face pressed close to the grass, even the clothed lines of his figure were instinct with a vitality that somehow was different from that of other men. And some faint glow from it reached Darcy, some thrill, some vibration from that charged recumbent body passed to him, and for a moment he understood as he had not understood before, despite his persistent questions and the candid answers they received, how real, and how realized by Frank, his idea was.

Then suddenly the muscles in Frank's neck became stiff and alert, and he half-raised his head.

"The Pan-pipes, the Pan-pipes," he whispered. "Close, oh, so close."

Very slowly, as if a sudden movement might interrupt the melody, he raised himself and leaned on the elbow of his bent arm. His eyes opened wider, the lower lids drooped as if he focussed his eyes on something very far away, and the smile on his face broadened and quivered like sunlight on still water, till the exultance of its happiness was scarcely human. So he remained motionless and rapt for some minutes, then the look of listening died from his face, and he bowed his head, satisfied.

"Ah, that was good," he said. "How is it possible you did not hear? Oh, you poor fellow! Did you really hear nothing?"

A week of this outdoor and stimulating life did wonders in restoring to Darcy the vigor and health which his weeks of fever had filched from him, and as his normal activity and higher pressure of vitality returned, he seemed to himself to fall even more under the spell which the miracle of Frank's youth cast over him. Twenty times a day he found himself saying to himself suddenly at the end of some ten minutes silent resistance to the absurdity of Frank's idea: "But it isn't possible; it can't be possible," and from the fact of his having to assure himself so frequently of this, he knew that he was struggling and arguing with a conclusion which already had taken root in his mind. For in any case a visible living miracle confronted him, since it was equally impossible that this youth, this boy, trembling on the verge of manhood, was thirty-five.

Yet such was the fact.

July was ushered in by a couple of days of blustering and fretful rain, and Darcy, unwilling to risk a chill, kept to the house. But to Frank this weeping change of weather seemed to have no bearing on the behavior of man, and he spent his days exactly as he did under the suns of June, lying in his hammock, stretched on the dripping grass, or making huge rambling excursions into the forest, the birds hopping from tree to tree after him, to return in the evening, drenched and soaked, but with the same unquenchable flame of joy burning within him.

"Catch cold?" he would ask; "I've forgotten how to do it, I think I suppose it makes one's body more sensible always to sleep out-of-doors. People who live indoors always remind me of something peeled and skinless."

"Do you mean to say you slept out-of-doors last night in that deluge?" asked Darcy. "And where, may I ask?"

Frank thought a moment.

"I slept in the hammock till nearly dawn," he said. "For I remember the light blinked in the east when I awoke. Then I went—where did I go—oh, yes, to the meadow where the Pan-pipes sounded so close a week ago. You were with me, do you remember? But I always have a rug if it is wet."

And he went whistling upstairs.

Somehow that little touch, his obvious effort to recall where he had slept, brought strangely home to Darcy the wonderful romance of which he was the still half-incredulous beholder. Sleep till close on dawn in a hammock, then the tramp—or probably scamper—underneath the windy and weeping heavens to the remote and lonely meadow by the weir! The picture of other such nights rose before him; Frank sleeping perhaps by the bathing-place under the filtered twilight of the stars, or the white blaze of moon-shine, a stir and awakening at some dead hour, perhaps a space of silent wide-eyed thought, and then awandering through the hushed woods to some other dormitory, alone with his happiness, alone with the joy and the life that suffused and enveloped him, without other thought or desire or aim except the hourly and never-ceasing communion with the joy of nature.

They were in the middle of dinner that night, talking on indifferent subjects, when Darcy suddenly broke off in the middle of a sentence.

"I've got it," he said. "At last I've got it."

"Congratulate you," said Frank. "But what?"

"The radical unsoundness of your idea. It is this: 'All Nature from highest to lowest is full, crammed full of suffering; every living organism in Nature preys on another, yet in your aim to get close to, to be one with Nature, you leave suffering altogether out; you run away from it, you refuse to recognize it. And you are waiting, you say, for the final revelation."

Frank's brow clouded slightly.

"Well," he asked, rather wearily.

"Cannot you guess then when the final revelation will be? In joy you are supreme, I grant you that; I did not know a man could be so master of it. You have learned perhaps practically all that Nature can teach. And if, as you think, the final revelation is coming to you, it will be the revelation of horror, suffering, death, pain in all its hideous forms. Suffering does exist: you hate it and fear it."

Frank held up his hand.

"Stop; let me think," he said.

There was silence for a long minute.

"That never struck me," he said at length. "It is possible that what you suggest is true. Does the sight of Pan mean that, do you think? Is it that Nature, take it altogether, suffers horribly, suffers to a hideous inconceivable extent? Shall I be shown all the suffering?" He got up and came round to where Darcy sat.

"If it is so, so be it," he said. "Because, my dear fellow, I am near, so splendidly near to the final revelation. Today the pipes have sounded almost without pause. I have even heard the rustle in the bushes, I believe, of Pan's coming. I have seen, yes, I saw today, the bushes pushed aside as if by a hand, and piece of a face, not human, peered through. But I was not frightened, at least I did not run away this time."

He took a turn up to the window and back again.

"Yes, there is suffering all through," he said, "and I have left it all out of my search. Perhaps, as you say, the revelation will be that. And in that case, it will be good-bye. I have gone on one line. I shall have gone too far along one road, without having explored the other. But I can't go back now. I wouldn't if I could; not a step would I retrace! In any case, whatever the revelation is, it will be God. I'm sure of that."

The rainy weather soon passed, and with the return of the sun Darcy again joined Frank in long rambling days. It grew extraordinarily hotter, and with the fresh bursting of life, after the rain, Frank's vitality seemed to blaze higher and higher. Then, as is the habit of the English weather, one evening clouds began to bank themselves up in the west, the sun went down in a glare of coppery thunder-rack, and the whole earth broiling under an unspeakable oppression and sultriness paused and panted for the storm. After sunset the remote fires of lightning began to wink and flicker on the horizon, but when bed-time came the storm seemed to have moved no nearer, though a very low unceasing noise of thunder was audible. Weary and oppressed by the stress of the day, Darcy fell at once into a heavy uncomforting sleep.

He woke suddenly into full consciousness, with the din of some appalling explosion of thunder in his ears, and sat up in bed with racing heart. Then for a moment, as he recovered himself from the panic-land which lies between sleeping and waking, there was silence, except for the steady hissing of rain on the shrubs outside his window. But suddenly that silence was shattered and shredded into fragments by a scream from somewhere close at hand outside in the black garden, a scream of supreme and despairing terror. Again and once again it shrilled up, and then a babble of awful words was interjected. A quivering sobbing voice that he knew said:

"My God, oh, my God; oh, Christ!"

And then followed a little mocking, bleating laugh. Then was silence again; only the rain hissed on the shrubs.

All this was but the affair of a moment, and without pause either to put on clothes or light a candle, Darcy was already fumbling at his door-handle. Even as he opened it he met a terror-stricken face outside, that of the man-servant who carried a light.

"Did you hear?" he asked.

The man's face was bleached to a dull shining whiteness. "Yes, sir," he said. "It was the master's voice."

Together they hurried down the stairs and through the dining-room where an orderly table for breakfast had already been laid, and out on to the terrace. The rain for the moment had been utterly stayed, as if the tap of the heavens had been turned off, and under the lowering black sky, not quite dark, since the moon rode somewhere serene behind the conglomerated thunder-clouds, Darcy stumbled into the garden, followed by the servant with the candle. The monstrous leaping shadow of himself was cast before him on the lawn; lost and wandering odours of rose and lily and damp earth were thick about him, but more pungent was some sharp and acrid smell that suddenly reminded him of a certain chalet in which he had once taken refuge in the Alps. In the blackness of the hazy light from the sky, and the vague tossing of the candle behind him, he saw that the hammock in which Frank so often lay was tenanted. A gleam of white shirt was there, as if a man were sitting up in it, but across that there was an obscure dark shadow, and as he approached the acrid odor grew more intense.

He was now only some few yards away, when suddenly the black shadow seemed to jump into the air, then came down with tappings of hard hoofs on the brick path that ran down the pergola, and with frolicsome skippings galloped off into the bushes. When that was gone Darcy could see quite clearly that a shirted figure sat up in the hammock. For one moment, from sheer terror of the unseen, he hung on his step, and the servant joining him they walked together to the hammock.

It was Frank. He was in shirt and trousers only, and he sat up with braced arms. For one half-second he stared at them, his face a mask of horrible contorted terror. His upper lip was drawn back so that the gums of the teeth appeared, and his eyes were focussed not on the two who approached him, but on something quite close to him; his nostrils were widely expanded, as if he panted for breath, and terror incarnate and repulsion and deathly anguish ruled dreadful lines on his smooth cheeks and forehead. Then even as they looked the body sank backwards, and the ropes of the hammock wheezed and strained.

Darcy lifted him out and carried him indoors. Once he thought there was a faint convulsive stir of the limbs that lay with so dead a weight in his arms, but when they got inside, there was no trace of life. But the look of supreme terror and agony of fear had gone from his face, a boy tired with play but still smiling in his sleep was the burden he laid on the floor. His eyes had closed, and the beautiful mouth lay in smiling curves, even as when a few mornings ago, in the meadow by the weir, it had quivered to the music of the unheard melody of Pan's pipes. Then they looked further.

Frank had come back from his bathe before dinner that night in his usual costume of shirt and trousers only. He had not dressed, and during dinner, so Darcy remembered, he had rolled up the sleeves of his shirt to above the elbow. Later, as they sat and talked after dinner on the close sultriness of the evening, he had unbuttoned the front of his shirt to let what little breath of wind there was play on his skin. The sleeves were rolled up now, the front of the shirt was unbuttoned, and on his arms and on the brown skin of his chest were strange discolorations which grew momently more clear and defined, till they saw that the marks were pointed prints, as if caused by the hoofs of some monstrous goat that had leaped and stamped upon him.

THE STORY OF A PANIC

E. M. Forster

first published in The Independent Review (March 1904)

I.

Eustace's career—if career it can be called—certainly dates from that afternoon in the chestnut woods above Ravello. I confess at once that I am a plain, simple man, with no pretensions to literary style. Still, I do flatter myself that I can tell a story without exaggerating, and I have therefore decided to give an unbiassed account of the extraordinary events of eight years ago.

Ravello is a delightful place with a delightful little hotel in which we met some charming people. There were the two Miss Robinsons, who had been there for six weeks with Eustace, their nephew, then a boy of about fourteen. Mr. Sandbach had also been there some time. He had held a curacy in the north of England, which he had been compelled to resign on account of ill-health, and while he was recruiting at Ravello he had taken in hand Eustace's education—which was then sadly deficient—and was endeavoring to fit him for one of our great public schools. Then there was Mr. Leyland, a would-be artist, and, finally, there was the nice landlady, Signora Scafetti, and the nice English-speaking waiter, Emmanuele—though at the time of which I am speaking Emmanuele was away, visiting a sick father.

To this little circle, I, my wife, and my two daughters made, I venture to think, a not unwelcome addition. But though I liked most of the company well enough, there were two of them to whom I did not take at all. They were the artist, Leyland, and the Miss Robinsons' nephew, Eustace.

Leyland was simply conceited and odious, and, as those qualities will be amply illustrated in my narrative, I need not enlarge upon them here. But Eustace was something besides: he was indescribably repellent.

I am fond of boys as a rule, and was quite disposed to be friendly. I and my daughters offered to take him out—'No, walking was such a fag.' Then I asked him to come and bathe—' No, he could not swim.'

"Every English boy should be able to swim," I said, "I will teach you myself."

"There, Eustace dear," said Miss Robinson; "here is a chance for you."

But he said he was afraid of the water!—a boy afraid!—and of course I said no more.

I would not have minded so much if he had been a really studious boy, but he neither played hard nor worked hard. His favorite occupations were lounging on the terrace in an easy chair and loafing along the high road, with his feet shuffling up the dust and his shoulders stooping forward. Naturally enough, his features were pale, his chest contracted, and his muscles undeveloped. His aunts thought him delicate; what he really needed was discipline.

That memorable day we all arranged to go for a picnic up in the chestnut woods—all, that is, except Janet, who stopped behind to finish her water-color of the Cathedral—not a very successful attempt, I am afraid.

I wander off into these irrelevant details, because in my mind I cannot separate them from an account of the day; and it is the same with the conversation during the picnic: all is imprinted on my brain together. After a couple of hours' ascent, we left the donkeys that had carried the Miss Robinsons and my wife, and all proceeded on foot to the head of the valley—Vallone Fontana Caroso is its proper name, I find.

I have visited a good deal of fine scenery before and since, but have found little that has pleased me more. The valley ended in a vast hollow, shaped like a cup, into which radiated ravines from the precipitous hills around. Both the valley and the ravines and the ribs of hill that divided the ravines were covered with leafy chestnut, so that the general appearance was that of a many fingered green hand, palm upwards, which was clutching, convulsively to keep us in its grasp. Far down the valley we could see Ravello and the sea, but that was the only sign of another world.

"Oh, what a perfectly lovely place," said my daughter Rose. "What a picture it would make!"

"Yes," said Mr. Sandbach. "Many a famous European gallery would be proud to have a landscape a tithe as beautiful as this upon its walls."

"On the contrary," said Leyland, "it would make a very poor picture. Indeed, it is not paintable at all."

"And why is that?" said Rose, with far more deference than he deserved.

"Look, in the first place," he replied, "how intolerably straight against the sky is the line of the hill. It would need breaking up and diversifying. And where we are standing the whole thing is out of perspective. Besides, all the coloring is monotonous and crude."

"I do not know anything about pictures," I put in, "and I do not pretend to know: but I know what is beautiful when I see it, and I am thoroughly content with this."

"Indeed, who could help being contented!" said the elder Miss Robinson and Mr. Sandbach said the same.

"Ah!" said Leyland, "you all confuse the artistic view of nature with the photographic."

Poor Rose had brought her camera with her, so I thought this positively rude. I did not wish any unpleasantness; so I merely turned away and assisted my wife and Miss Mary Robinson to put out the lunch—not a very nice lunch.

"Eustace, dear," said his aunt, "come and help us here."

He was in a particularly bad temper that morning. He had, as usual, not wanted to come, and his aunts had nearly allowed him to stop at the hotel to vex Janet. But I, with their permission, spoke to him rather sharply on the subject of exercise; and the result was that he had come, but was even more taciturn and moody than usual.

Obedience was not his strong point. He invariably questioned every command, and only executed it grumbling. I should always insist on prompt and cheerful obedience, if I had a son.

"I'm—coming—Aunt—Mary," he at last replied, and dawdled to cut a piece of wood to make a whistle, taking care not to arrive till we had finished.

"Well, well, sir!" said I, "you stroll in at the end and profit by our labors." He sighed, for he could not endure being chaffed. Miss Mary, very unwisely, insisted on giving him the wing of the chicken, in spite of all my attempts to prevent her. I remember that I had a moment's vexation when I thought that, instead of enjoying the sun, and the air, and the woods, we were all engaged in wrangling over the diet of a spoilt boy.

But, after lunch, he was a little less in evidence. He withdrew to a tree trunk, and began to loosen the bark from his whistle. I was thankful to see him employed, for once in a way. We reclined, and took a dolce far niente.

Those sweet chestnuts of the South are puny striplings compared with our robust Northerners. But they clothed the contours of the hills and valleys in a most pleasing way, their veil being only broken by two clearings, in one of which we were sitting.

And because these few trees were cut down, Leyland burst into a petty indictment of the proprietor.

"All the poetry is going from Nature," he cried, "her lakes and marshes are drained, her seas banked up, her forests cut down. Everywhere we see the vulgarity of desolation spreading."

I have had some experience of estates, and answered that cutting was very necessary for the health of the larger trees. Besides, it was unreasonable to expect the proprietor to derive no income from his lands.

"If you take the commercial side of landscape, you may feel pleasure in the owner's activity. But to me the mere thought that a tree is convertible into cash is disgusting."

"I see no reason," I observed politely, "to despise the gifts of Nature, because they are of value."

It did not stop him. "It is no matter," he went on, "we are all hopelessly steeped in vulgarity. I do not except myself. It is through us, and to our shame, that the Nereids have left the waters and the Oreads the mountains, that the woods no longer give shelter to Pan."

"Pan!" cried Mr. Sandbach, his mellow voice filling the valley as if it had been a great green church, "Pan is dead. That is why the woods do not shelter him." And he began to tell the striking story of the mariners who were sailing near the coast at the time of the birth of Christ, and three times heard a loud voice saying: "The great God Pan is dead."

"Yes. The great God Pan is dead," said Leyland. And he abandoned himself to that mock misery in which artistic people are so fond of indulging. His cigar went out, and he had to ask me for a match.

"How very interesting," said Rose. "I do wish I knew some ancient history."

"It is not worth your notice," said Mr. Sandbach. "Eh, Eustace?"

Eustace was finishing his whistle. He looked up, with the irritable frown in which his aunts allowed him to indulge, and made no reply.

The conversation turned to various topics and then died out. It was a cloudless afternoon in May, and the pale green of the young chestnut leaves made a pretty contrast with the dark blue of the sky. We were all sitting at the edge of the small clearing for the sake of the view, and the shade of the chestnut saplings behind us was manifestly insufficient. All sounds died away —at least that is my account: Miss Robinson says that the clamor of the birds was the first sign of uneasiness that she discerned. All sounds died away, except that, far in the distance, I could hear two boughs of a great chestnut grinding together as the tree swayed. The grinds grew shorter and shorter, and finally that sound stopped also. As I looked over the green fingers of the valley, everything was absolutely motionless and still; and that feeling of suspense which one so often experiences when Nature is in repose, began to steal over me.

Suddenly, we were all electrified by the excruciating noise of Eustace's whistle. I never heard any instrument give forth so ear-splitting and discordant a sound.

"Eustace, dear," said Miss Mary Robinson, "you might have thought of your poor Aunt Julia's head."

Leyland who had apparently been asleep, sat up.

"It is astonishing how blind a boy is to anything that is elevating or beautiful," he observed. "I should not have thought he could have found the wherewithal out here to spoil our pleasure like this."

Then the terrible silence fell upon us again. I was now standing up and watching a catspaw of wind that was running down one of the ridges opposite, turning the light green to dark as it traveled. A fanciful feeling of foreboding came over me; so I turned away, to find to my amazement, that all the others were also on their feet, watching it too.

It is not possible to describe coherently what happened next: but I, for one, am not ashamed to confess that, though the fair blue sky was above me, and the green spring woods beneath me, and the kindest of friends around me, yet I became terribly frightened, more frightened than I ever wish to become again, frightened in a way I never have known either before or after.

And in the eyes of the others, too, I saw blank, expressionless fear, while their mouths strove in vain to speak and their hands to gesticulate. Yet, all around us were prosperity, beauty, and peace, and all was motionless, save the catspaw of wind, now traveling up the ridge on which we stood.

Who moved first has never been settled. It is enough to say that in one second we were tearing away along the hillside. Leyland was in front, then Mr. Sandbach, then my wife. But I only saw for a brief moment; for I ran across the little clearing and through the woods and over the undergrowth and the rocks and down the dry torrent beds into the valley below. The sky might have been black as I ran, and the trees short grass, and the hillside a level road; for I saw nothing and heard nothing and felt nothing, since all the channels of sense and reason were blocked. It was not the spiritual fear that one has known at other times, but brutal overmastering physical fear, stopping up the ears, and dropping clouds before the eyes, and filling the mouth with foul tastes. And it was no ordinary humiliation that survived; for I had been afraid, not as a man, but as a beast.

II.

I cannot describe our finish any better than our start; for our fear passed away as it had come, without cause. Suddenly I was able to see, and hear, and cough, and clear my mouth. Looking back, I saw that the others were stopping too; and, in a short time, we were all together, though it was long before we could speak, and longer before we dared to.

No one was seriously injured. My poor wife had sprained her ankle, Leyland had torn one of his nails on a tree trunk, and I myself had scraped and damaged my ear. I never noticed it till I had stopped.

We were all silent, searching one another's faces. Suddenly Miss Mary Robinson gave a terrible shriek. "Oh, merciful heavens! where is Eustace?" And then she would have fallen, if Mr. Sandbach had not caught her.

"We must go back, we must go back at once," said my Rose, who was quite the most collected of the party. "But I hope—I feel he is safe."

Such was the cowardice of Leyland, that he objected. But, finding himself in a minority, and being afraid of being left alone, he gave in. Rose and I supported my poor wife, Mr. Sandbach and Miss Robinson helped Miss Mary, and we returned slowly and silently, taking forty minutes to ascend the path that we had descended in ten.

Our conversation was naturally disjointed, as no one wished to offer an opinion on what had happened. Rose was the most talkative: she startled us all by saying that she had very nearly stopped where she was.

"Do you mean to say that you weren't—that you didn't feel compelled to go?" said Mr. Sandbach.

"Oh, of course, I did feel frightened"—she was the first to use the word—"but I somehow felt that if I could stop on it would be quite different, that I shouldn't be frightened at all, so to speak." Rose never did express herself clearly: still, it is greatly to her credit that she, the youngest of us, should have held on so long at that terrible time.

"I should have stopped, I do believe," she continued, "if I had not seen mamma go."

Rose's experience comforted us a little about Eustace. But a feeling of terrible foreboding was on us all, as we painfully climbed the chestnut-covered slopes and neared the little clearing. When we reached it our tongues broke loose. There, at the further side, were the remains of our lunch, and close to them, lying motionless on his back, was Eustace.

With some presence of mind I at once cried out: "Hey, you young monkey! jump up!" But he made no reply, nor did he answer when his poor aunts spoke to him. And, to my unspeakable horror, I saw one of those green lizards dart out from under his shirt-cuff as we approached.

We stood watching him as he lay there so silently, and my ears began to tingle in expectation of the outbursts of lamentations and tears.

Miss Mary fell on her knees beside him and touched his hand, which was convulsively entwined in the long grass.

As she did so, he opened his eyes and smiled.

I have often seen that peculiar smile since, both on the possessor's face and on the photographs of him that are beginning to get into the illustrated papers. But, till then, Eustace had always worn a peevish, discontented frown; and we were all unused to this disquieting smile, which always seemed to be without adequate reason.

His aunts showered kisses on him, which he did not reciprocate, and then there was an awkward pause, Eustace seemed so natural and undisturbed, yet, if he had not had astonishing experiences himself, he ought to have been all the more astonished at our extraordinary behavior. My wife, with ready tact, endeavored to behave as if nothing had happened.

"Well, Mr. Eustace," she said, sitting down as she spoke, to ease her foot, "how have you been amusing yourself since we have been away?"

"Thank you, Mrs. Tytler, I have been very happy."

"And where have you been?"

"Here."

"And lying down all the time, you idle boy?"

"No, not all the time."

"What were you doing before?"

"Oh; standing or sitting."

"Stood and sat doing nothing! Don't you know the poem 'Satan finds some mischief still for—'"

"Oh, my dear madam, hush! hush!" Mr. Sandbach's voice broke in; and my wife, naturally mortified by the interruption, said no more and moved away. I was surprised to see Rose immediately take her place, and, with more freedom than she generally displayed, run her fingers through the boy's tousled hair.

"Eustace! Eustace!" she said, hurriedly, "tell me everything—every single thing."

Slowly he sat up—till then he had lain on his back.

"Oh, Rose," he whispered, and, my curiosity being aroused, I moved nearer to hear what he was going to say. As I did so, I caught sight of some goats' footmarks in the moist earth beneath the trees.

"Apparently you have had a visit from some goats," I observed. "I had no idea they fed up here."

Eustace laboriously got on to his feet and came to see; and when he saw the footmarks he lay down and rolled on them, as a dog rolls in dirt.

After that there was a grave silence, broken at length by the solemn speech of Mr. Sandbach.

"My dear friends," he said, "it is best to confess the truth bravely. I know that what I am going to say now is what you are all now feeling. The Evil One has been very near us in bodily form. Time may yet discover some injury that he has wrought among us. But, at present, for myself at all events, I wish to offer up thanks for a merciful deliverance."

With that he knelt down, and, as the others knelt, I knelt too, though I do not believe in the Devil being allowed to assail us in visible form, as I told Mr. Sandbach afterwards. Eustace came too, and knelt quietly enough between his aunts after they had beckoned to him. But when it was over he at once got up, and began hunting for something.

"Why! Someone has cut my whistle in two," he said. (I had seen Leyland with an open knife in his hand—a superstitious act which I could hardly approve.)

"Well, it doesn't matter," he continued.

"And why doesn't it matter?" said Mr. Sandbach, who has ever since tried to entrap Eustace into an account of that mysterious hour.

"Because I don't want it any more."

"Why?"

At that he smiled; and, as no one seemed to have anything more to say, I set off as fast as I could through the wood, and hauled up a donkey to carry my poor wife home. Nothing occurred in my absence, except that Rose had again asked Eustace to tell her what had happened; and he, this time, had turned away his head, and had not answered her a single word.

As soon as I returned, we all set off. Eustace walked with difficulty, almost with pain, so that, when we reached the other donkeys, his aunts wished him to mount one of them and ride all the way home. I make it a rule never to interfere between relatives, but I put my foot down at this. As it turned out, I was perfectly right, for the healthy exercise, I suppose, began to thaw Eustace's sluggish blood and loosen his stiffened muscles. He stepped out manfully, for the first time in his life, holding his head up and taking deep draughts of air into his chest. I observed with satisfaction to Miss Mary

Robinson, that Eustace was at last taking some pride in his personal appearance.

Mr. Sandbach sighed, and said that Eustace must be carefully watched, for we none of us understood him yet. Miss Mary Robinson being very much—over much, I think—guided by him, sighed too.

"Come, come. Miss Robinson," I said, "there's nothing wrong with Eustace. Our experiences are mysterious, not his. He was astonished at our sudden departure, that's why he was so strange when we returned. He's right enough—improved, if anything."

"And is the worship of athletics, the cult of insensate activity, to be counted as an improvement?" put in Leyland, fixing a large, sorrowful eye on Eustace, who had stopped to scramble on to a rock to pick some cyclamen. "The passionate desire to rend from Nature the few beauties that have been still left her—that is to be counted as an improvement too?"

It is mere waste of time to reply to such remarks, especially when they come from an unsuccessful artist, suffering from a damaged finger. I changed the conversation by asking what we should say at the hotel. After some discussion, it was agreed that we should say nothing, either there or in our letters home. Importunate truth-telling, which brings only bewilderment and discomfort to the hearers, is, in my opinion, a mistake; and, after a long discussion, I managed to make Mr. Sandbach acquiesce in my view.

Eustace did not share in our conversation. He was racing about, like a real boy, in the wood to the right. A strange feeling of shame; prevented us from openly mentioning our fright to him. Indeed, it seemed almost reasonable to conclude that it had made but little impression on him. So it disconcerted us when he bounded back with an armful of flowering acanthus, calling out:

"Do you suppose Gennaro'll be there when we get back?"

Gennaro was the stop-gap waiter, a clumsy, impertinent fisher-lad, who had been had up from Minori in the absence of the nice English-speaking Emmanuele. It was to him that we owed our scrappy lunch; and I could not conceive why Eustace desired to see him, unless it was to make mock with him of our behavior.

"Yes, of course he will be there," said Miss Robinson. "Why do you ask, dear?"

"Oh, I thought I'd like to see him."

"And why?" snapped Mr. Sandbach.

"Because, because I do, I do; because, because I do." He danced away into the darkening wood to the rhythm of his words.

"This is very extraordinary," said Mr. Sandbach. "Did he like Gennaro before?"

"Gennaro has only been here two days," said Rose, "and I know that they haven't spoken to each other a dozen times."

Each time Eustace returned from the wood his spirits were higher. Once he came whooping down on us as a wild Indian, and another time he made believe to be a dog. The last time he came back with a poor dazed hare, too frightened to move, sitting on his arm. He was getting too uproarious, I thought; and we were all glad to leave the wood, and start upon the steep staircase path that leads down into Ravello. It was late and turning dark; and we made all the speed we could, Eustace scurrying in front of us like a goat.

Just where the staircase path debouches on the white high road, the next extraordinary incident of this extraordinary day occurred. Three old women were standing by the wayside. They, like ourselves, had come down from the woods, and they were resting their heavy bundles of fuel on the low parapet of the road. Eustace stopped in front of them, and, after a moment's deliberation, stepped forward and—kissed the left-hand one on the cheek!

"My good fellow!" exclaimed Mr. Sandbach, "are you quite crazy?"

Eustace said nothing, but offered the old woman some of his flowers, and then hurried on. I looked back; and the old woman's companions seemed as much astonished at the proceeding as we were. But she herself had put the flowers in her bosom, and was murmuring blessings.

This salutation of the old lady was the first example of Eustace's strange behavior, and we were both surprised and alarmed. It was useless talking to him, for he either made silly replies, or else bounded away without replying at all.

He made no reference on the way home to Gennaro, and I hoped that that was forgotten. But, when we came to the Piazza, in front of the Cathedral, he screamed out: "Gennaro! Gennaro!" at the top of his voice, and began running up the little alley that led to the hotel. Sure enough, there was Gennaro at the end of it, with his arms and legs sticking out of the nice little English-speaking waiter's dress suit, and a dirty fisherman's cap on his head —for, as the poor landlady truly said, however much she superintended his toilette, he always managed to introduce something incongruous into it before he had done.

Eustace sprang to meet him, and leapt right up into his arms, and put his own arms round his neck. And this in the presence, not only of us, but also of the landlady, the chambermaid, the facchino,[20] and of two American ladies who were coming for a few days' visit to the little hotel.

I always make a point of behaving pleasantly to Italians, however little they may deserve it; but this habit of promiscuous intimacy was perfectly intolerable and could only lead to familiarity and mortification for all. Taking Miss Robinson aside, I asked her permission to speak seriously to Eustace on the subject of intercourse with social inferiors. She granted it; but I determined to wait till the absurd boy had calmed down a little from the excitement of the day. Meanwhile, Gennaro, instead of attending to the wants of the two new ladies, carried Eustace into the house, as if it was the most natural thing in the world.

"*Ho capito*," I heard him say as he passed me. "*Ho capito*" is the Italian for "I have understood;" but, as Eustace had not spoken to him, I could not see the

---

[20] a porter, one who carries luggage

force of the remark. It served to increase our bewilderment, and, by the time we sat down at the dinner-table, our imaginations and our tongues were alike exhausted.

I omit from this account the various comments that were made, as few of them seem worthy of being recorded. But, for three or four hours, seven of us were pouring forth our bewilderment in a stream of appropriate and inappropriate exclamations. Some traced a connection between our behavior in the afternoon and the behavior of Eustace now. Others saw no connexion at all. Mr. Sandbach still held to the possibility of infernal influences, and also said that he ought to have a doctor. Leyland only saw the development of "that unspeakable Philistine, the boy." Rose maintained, to my surprise, that everything was excusable; while I began to see that the young gentleman wanted a sound thrashing. The poor Miss Robinsons swayed helplessly about between these diverse opinions; inclining now to careful supervision, now to acquiescence, now to corporal chastisement, now to Eno's Fruit Salt.

Dinner passed off fairly well, though Eustace was terribly fidgety, Gennaro as usual dropping the knives and spoons, and hawking and clearing his throat. He only knew a few words of English, and we were all reduced to Italian for making known our wants. Eustace, who had picked up a little somehow, asked for some oranges. To my annoyance, Gennaro, in his answer made use of the second person singular—a form only used when addressing those who are both intimates and equals. Eustace had brought it on himself; but an impertinence of this kind was an affront to us all, and I was determined to speak, and to speak at once.

When I heard him clearing the table I went in, and, summoning up my Italian, or rather Neapolitan—the Southern dialects are execrable—I said, "Gennaro! I heard you address Signor Eustace with 'Tu.'"

"It is true."

"You are not right. You must use 'Lei' or 'Voi'—more polite forms. And remember that, though Signor Eustace is sometimes silly and foolish—this afternoon for example—yet you must always behave respectfully to him; for he is a young English gentleman, and you are a poor Italian fisher-boy."

I know that speech sounds terribly snobbish, but in Italian one can say things that one would never dream of saying in English. Besides, it is no good speaking delicately to persons of that class. Unless you put things plainly, they take a vicious pleasure in misunderstanding you.

An honest English fisherman would have landed me one in the eye in a minute for such a remark, but the wretched down-trodden Italians have no pride. Gennaro only sighed, and said: "It is true."

"Quite so," I said, and turned to go. To my indignation I heard him add: "But sometimes it is not important."

"What do you mean?" I shouted.

He came close up to me with horrid gesticulating fingers.

"Signor Tytler, I wish to say this. If Eustazio asks me to call him 'Voi,' I will call him 'Voi.' Otherwise, no."

With that he seized up a tray of dinner things, and fled from the room with them; and I heard two more wine-glasses go on the court-yard floor.

I was now fairly angry, and strode out to interview Eustace. But he had gone to bed, and the landlady, to whom I also wished to speak, was engaged. After more vague wonderings, obscurely expressed owing to the presence of Janet and the two American ladies, we all went to bed, too, after a harassing and most extraordinary day.

III.

But the day was nothing to the night.

I suppose I had slept for about four hours, when I woke suddenly thinking I heard a noise in the garden. And, immediately, before my eyes were open, cold terrible fear seized me—not fear of something that was happening, like the fear in the wood, but fear of something that might happen.

Our room was on the first floor, looking out on to the garden—or terrace, it was rather: a wedge-shaped block of ground covered with roses and vines, and intersected with little asphalt paths. It was bounded on the small side by the house; round the two long sides ran a wall, only three feet above the terrace level, but with a good twenty feet drop over it into the olive yards, for the ground fell very precipitously away.

Trembling all over I stole to the window. There, pattering up and down the asphalt, paths, was something white. I was too much alarmed to see clearly; and in the uncertain light of the stars the thing took all manner of curious shapes. Now it was a great dog, now an enormous white bat, now a mass of quickly traveling cloud. It would bounce like a ball, or take short flights like a bird, or glide slowly; like a wraith. It gave no sound—save the pattering sound of what, after all, must be human feet. And at last the obvious explanation forced itself upon my disordered mind; and I realized that Eustace had got out of bed, and that we were in for something more.

I hastily dressed myself, and went down into the dining-room which opened upon the terrace. The door was already unfastened. My terror had almost entirely passed away, but for quite five minutes I struggled with a curious cowardly feeling, which bade me not interfere with the poor strange boy, but leave him to his ghostly patterings, and merely watch him from the window, to see he took no harm.

But better impulses prevailed and, opening the door, I called out:

"Eustace! what on earth are you doing? Come in at once."

He stopped his antics, and said: "I hate my bedroom. I could not stop in it, it is too small."

"Come! come! I'm tired of affectation. You've never complained of it before."

"Besides I can't see anything—no flowers, no leaves, no sky: only a stone wall." The outlook of Eustace's room certainly was limited; but, as I told him, he had never complained of it before.

"Eustace, you talk like a child. Come in! Prompt obedience, if you please."

He did not move.

"Very well: I shall carry you in by force." I added, and made a few steps towards him. But I was soon convinced of the futility of pursuing a boy through a tangle of asphalt paths, and went in instead, to call Mr. Sandbach and Leyland to my aid.

When I returned with them he was worse than ever. He would not even answer us when we spoke, but began singing and chattering to himself in a most alarming way.

"It's a case for the doctor now," said Mr. Sandbach, gravely tapping his forehead.

He had stopped his running and was singing, first low, then loud—singing five-finger exercises, scales, hymn tunes, scraps of Wagner—anything that came into his head. His voice—a very untuneful voice—grew stronger and stronger, and he ended with a tremendous shout which boomed like a gun among the mountains, and awoke everyone who was still sleeping in the hotel. My poor wife and the two girls appeared at their respective windows, and the American ladies were heard violently ringing their bell.

"Eustace," we all cried, "stop! stop, dear boy, and come into the house."

He shook his head, and started off again—talking this time. Never have I listened to such an extraordinary speech. At any other time it would have been ludicrous, for here was a boy, with no sense of beauty and a puerile command of words, attempting to tackle themes which the greatest poets have found almost beyond their power. Eustace Robinson, aged fourteen, was standing in his nightshirt saluting, praising, and blessing, the great forces and manifestations of Nature.

He spoke first of night and the stars and planets above his head, of the swarms of fire-flies below him, of the invisible sea below the fire-flies, of the great rocks covered with anemones and shells that were slumbering in the invisible sea. He spoke of the rivers and water-falls, of the ripening bunches of grapes, of the smoking cone of Vesuvius and the hidden fire-channels that made the smoke, of the myriads of lizards who were lying curled up in the crannies of the sultry earth, of the showers of white rose-leaves that were tangled in his hair. And then he spoke of the rain and the wind by which all things are changed, of the air through which all things live, and of the woods in which all things can be hidden.

Of course, it was all absurdly high fainting: yet I could have kicked Leyland for audibly observing that it was "a diabolical caricature of all that was most holy and beautiful in life."

"And then,"—Eustace was going on in the pitiable conversational doggerel which was his only mode of expression—"and then there are men, but I can't make them out so well." He knelt down by the parapet, and rested his head on his arms.

"Now's the time," whispered Leyland. I hate stealth, but we darted forward and endeavored to catch hold of him from behind. He was away in a twinkling, but turned round at once to look at us. As far as I could see in the starlight, he was crying. Leyland rushed at him again, and we tried to corner him among the asphalt paths, but without the slightest approach to success.

We returned, breathless and discomfited, leaving him to his madness in the further corner of the terrace. But my Rose had an inspiration.

"Papa," she called from the window, "if you get Gennaro, he might be able to catch him for you."

I had no wish to ask a favor of Gennaro, but, as the landlady had by now appeared on the scene, I begged her to summon him from the charcoal-bin in which he slept, and make him try what he could do.

She soon returned, and was shortly followed by Gennaro, attired in a dress coat, without either waistcoat, shirt, or vest, and a ragged pair of what had been trousers, cut short above the knees for purposes of wading. The landlady, who had quite picked up English ways, rebuked him for the incongruous and even indecent appearance which he presented.

"I have a coat and I have trousers. What more do you desire?"

"Never mind, Signora Scafetti," I put in, "As there are no ladies here, it is not of the slightest consequence." Then, turning to Gennaro, I said: "The aunts of Signor Eustace wish you to fetch him into the house."

He did not answer.

"Do you hear me? He is not well. I order you to fetch him into the house."

"Fetch! fetch!" said Signora Scafetti, and shook him roughly by the arm.

"Eustazio is well where he is."

"Fetch! fetch!" Signora Scafetti screamed, and let loose a flood of Italian, most of which, I am glad to say, I could not follow. I glanced up nervously at the girls' window, but they hardly know as much as I do, and I am thankful to say that none of us caught one word of Gennaro's answer.

The two yelled and shouted at each other for quite ten minutes, at the end of which Gennaro rushed back to his charcoal-bin and Signora Scafetti burst into tears, as well she might, for she greatly valued her English guests.

"He says," she sobbed, "that Signer Eustace is well where he is, and that he will not fetch him. I can do no more."

But I could, for, in my stupid British way, I have got some insight into the Italian character. I followed Mr. Gennaro to his place of repose, and found him wriggling down on to a dirty sack.

"I wish you to fetch Signor Eustace to me," I began.

He hurled at me an unintelligible reply.

"If you fetch him, I will give you this." And out of my pocket I took a new ten lira note.

This time he did not answer.

"This note is equal to ten lire in silver," I continued, for I knew that the poor-class Italian is unable to conceive of a single large sum.

"I know it."

"That is, two hundred soldi."

"I do not desire them. Eustazio is my friend."

I put the note into my pocket.

"Besides, you would not give it me."

"I am an Englishman. The English always do what they promise."

"That is true." It is astonishing how the most dishonest of nations trust us. Indeed they often trust us more than we trust one another. Gennaro knelt up on his sack. It was too dark to see his face, but I could feel his warm garlicky breath coming out in gasps, and I knew that the eternal avarice of the South had laid hold upon him.

"I could not fetch Eustazio to the house. He might die there."

"You need not do that," I replied patiently. "You need only bring him to me; and I will stand outside in the garden." And to this, as if it were something quite different, the pitiable youth consented.

"But give me first the ten lire."

"No,"—for I knew the kind of person with whom I had to deal. Once faithless, always faithless.

We returned to the terrace, and Gennaro, without a single word, pattered off towards the pattering that could be heard at the remoter end. Mr. Sandbach, Leyland, and myself moved away a little from the house, and stood in the shadow of the white climbing roses, practically invisible.

We heard "Eustazio" called, followed by absurd cries of pleasure from the poor boy. The pattering ceased, and we heard them talking. Their voices got nearer, and presently I could discern them through the creepers, the grotesque figure of the young man, and the slim little white-robed boy. Gennaro had his arm round Eustace's neck, and Eustace was talking away in his fluent, slip-shod Italian.

"I understand almost everything," I heard him say. "The trees, hills, stars, water, I can see all. But isn't it odd! I can't make out men a bit. Do you know what I mean?"

"*Ho capito*," said Gennaro gravely, and took his arm off Eustace's shoulder. But I made the new note crackle in my pocket; and he heard it. He stuck his hand out with a jerk; and the unsuspecting Eustace gripped it in his own.

"It is odd!" Eustace went on—they were quite close now—"It almost seems as if—as if—"

I darted out and caught hold of his arm, and Leyland got hold of the other arm, and Mr. Sandbach hung on to his feet. He gave shrill heart-piercing screams; and the white roses, which were falling early that year, descended in showers on him as we dragged him into the house.

As soon as we entered the house he stopped shrieking; but floods of tears silently burst forth, and spread over his upturned face.

"Not to my room," he pleaded. "It is so small."

His infinitely dolorous look filled me with strange pity, but what could I do? Besides, his window was the only one that had bars to it.

"Never mind, dear boy," said kind Mr. Sandbach. "I will bear you company till the morning."

At this his convulsive struggles began again. "Oh, please, not that. Anything but that. I will promise to lie still and not to cry more than I can help, if I am left alone."

So we laid him on the bed, and drew the sheets over him, and left him sobbing bitterly, and saying: "I nearly saw everything, and now I can see nothing at all."

We informed the Miss Robinsons of all that had happened, and returned to the dining-room, where we found Signora Scafetti and Gennaro whispering together. Mr. Sandbach got pen and paper, and began writing to the English doctor at Naples. I at once drew out the note, and flung it down on the table to Gennaro.

"Here is your pay," I said sternly, for I was thinking of the Thirty Pieces of Silver.

"Thank you very much, sir," said Gennaro, and grabbed it.

He was going off, when Leyland, whose interest and indifference were always equally misplaced, asked him what Eustace had meant by saying 'he could not make out men a bit.'

"I cannot say. Signor Eustazio—" (I was glad to observe a little deference at last) "has a subtle brain. He understands many things."

"But I heard you say you understood," Leyland persisted.

"I understand, but I cannot explain. I am a poor Italian fisher-lad. Yet, listen: I will try." I saw to my alarm that his manner was changing, and tried to stop him. But he sat down on the edge of the table and started off, with some absolutely incoherent remarks.

"It is sad," he observed at last. "What has happened is very sad. But what can I do? I am poor. It is not I."

I turned away in contempt. Leyland went on asking questions. He wanted to know who it was that Eustace had in his mind when he spoke.

"That is easy to say," Gennaro gravely answered. "It is you, it is I. It is all in this house, and many outside it. If he wishes for mirth, we discomfort him. If he asks to be alone, we disturb him. He longed for a friend, and found none for fifteen years. Then he found me, and the first night I—I who have been in the woods and understood things too—betray him to you, and send him in to die. But what could I do?"

"Gently, gently," said I.

"Oh, assuredly he will die. He will lie in the small room all night, and in the morning he will be dead. That I know for certain."

"There, that will do," said Mr. Sandbach. "I shall be sitting with him."

"Filomena Giusti sat all night with Caterina, but Caterina was dead in the morning. They would not let her out, though I begged, and prayed, and cursed, and beat the door, and climbed the wall. They were ignorant fools, and thought I wished to carry her away. And in the morning she was dead."

"What is all this?" I asked Signora Scafetti.

"All kinds of stories will get about," she replied, "and he, least of anyone, has reason to repeat them."

"And I am alive now," he went on, "because I had neither parents nor relatives nor friends, so that, when the first night came, I could run through the woods, and climb the rocks, and plunge into the water, until I had accomplished my desire!"

We heard a cry from Eustace's room—a faint but steady sound, like the sound of wind in a distant wood, heard by one standing in tranquillity.

"That," said Gennaro, "was the last noise of Caterina. I was hanging on to her window then, and it blew out past me."

And, lifting up his hand, in which my ten lira note was safely packed, he solemnly cursed Mr. Sandbach, and Leyland, and myself, and Fate, because Eustace was dying in the upstairs room. Such is the working of the Southern mind; and I verily believe that he would not have moved even then, had not Leyland, that unspeakable idiot, upset the lamp with his elbow. It was a patent self-extinguishing lamp, bought by Signora Scafetti, at my special request, to replace the dangerous thing that she was using. The result was, that it went out; and the mere physical change from light to darkness had more power over the ignorant animal nature of Gennaro than the most obvious dictates of logic and reason.

I felt, rather than saw, that he had left the room, and shouted out to Mr. Sandbach: "Have you got the key of Eustace's room in your pocket?" But Mr. Sandbach and Leyland were both on the floor, having mistaken each other for Gennaro, and some more precious time was wasted in finding a match. Mr. Sandbach had only just time to say that he had left the key in the door, in case the Miss Robinsons wished to pay Eustace a visit, when we heard a noise on the stairs, and there was Gennaro, carrying Eustace down.

We rushed out and blocked up the passage, and they lost heart and retreated to the upper landing.

"Now they are caught," cried Signora Scafetti. "There is no other way out."

We were cautiously ascending the staircase, when there was a terrific scream from my wife's room, followed by a heavy thud on the asphalt path. They had leapt out of her window.

I reached the terrace just in time to see Eustace jumping over the parapet of the garden wall. This time I knew for certain he would be killed. But he alighted in an olive tree, looking like a great white moth; and from the tree he slid on to the earth. And as soon as his bare feet touched the clods of earth he uttered a strange loud cry, such as I should not have thought the human voice could have produced, and disappeared among the trees below.

"He has understood and he is saved," cried Gennaro, who was still sitting on the asphalt path. "Now, instead of dying he will live!"

"And you, instead of keeping the ten lire, will give them up," I retorted, for at this theatrical remark I could contain myself no longer.

"The ten lire are mine," he hissed back, in a scarcely audible voice. He clasped his hand over his breast to protect his ill-gotten gains, and, as he did so, he swayed forward and fell upon his face on the path. He had not broken any limbs, and a leap like that would never have killed an Englishman, for the drop was not great. But those miserable Italians have no stamina. Something had gone wrong inside him, and he was dead.

The morning was still far off, but the morning breeze had begun, and more rose leaves fell on us as we carried him in. Signora Scafetti burst into screams at the sight of the dead body, and, far down the valley towards the sea, there still resounded the shouts and the laughter of the escaping boy.

THE MUSIC ON THE HILL

Saki

from *The Chronicles of Clovis* (1911)

Sylvia Seltoun ate her breakfast in the morning-room at Yessney with a pleasant sense of ultimate victory, such as a fervent Ironside might have permitted himself on the morrow of Worcester fight. She was scarcely pugnacious by temperament, but belonged to that more successful class of fighters who are pugnacious by circumstance. Fate had willed that her life should be occupied with a series of small struggles, usually with the odds slightly against her, and usually she had just managed to come through winning. And now she felt that she had brought her hardest and certainly her most important struggle to a successful issue. To have married Mortimer Seltoun, "Dead Mortimer" as his more intimate enemies called him, in the teeth of the cold hostility of his family, and in spite of his unaffected indifference to women, was indeed an achievement that had needed some determination and adroitness to carry through; yesterday she had brought her victory to its concluding stage by wrenching her husband away from Town and its group of satellite watering-places and "settling him down," in the vocabulary of her kind, in this remote wood-girt manor farm which was his country house.

"You will never get Mortimer to go," his mother had said carpingly, "but if he once goes he'll stay; Yessney throws almost as much a spell over him as Town does. One can understand what holds him to Town, but Yessney—" and the dowager had shrugged her shoulders.

There was a sombre almost savage wildness about Yessney that was certainly not likely to appeal to town-bred tastes, and Sylvia, notwithstanding her name, was accustomed to nothing much more sylvan than "leafy Kensington." She looked on the country as something excellent and wholesome in its way, which was apt to become troublesome if you encouraged it overmuch. Distrust of town life had been a new thing with her, born of her marriage with Mortimer, and she had watched with satisfaction the gradual fading of what she called "the Jermyn-Street-look" in his eyes as the woods and heather of Yessney had closed in on them yesternight. Her will-power and strategy had prevailed; Mortimer would stay. Outside the morning-room windows was a triangular slope of turf, which the indulgent might call a lawn, and beyond its low hedge of neglected fuchsia bushes a steeper slope of heather and bracken dropped down into cavernous combes overgrown with oak and yew.[21] In its wild open savagery there seemed a stealthy linking of the joy of life with the terror of unseen things. Sylvia smiled complacently as she gazed with a School-of-Art appreciation at the landscape, and then of a sudden she almost shuddered.

"It is very wild," she said to Mortimer, who had joined her; "one could almost think that in such a place the worship of Pan had never quite died out."

"The worship of Pan never has died out," said Mortimer. "Other newer gods have drawn aside his votaries from time to time, but he is the Nature-God to whom all must come back at last. He has been called the Father of all the Gods, but most of his children have been stillborn."

Sylvia was religious in an honest, vaguely devotional kind of way, and did not like to hear her beliefs spoken of as mere aftergrowths, but it was at least something new and hopeful to hear Dead Mortimer speak with such energy and conviction on any subject.

"You don't really believe in Pan?" she asked incredulously.

"I've been a fool in most things," said Mortimer quietly, "but I'm not such a fool as not to believe in Pan when I'm down here. And if you're wise you won't disbelieve in him too boastfully while you're in his country."

It was not till a week later, when Sylvia had exhausted the attractions of the woodland walks round Yessney, that she ventured on a tour of inspection of the farm buildings. A farmyard suggested in her mind a scene of cheerful bustle, with churns and flails and smiling dairymaids, and teams of horses drinking knee-deep in duck-crowded ponds. As she wandered among the gaunt grey buildings of Yessney manor farm her first impression was one of crushing stillness and desolation, as though she had happened on some lone deserted homestead long given over to owls and cobwebs; then came a sense of furtive watchful hostility, the same shadow of unseen things that seemed to lurk in the wooded combes and coppices. From behind heavy doors and shuttered windows came the restless stamp of hoof or rasp of chain halter, and at times a muffled bellow from some stalled beast. From a distant corner a shaggy dog watched her with intent unfriendly eyes; as she drew near it slipped quietly into its kennel, and slipped out again as noiselessly when she had passed by. A few hens, questing for food under a rick, stole away under a gate at her approach. Sylvia felt that if she had come across any human beings in this wilderness of barn and byre they would have fled wraith-like from her gaze. At last, turning a corner quickly, she came upon a living thing that did not fly from her. Astretch in a pool of mud was an enormous sow, gigantic beyond the town-woman's wildest computation of swine-flesh, and speedily alert to resent and if necessary repel the unwonted intrusion. It was

---

[21] A "combe" is a small valley, characterized by its steep and narrow form or as a hollow nestled on the side of a hill, devoid of flowing water.

Sylvia's turn to make an unobtrusive retreat. As she threaded her way past rickyards and cowsheds and long blank walls, she started suddenly at a strange sound - the echo of a boy's laughter, golden and equivocal. Jan, the only boy employed on the farm, a tow-headed, wizen-faced yokel, was visibly at work on a potato clearing half-way up the nearest hill-side, and Mortimer, when questioned, knew of no other probable or possible begetter of the hidden mockery that had ambushed Sylvia's retreat. The memory of that untraceable echo was added to her other impressions of a furtive sinister "something" that hung around Yessney.

Of Mortimer she saw very little; farm and woods and trout- streams seemed to swallow him up from dawn till dusk. Once, following the direction she had seen him take in the morning, she came to an open space in a nut copse, further shut in by huge yew trees, in the centre of which stood a stone pedestal surmounted by a small bronze figure of a youthful Pan. It was a beautiful piece of workmanship, but her attention was chiefly held by the fact that a newly cut bunch of grapes had been placed as an offering at its feet. Grapes were none too plentiful at the manor house, and Sylvia snatched the bunch angrily from the pedestal. Contemptuous annoyance dominated her thoughts as she strolled slowly homeward, and then gave way to a sharp feeling of something that was very near fright; across a thick tangle of undergrowth a boy's face was scowling at her, brown and beautiful, with unutterably evil eyes. It was a lonely pathway, all pathways round Yessney were lonely for the matter of that, and she sped forward without waiting to give a closer scrutiny to this sudden apparition. It was not till she had reached the house that she discovered that she had dropped the bunch of grapes in her flight.

"I saw a youth in the wood today," she told Mortimer that evening, "brown-faced and rather handsome, but a scoundrel to look at. A gipsy lad, I suppose."

"A reasonable theory," said Mortimer, "only there aren't any gipsies in these parts at present."

"Then who was he?" asked Sylvia, and as Mortimer appeared to have no theory of his own she passed on to recount her finding of the votive offering.

"I suppose it was your doing," she observed; "it's a harmless piece of lunacy, but people would think you dreadfully silly if they knew of it."

"Did you meddle with it in any way?" asked Mortimer.

"I - I threw the grapes away. It seemed so silly," said Sylvia, watching Mortimer's impassive face for a sign of annoyance.

"I don't think you were wise to do that," he said reflectively. "I've heard it said that the Wood Gods are rather horrible to those who molest them."

"Horrible perhaps to those that believe in them, but you see I don't," retorted Sylvia.

"All the same," said Mortimer in his even, dispassionate tone, "I should avoid the woods and orchards if I were you, and give a wide berth to the horned beasts on the farm."

It was all nonsense, of course, but in that lonely wood-girt spot nonsense seemed able to rear a bastard brood of uneasiness.

"Mortimer," said Sylvia suddenly, "I think we will go back to Town some time soon."

Her victory had not been so complete as she had supposed; it had carried her on to ground that she was already anxious to quit.

"I don't think you will ever go back to Town," said Mortimer. He seemed to be paraphrasing his mother's prediction as to himself.

Sylvia noted with dissatisfaction and some self-contempt that the course of her next afternoon's ramble took her instinctively clear of the network of woods. As to the horned cattle, Mortimer's warning was scarcely needed, for she had always regarded them as of doubtful neutrality at the best: her imagination unsexed the most matronly dairy cows and turned them into bulls liable to "see red" at any moment. The ram who fed in the narrow paddock below the orchards she had adjudged, after ample and cautious probation, to be of docile temper; today, however, she decided to leave his docility untested, for the usually tranquil beast was roaming with every sign of restlessness from corner to corner of his meadow. A low, fitful piping, as of some reedy flute, was coming from the depth of a neighboring copse, and there seemed to be some subtle connection between the animal's restless pacing and the wild music from the wood. Sylvia turned her steps in an upward direction and climbed the heather-clad slopes that stretched in rolling shoulders high above Yessney. She had left the piping notes behind her, but across the wooded combes at her feet the wind brought her another kind of music, the straining bay of hounds in full chase. Yessney was just on the outskirts of the Devon-and-Somerset country, and the hunted deer sometimes came that way. Sylvia could presently see a dark body, breasting hill after hill, and sinking again and again out of sight as he crossed the combes, while behind him steadily swelled that relentless chorus, and she grew tense with the excited sympathy that one feels for any hunted thing in whose capture one is not directly interested. And at last he broke through the outermost line of oak scrub and fern and stood panting in the open, a fat September stag carrying a well-furnished head. His obvious course was to drop down to the brown pools of undercombe, and thence make his way towards the red deer's favored sanctuary, the sea. To Sylvia's surprise, however, he turned his head to the upland slope and came lumbering resolutely onward over the heather. "It will be dreadful," she thought, "the hounds will pull him down under my very eyes." But the music of the pack seemed to have died away for a moment, and in its place she heard again that wild piping, which rose now on this side, now on that, as though urging the failing stag to a final effort. Sylvia stood well aside from his path, half hidden in a thick growth of whortle bushes, and watched him swing stiffly upward, his flanks dark with sweat, the coarse hair on his neck showing light by contrast. The pipe music shrilled suddenly around her, seeming to come from the bushes at her very feet, and at the same moment the great beast slewed round and bore directly down upon her. In an instant her pity for the hunted animal was changed to wild terror at her own danger; the thick heather roots mocked her scrambling efforts at flight, and she looked frantically downward for a glimpse of oncoming hounds. The huge antler spikes were within a few yards of her, and in a flash of numbing fear she remembered Mortimer's warning, to beware of horned beasts on the farm. And then with a quick throb of joy she saw that she was not alone; a human figure stood a few paces aside, knee-deep in the whortle bushes.

"Drive it off!" she shrieked. But the figure made no answering movement.

The antlers drove straight at her breast, the acrid smell of the hunted animal was in her nostrils, but her eyes were filled with the horror of something she saw other than her oncoming death. And in her ears rang the echo of a boy's laughter, golden and equivocal.

GOBLIN MARKET

Christina Rossetti

from *Goblin Market and Other Poems* (1862)

Morning and evening
Maids heard the goblins cry:
"Come buy our orchard fruits,
Come buy, come buy:
Apples and quinces,
Lemons and oranges,
Plump unpecked cherries,
Melons and raspberries,
Bloom-down-cheeked peaches,
Swart-headed mulberries,
Wild free-born cranberries,
Crab-apples, dewberries,
Pine-apples, blackberries,
Apricots, strawberries;—
All ripe together
In summer weather,—
Morns that pass by,
Fair eves that fly;
Come buy, come buy:
Our grapes fresh from the vine,
Pomegranates full and fine,
Dates and sharp bullaces,
Rare pears and greengages,
Damsons and bilberries,
Taste them and try:
Currants and gooseberries,
Bright-fire-like barberries,
Figs to fill your mouth,
Citrons from the South,
Sweet to tongue and sound to eye;
Come buy, come buy."

Evening by evening
Among the brookside rushes,
Laura bowed her head to hear,
Lizzie veiled her blushes:
Crouching close together
In the cooling weather,
With clasping arms and cautioning lips,
With tingling cheeks and finger tips.
"Lie close," Laura said,
Pricking up her golden head:
"We must not look at goblin men,
We must not buy their fruits:
Who knows upon what soil they fed
Their hungry thirsty roots?"
"Come buy," call the goblins
Hobbling down the glen.

"Oh," cried Lizzie, "Laura, Laura,
You should not peep at goblin men."
Lizzie covered up her eyes,
Covered close lest they should look;
Laura reared her glossy head,
And whispered like the restless brook:
"Look, Lizzie, look, Lizzie,
Down the glen tramp little men.
One hauls a basket,
One bears a plate,
One lugs a golden dish
Of many pounds weight.
How fair the vine must grow
Whose grapes are so luscious;
How warm the wind must blow
Through those fruit bushes."
"No," said Lizzie, "No, no, no;
Their offers should not charm us,
Their evil gifts would harm us."
She thrust a dimpled finger
In each ear, shut eyes and ran:
Curious Laura chose to linger
Wondering at each merchant man.
One had a cat's face,
One whisked a tail,
One tramped at a rat's pace,
One crawled like a snail,
One like a wombat prowled obtuse and furry,

One like a ratel tumbled hurry skurry.
She heard a voice like voice of doves
Cooing all together:
They sounded kind and full of loves
In the pleasant weather.

Laura stretched her gleaming neck
Like a rush-imbedded swan,
Like a lily from the beck,
Like a moonlit poplar branch,
Like a vessel at the launch
When its last restraint is gone.

Backwards up the mossy glen
Turned and trooped the goblin men,
With their shrill repeated cry,
"Come buy, come buy."
When they reached where Laura was
They stood stock still upon the moss,
Leering at each other,
Brother with queer brother;
Signaling each other,
Brother with sly brother.
One set his basket down,
One reared his plate;
One began to weave a crown
Of tendrils, leaves, and rough nuts brown
(Men sell not such in any town);
One heaved the golden weight
Of dish and fruit to offer her:
"Come buy, come buy," was still their cry.
Laura stared but did not stir,
Longed but had no money:
The whisk-tailed merchant bade her taste
In tones as smooth as honey,
The cat-faced purr'd,
The rat-faced spoke a word
Of welcome, and the snail-paced even was heard;
One parrot-voiced and jolly
Cried "Pretty Goblin" still for "Pretty Polly;"—
One whistled like a bird.

But sweet-tooth Laura spoke in haste
"Good folk, I have no coin;
To take were to purloin:

I have no copper in my purse,
I have no silver either,
And all my gold is on the furze
That shakes in windy weather
Above the rusty heather."
"You have much gold upon your head,"
They answered all together:
"Buy from us with a golden curl."
She clipped a precious golden lock,
She dropped a tear more rare than pearl,
Then sucked their fruit globes fair or red:
Sweeter than honey from the rock,
Stronger than man-rejoicing wine,
Clearer than water flowed that juice;
She never tasted such before,
How should it cloy with length of use?
She sucked and sucked and sucked the more
Fruits which that unknown orchard bore;
She sucked until her lips were sore;
Then flung the emptied rinds away
But gathered up one kernel stone,
And knew not was it night or day
As she turned home alone.

Lizzie met her at the gate
Full of wise upbraidings:
"Dear, you should not stay so late,
Twilight is not good for maidens;
Should not loiter in the glen
In the haunts of goblin men.
Do you not remember Jeanie,
How she met them in the moonlight,
Took their gifts both choice and many,
Ate their fruits and wore their flowers
Plucked from bowers
Where summer ripens at all hours?
But ever in the noonlight
She pined and pined away;
Sought them by night and day,
Found them no more, but dwindled and grew grey;
Then fell with the first snow,
While to this day no grass will grow
Where she lies low:
I planted daisies there a year ago
That never blow.

You should not loiter so."
"Nay, hush," said Laura:
"Nay, hush, my sister:
I ate and ate my fill,
Yet my mouth waters still;
Tomorrow night I will
Buy more:" and kissed her:
"Have done with sorrow;
I'll bring you plums tomorrow
Fresh on their mother twigs,
Cherries worth getting;
You cannot think what figs
My teeth have met in,
What melons icy-cold
Piled on a dish of gold
Too huge for me to hold,
What peaches with a velvet nap,
Pellucid grapes without one seed:
Odorous indeed must be the mead
Whereon they grow, and pure the wave they drink
With lilies at the brink,
And sugar-sweet their sap."

Golden head by golden head,
Like two pigeons in one nest
Folded in each other's wings,
They lay down in their curtained bed:
Like two blossoms on one stem,
Like two flakes of new-fall'n snow,
Like two wands of ivory
Tipped with gold for awful kings.
Moon and stars gazed in at them,
Wind sang to them lullaby,
Lumbering owls forbore to fly,
Not a bat flapped to and fro
Round their rest:
Cheek to cheek and breast to breast
Locked together in one nest.

Early in the morning
When the first cock crowed his warning,
Neat like bees, as sweet and busy,
Laura rose with Lizzie:
Fetched in honey, milked the cows,
Aired and set to rights the house,

Kneaded cakes of whitest wheat,
Cakes for dainty mouths to eat,
Next churned butter, whipped up cream,
Fed their poultry, sat and sewed;
Talked as modest maidens should:
Lizzie with an open heart,
Laura in an absent dream,
One content, one sick in part;
One warbling for the mere bright day's delight,
One longing for the night.

At length slow evening came:
They went with pitchers to the reedy brook;
Lizzie most placid in her look,
Laura most like a leaping flame.
They drew the gurgling water from its deep;
Lizzie plucked purple and rich golden flags,
Then turning homeward said: "The sunset flushes
Those furthest loftiest crags;
Come, Laura, not another maiden lags,
No willful squirrel wags,
The beasts and birds are fast asleep."
But Laura loitered still among the rushes
And said the bank was steep.

And said the hour was early still
The dew not fall'n, the wind not chill:
Listening ever, but not catching
The customary cry,
"Come buy, come buy,"
With its iterated jingle
Of sugar-baited words:
Not for all her watching
Once discerning even one goblin
Racing, whisking, tumbling, hobbling;
Let alone the herds
That used to tramp along the glen,
In groups or single,
Of brisk fruit-merchant men.

Till Lizzie urged, "O Laura, come;
I hear the fruit-call but I dare not look:
You should not loiter longer at this brook:
Come with me home.
The stars rise, the moon bends her arc,

Each glowworm winks her spark,
Let us get home before the night grows dark:
For clouds may gather
Though this is summer weather,
Put out the lights and drench us through;
Then if we lost our way what should we do?"

Laura turned cold as stone
To find her sister heard that cry alone,
That goblin cry,
"Come buy our fruits, come buy."
Must she then buy no more such dainty fruit?
Must she no more such succous pasture find,
Gone deaf and blind?
Her tree of life drooped from the root:
She said not one word in her heart's sore ache;
But peering thro' the dimness, nought discerning,
Trudged home, her pitcher dripping all the way;
So crept to bed, and lay
Silent till Lizzie slept;
Then sat up in a passionate yearning,
And gnashed her teeth for baulked desire, and wept
As if her heart would break.

Day after day, night after night,
Laura kept watch in vain
In sullen silence of exceeding pain.
She never caught again the goblin cry:
"Come buy, come buy;"—
She never spied the goblin men
Hawking their fruits along the glen:
But when the noon waxed bright
Her hair grew thin and grey;
She dwindled, as the fair full moon doth turn
To swift decay and burn
Her fire away.

One day remembering her kernel-stone
She set it by a wall that faced the south;
Dewed it with tears, hoped for a root,
Watched for a waxing shoot,
But there came none;
It never saw the sun,
It never felt the trickling moisture run:
While with sunk eyes and faded mouth

She dreamed of melons, as a traveler sees
False waves in desert drouth
With shade of leaf-crowned trees,
And burns the thirstier in the sandful breeze.

She no more swept the house,
Tended the fowls or cows,
Fetched honey, kneaded cakes of wheat,
Brought water from the brook:
But sat down listless in the chimney-nook
And would not eat.

Tender Lizzie could not bear
To watch her sister's cankerous care
Yet not to share.
She night and morning
Caught the goblins' cry:
"Come buy our orchard fruits,
Come buy, come buy:"—
Beside the brook, along the glen,
She heard the tramp of goblin men,
The voice and stir
Poor Laura could not hear;
Longed to buy fruit to comfort her,
But feared to pay too dear.
She thought of Jeanie in her grave,
Who should have been a bride;
But who for joys brides hope to have
Fell sick and died
In her gay prime,
In earliest Winter time
With the first glazing rime,
With the first snow-fall of crisp Winter time.

Till Laura dwindling
Seemed knocking at Death's door:
Then Lizzie weighed no more
Better and worse;
But put a silver penny in her purse,
Kissed Laura, crossed the heath with clumps of furze
At twilight, halted by the brook:
And for the first time in her life
Began to listen and look.

Laughed every goblin

When they spied her peeping:
Came towards her hobbling,
Flying, running, leaping,
Puffing and blowing,
Chuckling, clapping, crowing,
Clucking and gobbling,
Mopping and mowing,
Full of airs and graces,
Pulling wry faces,
Demure grimaces,
Cat-like and rat-like,
Ratel- and wombat-like,
Snail-paced in a hurry,
Parrot-voiced and whistler,
Helter skelter, hurry skurry,
Chattering like magpies,
Fluttering like pigeons,
Gliding like fishes,—
Hugged her and kissed her:
Squeezed and caressed her:
Stretched up their dishes,
Panniers, and plates:
"Look at our apples
Russet and dun,
Bob at our cherries,
Bite at our peaches,
Citrons and dates,
Grapes for the asking,
Pears red with basking
Out in the sun,
Plums on their twigs;
Pluck them and suck them,
Pomegranates, figs."—

"Good folk," said Lizzie,
Mindful of Jeanie:
"Give me much and many:"—
Held out her apron,
Tossed them her penny.
"Nay, take a seat with us,
Honor and eat with us,"
They answered grinning:
"Our feast is but beginning.
Night yet is early,
Warm and dew-pearly,

Wakeful and starry:
Such fruits as these
No man can carry;
Half their bloom would fly,
Half their dew would dry,
Half their flavor would pass by.
Sit down and feast with us,
Be welcome guest with us,
Cheer you and rest with us."—
"Thank you," said Lizzie: "But one waits
At home alone for me:
So without further parleying,
If you will not sell me any
Of your fruits though much and many,
Give me back my silver penny
I tossed you for a fee."—
They began to scratch their pates,
No longer wagging, purring,
But visibly demurring,
Grunting and snarling.
One called her proud,
Cross-grained, uncivil;
Their tones waxed loud,
Their looks were evil.
Lashing their tails
They trod and hustled her,
Elbowed and jostled her,
Clawed with their nails,
Barking, mewing, hissing, mocking,
Tore her gown and soiled her stocking,
Twitched her hair out by the roots,
Stamped upon her tender feet,
Held her hands and squeezed their fruits
Against her mouth to make her eat.

White and golden Lizzie stood,
Like a lily in a flood,—
Like a rock of blue-veined stone
Lashed by tides obstreperously,—
Like a beacon left alone
In a hoary roaring sea,
Sending up a golden fire,—
Like a fruit-crowned orange-tree
White with blossoms honey-sweet
Sore beset by wasp and bee,—

Like a royal virgin town
Topped with gilded dome and spire
Close beleaguered by a fleet
Mad to tug her standard down.

One may lead a horse to water,
Twenty cannot make him drink.
Though the goblins cuffed and caught her,
Coaxed and fought her,
Bullied and besought her,
Scratched her, pinched her black as ink,
Kicked and knocked her,
Mauled and mocked her,
Lizzie uttered not a word;
Would not open lip from lip
Lest they should cram a mouthful in:
But laughed in heart to feel the drip
Of juice that syrupped all her face,
And lodged in dimples of her chin,
And streaked her neck which quaked like curd.
At last the evil people,
Worn out by her resistance,
Flung back her penny, kicked their fruit
Along whichever road they took,
Not leaving root or stone or shoot;
Some writhed into the ground,
Some dived into the brook
With ring and ripple,
Some scudded on the gale without a sound,
Some vanished in the distance.

In a smart, ache, tingle,
Lizzie went her way;
Knew not was it night or day;
Sprang up the bank, tore thro' the furze,
Threaded copse and dingle,
And heard her penny jingle
Bouncing in her purse,—
Its bounce was music to her ear.
She ran and ran
As if she feared some goblin man
Dogged her with gibe or curse
Or something worse:
But not one goblin scurried after,
Nor was she pricked by fear;

The kind heart made her windy-paced
That urged her home quite out of breath with haste
And inward laughter.

She cried "Laura," up the garden,
"Did you miss me?
Come and kiss me.
Never mind my bruises,
Hug me, kiss me, suck my juices
Squeezed from goblin fruits for you,
Goblin pulp and goblin dew.
Eat me, drink me, love me;
Laura, make much of me:
For your sake I have braved the glen
And had to do with goblin merchant men."

Laura started from her chair,
Flung her arms up in the air,
Clutched her hair:
"Lizzie, Lizzie, have you tasted
For my sake the fruit forbidden?
Must your light like mine be hidden,
Your young life like mine be wasted,
Undone in mine undoing,
And ruined in my ruin,
Thirsty, cankered, goblin-ridden?"—
She clung about her sister,
Kissed and kissed and kissed her:
Tears once again
Refreshed her shrunken eyes,
Dropping like rain
After long sultry drouth;
Shaking with aguish fear, and pain,
She kissed and kissed her with a hungry mouth.

Her lips began to scorch,
That juice was wormwood to her tongue,
She loathed the feast:
Writhing as one possessed she leaped and sung,
Rent all her robe, and wrung
Her hands in lamentable haste,
And beat her breast.
Her locks streamed like the torch
Borne by a racer at full speed,
Or like the mane of horses in their flight,

Or like an eagle when she stems the light
Straight toward the sun,
Or like a caged thing freed,
Or like a flying flag when armies run.

Swift fire spread through her veins, knocked at her heart,
Met the fire smoldering there
And overbore its lesser flame;
She gorged on bitterness without a name:
Ah! fool, to choose such part
Of soul-consuming care!
Sense failed in the mortal strife:
Like the watch-tower of a town
Which an earthquake shatters down,
Like a lightning-stricken mast,
Like a wind-uprooted tree
Spun about,
Like a foam-topped waterspout
Cast down headlong in the sea,
She fell at last;
Pleasure past and anguish past,
Is it death or is it life?

Life out of death.
That night long Lizzie watched by her,
Counted her pulse's flagging stir,
Felt for her breath,
Held water to her lips, and cooled her face
With tears and fanning leaves:
But when the first birds chirped about their eaves,
And early reapers plodded to the place
Of golden sheaves,
And dew-wet grass
Bowed in the morning winds so brisk to pass,
And new buds with new day
Opened of cup-like lilies on the stream,
Laura awoke as from a dream,
Laughed in the innocent old way,
Hugged Lizzie but not twice or thrice;
Her gleaming locks showed not one thread of grey,
Her breath was sweet as May
And light danced in her eyes.

Days, weeks, months, year
Afterwards, when both were wives

With children of their own;
Their mother-hearts beset with fears,
Their lives bound up in tender lives;
Laura would call the little ones
And tell them of her early prime,
Those pleasant days long gone
Of not-returning time:
Would talk about the haunted glen,
The wicked, quaint fruit-merchant men,
Their fruits like honey to the throat
But poison in the blood;
(Men sell not such in any town:)
Would tell them how her sister stood
In deadly peril to do her good,
And win the fiery antidote:
Then joining hands to little hands
Would bid them cling together,
"For there is no friend like a sister
In calm or stormy weather;
To cheer one on the tedious way,
To fetch one if one goes astray,
To lift one if one totters down
To strengthen whilst one stands."

The Bottle Imp

Robert Louis Stevenson

first published in the *New York Herald* (February–March 1891)

There was a man of the Island of Hawaii, whom I shall call Keawe; for the truth is, he still lives, and his name must be kept secret; but the place of his birth was not far from Honaunau, where the bones of Keawe the Great lie hidden in a cave. This man was poor, brave, and active; he could read and write like a schoolmaster; he was a first-rate mariner besides, sailed for some time in the island steamers, and steered a whaleboat on the Hamakua coast. At length it came in Keawe's mind to have a sight of the great world and foreign cities, and he shipped on a vessel bound to San Francisco.

This is a fine town, with a fine harbor, and rich people uncountable; and, in particular, there is one hill which is covered with palaces. Upon this hill Keawe was one day taking a walk with his pocket full of money, viewing the great houses upon either hand with pleasure, "What fine houses these are!" he was thinking, "and how happy must those people be who dwell in them, and take no care for the morrow!" The thought was in his mind when he came abreast of a house that was smaller than some others, but all finished and beautified like a toy; the steps of that house shone like silver, and the borders of the garden bloomed like garlands, and the windows were bright like diamond; and Keawe stopped and wondered at the excellence of all he saw. So stopping, he was aware of a man that looked forth upon him through a window so clear that Keawe could see him as you see a fish in a pool upon the reef. The man was elderly, with a bald head and a black beard; and his face was heavy with sorrow, and he bitterly sighed. And the truth of it is, that as Keawe looked in upon the man, and the man looked out upon Keawe, each envied the other.

All of a sudden, the man smiled and nodded, and beckoned Keawe to enter, and met him at the door of the house.

"This is a fine house of mine," said the man, and bitterly sighed. "Would you not care to view the chambers?"

So he led Keawe all over it, from the cellar to the roof, and there was nothing there that was not perfect of its kind, and Keawe was astonished.

"Truly," said Keawe, "this is a beautiful house; if I lived in the like of it, I should be laughing all day long. How comes it, then, that you should be sighing?"

"There is no reason," said the man, "why you should not have a house in all points similar to this, and finer, if you wish. You have some money, I suppose?"

"I have fifty dollars," said Keawe; "but a house like this will cost more than fifty dollars."

The man made a computation. "I am sorry you have no more," said he, "for it may raise you trouble in the future; but it shall be yours at fifty dollars."

"The house?" asked Keawe.

"No, not the house," replied the man; "but the bottle. For, I must tell you, although I appear to you so rich and fortunate, all my fortune, and this house itself and its garden, came out of a bottle not much bigger than a pint. This is it."

And he opened a lockfast place, and took out a round-bellied bottle with a long neck; the glass of it was white like milk, with changing rainbow colors in the grain. Withinsides something obscurely moved, like a shadow and a fire.

"This is the bottle," said the man; and, when Keawe laughed, "You do not believe me?" he added. "Try, then, for yourself. See if you can break it."

So Keawe took the bottle up and dashed it on the floor till he was weary; but it jumped on the floor like a child's ball, and was not injured.

"This is a strange thing," said Keawe. "For by the touch of it, as well as by the look, the bottle should be of glass."

"Of glass it is," replied the man, sighing more heavily than ever; "but the glass of it was tempered in the flames of hell. An imp lives in it, and that is the shadow we behold there moving: or so I suppose. If any man buy this bottle the imp is at his command; all that he desires—love, fame, money, houses like this house, ay, or a city like this city—all are his at the word uttered. Napoleon had this bottle, and by it he grew to be the king of the world; but he sold it at the last, and fell. Captain Cook had this bottle, and by it he found his way to so many islands; but he, too, sold it, and was slain upon Hawaii. For, once it is sold, the power goes and the protection; and unless a man remain content with what he has, ill will befall him."

"And yet you talk of selling it yourself?" Keawe said.

"I have all I wish, and I am growing elderly," replied the man. "There is one thing the imp cannot do—he cannot prolong life; and, it would not be fair to conceal from you, there is a drawback to the bottle; for if a man die before he sells it, he must burn in hell forever."

"To be sure, that is a drawback and no mistake," cried Keawe. "I would not meddle with the thing. I can do without a house, thank God; but there is one thing I could not be doing with one particle, and that is to be damned."

"Dear me, you must not run away with things," returned the man. "All you have to do is to use the power of the imp in moderation, and then sell it to someone else, as I do to you, and finish your life in comfort."

"Well, I observe two things," said Keawe. "All the time you keep sighing like a maid in love, that is one; and, for the other, you sell this bottle very cheap."

"I have told you already why I sigh," said the man. "It is because I fear my health is breaking up; and, as you said yourself, to die and go to the devil is a pity for anyone. As for why I sell so cheap, I must explain to you there is a peculiarity about the bottle. Long ago, when the devil brought it first upon earth, it was extremely expensive, and was sold first of all to Prester John for many millions of dollars; but it cannot be sold at all, unless sold at a loss. If you sell it for as much as you paid for it, back it comes to you again like a homing pigeon. It follows that the price has kept falling in these centuries, and the bottle is now remarkably cheap. I bought it myself from one of my great neighbors on this hill, and the price I paid was only ninety dollars. I could sell it for as high as eighty-nine dollars and ninety-nine cents, but not a penny dearer, or back the thing must come to me. Now, about this there are two bothers. First, when you offer a bottle so singular for eighty odd dollars, people suppose you to be jesting. And second—but there is no hurry about that—and I need not go into it. Only remember it must be coined money that you sell it for."

"How am I to know that this is all true?" asked Keawe.

"Some of it you can try at once," replied the man. "Give me your fifty dollars, take the bottle, and wish your fifty dollars back into your pocket. If that does not happen, I pledge you my honor I will cry off the bargain and restore your money."

"You are not deceiving me?" said Keawe.

The man bound himself with a great oath.

"Well, I will risk that much," said Keawe, "for that can do no harm." And he paid over his money to the man, and the man handed him the bottle.

"Imp of the bottle," said Keawe, "I want my fifty dollars back." And sure enough he had scarce said the word before his pocket was as heavy as ever.

"To be sure this is a wonderful bottle," said Keawe.

"And now good-morning to you, my fine fellow, and the devil go with you for me!" said the man.

"Hold on," said Keawe, "I don't want any more of this fun. Here, take your bottle back."

"You have bought it for less than I paid for it," replied the man, rubbing his hands. "It is yours now; and, for my part, I am only concerned to see the back of you." And with that he rang for his Chinese servant, and had Keawe shown out of the house.

Now, when Keawe was in the street, with the bottle under his arm, he began to think. "If all is true about this bottle, I may have made a losing bargain," thinks he. "But perhaps the man was only fooling me." The first thing he did was to count his money; the sum was exact—forty-nine dollars American money, and one Chili piece. "That looks like the truth," said Keawe. "Now I will try another part."

The streets in that part of the city were as clean as a ship's decks, and though it was noon, there were no passengers. Keawe set the bottle in the gutter and walked away. Twice he looked back, and there was the milky, round-bellied bottle where he left it. A third time he looked back, and turned a corner; but he had scarce done so, when something knocked upon his elbow, and behold! it was the long neck sticking up; and as for the round belly, it was jammed into the pocket of his pilot-coat.

"And that looks like the truth," said Keawe.

The next thing he did was to buy a cork-screw in a shop, and go apart into a secret place in the fields. And there he tried to draw the cork, but as often as he put the screw in, out it came again, and the cork as whole as ever.

"This is some new sort of cork," said Keawe, and all at once he began to shake and sweat, for he was afraid of that bottle.

On his way back to the portside, he saw a shop where a man sold shells and clubs from the wild islands, old heathen deities, old coined money, pictures from China and Japan, and all manner of things that sailors bring in their sea-chests. And here he had an idea. So he went in and offered the bottle for a hundred dollars. The man of the shop laughed at him at the first, and offered him five; but, indeed, it was a curious bottle—such glass was never blown in any human glassworks, so prettily the colors shone under the milky white, and so strangely the shadow hovered in the midst; so, after he had disputed awhile after the manner of his kind, the shop-man gave Keawe sixty silver dollars for the thing, and set it on a shelf in the midst of his window.

"Now," said Keawe, "I have sold that for sixty which I bought for fifty—or, to say truth, a little less, because one of my dollars was from Chili. Now I shall know the truth upon another point."

So he went back on board his ship, and, when he opened his chest, there was the bottle, and had come more quickly than himself. Now Keawe had a mate on board whose name was Lopaka.

"What ails you?" said Lopaka, "that you stare in your chest?"

They were alone in the ship's forecastle, and Keawe bound him to secrecy, and told all.

"This is a very strange affair," said Lopaka; "and I fear you will be in trouble about this bottle. But there is one point very clear—that you are sure of the trouble, and you had better have the profit in the bargain. Make up your mind what you want with it; give the order, and if it is done as you desire, I will buy the bottle myself; for I have an idea of my own to get a schooner, and go trading through the islands."

"That is not my idea," said Keawe; "but to have a beautiful house and garden on the Kona Coast, where I was born, the sun shining in at the door, flowers in the garden, glass in the windows, pictures on the walls, and toys and fine carpets on the tables, for all the world like the house I was in this day—only a storey higher, and with balconies all about like the King's palace; and to live there without care and make merry with my friends and relatives."

"Well," said Lopaka, "let us carry it back with us to Hawaii; and if all comes true, as you suppose, I will buy the bottle, as I said, and ask a schooner."

Upon that they were agreed, and it was not long before the ship returned to Honolulu, carrying Keawe and Lopaka, and the bottle. They were scarce come ashore when they met a friend upon the beach, who began at once to condole with Keawe.

"I do not know what I am to be condoled about," said Keawe.

"Is it possible you have not heard," said the friend, "your uncle—that good old man—is dead, and your cousin—that beautiful boy—was drowned at sea?"

Keawe was filled with sorrow, and, beginning to weep and to lament, he forgot about the bottle. But Lopaka was thinking to himself, and presently, when Keawe's grief was a little abated, "I have been thinking," said Lopaka. "Had not your uncle lands in Hawaii, in the district of Kau?"

"No," said Keawe, "not in Kau; they are on the mountain-side—a little way south of Hookena."

"These lands will now be yours?" asked Lopaka.

"And so they will," says Keawe, and began again to lament for his relatives.

"No," said Lopaka, "do not lament at present. I have a thought in my mind. How if this should be the doing of the bottle? For here is the place ready for your house."

"If this be so," cried Keawe, "it is a very ill way to serve me by killing my relatives. But it may be, indeed; for it was in just such a station that I saw the house with my mind's eye."

"The house, however, is not yet built," said Lopaka.

"No, nor like to be!" said Keawe; "for though my uncle has some coffee and ava and bananas, it will not be more than will keep me in comfort; and the rest of that land is the black lava."

"Let us go to the lawyer," said Lopaka; "I have still this idea in my mind."

Now, when they came to the lawyer's, it appeared Keawe's uncle had grown monstrous rich in the last days, and there was a fund of money.

"And here is the money for the house!" cried Lopaka.

"If you are thinking of a new house," said the lawyer, "here is the card of a new architect, of whom they tell me great things."

"Better and better!" cried Lopaka. "Here is all made plain for us. Let us continue to obey orders."

So they went to the architect, and he had drawings of houses on his table.

"You want something out of the way," said the architect. "How do you like this?" and he handed a drawing to Keawe.

Now, when Keawe set eyes on the drawing, he cried out aloud, for it was the picture of his thought exactly drawn.

"I am in for this house," thought he. "Little as I like the way it comes to me, I am in for it now, and I may as well take the good along with the evil."

So he told the architect all that he wished, and how he would have that house furnished, and about the pictures on the wall and the knick-knacks on the tables; and he asked the man plainly for how much he would undertake the whole affair.

The architect put many questions, and took his pen and made a computation; and when he had done he named the very sum that Keawe had inherited.

Lopaka and Keawe looked at one another and nodded.

"It is quite clear," thought Keawe, "that I am to have this house, whether or no. It comes from the devil, and I fear I will get little good by that; and of one thing I am sure, I will make no more wishes as long as I have this bottle. But with the house I am saddled, and I may as well take the good along with the evil."

So he made his terms with the architect, and they signed a paper; and Keawe and Lopaka took ship again and sailed to Australia; for it was concluded between them they should not interfere at all, but leave the architect and the bottle imp to build and to adorn that house at their own pleasure.

The voyage was a good voyage, only all the time Keawe was holding in his breath, for he had sworn he would utter no more wishes, and take no more favors from the devil. The time was up when they got back. The architect told them that the house was ready, and Keawe and Lopaka took a passage in the *Hall*, and went down Kona way to view the house, and see if all had been done fitly according to the thought that was in Keawe's mind.

Now the house stood on the mountain side, visible to ships. Above, the forest ran up into the clouds of rain; below, the black lava fell in cliffs, where the kings of old lay buried. A garden bloomed about that house with every hue of flowers; and there was an orchard of papaya on the one hand and an orchard of breadfruit on the other, and right in front, toward the sea, a ship's mast had been rigged up and bore a flag. As for the house, it was three stories high, with great chambers and broad balconies on each. The windows were of glass, so excellent that it was as clear as water and as bright as day. All manner of furniture adorned the chambers. Pictures hung upon the wall in golden frames: pictures of ships, and men fighting, and of the most beautiful women, and of singular places; nowhere in the world are there pictures of so bright a color as those Keawe found hanging in his house. As for the knick-knacks, they were extraordinary fine; chiming clocks and musical boxes, little men with nodding heads, books filled with pictures, weapons of price from all quarters of the world, and the most elegant puzzles to entertain the leisure of a solitary man. And as no one would care to live in such chambers, only to walk through and view them, the balconies were made so broad that a whole town might have lived upon them in delight; and Keawe knew not which to prefer, whether the back porch, where you got the land breeze, and looked upon the orchards and the flowers, or the front balcony, where you could drink the wind of the sea, and look down the steep wall of the mountain and see the *Hall* going by once a week or so between Hookena and the hills of Pele, or the schooners plying up the coast for wood and ava and bananas.

When they had viewed all, Keawe and Lopaka sat on the porch.

"Well," asked Lopaka, "is it all as you designed?"

"Words cannot utter it," said Keawe. "It is better than I dreamed, and I am sick with satisfaction."

"There is but one thing to consider," said Lopaka; "all this may be quite natural, and the bottle imp have nothing whatever to say to it. If I were to buy the bottle, and got no schooner after all, I should have put my hand in the fire for nothing. I gave you my word, I know; but yet I think you would not grudge me one more proof."

"I have sworn I would take no more favors," said Keawe. "I have gone already deep enough."

"This is no favor I am thinking of," replied Lopaka. "It is only to see the imp himself. There is nothing to be gained by that, and so nothing to be ashamed of; and yet, if I once saw him, I should be sure of the whole matter. So indulge me so far, and let me see the imp; and, after that, here is the money in my hand, and I will buy it."

"There is only one thing I am afraid of," said Keawe. "The imp may be very ugly to view; and if you once set eyes upon him you might be very undesirous of the bottle."

"I am a man of my word," said Lopaka. "And here is the money betwixt us."

"Very well," replied Keawe. "I have a curiosity myself. So come, let us have one look at you, Mr. Imp."

Now as soon as that was said, the imp looked out of the bottle, and in again, swift as a lizard; and there sat Keawe and Lopaka turned to stone. The night had quite come, before either found a thought to say or voice to say it with; and then Lopaka pushed the money over and took the bottle.

"I am a man of my word," said he, "and had need to be so, or I would not touch this bottle with my foot. Well, I shall get my schooner and a dollar or two for my pocket; and then I will be rid of this devil as fast as I can. For to tell you the plain truth, the look of him has cast me down."

"Lopaka," said Keawe, "do not you think any worse of me than you can help; I know it is night, and the roads bad, and the pass by the tombs an ill place to go by so late, but I declare since I have seen that little face, I cannot eat or sleep or pray till it is gone from me. I will give you a lantern and a basket to put the bottle in, and any picture or fine thing in all my house that takes your fancy;—and be gone at once, and go sleep at Hookena with Nahinu."

"Keawe," said Lopaka, "many a man would take this ill; above all, when I am doing you a turn so friendly, as to keep my word and buy the bottle; and for that matter, the night and the dark, and the way by the tombs, must be all tenfold more dangerous to a man with such a sin upon his conscience, and such a bottle under his arm. But for my part, I am so extremely terrified myself, I have not the heart to blame you. Here I go then; and I pray God you may be happy in your house, and I fortunate with my schooner, and both get to heaven in the end in spite of the devil and his bottle."

So Lopaka went down the mountain; and Keawe stood in his front balcony, and listened to the clink of the horse's shoes, and watched the lantern go shining down the path, and along the cliff of caves where the old dead are buried; and all the time he trembled and clasped his hands, and prayed for his friend, and gave glory to God that he himself was escaped out of that trouble.

But the next day came very brightly, and that new house of his was so delightful to behold that he forgot his terrors. One day followed another, and Keawe dwelt there in perpetual joy. He had his place on the back porch; it was there he ate and lived, and read the stories in the Honolulu newspapers; but when anyone came by they would go in and view the chambers and the pictures. And the fame of the house went far and wide; it was called *Ka-Hale Nui*—the Great House—in all Kona; and sometimes the Bright House, for Keawe kept a Chinaman, who was all day dusting and furbishing; and the glass, and the gilt, and the fine stuffs, and the pictures, shone as bright as the morning. As for Keawe himself, he could not walk in the chambers without singing, his heart was so enlarged; and when ships sailed by upon the sea, he would fly his colors on the mast.

So time went by, until one day Keawe went upon a visit as far as Kailua to certain of his friends. There he was well feasted; and left as soon as he could the next morning, and rode hard, for he was impatient to behold his beautiful house; and, besides, the night then coming on was the night in which the dead of old days go abroad in the sides of Kona; and having already meddled with the devil, he was the more chary of meeting with the dead. A little beyond Honaunau, looking far ahead, he was aware of a woman bathing in the edge of the sea; and she seemed a well-grown girl, but he thought no more of it. Then he saw her white shift flutter as she put it on, and then her red holoku; and by the time he came abreast of her she was done with her toilet, and had come up from the sea, and stood by the track-side in her red holoku, and she was all freshened with the bath, and her eyes shone and were kind. Now Keawe no sooner beheld her than he drew rein.

"I thought I knew everyone in this country," said he. "How comes it that I do not know you?"

"I am Kokua, daughter of Kiano," said the girl, "and I have just returned from Oahu. Who are you?"

"I will tell you who I am in a little," said Keawe, dismounting from his horse, "but not now. For I have a thought in my mind, and if you knew who I was, you might have heard of me, and would not give me a true answer. But tell me, first of all, one thing: Are you married?"

At this Kokua laughed out aloud. "It is you who ask questions," she said. "Are you married yourself?"

"Indeed, Kokua, I am not," replied Keawe, "and never thought to be until this hour. But here is the plain truth. I have met you here at the roadside, and I saw your eyes, which are like the stars, and my heart went to you as swift as a bird. And so now, if you want none of me, say so, and I will go on to my own place; but if you think me no worse than any other young man, say so, too, and I will turn aside to your father's for the night, and tomorrow I will talk with the good man."

Kokua said never a word, but she looked at the sea and laughed.

"Kokua," said Keawe, "if you say nothing, I will take that for the good answer; so let us be stepping to your father's door."

She went on ahead of him, still without speech; only sometimes she glanced back and glanced away again, and she kept the strings of her hat in her mouth.

Now, when they had come to the door, Kiano came out on his verandah, and cried out and welcomed Keawe by name. At that the girl looked over, for the fame of the great house had come to her ears; and, to be sure, it was a great temptation. All that evening they were very merry together; and the girl was as bold as brass under the eyes of her parents, and made a mock of Keawe, for she had a quick wit. The next day he had a word with Kiano, and found the girl alone.

"Kokua," said he, "you made a mock of me all the evening; and it is still time to bid me go. I would not tell you who I was, because I have so fine a house, and I feared you would think too much of that house and too little of the man that loves you. Now you know all, and if you wish to have seen the last of me, say so at once."

"No," said Kokua; but this time she did not laugh, nor did Keawe ask for more.

This was the wooing of Keawe; things had gone quickly; but so an arrow goes, and the ball of a rifle swifter still, and yet both may strike the target. Things had gone fast, but they had gone far also, and the thought of Keawe rang in the maiden's head; she heard his voice in the breach of the surf upon the lava, and for this young man that she had seen but twice she would have left father and mother and her native islands. As for Keawe himself, his horse flew up the path of the mountain under the cliff of tombs, and the sound of the hoofs, and the sound of Keawe singing to himself for pleasure, echoed in the caverns of the dead. He came to the Bright House, and still he was singing. He sat and ate in the broad balcony, and the Chinaman wondered at his master, to hear how he sang between the mouthfuls. The sun went down into the sea, and the night came; and Keawe walked the balconies by lamplight, high on the mountains, and the voice of his singing startled men on ships.

"Here am I now upon my high place," he said to himself. "Life may be no better; this is the mountain top; and all shelves about me toward the worse. For the first time I will light up the chambers, and bathe in my fine bath with the hot water and the cold, and sleep alone in the bed of my bridal chamber."

So the Chinaman had word, and he must rise from sleep and light the furnaces; and as he wrought below, beside the boilers, he heard his master singing and rejoicing above him in the lighted chambers. When the water began to be hot the Chinaman cried to his master; and Keawe went into the bathroom; and the Chinaman heard him sing as he filled the marble basin; and heard him sing, and the singing broken, as he undressed; until of a sudden, the song ceased. The Chinaman listened, and listened; he called up the house to Keawe to ask if all were well, and Keawe answered him "Yes," and bade him go to bed; but there was no more singing in the Bright House; and all night long, the Chinaman heard his master's feet go round and round the balconies without repose.

Now the truth of it was this: as Keawe undressed for his bath, he spied upon his flesh a patch like a patch of lichen on a rock, and it was then that he stopped singing. For he knew the likeness of that patch, and knew that he was stricken with leprosy.

Now, it is a sad thing for any man to fall into this sickness. And it would be a sad thing for anyone to leave a house so beautiful and so commodious, and depart from all his friends to the north coast of Molokai between the mighty cliff and the sea-breakers. But what was that to the case of the man Keawe, he who had met his love but yesterday, and won her but that morning, and now saw all his hopes break, in a moment, like a piece of glass?

Awhile he sat upon the edge of the bath; then sprang, with a cry, and ran outside; and to and fro, to and fro, along the balcony, like one despairing.

"Very willingly could I leave Hawaii, the home of my fathers," Keawe was thinking. "Very lightly could I leave my house, the high-placed, the many-windowed, here upon the mountains. Very bravely could I go to Molokai, to Kalaupapa by the cliffs, to live with the smitten and to sleep there, far from my fathers. But what wrong have I done, what sin lies upon my soul, that I should have encountered Kokua coming cool from the sea-water in the evening? Kokua, the soul ensnarer! Kokua, the light of my life! Her may I never wed, her may I look upon no longer, her may I no more handle with my loving hand; and it is for this, it is for you, O Kokua! that I pour my lamentations!"

Now you are to observe what sort of a man Keawe was, for he might have dwelt there in the Bright House for years, and no one been the wiser of his sickness; but he reckoned nothing of that, if he must lose Kokua. And again, he might have wed Kokua even as he was; and so many would have done, because they have the souls of pigs; but Keawe loved the maid manfully, and he would do her no hurt and bring her in no danger.

A little beyond the midst of the night, there came in his mind the recollection of that bottle. He went round to the back porch, and called to memory the day when the devil had looked forth; and at the thought ice ran in his veins.

"A dreadful thing is the bottle," thought Keawe, "and dreadful is the imp, and it is a dreadful thing to risk the flames of hell. But what other hope have

I to cure my sickness or to wed Kokua? What!" he thought, "would I beard the devil once, only to get me a house, and not face him again to win Kokua?"

Thereupon he called to mind it was the next day the *Hall* went by on her return to Honolulu. "There must I go first," he thought, "and see Lopaka. For the best hope that I have now is to find that same bottle I was so pleased to be rid of."

Never a wink could he sleep; the food stuck in his throat; but he sent a letter to Kiano, and about the time when the steamer would be coming, rode down beside the cliff of the tombs. It rained; his horse went heavily; he looked up at the black mouths of the caves, and he envied the dead that slept there and were done with trouble; and called to mind how he had galloped by the day before, and was astonished. So he came down to Hookena, and there was all the country gathered for the steamer as usual. In the shed before the store they sat and jested and passed the news; but there was no matter of speech in Keawe's bosom, and he sat in their midst and looked without on the rain falling on the houses, and the surf beating among the rocks, and the sighs arose in his throat.

"Keawe of the Bright House is out of spirits," said one to another. Indeed, and so he was, and little wonder.

Then the *Hall* came, and the whaleboat carried him on board. The after-part of the ship was full of Haoles who had been to visit the volcano, as their custom is;[22] and the midst was crowded with Kanakas, and the forepart with wild bulls from Hilo and horses from Kau; but Keawe sat apart from all in his sorrow, and watched for the house of Kiano. There it sat, low upon the shore in the black rocks, and shaded by the cocoa palms, and there by the door was a red holoku, no greater than a fly, and going to and fro with a fly's busyness. "Ah, queen of my heart," he cried, "I'll venture my dear soul to win you!"

Soon after, darkness fell, and the cabins were lit up, and the Haoles sat and played at the cards and drank whiskey as their custom is; but Keawe walked the deck all night; and all the next day, as they steamed under the lee of Maui or of Molokai, he was still pacing to and fro like a wild animal in a menagerie.

Towards evening they passed Diamond Head, and came to the pier of Honolulu. Keawe stepped out among the crowd and began to ask for Lopaka. It seemed he had become the owner of a schooner—none better in the islands—and was gone upon an adventure as far as Pola-Pola or Kahiki; so there was no help to be looked for from Lopaka. Keawe called to mind a friend of his, a lawyer in the town (I must not tell his name), and inquired of him. They said he was grown suddenly rich, and had a fine new house upon Waikiki shore; and this put a thought in Keawe's head, and he called a hack and drove to the lawyer's house.

---

22 "Haoles" are non-natives in Hawaii, typically white.

The house was all brand new, and the trees in the garden no greater than walking-sticks, and the lawyer, when he came, had the air of a man well pleased.

"What can I do to serve you?" said the lawyer.

"You are a friend of Lopaka's," replied Keawe, "and Lopaka purchased from me a certain piece of goods that I thought you might enable me to trace."

The lawyer's face became very dark. "I do not profess to misunderstand you, Mr. Keawe," said he, "though this is an ugly business to be stirring in. You may be sure I know nothing, but yet I have a guess, and if you would apply in a certain quarter I think you might have news."

And he named the name of a man, which, again, I had better not repeat. So it was for days, and Keawe went from one to another, finding everywhere new clothes and carriages, and fine new houses and men everywhere in great contentment, although, to be sure, when he hinted at his business their faces would cloud over.

"No doubt I am upon the track," thought Keawe. "These new clothes and carriages are all the gifts of the little imp, and these glad faces are the faces of men who have taken their profit and got rid of the accursed thing in safety. When I see pale cheeks and hear sighing, I shall know that I am near the bottle."

So it befell at last that he was recommended to a Haole in Beritania Street. When he came to the door, about the hour of the evening meal, there were the usual marks of the new house, and the young garden, and the electric light shining in the windows; but when the owner came, a shock of hope and fear ran through Keawe; for here was a young man, white as a corpse, and black about the eyes, the hair shedding from his head, and such a look in his countenance as a man may have when he is waiting for the gallows.

"Here it is, to be sure," thought Keawe, and so with this man he noways veiled his errand. "I am come to buy the bottle," said he.

At the word, the young Haole of Beritania Street reeled against the wall.

"The bottle!" he gasped. "To buy the bottle!" Then he seemed to choke, and seizing Keawe by the arm carried him into a room and poured out wine in two glasses.

"Here is my respects," said Keawe, who had been much about with Haoles in his time. "Yes," he added, "I am come to buy the bottle. What is the price by now?"

At that word the young man let his glass slip through his fingers, and looked upon Keawe like a ghost.

"The price," says he; "the price! You do not know the price?"

"It is for that I am asking you," returned Keawe. "But why are you so much concerned? Is there anything wrong about the price?"

"It has dropped a great deal in value since your time, Mr. Keawe," said the young man stammering.

"Well, well, I shall have the less to pay for it," says Keawe. "How much did it cost you?"

The young man was as white as a sheet. "Two cents," said he.

"What?" cried Keawe, "two cents? Why, then, you can only sell it for one. And he who buys it—" The words died upon Keawe's tongue; he who bought it could never sell it again, the bottle and the bottle imp must abide with him until he died, and when he died must carry him to the red end of hell.

The young man of Beritania Street fell upon his knees. "For God's sake buy it!" he cried. "You can have all my fortune in the bargain. I was mad when I bought it at that price. I had embezzled money at my store; I was lost else; I must have gone to jail."

"Poor creature," said Keawe, "you would risk your soul upon so desperate an adventure, and to avoid the proper punishment of your own disgrace; and you think I could hesitate with love in front of me. Give me the bottle, and the change which I make sure you have all ready. Here is a five-cent piece."

It was as Keawe supposed; the young man had the change ready in a drawer; the bottle changed hands, and Keawe's fingers were no sooner clasped upon the stalk than he had breathed his wish to be a clean man. And, sure enough, when he got home to his room, and stripped himself before a glass, his flesh was whole like an infant's. And here was the strange thing: he had no sooner seen this miracle, than his mind was changed within him, and he cared naught for the Chinese Evil, and little enough for Kokua; and had but the one thought, that here he was bound to the bottle imp for time and for eternity, and had no better hope but to be a cinder for ever in the flames of hell. Away ahead of him he saw them blaze with his mind's eye, and his soul shrank, and darkness fell upon the light.

When Keawe came to himself a little, he was aware it was the night when the band played at the hotel. Thither he went, because he feared to be alone; and there, among happy faces, walked to and fro, and heard the tunes go up and down, and saw Berger beat the measure, and all the while he heard the flames crackle, and saw the red fire burning in the bottomless pit. Of a sudden the band played *Hiki-ao-ao*; that was a song that he had sung with Kokua, and at the strain courage returned to him.

"It is done now," he thought, "and once more let me take the good along with the evil."

So it befell that he returned to Hawaii by the first steamer, and as soon as it could be managed he was wedded to Kokua, and carried her up the mountain side to the Bright House.

Now it was so with these two, that when they were together, Keawe's heart was stilled; but so soon as he was alone he fell into a brooding horror, and heard the flames crackle, and saw the red fire burn in the bottomless pit. The girl, indeed, had come to him wholly; her heart leapt in her side at sight of him, her hand clung to his; and she was so fashioned from the hair upon her head to the nails upon her toes that none could see her without joy. She was pleasant in her nature. She had the good word always. Full of song she was, and went to and fro in the Bright House, the brightest thing in its three storeys, carolling like the birds. And Keawe beheld and heard her with delight, and then must shrink upon one side, and weep and groan to think upon the price that he had paid for her; and then he must dry his eyes, and wash his face, and go and sit with her on the broad balconies, joining in her songs, and, with a sick spirit, answering her smiles.

There came a day when her feet began to be heavy and her songs more rare; and now it was not Keawe only that would weep apart, but each would sunder from the other and sit in opposite balconies with the whole width of the Bright House betwixt. Keawe was so sunk in his despair, he scarce observed the change, and was only glad he had more hours to sit alone and brood upon his destiny, and was not so frequently condemned to pull a smiling face on a sick heart. But one day, coming softly through the house, he heard the sound of a child sobbing, and there was Kokua rolling her face upon the balcony floor, and weeping like the lost.

"You do well to weep in this house, Kokua," he said. "And yet I would give the head off my body that you (at least) might have been happy."

"Happy!" she cried. "Keawe, when you lived alone in your Bright House, you were the word of the island for a happy man; laughter and song were in your mouth, and your face was as bright as the sunrise. Then you wedded poor Kokua; and the good God knows what is amiss in her—but from that day you have not smiled. Oh!" she cried, "what ails me? I thought I was pretty, and I knew I loved him. What ails me that I throw this cloud upon my husband?"

"Poor Kokua," said Keawe. He sat down by her side, and sought to take her hand; but that she plucked away. "Poor Kokua," he said, again. "My poor child—my pretty. And I had thought all this while to spare you! Well, you shall know all. Then, at least, you will pity poor Keawe; then you will understand how much he loved you in the past—that he dared hell for your possession—and how much he loves you still (the poor condemned one), that he can yet call up a smile when he beholds you."

With that, he told her all, even from the beginning.

"You have done this for me?" she cried "Ah, well, then what do I care!"—and she clasped and wept upon him.

"Ah, child!" said Keawe, "and yet, when I consider of the fire of hell, I care a good deal!"

"Never tell me," said she; "no man can be lost because he loved Kokua, and no other fault. I tell you, Keawe, I shall save you with these hands, or perish in your company. What! you loved me, and gave your soul, and you think I will not die to save you in return?"

"Ah, my dear! you might die a hundred times, and what difference would that make?" he cried, "except to leave me lonely till the time comes of my damnation?"

"You know nothing," said she. "I was educated in a school in Honolulu; I am no common girl. And I tell you, I shall save my lover. What is this you say about a cent? But all the world is not American. In England they have a piece they call a farthing, which is about half a cent. Ah! sorrow!" she cried, "that makes it scarcely better, for the buyer must be lost, and we shall find none so brave as my Keawe! But, then, there is France; they have a small coin there which they call a centime, and these go five to the cent or there-about. We could not do better. Come, Keawe, let us go to the French islands; let us go to Tahiti, as fast as ships can bear us. There we have four centimes, three centimes, two centimes, one centime; four possible sales to come and go on; and two of us to push the bargain. Come, my Keawe! kiss me, and banish care. Kokua will defend you."

"Gift of God!" he cried. "I cannot think that God will punish me for desiring aught so good! Be it as you will, then; take me where you please: I put my life and my salvation in your hands."

Early the next day Kokua was about her preparations. She took Keawe's chest that he went with sailoring; and first she put the bottle in a corner; and then packed it with the richest of their clothes and the bravest of the knick-knacks in the house. "For," said she, "we must seem to be rich folks, or who will believe in the bottle?" All the time of her preparation she was as gay as a bird; only when she looked upon Keawe, the tears would spring in her eye, and she must run and kiss him. As for Keawe, a weight was off his soul; now that he had his secret shared, and some hope in front of him, he seemed like a new man, his feet went lightly on the earth, and his breath was good to him again. Yet was terror still at his elbow; and ever and again, as the wind blows out a taper, hope died in him, and he saw the flames toss and the red fire burn in hell.

It was given out in the country they were gone pleasuring to the States, which was thought a strange thing, and yet not so strange as the truth, if any could have guessed it. So they went to Honolulu in the *Hall*, and thence in the *Umatilla* to San Francisco with a crowd of Haoles, and at San Francisco took their passage by the mail brigantine, the *Tropic Bird*, for Papeete, the chief place of the French in the south islands. Thither they came, after a pleasant voyage, on a fair day of the Trade Wind, and saw the reef with the surf breaking, and Motuiti with its palms, and the schooner riding within-side, and the white houses of the town low down along the shore among green trees, and overhead the mountains and the clouds of Tahiti, the wise island.

It was judged the most wise to hire a house, which they did accordingly, opposite the British Consul's, to make a great parade of money, and themselves conspicuous with carriages and horses. This it was very easy to do, so long as they had the bottle in their possession; for Kokua was more bold than Keawe, and, whenever she had a mind, called on the imp for twenty or a hundred dollars. At this rate they soon grew to be remarked in the town; and the strangers from Hawaii, their riding and their driving, the fine holokus and the rich lace of Kokua, became the matter of much talk.

They got on well after the first with the Tahitian language, which is indeed like to the Hawaiian, with a change of certain letters; and as soon as they had any freedom of speech, began to push the bottle. You are to consider it was not an easy subject to introduce; it was not easy to persuade people you were in earnest, when you offered to sell them for four centimes the spring of health and riches inexhaustible. It was necessary besides to explain the dangers of the bottle; and either people disbelieved the whole thing and laughed, or they thought the more of the darker part, became overcast with gravity, and drew away from Keawe and Kokua, as from persons who had dealings with the devil. So far from gaining ground, these two began to find they were avoided in the town; the children ran away from them screaming, a thing intolerable to Kokua; Catholics crossed themselves as they went by; and all persons began with one accord to disengage themselves from their advances.

Depression fell upon their spirits. They would sit at night in their new house, after a day's weariness, and not exchange one word, or the silence would be broken by Kokua bursting suddenly into sobs. Sometimes they would pray together; sometimes they would have the bottle out upon the floor, and sit all evening watching how the shadow hovered in the midst. At such times they would be afraid to go to rest. It was long ere slumber came to them, and, if either dozed off, it would be to wake and find the other silently weeping in the dark, or, perhaps, to wake alone, the other having fled from the house and the neighborhood of that bottle, to pace under the bananas in the little garden, or to wander on the beach by moonlight.

One night it was so when Kokua awoke. Keawe was gone. She felt in the bed and his place was cold. Then fear fell upon her, and she sat up in bed. A little moonshine filtered through the shutters. The room was bright, and she could spy the bottle on the floor. Outside it blew high, the great trees of the avenue cried aloud, and the fallen leaves rattled in the verandah. In the midst of this Kokua was aware of another sound; whether of a beast or of a man she could scarce tell, but it was as sad as death, and cut her to the soul. Softly she arose, set the door ajar, and looked forth into the moonlit yard. There, under the bananas, lay Keawe, his mouth in the dust, and as he lay he moaned.

It was Kokua's first thought to run forward and console him; her second potently withheld her. Keawe had borne himself before his wife like a brave man; it became her little in the hour of weakness to intrude upon his shame. With the thought she drew back into the house.

"Heaven!" she thought, "how careless have I been—how weak! It is he, not I, that stands in this eternal peril; it was he, not I, that took the curse upon his soul. It is for my sake, and for the love of a creature of so little worth and such poor help, that he now beholds so close to him the flames of hell—ay, and smells the smoke of it, lying without there in the wind and moonlight. Am I so dull of spirit that never till now I have surmised my duty, or have I seen it before and turned aside? But now, at least, I take up my soul in both the hands of my affection; now I say farewell to the white steps of heaven and the waiting faces of my friends. A love for a love, and let mine be equalled with Keawe's! A soul for a soul, and be it mine to perish!"

She was a deft woman with her hands, and was soon appareled. She took in her hands the change—the precious centimes they kept ever at their side; for this coin is little used, and they had made provision at a Government office. When she was forth in the avenue clouds came on the wind, and the moon was blackened. The town slept, and she knew not whither to turn till she heard one coughing in the shadow of the trees.

"Old man," said Kokua, "what do you here abroad in the cold night?"

The old man could scarce express himself for coughing, but she made out that he was old and poor, and a stranger in the island.

"Will you do me a service?" said Kokua. "As one stranger to another, and as an old man to a young woman, will you help a daughter of Hawaii?"

"Ah," said the old man. "So you are the witch from the eight islands, and even my old soul you seek to entangle. But I have heard of you, and defy your wickedness."

"Sit down here," said Kokua, "and let me tell you a tale." And she told him the story of Keawe from the beginning to the end.

"And now," said she, "I am his wife, whom he bought with his soul's welfare. And what should I do? If I went to him myself and offered to buy it, he would refuse. But if you go, he will sell it eagerly; I will await you here; you will buy it for four centimes, and I will buy it again for three. And the Lord strengthen a poor girl!"

"If you meant falsely," said the old man, "I think God would strike you dead."

"He would!" cried Kokua. "Be sure he would. I could not be so treacherous —God would not suffer it."

"Give me the four centimes and await me here," said the old man.

Now, when Kokua stood alone in the street, her spirit died. The wind roared in the trees, and it seemed to her the rushing of the flames of hell; the shadows tossed in the light of the street lamp, and they seemed to her the snatching hands of evil ones. If she had had the strength, she must have run away, and if she had had the breath she must have screamed aloud; but, in truth, she could do neither, and stood and trembled in the avenue, like an affrighted child.

Then she saw the old man returning, and he had the bottle in his hand.

"I have done your bidding," said he. "I left your husband weeping like a child; tonight he will sleep easy." And he held the bottle forth.

"Before you give it me," Kokua panted, "take the good with the evil—ask to be delivered from your cough."

"I am an old man," replied the other, "and too near the gate of the grave to take a favor from the devil. But what is this? Why do you not take the bottle? Do you hesitate?"

"Not hesitate!" cried Kokua. "I am only weak. Give me a moment. It is my hand resists, my flesh shrinks back from the accursed thing. One moment only!"

The old man looked upon Kokua kindly. "Poor child!" said he, "you fear; your soul misgives you. Well, let me keep it. I am old, and can never more be happy in this world, and as for the next—"

"Give it me!" gasped Kokua. "There is your money. Do you think I am so base as that? Give me the bottle."

"God bless you, child," said the old man.

Kokua concealed the bottle under her holoku, said farewell to the old man, and walked off along the avenue, she cared not whither. For all roads were now the same to her, and led equally to hell. Sometimes she walked, and sometimes ran; sometimes she screamed out loud in the night, and sometimes lay by the wayside in the dust and wept. All that she had heard of hell came back to her; she saw the flames blaze, and she smelt the smoke, and her flesh withered on the coals.

Near day she came to her mind again, and returned to the house. It was even as the old man said—Keawe slumbered like a child. Kokua stood and gazed upon his face.

"Now, my husband," said she, "it is your turn to sleep. When you wake it will be your turn to sing and laugh. But for poor Kokua, alas! that meant no evil—for poor Kokua no more sleep, no more singing, no more delight, whether in earth or heaven."

With that she lay down in the bed by his side, and her misery was so extreme that she fell in a deep slumber instantly.

Late in the morning her husband woke her and gave her the good news. It seemed he was silly with delight, for he paid no heed to her distress, ill though she dissembled it. The words stuck in her mouth, it mattered not; Keawe did the speaking. She ate not a bite, but who was to observe it? for Keawe cleared the dish. Kokua saw and heard him, like some strange thing in a dream; there were times when she forgot or doubted, and put her hands to her brow; to know herself doomed and hear her husband babble, seemed so monstrous.

All the while Keawe was eating and talking, and planning the time of their return, and thanking her for saving him, and fondling her, and calling her the true helper after all. He laughed at the old man that was fool enough to buy that bottle.

"A worthy old man he seemed," Keawe said. "But no one can judge by appearances. For why did the old reprobate require the bottle?"

"My husband," said Kokua, humbly, "his purpose may have been good."

Keawe laughed like an angry man.

"Fiddle-de-dee!" cried Keawe. "An old rogue, I tell you; and an old ass to boot. For the bottle was hard enough to sell at four centimes; and at three it will be quite impossible. The margin is not broad enough, the thing begins to smell of scorching—brrr!" said he, and shuddered. "It is true I bought it myself at a cent, when I knew not there were smaller coins. I was a fool for my pains; there will never be found another: and whoever has that bottle now will carry it to the pit."

"O my husband!" said Kokua. "Is it not a terrible thing to save oneself by the eternal ruin of another? It seems to me I could not laugh. I would be humbled. I would be filled with melancholy. I would pray for the poor holder."

Then Keawe, because he felt the truth of what she said, grew the more angry. "Heighty-teighty!" cried he. "You may be filled with melancholy if you please. It is not the mind of a good wife. If you thought at all of me, you would sit shamed."

Thereupon he went out, and Kokua was alone.

What chance had she to sell that bottle at two centimes? None, she perceived. And if she had any, here was her husband hurrying her away to a country where there was nothing lower than a cent. And here—on the morrow of her sacrifice—was her husband leaving her and blaming her.

She would not even try to profit by what time she had, but sat in the house, and now had the bottle out and viewed it with unutterable fear, and now, with loathing, hid it out of sight.

By-and-by, Keawe came back, and would have her take a drive.

"My husband, I am ill," she said. "I am out of heart. Excuse me, I can take no pleasure."

Then was Keawe more wroth than ever. With her, because he thought she was brooding over the case of the old man; and with himself, because he thought she was right, and was ashamed to be so happy.

"This is your truth," cried he, "and this your affection! Your husband is just saved from eternal ruin, which he encountered for the love of you—and you can take no pleasure! Kokua, you have a disloyal heart."

He went forth again furious, and wandered in the town all day. He met friends, and drank with them; they hired a carriage and drove into the country, and there drank again. All the time Keawe was ill at ease, because he was taking this pastime while his wife was sad, and because he knew in his heart that she was more right than he; and the knowledge made him drink the deeper.

Now there was an old brutal Haole drinking with him, one that had been a boatswain of a whaler, a runaway, a digger in gold mines, a convict in prisons. He had a low mind and a foul mouth; he loved to drink and to see others drunken; and he pressed the glass upon Keawe. Soon there was no more money in the company.

"Here, you!" says the boatswain, "you are rich, you have been always saying. You have a bottle or some foolishness."

"Yes," says Keawe, "I am rich; I will go back and get some money from my wife, who keeps it."

"That's a bad idea, mate," said the boatswain. "Never you trust a petticoat with dollars. They're all as false as water; you keep an eye on her."

Now, this word struck in Keawe's mind; for he was muddled with what he had been drinking.

"I should not wonder but she was false, indeed," thought he. "Why else should she be so cast down at my release? But I will show her I am not the man to be fooled. I will catch her in the act."

Accordingly, when they were back in town, Keawe bade the boatswain wait for him at the corner, by the old calaboose, and went forward up the avenue alone to the door of his house. The night had come again; there was a light within, but never a sound; and Keawe crept about the corner, opened the back door softly, and looked in.

There was Kokua on the floor, the lamp at her side; before her was a milk-white bottle, with a round belly and a long neck; and as she viewed it, Kokua wrung her hands.

A long time Keawe stood and looked in the doorway. At first he was struck stupid; and then fear fell upon him that the bargain had been made amiss, and the bottle had come back to him as it came at San Francisco; and at that his knees were loosened, and the fumes of the wine departed from his head like mists off a river in the morning. And then he had another thought; and it was a strange one, that made his cheeks to burn.

"I must make sure of this," thought he.

So he closed the door, and went softly round the corner again, and then came noisily in, as though he were but now returned. And, lo! by the time he opened the front door no bottle was to be seen; and Kokua sat in a chair and started up like one awakened out of sleep.

"I have been drinking all day and making merry," said Keawe. "I have been with good companions, and now I only come back for money, and return to drink and carouse with them again."

Both his face and voice were as stern as judgment, but Kokua was too troubled to observe.

"You do well to use your own, my husband," said she, and her words trembled.

"O, I do well in all things," said Keawe, and he went straight to the chest and took out money. But he looked besides in the corner where they kept the bottle, and there was no bottle there.

At that the chest heaved upon the floor like a sea-billow, and the house span about him like a wreath of smoke, for he saw he was lost now, and there was no escape. "It is what I feared," he thought. "It is she who has bought it."

And then he came to himself a little and rose up; but the sweat streamed on his face as thick as the rain and as cold as the well-water.

"Kokua," said he, "I said to you today what ill became me. Now I return to carouse with my jolly companions," and at that he laughed a little quietly. "I will take more pleasure in the cup if you forgive me."

She clasped his knees in a moment; she kissed his knees with flowing tears.

"O," she cried, "I asked but a kind word!"

"Let us never one think hardly of the other," said Keawe, and was gone out of the house.

Now, the money that Keawe had taken was only some of that store of centime pieces they had laid in at their arrival. It was very sure he had no mind to be drinking. His wife had given her soul for him, now he must give his for hers; no other thought was in the world with him.

At the corner, by the old calaboose, there was the boatswain waiting.

"My wife has the bottle," said Keawe, "and, unless you help me to recover it, there can be no more money and no more liquor tonight."

"You do not mean to say you are serious about that bottle?" cried the boatswain.

"There is the lamp," said Keawe. "Do I look as if I was jesting?"

"That is so," said the boatswain. "You look as serious as a ghost."

"Well, then," said Keawe, "here are two centimes; you must go to my wife in the house, and offer her these for the bottle, which (if I am not much mistaken) she will give you instantly. Bring it to me here, and I will buy it back from you for one; for that is the law with this bottle, that it still must be sold for a less sum. But whatever you do, never breathe a word to her that you have come from me."

"Mate, I wonder are you making a fool of me?" asked the boatswain.

"It will do you no harm if I am," returned Keawe.

"That is so, mate," said the boatswain.

"And if you doubt me," added Keawe, "you can try. As soon as you are clear of the house, wish to have your pocket full of money, or a bottle of the best rum, or what you please, and you will see the virtue of the thing."

"Very well, Kanaka," says the boatswain. "I will try; but if you are having your fun out of me, I will take my fun out of you with a belaying pin."

So the whaler-man went off up the avenue; and Keawe stood and waited. It was near the same spot where Kokua had waited the night before; but Keawe was more resolved, and never faltered in his purpose; only his soul was bitter with despair.

It seemed a long time he had to wait before he heard a voice singing in the darkness of the avenue. He knew the voice to be the boatswain's; but it was strange how drunken it appeared upon a sudden.

Next, the man himself came stumbling into the light of the lamp. He had the devil's bottle buttoned in his coat; another bottle was in his hand; and even as he came in view he raised it to his mouth and drank.

"You have it," said Keawe. "I see that."

"Hands off!" cried the boatswain, jumping back. "Take a step near me, and I'll smash your mouth. You thought you could make a cat's-paw of me, did you?"

"What do you mean?" cried Keawe.

"Mean?" cried the boatswain. "This is a pretty good bottle, this is; that's what I mean. How I got it for two centimes I can't make out; but I'm sure you shan't have it for one."

"You mean you won't sell?" gasped Keawe.

"No, *sir*!" cried the boatswain. "But I'll give you a drink of the rum, if you like."

"I tell you," said Keawe, "the man who has that bottle goes to hell."

"I reckon I'm going anyway," returned the sailor; "and this bottle's the best thing to go with I've struck yet. No, sir!" he cried again, "this is my bottle now, and you can go and fish for another."

"Can this be true?" Keawe cried. "For your own sake, I beseech you, sell it me!"

"I don't value any of your talk," replied the boatswain. "You thought I was a flat; now you see I'm not; and there's an end. If you won't have a swallow of the rum, I'll have one myself. Here's your health, and good-night to you!"

So off he went down the avenue towards town, and there goes the bottle out of the story.

But Keawe ran to Kokua light as the wind; and great was their joy that night; and great, since then, has been the peace of all their days in the Bright House.

TRANSFORMATION

Mary Shelley

first published in *The Keepsake for MDCCCXXXI* (1830)

> Forthwith this frame of mine was wrench'd
> With a woful agony,
> Which forced me to begin my tale,
> And then it set me free.
> Since then, at an uncertain hour,
> That agony returns;
> And till my ghastly tale is told
> This heart within me burns.
> Coleridge's Ancient Mariner.

I have heard it said, that, when any strange, supernatural, and necromantic adventure has occurred to a human being, that being, however desirous he may be to conceal the same, feels at certain periods torn up as it were by an intellectual earthquake, and is forced to bare the inner depths of his spirit to another. I am a witness of the truth of this. I have dearly sworn to myself never to reveal to human ears the horrors to which I once, in excess of fiendly pride, delivered myself over. The holy man who heard my confession, and reconciled me to the church, is dead. None knows that once—

Why should it not be thus? Why tell a tale of impious tempting of Providence, and soul-subduing humiliation? Why? answer me, ye who are wise in the secrets of human nature! I only know that so it is; and in spite of strong resolve—of a pride that too much masters me—of shame, and even of fear, so to render myself odious to my species—I must speak.

Genoa! My birth-place—proud city! looking upon the blue waves of the Mediterranean sea—dost thou remember me in my boyhood, when thy cliffs and promontories, thy bright sky and gay vineyards, were my world? Happy time! when to the young heart the narrow-bounded universe, which leaves, by its very limitation, free scope to the imagination, enchains our physical energies, and, sole period in our lives, innocence and enjoyment are united. Yet, who can look back to childhood, and not remember its sorrows and its harrowing fears? I was born with the most imperious, haughty, tameless spirit, with which ever mortal was gifted. I quailed before my father only; and he, generous and noble, but capricious and tyrannical, at once fostered and checked the wild impetuosity of my character, making obedience necessary, but inspiring no respect for the motives which guided his commands. To be a man, free, independent; or, in better words, insolent and domineering, was the hope and prayer of my rebel heart.

My father had one friend, a wealthy Genoese noble, who in a political tumult was suddenly sentenced to banishment, and his property confiscated. The Marchese Torella went into exile alone. Like my father, he was a widower: he bad one child, the almost infant Juliet, who was left under my father's guardianship. I should certainly have been an unkind master to the lovely girl, but that I was forced by my position to become her protector. A variety of childish incidents all tended to one point,—to make Juliet see in me a rock of refuge; I in her, one, who must perish through the soft sensibility of her nature too rudely visited, but for my guardian care. We grew up together. The opening rose in May was not more sweet than this dear girl. An irradiation of beauty was spread over her face. Her form, her step, her voice—my heart weeps even now, to think of all of relying, gentle, loving, and pure, that was enshrined in that celestial tenement. When I was eleven and Juliet eight years of age, a cousin of mine, much older than either—he seemed to us a man—took great notice of my playmate; he called her his bride, and asked her to marry him. She refused, and he insisted, drawing her unwillingly towards him. With the countenance and emotions of a maniac I threw myself on him—I strove to draw his sword—I clung to his neck with the ferocious resolve to strangle him: he was obliged to call for assistance to disengage himself from me. On that night I led Juliet to the chapel of our house: I made her touch the sacred relics—I harrowed her child's heart, and profaned her child's lips with an oath, that she would be mine, and mine only.

Well, those days passed away. Torella returned in a few years, and became wealthier and more prosperous than ever. When I was seventeen my father died; he had been magnificent to prodigality; Torella rejoiced that my minority would afford an opportunity for repairing my fortunes. Juliet and I had been affianced beside my father's deathbed—Torella was to be a second parent to me.

I desired to see the world, and I was indulged. I went to Florence, to Rome, to Naples; thence I passed to Toulon, and at length reached what had long been the bourne of my wishes, Paris. There was wild work in Paris then. The poor king, Charles the Sixth, now sane, now mad, now a monarch, now an abject slave, was the very mockery of humanity. The queen, the dauphin, the Duke of Burgundy, alternately friends and foes now meeting in prodigal feasts, now shedding blood in rivalry—were blind to the miserable state of their country, and the dangers that impended over it, and gave themselves wholly up to dissolute enjoyment or savage strife. My character still followed me. I was arrogant and selfwilled; I loved display, and above all, I threw all control far from me. Who could control me in Paris? My young friends were eager to foster passions which furnished them with pleasures. I was deemed handsome—I was master of every knightly accomplishment. I was disconnected with any political party. I grew a favorite with all: my presumption and arrogance were pardoned in one so young: I became a spoiled child. Who could control me? not the letters and advice of Torella—only strong necessity visiting me in the abhorred shape of an empty purse. But there were means to refill this void. Acre after acre, estate after estate, I sold. My dress, my jewels, my horses and their caparisons, were almost unrivaled in gorgeous Paris, while the lands of my inheritance passed into possession of others.

The Duke of Orleans was waylaid and murdered by the Duke of Burgundy. Fear and terror possessed all Paris. The dauphin and the queen shut themselves up; every pleasure was suspended. I grew weary of this state of things, and my heart yearned for my boyhood's haunts. I was nearly a beggar, yet still I would go there, claim my bride, and rebuild my fortunes. A few happy ventures as a merchant would make me rich again. Nevertheless, I would not return in humble guise. My last act was to dispose of my remaining estate near Albaro for half its worth, for ready money. Then I despatched all kinds of artificers, arras, furniture of regal splendor, to fit up the last relic of my inheritance, my palace in Genoa. I lingered a little longer yet, ashamed at the part of the prodigal returned, which I feared I should play. I sent my horses. One matchless Spanish jennet I despatched to my promised bride; its caparisons flamed with jewels and cloth of gold. In every part I caused to be entwined the initials of Juliet and her Guido. My present found favor in hers and in her father's eyes.

Still to return a proclaimed spendthrift, the mark of impertinent wonder, perhaps of scorn, and to encounter singly the reproaches or taunts of my fellow-citizens, was no alluring prospect. As a shield between me and censure, I invited some few of the most reckless of my comrades to accompany me: thus I went armed against the world, hiding a rankling feeling, half fear and half penitence, by bravado and an insolent display of satisfied vanity.

I arrived in Genoa. I trod the pavement of my ancestral palace. My proud step was no interpreter of my heart, for I deeply felt that, though surrounded by every luxury, I was a beggar. The first step I took in claiming Juliet must widely declare me such. I read contempt or pity in the looks of all. I fancied, so apt is conscience to imagine what it deserves, that rich and poor, young and old, all regarded me with derision. Torella came not near me. No wonder that my second father should expect a son's deference from me in waiting first on him. But, galled and stung by a sense of my follies and demerit, I strove to throw the blame on others. We kept nightly orgies in Palazzo Carega. To sleepless, riotous nights, followed listless, supine mornings. At the Ave Maria we showed our dainty persons in the streets, scoffing at the sober citizens, casting insolent glances on the shrinking women. Juliet was not among them —no, no; if she had been there, shame would have driven me away, if love had not brought me to her feet.

I grew tired of this. Suddenly I paid the Marchese a visit. He was at his villa, one among the many which deck the suburb of San Pietro d'Arena. It was the month of May—a month of May in that garden of the world the blossoms of the fruit trees were fading among thick, green foliage; the vines were shooting forth; the ground strewed with the fallen olive blooms; the fire-fly was in the myrtle hedge; heaven and earth wore a mantle of surpassing beauty. Torella welcomed me kindly, though seriously; and even his shade of displeasure soon wore away. Some resemblance to my father—some look and tone of youthful ingenuousness, lurking still in spite of my misdeeds, softened the good old man's heart. He sent for his daughter—he presented me to her as her betrothed. The chamber became hallowed by a holy light as she entered. Hers was that cherub look, those large, soft eyes, full dimpled cheeks, and mouth of infantine sweetness, that expresses the rare union of happiness and love. Admiration first possessed me; she is mine! was the second proud emotion, and my lips curled with haughty triumph. I had not been the *enfant gate* of the beauties of France not to have learnt the art of pleasing the soft heart of woman.[23] If towards men I was overbearing, the deference I paid to them was the more in contrast. I commenced my courtship by the display of a thousand gallantries to Juliet, who, vowed to me from infancy, had never admitted the devotion of others; and who, though accustomed to expressions of admiration, was uninitiated in the language of lovers.

For a few days all went well. Torella never alluded to my extravagance; he treated me as a favorite son. But the time came, as we discussed the preliminaries to my union with his daughter, when this fair face of things should be overcast. A contract had been drawn up in my father's lifetime. I had rendered this, in fact, void, by having squandered the whole of the wealth which was to have been shared by Juliet and myself. Torella, in consequence, chose to consider this bond as cancelled, and proposed another, in which, though the wealth he bestowed was immeasurably increased, there were so many restrictions as to the mode of spending it, that I, who saw independence only in free career being given to my own imperious will, taunted him as taking advantage of my situation, and refused utterly to subscribe to his conditions. The old man mildly strove to recall me to reason. Roused pride became the tyrant of my thought: I listened with indignation— I repelled him with disdain.

"Juliet, thou art mine! Did we not interchange vows in our innocent childhood? are we not one in the sight of God? and shall thy cold-hearted, cold-blooded father divide us? Be generous, my love, be just; take not away a gift, last treasure of thy Guido—retract not thy vows—let us defy the world, and setting at nought the calculations of age, find in our mutual affection a refuge from every ill."

---

[23] *enfant gate*, or "pampered darling"

Fiend I must have been, with such sophistry to endeavor to poison that sanctuary of holy thought and tender love. Juliet shrank from me affrighted. Her father was the best and kindest of men, and she strove to show me how, in obeying him, every good would follow. He would receive my tardy submission with warm affection; and generous pardon would follow my repentance. Profitless words for a young and gentle daughter to use to a man accustomed to make his will, law; and to feel in his own heart a despot so terrible and stern, that he could yield obedience to nought save his own imperious desires! My resentment grew with resistance; my wild companions were ready to add fuel to the flame. We laid a plan to carry off Juliet. At first it appeared to be crowned with success. Midway, on our return, we were overtaken by the agonized father and his attendants. A conflict ensued. Before the city guard came to decide the victory in favor of our antagonists, two of Torella's servitors were dangerously wounded.

This portion of my history weighs most heavily with me. Changed man as I am, I abhor myself in the recollection. May none who hear this tale ever have felt as I. A horse driven to fury by a rider armed with barbed spurs, was not more a slave than I, to the violent tyranny of my temper. A fiend possessed my soul, irritating it to madness. I felt the voice of conscience within me; but if I yielded to it for a brief interval, it was only to be a moment after torn, as by a whirlwind, away—borne along on the stream of desperate rage—the plaything of the storms engendered by pride. I was imprisoned, and, at the instance of Torella, set free. Again I returned to carry off both him and his child to France; which hapless country, then preyed on by freebooters and gangs of lawless soldiery, offered a grateful refuge to a criminal like me. Our plots were discovered. I was sentenced to banishment; and, as my debts were already enormous, my remaining property was put in the hands of commissioners for their payment. Torella again offered his mediation, requiring only my promise not to renew my abortive attempts on himself and his daughter. I spurned his offers, and fancied that I triumphed when I was thrust out from Genoa, a solitary and penniless exile. My companions were gone: they had been dismissed the city some weeks before, and were already in France. I was alone—friendless; with nor sword at my side, nor ducat in my purse.

I wandered along the seashore, a whirlwind of passion possessing and tearing my soul. It was as if a live coal had been set burning in my breast. At first I meditated on what *I should do*. I would join a band of freebooters. Revenge!—the word seemed balm to me:—I hugged it—caressed it—till, like a serpent, it stung me. Then again I would abjure and despise Genoa, that little corner of the world. I would return to Paris, where so many of my friends swarmed; where my services would be eagerly accepted; where I would carve out fortune with my sword, and might, through success, make my paltry birth-place, and the false Torella, rue the day when they drove me, a new Coriolanus, from her walls. I would return to Paris—thus, on foot—a beggar—and present myself in my poverty to those I had formerly entertained sumptuously? There was gall in the mere thought of it.

The reality of things began to dawn upon my mind, bringing despair in its train. For several months I had been a prisoner: the evils of my dungeon had whipped my soul to madness, but they had subdued my corporeal frame. I was weak and wan. Torella. had used a thousand artifices to administer to my comfort; I had detected and scorned them all—and I reaped the harvest of my obduracy. What was to be done? Should I crouch before my foe, and sue for forgiveness?—Die rather ten thousand deaths!—Never should they obtain that victory! Hate—I swore eternal hate! Hate from whom?—to whom?— From a wandering outcast to a mighty noble. I and my feelings were nothing to them: already had they forgotten one so unworthy. And Juliet!—her angel-face and sylphlike form gleamed among the clouds of my despair with vain beauty; for I had lost her—the glory and flower of the world! Another will call her his!—that smile of paradise will bless another!

Even now my heart fails within me when I recur to this rout of grim-visaged ideas. Now subdued almost to tears, now raving in my agony, still I wandered along the rocky shore, which grew at each step wilder and more desolate. Hanging rocks and hoar precipices overlooked the tideless ocean; black caverns yawned; and for ever, among the seaworn recesses, murmured and dashed the unfruitful waters. Now my way was almost barred by an abrupt promontory, now rendered nearly impracticable by fragments fallen from the cliff. Evening was at hand, when, seaward, arose, as if on the waving of a wizard's wand, a murky web of clouds, blotting the late azure sky, and darkening and disturbing the till now placid deep. The clouds had strange fantastic shapes; and they changed, and mingled, and seemed to be driven about by a mighty spell. The waves raised their white crests; the thunder first muttered, then roared from across the waste of waters, which took a deep purple dye, flecked with foam. The spot where I stood, looked, on one side, to the wide-spread ocean; on the other, it was barred by a rugged promontory. Round this cape suddenly came, driven by the wind, a vessel. In vain the mariners tried to force a path for her to the open sea—the gale drove her on the rocks. It will perish!—all on board will perish!—Would I were among them! And to my young heart the idea of death came for the first time blended with that of joy. It was an awful sight to behold that vessel struggling with her fate. Hardly could I discern the sailors, but I heard them. It was soon all over!—A rock, just covered by the tossing waves, and so unperceived, lay in wait for its prey. A crash of thunder broke over my head at the moment that, with a frightful shock, the skiff dashed upon her unseen enemy. In a brief space of time she went to pieces. There I stood in safety; and there were my fellow-creatures, battling, how hopelessly, with annihilation. Methought I saw them struggling—too truly did I hear their shrieks, conquering the barking surges in their shrill agony. The dark breakers threw hither and thither the fragments of the wreck: soon it disappeared. I had been fascinated to gaze till the end: at last I sank on my knees—I covered my face with my hands: I again looked up; something was floating on the billows towards the shore. It neared and neared. Was that a human form?—It grew more distinct; and at last a mighty wave, lifting the whole freight, lodged it upon a rock. A human being bestriding a sea-chest!—A human being!—Yet was it one? Surely never such had existed before—a misshapen dwarf, with squinting eyes, distorted features, and body deformed, till it became a horror to behold. My blood, lately warming towards a fellow-being so snatched from a watery tomb, froze in my heart. The dwarf got off his chest; he tossed his straight, straggling hair from his odious visage:

"By St. Beelzebub!" he exclaimed, "I have been well bested." He looked round and saw me. "Oh, by the fiend! here is another ally of the mighty one. To what saint did you offer prayers, friend—if not to mine? Yet I remember you not on board."

I shrank from the monster and his blasphemy. Again he questioned me, and I muttered some inaudible reply. He continued:—

"Your voice is drowned by this dissonant roar. What a noise the big ocean makes! Schoolboys bursting from their prison are not louder than these waves set free to play. They disturb me. I will no more of their ill-timed brawling.—Silence, hoary One!—Winds, avaunt!—to your homes! Clouds, fly to the antipodes, and leave our heaven clear!"

As he spoke, he stretched out his two long lank arms, that looked like spider's claws, and seemed to embrace with them the expanse before him. Was it a miracle? The clouds became broken, and fled; the azure sky first peeped out, and then was spread a calm field of blue above us; the stormy gale was exchanged to the softly breathing west; the sea grew calm; the waves dwindled to riplets.

"I like obedience even in these stupid elements," said the dwarf. "How much more in the tameless mind of man! It was a well got up storm, you must allow—and all of my own making."

It was tempting Providence to interchange talk with this magician. But *Power*, in all its shapes, is venerable to man. Awe, curiosity, a clinging fascination, drew me towards him.

"Come, don't be frightened, friend," said the wretch: "I am good humored when pleased; and something does please me in your well proportioned body and handsome face, though you look a little woebegone. You have suffered a land—I, a sea wreck. Perhaps I can allay the tempest of your fortunes as I did my own. Shall we be friends?"—And he held out his hand; I could not touch it. "Well, then, companions—that will do as well. And now, while I rest after the buffeting I underwent just now, tell me why, young and gallant as you seem, you wander thus alone and downcast on this wild seashore."

The voice of the wretch was screeching and horrid, and his contortions as he spoke were frightful to behold. Yet he did gain a kind of influence over me, which I could not master, and I told him my tale. When it was ended, he laughed long and loud: the rocks echoed back the sound: hell seemed yelling around me.

"Oh, thou cousin of Lucifer!" said he; "so thou too hast fallen through thy pride; and, though bright as the son of Morning, thou art ready to give up thy good looks, thy bride, and thy well-being, rather than submit thee to the tyranny of good. I honor thy choice, by my soul!—So thou hast fled, and yield the day; and mean to starve on these rocks, and to let the birds peck out thy dead eyes, while thy enemy and thy betrothed rejoice in thy ruin. Thy pride is strangely akin to humility, methinks."

As he spoke, a thousand fanged thoughts stung me to the heart.

"What would you that I should do?" I cried.

"I!—Oh, nothing, but lie down and say your prayers before you die. But, were I you, I know the deed that should be done."

I drew near him. His supernatural powers made him an oracle in my eyes; yet a strange unearthly thrill quivered through my frame as I said, "Speak!—teach me—what act do you advise?"

"Revenge thyself, man!—humble thy enemies!—set thy foot on the old man's neck, and possess thyself of his daughter!"

"To the east and west I turn," cried I, "and see no means! Had I gold, much could I achieve; but, poor and single, I am powerless."

The dwarf had been seated on his chest as he listened to my story. Now he got off; he touched a spring; it flew open!—What a mine of wealth—of blazing jewels, beaming gold, and pale silver—was displayed therein. A mad desire to possess this treasure was born within me.

"Doubtless," I said, "one so powerful as you could do all things."

"Nay," said the monster, humbly, "I am less omnipotent than I seem. Some things I possess which you may covet; but I would give them all for a small share, or even for a loan of what is yours."

"My possessions are at your service," I replied, bitterly—"my poverty, my exile, my disgrace—I make a free gift of them all."

"Good! I thank you. Add one other thing to your gift, and my treasure is yours."

"As nothing is my sole inheritance, what besides nothing would you have?"

"Your comely face and well-made limbs."

I shivered. Would this all-powerful monster murder me? I had no dagger. I forgot to pray—but I grew pale.

"I ask for a loan, not a gift," said the frightful thing: "lend me your body for three days—you shall have mine to cage your soul the while, and, in payment, my chest. What say you to the bargain?—Three short days."

We are told that it is dangerous to hold unlawful talk; and well do I prove the same. Tamely written down, it may seem incredible that I should lend any ear to this proposition; but, in spite of his unnatural ugliness, there was something fascinating in a being whose voice could govern earth, air, and sea. I felt a keen desire to comply; for with that chest I could command the world. My only hesitation resulted from a fear that he would not be true to his bargain. Then, I thought, I shall soon die here on these lonely sands, and the limbs he covets will be mine no more:—it is worth the chance. And, besides, I knew that, by all the rules of art-magic, there were formula and oaths which none of its practisers dared break. I hesitated to reply; and he went on, now displaying his wealth, now speaking of the petty price he demanded, till it seemed madness to refuse. Thus is it: place our bark in the current of the stream, and down, over fall and cataract it is hurried; give up our conduct to the wild torrent of passion, and we are away, we know not whither.

He swore many an oath, and I adjured him by many a sacred name; till I saw this wonder of power, this ruler of the elements, shiver like an autumn leaf before my words; and as if the spirit spake unwillingly and per force within him, at last, lie, with broken voice, revealed the spell whereby he might be obliged, did he wish to play me false, to render up the unlawful spoil. Our warm life-blood must mingle to make and to mar the charm.

Enough of this unholy theme. I was persuaded—the thing was done. The morrow dawned upon me as I lay upon the shingles, and I knew not my own shadow as it fell from me. I felt myself changed to a shape of horror, and cursed my easy faith and blind credulity. The chest was there—there the gold and precious stones for which I had sold the frame of flesh which nature had given me. The sight a little stilled my emotions: three days would soon be gone.

They did pass. The dwarf had supplied me with a plenteous store of food. At first I could hardly walk, so strange and out of joint were all my limbs; and my voice—it was that of the fiend. But I kept silent, and turned my face to the sun, that I might not see my shadow, and counted the hours, and ruminated on my future conduct. To bring Torella to my feet—to possess my Juliet in spite of him—all this my wealth could easily achieve. During dark night I slept, and dreamt of the accomplishment of my desires. Two suns had set—the third dawned. I was agitated, fearful. Oh expectation, what a frightful thing art thou, when kindled more by fear than hope! How dost thou twist thyself round the heart, torturing its pulsations! How dost thou dart unknown pangs all through our feeble mechanism, now seeming to shiver us like broken glass, to nothingness now giving us a fresh strength, which can do nothing, and so torments us by a sensation, such as the strong man must feel who cannot break his fetters, though they bend in his grasp. Slowly paced the bright, bright orb up the eastern sky; long it lingered in the zenith, and still more slowly wandered down the west: it touched the horizon's verge—it was lost! Its glories were on the summits of the cliff—they grew dun and gray. The evening star shone bright. He will soon be here.

He came not!—By the living heavens, he came not!—and night dragged out its weary length, and, in its decaying age, "day began to grizzle its dark hair;"[24] and the sun rose again on the most miserable wretch that ever upbraided its light. Three days thus I passed. The jewels and the gold—oh, how I abhorred them!

---

[24] Quoting Lord Byron's 1822 poem "Werner."

Well, well—I will not blacken these pages with demoniac ravings. All too terrible were the thoughts, the raging tumult of ideas that filled my soul. At the end of that time I slept; I had not before since the third sunset; and I dreamt that I was at Juliet's feet, and she smiled, and then she shrieked—for she saw my transformation—and again she smiled, for still her beautiful lover knelt before her. But it was not I—it was he, the fiend, arrayed in my limbs, speaking with my voice, winning her with my looks of love. I strove to warn her, but my tongue refused its office; I strove to tear him from her, but I was rooted to the ground—I awoke with the agony. There were the solitary hoar precipices—there the plashing sea, the quiet strand, and the blue sky over all. What did it mean? was my dream but a mirror of the truth? was he wooing and winning my betrothed? I would on the instant back to Genoa—but I was banished. I laughed—the dwarf's yell burst from my lips—I banished! O, no! they had not exiled the foul limbs I wore; I might with these enter, without fear of incurring the threatened penalty of death, my own, my native city.

I began to walk towards Genoa. I was somewhat accustomed to my distorted limbs; none were ever so ill adapted for a straight-forward movement; it was with infinite difficulty that I proceeded. Then, too, I desired to avoid all the hamlets strewed here and there on the sea-beach, for I was unwilling to make a display of my hideousness. I was not quite sure that, if seen, the mere boys would not stone me to death as I passed, for a monster: some ungentle salutations I did receive from the few peasants or fishermen I chanced to meet. But it was dark night before I approached Genoa. The weather was so balmy and sweet that it struck me that the Marchese and his daughter would very probably have quitted the city for their country retreat. It was from Villa Torella that I had attempted to carry off Juliet; I had spent many an hour reconnoitering the spot, and knew each inch of ground in its vicinity. It was beautifully situated, embosomed in trees, on the margin of a stream. As I drew near, it became evident that my conjecture was right; nay, moreover, that the hours were being then devoted to feasting and merriment. For the house was lighted up; strains of soft and gay music were wafted towards me by the breeze. My heart sank within me. Such was the generous kindness of Torella's heart that I felt sure that he would not have indulged in public manifestations of rejoicing just after my unfortunate banishment, but for a cause I dared not dwell upon.

The country people were all alive and flocking about; it became necessary that I should study to conceal myself; and yet I longed to address some one, or to hear others discourse, or in any way to gain intelligence of what was really going on. At length, entering the walks that were in immediate vicinity to the mansion, I found one dark enough to veil my excessive frightfulness; and yet others as well as I were loitering in its shade. I soon gathered all I wanted to know—all that first made my very heart die with horror, and then boil with indignation. Tomorrow Juliet was to be given to the penitent, reformed, beloved Guido—tomorrow my bride was to pledge her vows to a fiend from hell! And I did this!—my accursed pride—my demoniac violence and wicked self-idolatry had caused this act. For if I had acted as the wretch who had stolen my form had acted—if, with a mien at once yielding and dignified, I had presented myself to Torella, saying, I have done wrong, forgive me; I am unworthy of your angel-child, but permit me to claim her hereafter, when my altered conduct shall manifest that I abjure my vices, and endeavour to become in some sort worthy of her. I go to serve against the infidels; and when my zeal for religion and my true penitence for the past shall appear to you to cancel my crimes, permit me again to call myself your son. Thus had he spoken; and the penitent was welcomed even as the prodigal son of scripture: the fatted calf was killed for him; and he, still pursuing the same path, displayed such open-hearted regret for his follies, so humble a concession of all his rights, and so ardent a resolve to reacquire them by a life of contrition and virtue, that he quickly conquered the kind, old man; and full pardon, and the gift of his lovely child, followed in swift succession.

O! had an angel from Paradise whispered to me to act thus! But now, what would be the innocent Juliet's fate? Would God permit the foul union —or, some prodigy destroying it, link the dishonored name of Carega with the worst of crimes? Tomorrow at dawn they were to be married: there was but one way to prevent this—to meet mine enemy, and to enforce the ratification of our agreement. I felt that this could only be done by a mortal struggle. I had no sword—if indeed my distorted arms could wield a soldier's weapon—but I had a dagger, and in that lay my every hope. There was no time for pondering or balancing nicely the question: I might die in the attempt; but besides the burning jealousy and despair of my own heart, honor, mere humanity, demanded that I should fall rather than not destroy the machinations of the fiend.

The guests departed—the lights began to disappear; it was evident that the inhabitants of the villa were seeking repose. I hid myself among the trees —the garden grew desert—the gates were closed—I wandered round and came under a window—ah! well did I know the same!—a soft twilight glimmered in the room—the curtains were half withdrawn. It was the temple of innocence and beauty. Its magnificence was tempered, as it were, by the slight disarrangements occasioned by its being dwelt in, and all the objects scattered around displayed the taste of her who hallowed it by her presence. I saw her enter with a quick light step—I saw her approach the window—she drew back the curtain yet further, and looked out into the night. Its breezy freshness played among her ringlets, and wafted them from the transparent marble of her brow. She clasped her hands, she raised her eyes to Heaven. I heard her voice. Guido! she softly murmured, Mine own Guido! and then, as if overcome by the fullness of her own heart, she sank on her knees:—her upraised eyes—her negligent but graceful attitude—the beaming thankfulness that lighted up her face—oh, these are tame words! Heart of mine, thou imagest ever, though thou canst not portray, the celestial beauty of that child of light and love.

I heard a step—a quick firm step along the shady avenue. Soon I saw a cavalier, richly dressed, young and, methought, graceful to look on, advance. —I hid myself yet closer.—The youth approached; he paused beneath the window. She arose, and again looking out she saw him, and said—I cannot, no, at this distant time I cannot record her terms of soft silver tenderness; to me they were spoken, but they were replied to by him.

"I will not go," he cried: "here where you have been, where your memory glides like some Heaven-visiting ghost, I will pass the long hours till we meet, never, my Juliet, again, day or night, to part. But do thou, my love, retire; the cold morn and fitful breeze will make thy cheek pale, and fill with languor thy love-lighted eyes. Ah, sweetest! could I press one kiss upon them, I could, methinks, repose."

And then he approached still nearer, and methought lie was about to clamber into her chamber. I had hesitated, not to terrify her; now I was no longer master of myself. I rushed forward—I threw myself on him—I tore him away—I cried, "O loathsome and foul-shaped wretch!"

I need not repeat epithets, all tending, as it appeared, to rail at a person I at present feel some partiality for. A shriek rose from Juliet's lips. I neither heard nor saw—I *felt* only mine enemy, whose throat I grasped, and my dagger's hilt; he struggled, but could not escape: at length hoarsely he breathed these words: "Do!—strike home! destroy this body—you will still live: may your life be long and merry!"

The descending dagger was arrested at the word, and he, feeling my hold relax, extricated himself and drew his sword, while the uproar in the house, and flying of torches from one room to the other, showed that soon we should be separated—and I—oh! far better die: so that he did not survive, I cared not. In the midst of my frenzy there was much calculation:—fall I might, and so that he did not survive, I cared not for the death-blow I might deal against myself. While still, therefore, he thought I paused, and while I saw the villainous resolve to take advantage of my hesitation, in the sudden thrust he made at me, I threw myself on his sword, and at the same moment plunged my dagger, with a true desperate aim, in his side. We fell together, rolling over each other, and the tide of blood that flowed from the gaping wound of each mingled on the grass. More I know not—I fainted.

Again I returned to life: weak almost to death, I found myself stretched upon a bed—Juliet was kneeling beside it. Strange! my first broken request was for a mirror. I was so wan and ghastly, that my poor girl hesitated, as she told me afterwards; but, by the mass! I thought myself a right proper youth when I saw the dear reflection of my own well-known features. I confess it is a weakness, but I avow it, I do entertain a considerable affection for the countenance and limbs I behold, whenever I look at a glass; and have more mirrors in my house, and consult them oftener than any beauty in Venice. Before you too much condemn me, permit me to say that no one better knows than I the value of his own body; no one, probably, except myself, ever having had it stolen from him.

Incoherently I at first talked of the dwarf and his crimes, and reproached Juliet for her too easy admission of his love. She thought me raving, as well she might, and yet it was some time before I could prevail on myself to admit that the Guido whose penitence had won her back for me was myself; and while I cursed bitterly the monstrous dwarf, and blest the well-directed blow that had deprived him of life, I suddenly checked myself when I heard her say —Amen! knowing that him whom she reviled was my very self. A little reflection taught me silence—a little practice enabled me to speak of that frightful night without any very excessive blunder. The wound I had given myself was no mockery of one—it was long before I recovered—and as the benevolent and generous Torella sat beside me, talking such wisdom as might win friends to repentance, and mine own dear Juliet hovered near me, administering to my wants, and cheering me by her smiles, the work of my bodily cure and mental reform went on together. I have never, indeed, wholly recovered my strength my cheek is paler since—my person a little bent. Juliet sometimes ventures to allude bitterly to the malice that caused this change, but I kiss her on the moment, and tell her all is for the best. I am a fonder and more faithful husband—and true is this—but for that wound, never had I called her mine.

I did not revisit the seashore, nor seek for the fiend's treasure; yet, while I ponder on the past, I often think, and my confessor was not backward in favoring the idea, that it might be a good rather than an evil spirit, sent by my guardian angel, to show me the folly and misery of pride. So well at least did I learn this lesson, roughly taught as I was, that I am known now by all my friends and fellow-citizens by the name of Guido il Cortese.

/

Laura Silver Bell

J. Sheridan Le Fanu

first published in *Belgravia Annual* (December 1871)

In the five Northumbrian counties you will scarcely find so bleak, ugly, and yet, in a savage way, so picturesque a moor as Dardale Moss. The moor itself spreads north, south, east, and west, a great undulating sea of black peat and heath.

What we may term its shores are wooded wildly with birch, hazel, and dwarf-oak. No towering mountains surround it, but here and there you have a rocky knoll rising among the trees, and many a wooded promontory of the same pretty, because utterly wild, forest, running out into its dark level.

Habitations are thinly scattered in this barren territory, and a full mile away from the meanest was the stone cottage of Mother Carke.

Let not my southern reader who associates ideas of comfort with the term "cottage" mistake. This thing is built of shingle, with low walls. Its thatch is hollow; the peat-smoke curls stingily from its stunted chimney. It is worthy of its savage surroundings.

The primitive neighbors remark that no rowan-tree grows near, nor holly, nor bracken, and no horseshoe is nailed on the door.

Not far from the birches and hazels that straggle about the rude wall of the little enclosure, on the contrary, they say, you may discover the broom and the rag-wort, in which witches mysteriously delight. But this is perhaps a scandal.

Mall Carke was for many a year the *sage femme* of this wild domain.[25] She has renounced practice, however, for some years; and now, under the rose, she dabbles, it is thought, in the black art, in which she has always been secretly skilled, tells fortunes, practices charms, and in popular esteem is little better than a witch.

Mother Carke has been away to the town of Willarden, to sell knit stockings, and is returning to her rude dwelling by Dardale Moss. To her right, as far away as the eye can reach, the moor stretches. The narrow track she has followed here tops a gentle upland, and at her left a sort of jungle of dwarf-oak and brushwood approaches its edge. The sun is sinking blood-red

---

²⁵ "*Sage femme*" or midwife.

in the west. His disk has touched the broad black level of the moor, and his parting beams glare athwart the gaunt figure of the old beldame, as she strides homeward stick in hand, and bring into relief the folds of her mantle, which gleam like the draperies of a bronze image in the light of a fire. For a few moments this light floods the air—tree, gorse, rock, and bracken glare; and then it is out, and gray twilight over everything.

All is still and sombre. At this hour the simple traffic of the thinly-peopled country is over, and nothing can be more solitary.

From this jungle, nevertheless, through which the mists of evening are already creeping, she sees a gigantic man approaching her.

In that poor and primitive country robbery is a crime unknown. She, therefore, has no fears for her pound of tea, and pint of gin, and sixteen shillings in silver which she is bringing home in her pocket. But there is something that would have frighted another woman about this man.

He is gaunt, sombre, bony, dirty, and dressed in a black suit which a beggar would hardly care to pick out of the dust.

This ill-looking man nodded to her as he stepped on the road.

"I don't know you," she said.

He nodded again.

"I never sid ye neyawheere," she exclaimed sternly.

"Fine evening, Mother Carke," he says, and holds his snuff-box toward her.

She widened the distance between them by a step or so, and said again sternly and pale,

"I hev nowt to say to thee, whoe'er thou beest."

"You know Laura Silver Bell?"

"That's a byneyam; the lass's neyam is Laura Lew," she answered, looking straight before her.

"One name's as good as another for one that was never christened, mother."

"How know ye that?" she asked grimly; for it is a received opinion in that part of the world that the fairies have power over those who have never been baptized.

The stranger turned on her a malignant smile.

"There is a young lord in love with her," the stranger says, "and I'm that lord. Have her at your house tomorrow night at eight o'clock, and you must stick cross pins through the candle, as you have done for many a one before, to bring her lover thither by ten, and her fortune's made. And take this for your trouble."

He extended his long finger and thumb toward her, with a guinea temptingly displayed.

"I have nowt to do wi' thee. I nivver sid thee afoore. Git thee awa'! I earned nea goold o' thee, and I'll tak' nane. Awa' wi' thee, or I'll find ane that will mak' thee!"

The old woman had stopped, and was quivering in every limb as she thus spoke.

He looked very angry. Sulkily he turned away at her words, and strode slowly toward the wood from which he had come; and as he approached it, he seemed to her to grow taller and taller, and stalked into it as high as a tree.

"I conceited there would come something o't", she said to herself. "Farmer Lew must git it done nesht Sunda'. The a'ad awpy!"

Old Farmer Lew was one of that sect who insist that baptism shall be but once administered, and not until the Christian candidate had attained to adult years. The girl had indeed for some time been of an age not only, according to this theory, to be baptized, but if need be to be married.

Her story was a sad little romance. A lady some seventeen years before had come down and paid Farmer Lew for two rooms in his house. She told him that her husband would follow her in a fortnight, and that he was in the mean time delayed by business in Liverpool.

In ten days after her arrival her baby was born, Mall Carke acting as *sage femme* on the occasion; and on the evening of that day the poor young mother died. No husband came; no wedding-ring, they said, was on her finger. About fifty pounds was found in her desk, which Farmer Lew, who was a kind old fellow and had lost his two children, put in bank for the little girl, and resolved to keep her until a rightful owner should step forward to claim her.

They found half-a-dozen love-letters signed "Francis," and calling the dead woman "Laura."

So Farmer Lew called the little girl Laura; and her *sobriquet* of "Silver Bell" was derived from a tiny silver bell, once gilt, which was found among her poor mother's little treasures after her death, and which the child wore on a ribbon round her neck.

Thus, being very pretty and merry, she grew up as a North-country farmer's daughter; and the old man, as she needed more looking after, grew older and less able to take care of her; so she was, in fact, very nearly her own mistress, and did pretty much in all things as she liked.

Old Mall Carke, by some caprice for which no one could account, cherished an affection for the girl, who saw her often, and paid her many a small fee in exchange for the secret indications of the future.

It was too late when Mother Carke reached her home to look for a visit from Laura Silver Bell that day.

About three o'clock next afternoon, Mother Carke was sitting knitting, with her glasses on, outside her door on the stone bench, when she saw the pretty girl mount lightly to the top of the stile at her left under the birch, against the silver stem of which she leaned her slender hand, and called,

"Mall, Mall! Mother Carke, are ye alane all by yersel'?"

"Ay, Laura lass, we can be clooas enoo, if ye want a word wi' me," says the old woman, rising, with a mysterious nod, and beckoning her stiffly with her long fingers.

The girl was, assuredly, pretty enough for a "lord" to fall in love with. Only look at her. A profusion of brown rippling hair, parted low in the middle of her forehead, almost touched her eyebrows, and made the pretty oval of her face, by the breadth of that rich line, more marked. What a pretty little nose! what scarlet lips, and large, dark, long-fringed eyes!

Her face is transparently tinged with those clear Murillo tints which appear in deeper dyes on her wrists and the backs of her hands. These are the beautiful gipsy-tints with which the sun dyes young skins so richly.

The old woman eyes all this, and her pretty figure, so round and slender, and her shapely little feet, cased in the thick shoes that can't hide their comely proportions, as she stands on the top of the stile. But it is with a dark and saturnine aspect.

"Come, lass, what stand ye for atoppa t' wall, whar folk may chance to see thee? I hev a thing to tell thee, lass."

She beckoned her again.

"An' I hev a thing to tell *thee*, Mall."

"Come hidder," said the old woman peremptorily.

"But ye munna gie me the creepin's."[26] "I winna look again into the glass o' water, mind ye."

The old woman smiled grimly, and changed her tone.

"Now, hunny, git tha down, and let ma see thy canny feyace," and she beckoned her again.

Laura Silver Bell did get down, and stepped lightly toward the door of the old woman's dwelling.

"Tak this," said the girl, unfolding a piece of bacon from her apron, "and I hev a silver sixpence to gie thee, when I'm gaen away heyam."

They entered the dark kitchen of the cottage, and the old woman stood by the door, lest their conference should be lighted on by surprise.

"Afoore ye begin," said Mother Carke (I soften her patois), "I mun tell ye there's ill folk watchin' ye. What's auld Farmer Lew about, he doesna get t' sir to baptize thee?[27] If he lets Sunda' next pass, I'm afeared ye'll never be sprinkled nor signed wi' cross, while there's a sky aboon us."

"Agoy!" exclaims the girl, "who's lookin' after me?"

"A big black fella, as high as the kipples, came out o' the wood near Deadman's Grike, just after the sun gaed down yester e'en; I knew weel what he was, for his feet ne'er touched the road while he made as if he walked beside me. And he wanted to gie me snuff first, and I wouldna hev that; and then he offered me a gowden guinea, but I was no sic awpy, and to bring you here tonight, and cross the candle wi' pins, to call your lover in. And he said he's a great lord, and in luve wi' thee."

"And you refused him?"

"Well for thee I did, lass," says Mother Carke.

---

26 "Gie me the creepin's" or, "make me tremble."

27 Referencing the clergyman.

"Why, it's every word true!" cries the girl vehemently, starting to her feet, for she had seated herself on the great oak chest.

"True, lass? Come, say what ye mean," demanded Mall Carke, with a dark and searching gaze.

"Last night I was coming heyam from the wake, wi' auld farmer Dykes and his wife and his daughter Nell, and when we came to the stile, I bid them good-night, and we parted."

"And ye came by the path alone in the night-time, did ye?" exclaimed old Mall Carke sternly.

"I wasna afeared, I don't know why; the path heyam leads down by the wa'as o' auld Hawarth Castle."

"I knaa it weel, and a dowly path it is; ye'll keep indoors o' nights for a while, or ye'll rue it. What saw ye?"

"No freetin, mother; nowt I was feared on."

"Ye heard a voice callin' yer neyame?"

"I heard nowt that was dow, but the hullyhoo in the auld castle wa's," answered the pretty girl. "I heard nor sid nowt that's dow, but mickle that's conny and gladsome. I heard singin' and laughin' a long way off, I consaited; and I stopped a bit to listen. Then I walked on a step or two, and there, sure enough in the Pie-Mag field, under the castle wa's, not twenty steps away, I sid a grand company; silks and satins, and men wi' velvet coats, wi' gowd-lace striped over them, and ladies wi' necklaces that would dazzle ye, and fans as big as griddles; and powdered footmen, like what the shirra hed behind his coach, only these was ten times as grand."

"It was full moon last night," said the old woman.

"Sa bright 'twould blind ye to look at it," said the girl.

"Never an ill sight but the deaul finds a light," quoth the old woman. "There's a rinnin brook thar—you were at this side, and they at that; did they try to mak ye cross over?"

"Agoy! didn't they? Nowt but civility and kindness, though. But ye mun let me tell it my own way. They was talkin' and laughin', and eatin', and drinkin' out o' long glasses and goud cups, seated on the grass, and music was playin'; and I keekin' behind a bush at all the grand doin's; and up they gits to dance; and says a tall fella I didna see afoore, 'Ye mun step across, and dance wi' a young lord that's faan in luv wi' thee, and that's mysel',' and sure enow I keeked at him under my lashes and a conny lad he is, to my teyaste, though he be dressed in black, wi' sword and sash, velvet twice as fine as they sells in the shop at Gouden Friars; and keekin' at me again fra the corners o' his een. And the same fella telt me he was mad in luv wi' me, and his fadder was there, and his sister, and they came all the way from Catstean Castle to see me that night; and that's t' other side o' Gouden Friars."

"Come, lass, yer no mafflin; tell me true. What was he like? Was his feyace grimed wi' sut? a tall fella wi' wide shouthers, and lukt like an ill-thing, wi' black clothes amaist in rags?"

"His feyace was long, but weel-faured, and darker nor a gipsy; and his clothes were black and grand, and made o' velvet, and he said he was the young lord himsel'; and he lukt like it."

"That will be the same fella I sid at Deadman's Grike," said Mall Carke, with an anxious frown.

"Hoot, mudder! how cud that be?" cried the lass, with a toss of her pretty head and a smile of scorn. But the fortune-teller made no answer, and the girl went on with her story.

"When they began to dance," continued Laura Silver Bell, "he urged me again, but I wudna step o'er; 'twas partly pride, coz I wasna dressed fine enough, and partly contrariness, or something, but gaa I wudna, not a fut. No but I more nor half wished it a' the time."

"Weel for thee thou dudstna cross the brook."

"Hoity-toity, why not?"

"Keep at heyame after nightfall, and don't ye be walking by yersel' by daylight or any light lang lonesome ways, till after ye're baptized," said Mall Carke.

"I'm like to be married first."

"Tak care *that* marriage won't hang i' the bell-ropes," said Mother Carke.

"Leave me alane for that. The young lord said he was maist daft wi' luv o' me. He wanted to gie me a conny ring wi' a beautiful stone in it. But, drat it, I was sic an awpy I wudna tak it, and he a young lord!"

"Lord, indeed! are ye daft or dreamin'? Those fine folk, what were they? I'll tell ye. Dobies and fairies; and if ye don't du as yer bid, they'll tak ye, and ye'll never git out o' their hands again while grass grows," said the old woman grimly.

"Od wite it!" replies the girl impatiently, "who's daft or dreamin' noo? I'd a bin dead wi' fear, if 'twas any such thing. It cudna be; all was sa luvesome, and bonny, and shaply."

"Weel, and what do ye want o' me, lass?" asked the old woman sharply.

"I want to know—here's t' sixpence—what I sud du," said the young lass. "'Twud be a pity to lose such a marrow, hey?"

"Say yer prayers, lass; *I* can't help ye," says the old woman darkly. "If ye gaa wi' *the* people, ye'll never come back. Ye munna talk wi' them, nor eat wi' them, nor drink wi' them, nor tak a pin's-worth by way o' gift fra them—mark weel what I say—or ye're *lost!*"

The girl looked down, plainly much vexed.

The old woman stared at her with a mysterious frown steadily, for a few seconds.

"Tell me, lass, and tell me true, are ye in luve wi' that lad?"

"What for sud I?" said the girl with a careless toss of her head, and blushing up to her very temples.

"I see how it is," said the old woman, with a groan, and repeated the words, sadly thinking; and walked out of the door a step or two, and looked jealously round. "The lass is witched, the lass is witched!"

"Did ye see him since?" asked Mother Carke, returning.

The girl was still embarrassed; and now she spoke in a lower tone, and seemed subdued.

"I thought I sid him as I came here, walkin' beside me among the trees; but I consait it was only the trees themsels that lukt like rinnin' one behind another, as I walked on."

"I can tell thee nowt, lass, but what I telt ye afoore," answered the old woman peremptorily. "Get ye heyame, and don't delay on the way; and say yer prayers as ye gaa; and let none but good thoughts come nigh ye; and put nayer foot autside the door-steyan again till ye gaa to be christened; and get that done a Sunda' next."

And with this charge, given with grizzly earnestness, she saw her over the stile, and stood upon it watching her retreat, until the trees quite hid her and her path from view.

The sky grew cloudy and thunderous, and the air darkened rapidly, as the girl, a little frightened by Mall Carke's view of the case, walked homeward by the lonely path among the trees.

A black cat, which had walked close by her—for these creatures sometimes take a ramble in search of their prey among the woods and thickets—crept from under the hollow of an oak, and was again with her. It seemed to her to grow bigger and bigger as the darkness deepened, and its green eyes glared as large as halfpennies in her affrighted vision as the thunder came booming along the heights from the Willarden-road.

She tried to drive it away; but it growled and hissed awfully, and set up its back as if it would spring at her, and finally it skipped up into a tree, where they grew thickest at each side of her path, and accompanied her, high over head, hopping from bough to bough as if meditating a pounce upon her shoulders. Her fancy being full of strange thoughts, she was frightened, and she fancied that it was haunting her steps, and destined to undergo some hideous transformation, the moment she ceased to guard her path with prayers.

She was frightened for a while after she got home. The dark looks of Mother Carke were always before her eyes, and a secret dread prevented her passing the threshold of her home again that night.

Next day it was different. She had got rid of the awe with which Mother Carke had inspired her. She could not get the tall dark-featured lord, in the black velvet dress, out of her head. He had "taken her fancy"; she was growing to love him. She could think of nothing else.

Bessie Hennock, a neighbor's daughter, came to see her that day, and proposed a walk toward the ruins of Hawarth Castle, to gather "blaebirries." So off the two girls went together.

In the thicket, along the slopes near the ivied walls of Hawarth Castle, the companions began to fill their baskets. Hours passed. The sun was sinking near the west, and Laura Silver Bell had not come home.

Over the hatch of the farm-house door the maids leant ever and anon with outstretched necks, watching for a sign of the girl's return, and wondering, as the shadows lengthened, what had become of her.

At last, just as the rosy sunset gilding began to overspread the landscape, Bessie Hennock, weeping into her apron, made her appearance without her companion.

Her account of their adventures was curious.

I will relate the substance of it more connectedly than her agitation would allow her to give it, and without the disguise of the rude Northumbrian dialect.

The girl said, that, as they got along together among the brambles that grow beside the brook that bounds the Pie-Mag field, she on a sudden saw a very tall big-boned man, with an ill-favored smirched face, and dressed in worn and rusty black, standing at the other side of a little stream. She was frightened; and while looking at this dirty, wicked, starved figure, Laura Silver Bell touched her, gazing at the same tall scarecrow, but with a countenance full of confusion and even rapture. She was peeping through the bush behind which she stood, and with a sigh she said:

"Is na that a conny lad? Agoy! See his bonny velvet clothes, his sword and sash; that's a lord, I can tell ye; and weel I know who he follows, who he luves, and who he'll wed."

Bessie Hennock thought her companion daft.

"See how luvesome he luks!" whispered Laura.

Bessie looked again, and saw him gazing at her companion with a malignant smile, and at the same time he beckoned her to approach.

"Darrat ta! gaa not near him! he'll wring thy neck!" gasped Bessie in great fear, as she saw Laura step forward with a look of beautiful bashfulness and joy.

She took the hand he stretched across the stream, more for love of the hand than any need of help, and in a moment was across and by his side, and his long arm about her waist.

"Fares te weel, Bessie, I'm gain my ways," she called, leaning her head to his shoulder; "and tell gud Fadder Lew I'm gain my ways to be happy, and may be, at lang last, I'll see him again."

And with a farewell wave of her hand, she went away with her dismal partner; and Laura Silver Bell was never more seen at home, or among the "coppies" and "wickwoods," the bonny fields and bosky hollows, by Dardale Moss.

Bessie Hennock followed them for a time.

She crossed the brook, and though they seemed to move slowly enough, she was obliged to run to keep them in view; and she all the time cried to her continually, "Come back, come back, bonnie Laurie!" until, getting over a bank, she was met by a white-faced old man, and so frightened was she, that she thought she fainted outright. At all events, she did not come to herself until the birds were singing their vespers in the amber light of sunset, and the day was over.

No trace of the direction of the girl's flight was ever discovered. Weeks and months passed, and more than a year.

At the end of that time, one of Mall Carke's goats died, as she suspected, by the envious practices of a rival witch who lived at the far end of Dardale Moss.

All alone in her stone cabin the old woman had prepared her charm to ascertain the author of her misfortune.

The heart of the dead animal, stuck all over with pins, was burnt in the fire; the windows, doors, and every other aperture of the house being first carefully stopped. After the heart, thus prepared with suitable incantations, is consumed in the fire, the first person who comes to the door or passes by it is the offending magician.

Mother Carke completed these lonely rites at dead of night. It was a dark night, with the glimmer of the stars only, and a melancholy night-wind was soughing through the scattered woods that spread around.

After a long and dead silence, there came a heavy thump at the door, and a deep voice called her by name.

She was startled, for she expected no man's voice; and peeping from the window, she saw, in the dim light, a coach and four horses, with gold-laced footmen, and coachman in wig and cocked hat, turned out as if for a state occasion.

She unbarred the door; and a tall gentleman, dressed in black, waiting at the threshold, entreated her, as the only *sage femme* within reach, to come in the coach and attend Lady Lairdale, who was about to give birth to a baby, promising her handsome payment.

Lady Lairdale! She had never heard of her.

"How far away is it?"

"Twelve miles on the old road to Golden Friars."

Her avarice is roused, and she steps into the coach. The footman claps-to the door; the glass jingles with the sound of a laugh. The tall dark-faced gentleman in black is seated opposite; they are driving at a furious pace; they have turned out of the road into a narrower one, dark with thicker and loftier forest than she was accustomed to. She grows anxious; for she knows every road and by-path in the country round, and she has never seen this one.

He encourages her. The moon has risen above the edge of the horizon, and she sees a noble old castle. Its summit of tower, watchtower and battlement, glimmers faintly in the moonlight. This is their destination.

She feels on a sudden all but overpowered by sleep; but although she nods, she is quite conscious of the continued motion, which has become even rougher.

She makes an effort, and rouses herself. What has become of the coach, the castle, the servants? Nothing but the strange forest remains the same.

She is jolting along on a rude hurdle, seated on rushes, and a tall, big-boned man, in rags, sits in front, kicking with his heel the ill-favoured beast that pulls them along, every bone of which sticks out, and holding the halter which serves for reins. They stop at the door of a miserable building of loose stone, with a thatch so sunk and rotten, that the roof-tree and couples protrude in crooked corners, like the bones of the wretched horse, with enormous head and ears, that dragged them to the door.

The long gaunt man gets down, his sinister face grimed like his hands.

It was the same grimy giant who had accosted her on the lonely road near Deadman's Grike. But she feels that she "must go through with it" now, and she follows him into the house.

Two rushlights were burning in the large and miserable room, and on a coarse ragged bed lay a woman groaning piteously.

"That's Lady Lairdale," says the gaunt dark man, who then began to stride up and down the room rolling his head, stamping furiously, and thumping one hand on the palm of the other, and talking and laughing in the corners, where there was no one visible to hear or to answer.

Old Mall Carke recognized in the faded half-starved creature who lay on the bed, as dark now and grimy as the man, and looking as if she had never in her life washed hands or face, the once blithe and pretty Laura Lew.

The hideous being who was her mate continued in the same odd fluctuations of fury, grief, and merriment; and whenever she uttered a groan, he parodied it with another, as Mother Carke thought, in saturnine derision.

At length he strode into another room, and banged the door after him.

In due time the poor woman's pains were over, and a daughter was born.

Such an imp! with long pointed ears, flat nose, and enormous restless eyes and mouth. It instantly began to yell and talk in some unknown language, at the noise of which the father looked into the room, and told the sage femme that she should not go unrewarded.

The sick woman seized the moment of his absence to say in the ear of Mall Carke:

"If ye had not been at ill work tonight, he could not hev fetched ye. Tak no more now than your rightful fee, or he'll keep ye here."

At this moment he returned with a bag of gold and silver coins, which he emptied on the table, and told her to help herself.

She took four shillings, which was her primitive fee, neither more nor less; and all his urgency could not prevail with her to take a farthing more. He looked so terrible at her refusal, that she rushed out of the house.

He ran after her.

"You'll take your money with you," he roared, snatching up the bag, still half full, and flung it after her.

It lighted on her shoulder; and partly from the blow, partly from terror, she fell to the ground; and when she came to herself, it was morning, and she was lying across her own door-stone.

It is said that she never more told fortune or practiced spell. And though all that happened sixty years ago and more, Laura Silver Bell, wise folk think, is still living, and will so continue till the day of doom among the fairies.

The Brownie of the Black Haggs

James Hogg

from *The Shepherd's Calendar: Tales Illustrative of Pastoral Occupations, Country Life, and Superstitions* (1828)

When the Sprots were Lairds of Wheelhope, which is now a long time ago, there was one of the ladies who was very badly spoken of in the country. People did not just openly assert that Lady Wheelhope (for every landward laird's wife was then styled Lady) was a witch, but every one had an aversion even at hearing her named; and when by chance she happened to be mentioned, old men would shake their heads and say, "Ah! let us alane o' her! The less ye meddle wi' her the better." Old wives would give over spinning, and, as a pretense for hearing what might be said about her, poke in the fire with the tongs, cocking up their ears all the while; and then, after some meaning coughs, hems, and haws, would haply say, "Hech-wow, sirs! An a' be true that's said!" or something equally wise and decisive.

In short, Lady Wheelhope was accounted a very bad woman. She was an inexorable tyrant in her family, quarreled with her servants, often cursing them, striking them, and turning them away; especially if they were religious, for she could not endure people of that character, but charged them with every thing bad. Whenever she found out that any of the servant men of the Laird's establishment were religious, she gave them up to the military, and got them shot; and several girls that were regular in their devotions, she was supposed to have got rid of by poison. She was certainly a wicked woman, else many good people were mistaken in her character; and the poor persecuted Covenanters were obliged to unite in their prayers against her.

As for the Laird, he was a big, dun-faced, pluffy body, that cared neither for good nor evil, and did not well know the one from the other. He laughed at his lady's tantrums and barley-hoods; and the greater the rage that she got into, the Laird thought it the better sport. One day, when two maid-servants came running to him, in great agitation, and told him that his lady had felled one of their companions, the Laird laughed heartily, and said he did not doubt it.

"Why, sir, how can you laugh?" said they. "The poor girl is killed."

"Very likely, very likely," said the Laird. "Well, it will teach her to take care who she angers again."

"And, sir, your lady will be hanged."

"Very likely; well, it will teach her how to strike so rashly again—Ha, ha, ha! Will it not, Jessy?"

But when this same Jessy died suddenly one morning, the Laird was greatly confounded, and seemed dimly to comprehend that there had been unfair play going. There was little doubt that she was taken off by poison; but whether the Lady did it through jealousy or not, was never divulged; but it greatly bamboozled and astonished the poor Laird, for his nerves failed him, and his whole frame became paralytic. He seems to have been exactly in the same state of mind with a collie that I once had. He was extremely fond of the gun as long as I did not kill any thing with it, (there being no game laws in Ettrick Forest in those days,) and he got a grand chase after the hares when I missed them. But there was one day that I chanced for a marvel to shoot one dead, a few paces before his nose. I'll never forget the astonishment that the poor beast manifested. He stared one while at the gun, and another while at the dead hare, and seemed to be drawing the conclusion, that if the case stood thus, there was no creature sure of its life. Finally, he took his tail between his legs, and ran away home, and never would face a gun all his life again.

So was it precisely with Laird Sprot of Wheelhope. As long as his lady's wrath produced only noise and uproar among the servants, he thought it fine sport; but when he saw what he believed the dreadful effects of it, he became like a barrel organ out of tune, and could only discourse one note, which he did to every one he met. "I wish she mayna hae gotten something she had been the waur of." This note he repeated early and late, night and day, sleeping and waking, alone and in company, from the moment that Jessy died till she was buried; and on going to the churchyard as chief mourner, he whispered it to her relatives by the way. When they came to the grave, he took his stand at the head, nor would he give place to the girl's father; but there he stood, like a huge post, as though he neither saw nor heard; and when he had lowered her head into the grave, and dropped the cord, he slowly lifted his hat with one hand, wiped his dim eyes with the back of the other, and said, in a deep tremulous tone, "Poor lassie! I wish she didna get something she had been the waur of."

This death made a great noise among the common people; but there was little protection for the life of the subject in those days; and provided a man or woman was a real Anti-Covenanter, they might kill a good many without being quarreled for it. So there was no one to take cognizance of the circumstances relating to the death of poor Jessy.

After this, the Lady walked softly for the space of two or three years. She saw that she had rendered herself odious, and had entirely lost her husband's countenance, which she liked worst of all. But the evil propensity could not be overcome; and a poor boy, whom the Laird, out of sheer compassion, had taken into his service, being found dead one morning, the country people could no longer be restrained; so they went in a body to the Sheriff, and insisted on an investigation. It was proved that she detested the boy, had often threatened him, and had given him brose and butter the afternoon before he died;[28] but notwithstanding of all this, the cause was ultimately dismissed, and the pursuers fined.

No one can tell to what height of wickedness she might now have proceeded, had not a check of a very singular kind been laid upon her. Among the servants that came home at the next term, was one who called himself Merodach; and a strange person he was. He had the form of a boy, but the features of one a hundred years old, save that his eyes had a brilliancy and restlessness, which were very extraordinary, bearing a strong resemblance to the eyes of a well-known species of monkey. He was froward and perverse, and disregarded the pleasure or displeasure of any person; but he performed his work well, and with apparent ease. From the moment he entered the house, the Lady conceived a mortal antipathy against him, and besought the Laird to turn him away. But the Laird would not consent; he never turned away any servant, and moreover he had hired this fellow for a trivial wage, and he neither wanted activity nor perseverance. The natural consequence of this refusal was, that the Lady instantly set herself to embitter Merodach's life as much as possible, in order to get early quit of a domestic every way so disagreeable. Her hatred of him was not like a common antipathy entertained by one human being against another,—she hated him as one might hate a toad or an adder; and his occupation of jotteryman (as the Laird termed his servant of all work) keeping him always about her hand, it must have proved highly annoying.

She scolded him, she raged at him; but he only mocked her wrath, and giggled and laughed at her, with the most provoking derision. She tried to fell him again and again, but never, with all her address, could she hit him; and never did she make a blow at him, that she did not repent it. She was heavy and unwieldy, and he as quick in his motions as a monkey; besides, he generally contrived that she should be in such an ungovernable rage, that when she flew at him, she hardly knew what she was doing. At one time she guided her blow towards him, and he at the same instant avoided it with such dexterity, that she knocked down the chief hind, or foresman; and then Merodach giggled so heartily, that, lifting the kitchen poker, she threw it at

---

[28] "Brose and butter" is a simple traditional Scottish dish made from brose (oats or oatmeal mixed with boiling water) and served with a pat of butter as a breakfast or a comfort meal.

him with a full design of knocking out his brains; but the missile only broke every article of crockery on the kitchen dresser.

She then hasted to the Laird, crying bitterly, and telling him she would not suffer that wretch Merodach, as she called him, to stay another night in the family.

"Why, then, put him away, and trouble me no more about him," said the Laird.

"Put him away!" exclaimed she; "I have already ordered him away a hundred times, and charged him never to let me see his horrible face again; but he only grins, and answers with some intolerable piece of impertinence."

The pertinacity of the fellow amused the Laird; his dim eyes turned upwards into his head with delight; he then looked two ways at once, turned round his back, and laughed till the tears ran down his dun cheeks; but he could only articulate, "You're fitted now."

The Lady's agony of rage still increasing from this derision, she upbraided the Laird bitterly, and said he was not worthy the name of man, if he did not turn away that pestilence, after the way he had abused her.

"Why, Shusy, my dear, what has he done to you?"

"What done to me! has he not caused me to knock down John Thomson? and I do not know if ever he will come to life again!"

"Have you felled your favorite John Thomson?" said the Laird, laughing more heartily than before; "you might have done a worse deed than that."

"And has he not broke every plate and dish on the whole dresser?" continued the Lady; "and for all this devastation, he only mocks at my displeasure,—absolutely mocks me,—and if you do not have him turned away, and hanged or shot for his deeds, you are not worthy the name of man."

"O alack! What a devastation among the cheena metal!" said the Laird; and calling on Merodach, he said, "Tell me, thou evil Merodach of Babylon, how thou dared'st knock down thy Lady's favorite servant, John Thomson?"

"Not I, your honor. It was my Lady herself, who got into such a furious rage at me, that she mistook her man, and felled Mr Thomson; and the good man's skull is fractured."

"That was very odd," said the Laird, chuckling; "I do not comprehend it. But then, what set you on smashing all my Lady's delft and cheena ware?— That was a most infamous and provoking action."

"It was she herself, your honor. Sorry would I be to break one dish belonging to the house. I take all the house servants to witness, that my Lady smashed all the dishes with a poker; and now lays the blame on me!"

The Laird turned his dim eyes on his lady, who was crying with vexation and rage, and seemed meditating another personal attack on the culprit, which he did not at all appear to shun, but rather to court. She, however, vented her wrath in threatenings of the most deep and desperate revenge, the creature all the while assuring her that she would be foiled, and that in all her encounters and contests with him, she would uniformly come to the worst; he was resolved to do his duty, and there before his master he defied her.

The Laird thought more than he considered it prudent to reveal; he had little doubt that his wife would find some means of wreaking her vengeance on the object of her displeasure; and he shuddered when he recollected one who had taken "something that she had been the waur of."

In a word, the Lady of Wheelhope's inveterate malignity against this one object, was like the rod of Moses, that swallowed up the rest of the serpents. All her wicked and evil propensities seemed to be superseded, if not utterly absorbed by it. The rest of the family now lived in comparative peace and quietness; for early and late her malevolence was venting itself against the jotteryman, and against him alone. It was a delirium of hatred and vengeance, on which the whole bent and bias of her inclination was set. She could not stay from the creature's presence, or, in the intervals when absent from him, she spent her breath in curses and execrations; and then, not able to rest, she ran again to seek him, her eyes gleaming with the anticipated delights of vengeance, while, ever and anon, all the ridicule and the harm redounded on herself.

Was it not strange that she could not get quit of this sole annoyance of her life? One would have thought she easily might. But by this time there was nothing farther from her wishes; she wanted vengeance, full, adequate, and delicious vengeance, on her audacious opponent. But he was a strange and terrible creature, and the means of retaliation constantly came, as it were, to his hand.

Bread and sweet milk was the only fare that Merodach cared for, and having bargained for that, he would not want it, though he often got it with a curse and with ill will. The Lady having, upon one occasion, intentionally kept back his wonted allowance for some days, on the Sabbath morning following, she set him down a bowl of rich sweet milk, well drugged with a deadly poison; and then she lingered in a little anteroom to watch the success of her grand plot, and prevent any other creature from tasting of the potion. Merodach came in, and the house-maid said to him, "There is your breakfast, creature."

"Oho! my Lady has been liberal this morning," said he; "but I am beforehand with her.—Here, little Missie, you seem very hungry today—take you my breakfast." And with that he set the beverage down to the Lady's little favorite spaniel. It so happened that the Lady's only son came at that instant into the anteroom seeking her, and teasing his mamma about something, which withdrew her attention from the hall-table for a space. When she looked again, and saw Missie lapping up the sweet milk, she burst from her hiding-place like a fury, screaming as if her head had been on fire, kicked the remainder of its contents against the wall, and lifting Missie in her bosom, retreated hastily, crying all the way.

"Ha, ha, ha—I have you now!" cried Merodach, as she vanished from the hall.

Poor Missie died immediately, and very privately; indeed, she would have died and been buried, and never one have seen her, save her mistress, had not

Merodach, by a luck that never failed him, looked over the wall of the flower garden, just as his lady was laying her favorite in a grave of her own digging. She, not perceiving her tormentor, plied on at her task, apostrophizing the insensate little carcass,—"Ah! poor dear little creature, thou hast had a hard fortune, and hast drank of the bitter potion that was not intended for thee; but he shall drink it three times double for thy sake!"

"Is that little Missie?" said the eldrich voice of the jotteryman, close at the Lady's ear. She uttered a loud scream, and sunk down on the bank. "Alack for poor Missie!" continued the creature in a tone of mockery, "my heart is sorry for Missie. What has befallen her—whose breakfast cup did she drink?"

"Hence with thee, fiend!" cried the Lady; "what right hast thou to intrude on thy mistress's privacy? Thy turn is coming yet; or may the nature of woman change within me!"

"It is changed already," said the creature, grinning with delight; "I have thee now, I have thee now! And were it not to show my superiority over thee, which I do every hour, I should soon see thee strapped like a mad cat, or a worrying bratch. What wilt thou try next?"

"I will cut thy throat, and if I die for it, will rejoice in the deed; a deed of charity to all that dwell on the face of the earth."

"I have warned thee before, dame, and I now warn thee again, that all thy mischief meditated against me will fall double on thine own head."

"I want none of your warning, fiendish cur. Hence with your elvish face, and take care of yourself."

It would be too disgusting and horrible to relate or read all the incidents that fell out between this unaccountable couple. Their enmity against each other had no end, and no mitigation; and scarcely a single day passed over on which the Lady's acts of malevolent ingenuity did not terminate fatally for some favorite thing of her own. Scarcely was there a thing, animate or inanimate, on which she set a value, left to her, that was not destroyed; and yet scarcely one hour or minute could she remain absent from her tormentor, and all the while, it seems, solely for the purpose of tormenting him. While all the rest of the establishment enjoyed peace and quietness from the fury of their termagant dame, matters still grew worse and worse between the fascinated pair. The Lady haunted the menial, in the same manner as the raven haunts the eagle,—for a perpetual quarrel, though the former knows that in every encounter she is to come off the loser. Noises were heard on the stairs by night, and it was whispered among the servants, that the Lady had been seeking Merodach's chamber, on some horrible intent. Several of them would have sworn that they had seen her passing and repassing on the stair after midnight, when all was quiet; but then it was likewise well known, that Merodach slept with well-fastened doors, and a companion in another bed in the same room, whose bed, too, was nearest the door. Nobody cared much what became of the jotteryman, for he was an unsocial and disagreeable person; but some one told him what they had seen, and hinted a suspicion of the Lady's intent. But the creature only bit his upper lip, winked with his eyes, and said, "She had better let that alone; she will be the first to rue that."

Not long after this, to the horror of the family and the whole country side, the Laird's only son was found murdered in his bed one morning, under circumstances that manifested the most fiendish cruelty and inveteracy on the part of his destroyer. As soon as the atrocious act was divulged, the Lady fell into convulsions, and lost her reason; and happy had it been for her had she never recovered the use of it, for there was blood upon her hand, which she took no care to conceal, and there was little doubt that it was the blood of her own innocent and beloved boy, the sole heir and hope of the family.

This blow deprived the Laird of all power of action; but the Lady had a brother, a man of the law, who came and instantly proceeded to an investigation of this unaccountable murder. Before the Sheriff arrived, the housekeeper took the Lady's brother aside, and told him he had better not go on with the scrutiny, for she was sure the crime would be brought home to her unfortunate mistress; and after examining into several corroborative circumstances, and viewing the state of the raving maniac, with the blood on her hand and arm, he made the investigation a very short one, declaring the domestics all exculpated.

The Laird attended his boy's funeral, and laid his head in the grave, but appeared exactly like a man walking in a trance, an automaton, without feelings or sensations, oftentimes gazing at the funeral procession, as on something he could not comprehend. And when the death-bell of the parish church fell a-tolling, as the corpse approached the kirk-stile, he cast a dim eye up towards the belfry, and said hastily, "What, what's that? Och ay, we're just in time, just in time." And often was he hammering over the name of "Evil Merodach, King of Babylon," to himself. He seemed to have some far-fetched conception that his unaccountable jotteryman was in some way connected with the death of his only son, and other lesser calamities, although the evidence in favour of Merodach's innocence was as usual quite decisive.

This grievous mistake of Lady Wheelhope can only be accounted for, by supposing her in a state of derangement, or rather under some evil influence, over which she had no control; and to a person in such a state, the mistake was not so very unnatural. The mansion-house of Wheelhope was old and irregular. The stair had four acute turns, and four landing-places, all the same. In the uppermost chamber slept the two domestics,—Merodach in the bed farthest in, and in the chamber immediately below that, which was exactly similar, slept the Young Laird and his tutor, the former in the bed farthest in; and thus, in the turmoil of her wild and raging passions, her own hand made herself childless.

Merodach was expelled the family forthwith, but refused to accept of his wages, which the man of law pressed upon him, for fear of farther mischief; but he went away in apparent sullenness and discontent, no one knowing whither.

When his dismissal was announced to the Lady, who was watched day and night in her chamber, the news had such an effect on her, that her whole frame seemed electrified; the horrors of remorse vanished, and another passion, which I neither can comprehend nor define, took the sole possession of her distempered spirit. "He *must* not go!—He *shall* not go!" she exclaimed. "No, no, no—he shall not—he shall not—he shall not!" and then she instantly set herself about making ready to follow him, uttering all the while the most diabolical expressions, indicative of anticipated vengeance.—"Oh, could I but snap his nerves one by one, and birl among his vitals! Could I but slice his heart off piecemeal in small messes, and see his blood lopper, and bubble, and spin away in purple slays; and then to see him grin, and grin, and grin, and grin! Oh—oh—oh—How beautiful and grand a sight it would be to see him grin, and grin, and grin!" And in such a style would she run on for hours together.

She thought of nothing, she spake of nothing, but the discarded jotteryman, whom most people now began to regard as a creature that was "not canny." They had seen him eat, and drink, and work, like other people; still he had that about him that was not like other men. He was a boy in form, and an antediluvian in feature. Some thought he was half-ape, some a wizard, some a kelpie, or a fairy, but most of all, that he was really and truly a Brownie. What he was I do not know, and therefore will not pretend to say; but be that as it may, in spite of locks and keys, watching and waking, the Lady of Wheelhope soon made her escape, and eloped after him. The attendants, indeed, would have made oath that she was carried away by some invisible hand, for it was impossible, they said, that she could have escaped on foot like other people; and this edition of the story took in the country; but sensible people viewed the matter in another light.

As for instance, when Wattie Blythe, the Laird's old shepherd, came in from the hill one morning, his wife Bessie thus accosted him.—"His presence be about us, Wattie Blythe! have ye heard what has happened at the ha'? Things are aye turning waur and waur there, and it looks like as if Providence had gi'en up our Laird's house to destruction. This grand estate maun now gang frae the Sprots; for it has finished them."

"Na, na, Bessie, it isna the estate that has finished the Sprots, but the Sprots that hae finished the estate, and themsells into the boot. They hae been a wicked and degenerate race, and aye the langer the waur, till they hae reached the utmost bounds o' earthly wickedness; and it's time the deil were looking after his ain."

"Ah, Wattie Blythe, ye never said a truer say. And that's just the very point where your story ends, and mine begins; for hasna the deil, or the fairies, or the brownies, ta'en away our Leddy bodily! and the haill country is running and riding in search o' her; and there is twenty hunder merks offered to the first that can find her, and bring her safe back. They hae ta'en her away, skin and bane, body and soul, and a', Wattie!"

"Hech-wow! but that is awesome! And where is it thought they have ta'en her to, Bessie?"

"O, they hae some guess at that frae her ain hints afore. It is thought they hae carried her after that Satan of a creature, wha wrought sae muckle wae about the house. It is for him they are a' looking, for they ken weel, that where they get the tane they will get the tither."

"Whew! Is that the gate o't, Bessie? Why, then, the awfu' story is nouther mair nor less than this, that the Leddy has made a 'lopement, as they ca't, and run away after a blackguard jotteryman. Hech-wow! wae's me for human frailty! But that's just the gate! When aince the deil gets in the point o' his finger, he will soon have in his haill hand. Ay, he wants but a hair to make a tether of, ony day! I hae seen her a braw sonsy lass; but even then I feared she was devoted to destruction, for she aye mockit at religion, Bessie, and that's no a good mark of a young body. And she made a' its servants her enemies; and think you these good men's prayers were a' to blaw away i' the wind, and be nae mair regarded? Na, na, Bessie, my woman, take ye this mark baith o' our ain bairns and ither folk's—If ever ye see a young body that disregards the Sabbath, and makes a mock at the ordinances o' religion, ye will never see that body come to muckle good.—A braw hand our Leddy has made o' her gibes and jeers at religion, and her mockeries o' the poor persecuted hill-folk!— sunk down by degrees into the very dregs o' sin and misery! run away after a scullion!"

"Fy, fy, Wattie, how can ye say sae? It was weel kenn'd that she hatit him wi' a perfect and mortal hatred, and tried to make away wi' him mae ways nor ane."

"Aha, Bessie; but nipping and scarting is Scots folk's wooing; and though it is but right that we suspend our judgments, there will naebody persuade me if she be found alang wi' the creature, but that she has run away after him in the natural way, on her twa shanks, without help either frae fairy or brownie."

"I'll never believe sic a thing of ony woman born, let be a leddy weel up in years."

"Od help ye, Bessie! ye dinna ken the stretch o' corrupt nature. The best o' us, when left to oursells, are nae better than strayed sheep, that will never find the way back to their ain pastures; and of a' things made o' mortal flesh, a wicked woman is the warst."

"Alack-a-day! we get the blame o' muckle that we little deserve. But, Wattie, keep ye a geyan sharp look-out about the cleuchs and the caves o' our hope; for the Leddy kens them a' geyan weel; and gin the twenty hunder merks wad come our way, it might gang a waur gate. It wad tocher a' our bonny lasses."

"Ay, weel I wat, Bessie, that's nae lee. And now, when ye bring me amind o't, I'm sair mista'en if I didna hear a creature up in the Brockholes this morning, skirling as if something war cutting its throat. It gars a' the hairs stand on my head when I think it may hae been our Leddy, and the droich of a creature murdering her. I took it for a battle of wulcats, and wished they might pu' out ane anither's thrapples; but when I think on it again, they war unco like some o' our Leddy's unearthly screams."

"His presence be about us, Wattie! Haste ye—pit on your bonnet—tak' your staff in your hand, and gang and see what it is."

"Shame fa' me, if I daur gang, Bessie."

"Hout, Wattie, trust in the Lord."

"Aweel, sae I do. But ane's no to throw himsell ower a linn, and trust that the Lord will kep him in a blanket. And it's nae muckle safer for an auld stiff man like me to gang away out to a wild remote place, where there is ae body murdering another.—What is that I hear, Bessie? Haud the lang tongue o' you, and rin to the door, and see what noise that is."

Bessie ran to the door, but soon returned, with her mouth wide open, and her eyes set in her head.

"It is them, Wattie! it is them! His presence be about us! What will we do?"

"Them? whaten them?"

"Why, that blackguard creature, coming here, leading our Leddy by the hair o' the head, and yerking her wi' a stick. I am terrified out o' my wits. What will we do?"

"We'll *see* what they *say*," said Wattie, manifestly in as great terror as his wife; and by a natural impulse, or as a last resource, he opened the Bible, not knowing what he did, and then hurried on his spectacles; but before he got two leaves turned over, the two entered,—a frightful-looking couple indeed. Merodach, with his old withered face, and ferret eyes, leading the Lady of Wheelhope by the long hair, which was mixed with grey, and whose face was all bloated with wounds and bruises, and having stripes of blood on her garments.

"How's this!—How's this, sirs?" said Wattie Blythe.

"Close that book, and I will tell you, goodman," said Merodach.

"I can hear what you hae to say wi' the beuk open, sir," said Wattie, turning over the leaves, pretending to look for some particular passage, but apparently not knowing what he was doing. "It is a shamefu' business this; but some will hae to answer for't. My Leddy, I am unco grieved to see you in sic a plight. Ye hae surely been dooms sair left to yoursell."

The Lady shook her head, uttered a feeble hollow laugh, and fixed her eyes on Merodach. But such a look! It almost frightened the simple aged couple out of their senses. It was not a look of love nor of hatred exclusively; neither was it of desire or disgust, but it was a combination of them all. It was such a look as one fiend would cast on another, in whose everlasting destruction he rejoiced. Wattie was glad to take his eyes from such countenances, and look into the Bible, that firm foundation of all his hopes and all his joy.

"I request that you will shut that book, sir," said the horrible creature; "or if you do not, I will shut it for you with a vengeance;" and with that he seized it, and flung it against the wall. Bessie uttered a scream, and Wattie was quite paralyzed; and although he seemed disposed to run after his best friend, as he called it, the hellish looks of the Brownie interposed, and glued him to his seat.

"Hear what I have to say first," said the creature, "and then pore your fill on that precious book of yours. One concern at a time is enough. I came to do you a service. Here, take this cursed, wretched woman, whom you style your Lady, and deliver her up to the lawful authorities, to be restored to her husband and her place in society. She has followed one that hates her, and never said one kind word to her in his life; and though I have beat her like a dog, still she clings to me, and will not depart, so enchanted is she with the laudable purpose of cutting my throat. Tell your master and her brother, that I am not to be burdened with their maniac. I have scourged—I have spurned and kicked her, afflicting her night and day, and yet from my side she will not depart. Take her. Claim the reward in full, and your fortune is made; and so farewell!"

The creature went away, and the moment his back was turned, the Lady fell a-screaming and struggling, like one in an agony, and, in spite of all the old couple's exertions, she forced herself out of their hands, and ran after the retreating Merodach. When he saw better would not be, he turned upon her, and, by one blow with his stick, struck her down; and, not content with that, continued to maltreat her in such a manner, as to all appearance would have killed twenty ordinary persons. The poor devoted dame could do nothing, but now and then utter a squeak like a half-worried cat, and writhe and grovel on the sward, till Wattie and his wife came up, and withheld her tormentor from further violence. He then bound her hands behind her back with a strong cord, and delivered her once more to the charge of the old couple, who contrived to hold her by that means, and take her home.

Wattie was ashamed to take her into the hall, but led her into one of the out-houses, whither he brought her brother to receive her. The man of the law was manifestly vexed at her reappearance, and scrupled not to testify his dissatisfaction; for when Wattie told him how the wretch had abused his sister, and that, had it not been for Bessie's interference and his own, the Lady would have been killed outright, he said, "Why, Walter, it is a great pity that he did *not* kill her outright. What good can her life now do to her, or of what value is her life to any creature living? After one has lived to disgrace all connected with them, the sooner they are taken off the better."

The man, however, paid old Walter down his two thousand merks, a great fortune for one like him in those days; and not to dwell longer on this unnatural story, I shall only add, very shortly, that the Lady of Wheelhope soon made her escape once more, and flew, as if drawn by an irresistible charm, to her tormentor. Her friends looked no more after her; and the last time she was seen alive, it was following the uncouth creature up the water of Daur, weary, wounded, and lame, while he was all the way beating her, as a piece of excellent amusement. A few days after that, her body was found among some wild haggs, in a place called Crook-burn, by a party of the persecuted Covenanters that were in hiding there, some of the very men whom she had exerted herself to destroy, and who had been driven, like David of old, to pray for a curse and earthly punishment upon her. They buried her like a dog at the Yetts of Keppel, and rolled three huge stones upon her grave, which are lying there to this day. When they found her corpse, it was mangled and wounded in a most shocking manner, the fiendish creature having manifestly tormented her to death. He was never more seen or heard of in this kingdom, though all that country-side was kept in terror for him many years afterwards; and to this day, they will tell you of The Brownie of the Black Haggs, which title he seems to have acquired after his disappearance.

This story was told to me by an old man named Adam Halliday, whose great-grandfather, Thomas Halliday, was one of those that found the body and buried it. It is many years since I heard it; but, however ridiculous it may appear, I remember it made a dreadful impression on my young mind. I never heard any story like it, save one of an old fox-hound that pursued a fox through the Grampians for a fortnight, and when at last discovered by the Duke of Athole's people, neither of them could run, but the hound was still continuing to walk after the fox, and when the latter lay down, the other lay down beside him, and looked at him steadily all the while, though unable to do him the least harm. The passion of inveterate malice seems to have influenced these two exactly alike. But, upon the whole, I scarcely believe the tale can be true.

ANCIENT LIGHTS

Algernon Blackwood

first published in *The Eye-Witness* (July 1912)

From Southwater, where he left the train, the road led due west. That he knew; for the rest he trusted to luck, being one of those born walkers who dislike asking the way. He had that instinct, and as a rule it served him well. "A mile or so due west along the sandy road till you come to a stile on the right; then across the fields. You'll see the red house straight before you." He glanced at the post-card's instructions once again, and once again he tried to decipher the scratched-out sentence—without success. It had been so elaborately inked over that no word was legible. Inked-out sentences in a letter were always enticing. He wondered what it was that had to be so very carefully obliterated.

The afternoon was boisterous, with a tearing, shouting wind that blew from the sea, across the Sussex weald. Massive clouds with rounded, piled-up edges, cannoned across gaping spaces of blue sky. Far away the line of Downs swept the horizon, like an arriving wave. Chanctonbury Ring rode their crest —a scudding ship, hull down before the wind. He took his hat off and walked rapidly, breathing great draughts of air with delight and exhilaration. The road was deserted; no horsemen, bicycles, or motors; not even a tradesman's cart; no single walker. But anyhow he would never have asked the way. Keeping a sharp eye for the stile, he pounded along, while the wind tossed the cloak against his face, and made waves across the blue puddles in the yellow road. The trees showed their under leaves of white. The bracken and the high new grass bent all one way. Great life was in the day, high spirits and dancing everywhere. And for a Croydon surveyor's clerk just out of an office this was like a holiday at the sea.

It was a day for high adventure, and his heart rose up to meet the mood of Nature. His umbrella with the silver ring ought to have been a sword, and his brown shoes should have been top-boots with spurs upon the heels. Where hid the enchanted Castle and the princess with the hair of sunny gold? His horse…

The stile came suddenly into view and nipped adventure in the bud. Everyday clothes took him prisoner again. He was a surveyor's clerk, middle-aged, earning three pounds a week, coming from Croydon to see about a client's proposed alterations in a wood—something to ensure a better view from the dining-room window. Across the fields, perhaps a mile away, he saw the red house gleaming in the sunshine; and resting on the stile a moment to get his breath he noticed a copse of oak and hornbeam on the right. "Aha," he told himself "so that must be the wood he wants to cut down to improve the view? I'll 'ave a look at it." There were boards up, of course, but there was an inviting little path as well. "I'm not a trespasser," he said; "it's part of my business, this is." He scrambled awkwardly over the gate and entered the copse. A little round would bring him to the field again.

But the moment he passed among the trees the wind ceased shouting and a stillness dropped upon the world. So dense was the growth that the sunshine only came through in isolated patches. The air was close. He mopped his forehead and put his green felt hat on, but a low branch knocked it off again at once, and as he stooped an elastic twig swung back and stung his face. There were flowers along both edges of the little path; glades opened on either side; ferns curved about in damper corners, and the smell of earth and foliage was rich and sweet. It was cooler here. What an enchanting little wood, he thought, turning down a small green glade where the sunshine flickered like silver wings. How it danced and fluttered and moved about! He put a dark blue flower in his buttonhole. Again his hat, caught by an oak branch as he rose, was knocked from his head, falling across his eyes. And this time he did not put it on again. Swinging his umbrella, he walked on with uncovered head, whistling rather loudly as he went. But the thickness of the trees hardly encouraged whistling, and something of his gaiety and high spirits seemed to leave him. He suddenly found himself treading circumspectly and with caution. The stillness in the wood was so peculiar.

There was a rustle among the ferns and leaves and something shot across the path ten yards ahead, stopped abruptly an instant with head cocked sideways to stare, then dived again beneath the underbrush with the speed of a shadow. He started like a frightened child, laughing the next second that a mere pheasant could have made him jump. In the distance he heard wheels upon the road, and wondered why the sound was pleasant. "Good old butcher's cart," he said to himself—then realized that he was going in the wrong direction and had somehow got turned round. For the road should be behind him, not in front.

And he hurriedly took another narrow glade that lost itself in greenness to the right. "That's my direction, of course," he said; "the trees has mixed me up a bit, it seems"—then found himself abruptly by the gate he had first climbed over. He had merely made a circle. Surprise became almost discomfiture then. And a man, dressed like a gamekeeper in browny green, leaned against the gate, hitting his legs with a switch. "I'm making for Mr. Lumley's farm," explained the walker. "This *is* his wood, I believe—" then stopped dead, because it was no man at all, but merely an effect of light and shade and foliage. He stepped back to reconstruct the singular illusion, but the wind shook the branches roughly here on the edge of the wood and the foliage refused to reconstruct the figure. The leaves all rustled strangely. And just then the sun went behind a cloud, making the whole wood look otherwise. Yet how the mind could be thus doubly deceived was indeed remarkable, for it almost seemed to him the man had answered, spoken—or was this the shuffling noise the branches made?—and had pointed with his switch to the notice-board upon the nearest tree. The words rang on in his head, but of course he had imagined them: "No, it's not his wood. It's ours." And some village wit, moreover, had changed the lettering on the weather-beaten board, for it read quite plainly, "Trespassers will be persecuted."

And while the astonished clerk read the words and chuckled, he said to himself, thinking what a tale he'd have to tell his wife and children later— "The blooming wood has tried to chuck me out. But I'll go in again. Why, it's only a matter of a square acre at most. I'm bound to reach the fields on the other side if I keep straight on." He remembered his position in the office. He had a certain dignity to maintain.

The cloud passed from below the sun, and light splashed suddenly in all manner of unlikely places. The man went straight on. He felt a touch of puzzling confusion somewhere; this way the copse had of shifting from sunshine into shadow doubtless troubled sight a little. To his relief at last, a new glade opened through the trees and disclosed the fields with a glimpse of the red house in the distance at the far end. But a little wicket gate that stood across the path had first to be climbed, and as he scrambled heavily over—for it would not open—he got the astonishing feeling that it slid off sideways beneath his weight, and towards the wood. Like the moving staircases at Harrod's and Earl's Court, it began to glide off with him. It was quite horrible. He made a violent effort to get down before it carried him into the trees, but his feet became entangled with the bars and umbrella, so that he fell heavily upon the farther side, arms spread across the grass and nettles, boots clutched between the first and second bars. He lay there a moment like a man crucified upside down, and while he struggled to get disentangled— feet, bars, and umbrella formed a regular net—he saw the little man in browny green go past him with extreme rapidity through the wood. The man was laughing. He passed across the glade some fifty yards away, and he was not alone this time. A companion like himself went with him. The clerk, now upon his feet again, watched them disappear into the gloom of green beyond. "They're tramps, not gamekeepers," he said to himself, half mortified, half angry. But his heart was thumping dreadfully, and he dared not utter all his thought.

He examined the wicket gate, convinced it was a trick gate somehow— then went hurriedly on again, disturbed beyond belief to see that the glade no longer opened into fields, but curved away to the right. What in the world had happened to him? His sight was so utterly at fault. Again the sun flamed out abruptly and lit the floor of the wood with pools of silver, and at the same moment a violent gust of wind passed shouting overhead. Drops fell clattering everywhere upon the leaves, making a sharp pattering as of many footsteps. The whole copse shuddered and went moving.

"Rain, by George," thought the clerk, and feeling for his umbrella, discovered he had lost it. He turned back to the gate and found it lying on the farther side. To his amazement he saw the fields at the far end of the glade, the red house, too, ashine in the sunset. He laughed then, for, of course, in his struggle with the gate, he had somehow got turned round—had fallen back instead of forwards. Climbing over, this time quite easily, he retraced his steps. The silver band, he saw, had been torn from the umbrella. No doubt his foot, a nail, or something had caught in it and ripped it off. The clerk began to run; he felt extraordinarily dismayed.

But, while he ran, the entire wood ran with him, round him, to and fro, trees shifting like living things, leaves folding and unfolding, trunks darting backwards and forwards, and branches disclosing enormous empty spaces, then closing up again before he could look into them. There were footsteps everywhere, and laughing, crying voices, and crowds of figures gathering just behind his back till the glade, he knew, was thick with moving life. The wind in his ears, of course, produced the voices and the laughter, while sun and clouds, plunging the copse alternately in shadow and bright dazzling light, created the figures. But he did not like it, and went as fast as ever his sturdy legs could take him. He was frightened now. This was no story for his wife and children. He ran like the wind. But his feet made no sound upon the soft mossy turf.

Then, to his horror, he saw that the glade grew narrow, nettles and weeds stood thick across it, it dwindled down into a tiny path, and twenty yards ahead it stopped finally and melted off among the trees. What the trick gate had failed to achieve, this twisting glade accomplished easily—carried him in bodily among the dense and crowding trees.

There was only one thing to do—turn sharply and dash back again, run headlong into the life that followed at his back, followed so closely too that now it almost touched him, pushing him in. And with reckless courage this was what he did. It seemed a fearful thing to do. He turned with a sort of violent spring, head down and shoulders forward, hands stretched before his face. He made the plunge; like a hunted creature he charged full tilt the other way, meeting the wind now in his face.

Good Lord! The glade behind him had closed up as well; there was no longer any path at all. Turning round and round, like an animal at bay, he searched for an opening, a way of escape, searched frantically, breathlessly, terrified now in his bones. But foliage surrounded him, branches blocked the way; the trees stood close and still, unshaken by a breath of wind; and the sun dipped that moment behind a great black cloud. The entire wood turned dark and silent. It watched him.

Perhaps it was this final touch of sudden blackness that made him act so foolishly, as though he had really lost his head. At any rate, without pausing to think, he dashed headlong in among the trees again. There was a sensation of being stiflingly surrounded and entangled, and that he *must* break out at all costs—out and away into the open of the blessed fields and air. He did this ill-considered thing, and apparently charged straight into an oak that deliberately moved into his path to stop him. He saw it shift across a good full yard, and being a measuring man, accustomed to theodolite and chain, he ought to know. He fell, saw stars, and felt a thousand tiny fingers tugging and pulling at his hands and neck and ankles. The stinging nettles, no doubt, were responsible for this. He thought of it later. At the moment it felt diabolically calculated.

But another remarkable illusion was not so easily explained. For all in a moment, it seemed, the entire wood went sliding past him with a thick deep rustling of leaves and laughter, myriad footsteps, and tiny little active, energetic shapes; two men in browny green gave him a mighty hoist—and he opened his eyes to find himself lying in the meadow beside the stile where first his incredible adventure had begun. The wood stood in its usual place and stared down upon him in the sunlight. There was the red house in the distance as before. Above him grinned the weather-beaten notice-board: "Trespassers will be prosecuted."

Disheveled in mind and body, and a good deal shaken in his official soul, the clerk walked slowly across the fields. But on the way he glanced once more at the postcard of instructions, and saw with dull amazement that the inked-out sentence was quite legible after all beneath the scratches made across it: "There *is* a short cut through the wood—the wood I want cut down —if you care to take it." Only "care" was so badly written, it looked more like another word; the "c" was uncommonly like "d."

"That's the copse that spoils my view of the Downs, you see," his client explained to him later, pointing across the fields, and referring to the ordnance map beside him. "I want it cut down and a path made so and so." His finger indicated direction on the map. "The Fairy Wood—it's still called, and it's far older than this house. Come now, if you're ready, Mr. Thomas, we might go out and have a look at it…"

The Washer of the Ford

William Sharp
(WRITING AS FIONA MACLEOD)

from *The Washer of the Ford and Other Legendary Moralities* (1896)

I.

When Torcall the Harper heard of the death of his friend, Aodh-of-the-Songs, he made a vow to mourn for him for three seasons—a green time, an apple time, and a snow time.

There was sorrow upon him because of that death. True, Aodh was not of his kindred, but the singer had saved the harper's life when his friend was fallen in the Field of Spears.

Torcall was of the people of the north—of the men of Lochlin. His song was of the fjords, and of strange gods, of the sword and the war-galley, of the red blood and the white breast, of Odin and Thor and Freya, of Balder and the Dream-God that sits in the rainbow, of the starry North, of the flames of pale blue and flushing rose that play around the Pole, of sudden death in battle, and of Valhalla.

Aodh was of the south isles, where these shake under the thunder of the western seas. His clan was of the isle that is now called Barra, and was then Iondû; but his mother was a woman out of a royal rath in Banba, as men of old called Eiré. She was so fair that a man died of his desire of her. He was named Ulad, and was a prince. "The Melancholy of Ulad" was long sung in his land after his end in the dark swamp, where he heard a singing, and went laughing glad to his death. Another man was made a prince because of her. This was Aodh the Harper, out of the Hebrid Isles. He won the heart out of her, and it was his from the day she heard his music and felt his eyes flame upon her. Before the child was born, she said, "He shall be the son of love. He shall be called Aodh. He shall be called Aodh-of-the-Songs." And so it was.

Sweet were his songs. He loved, and he sang, and he died.

And when Torcall that was his friend knew this sorrow, he arose and made his vow, and went out for evermore from the place where he was.

Since the hour of the Field of Spears he had been blind. Torcall Dall he was upon men's lips thereafter. His harp had a moonshine wind upon it from that day, it was said: a beautiful strange harping when he went down through the glen, or out upon the sandy machar by the shore, and played what the wind sang, and the grass whispered, and the tree murmured, and the sea muttered or cried hollowly in the dark.

Because there was no sight to his eyes, men said he saw and he heard. What was it he heard and he saw that they saw not and heard not? It was in the voice that was in the strings of his harp, so the rumor ran.

When he rose and went away from his place, the Maormor asked him if he went north, as the blood sang; or south, as the heart cried; or west, as the dead go; or east, as the light comes.

"I go east," answered Torcall Dall.

"And why so, Blind Harper?"

"For there is darkness always upon me, and I go where the light comes."

On that night of the nights, a fair wind blowing out of the west, Torcall the Harper set forth in a galley. It splashed in the moonshine as it was rowed swiftly by nine men.

"Sing us a song, O Torcall Dall!" they cried.

"Sing us a song, Torcall of Lochlin," said the man who steered. He and all his company were of the Gael: the Harper only was of the Northmen.

"What shall I sing?" he asked. "Shall it be of war that you love, or of women that twine you like silk o' the kine; or shall it be of death that is your meed; or of your dread, the Spears of the North?"

A low sullen growl went from beard to beard.

"We are under *geas*, Blind Harper,"[29] said the steersman, with downcast eyes because of his flaming wrath; "we are under bond to take you safe to the mainland, but we have sworn no vow to sit still under the lash of your tongue. 'Twas a wind-fleet arrow that sliced the sight out of your eyes: have a care lest a sudden sword-wind sweep the breath out of your body."

Torcall laughed a low, quiet laugh.

"Is it death I am fearing now—I who have washed my hands in blood, and had love, and known all that is given to man? But I will sing you a song, I will."

And with that he took his harp, and struck the strings.

> *There is a lonely stream afar in a lone dim land:*
> *It hath white dust for shore it has, white bones bestrew the strand:*
> *The only thing that liveth there is a naked leaping sword;*
> *But I, who a seer am, have seen the whirling hand*
> *Of the Washer of the Ford.*
> *A shadowy shape of cloud and mist, of gloom and dusk, she stands,*

---

[29] In Irish folklore, *geas* is an obligation or prohibition imposed through magic, similar to a spell or a curse.

> *The Washer of the Ford:*
> *She laughs, at times, and strews the dust through the hollow of her hands.*
> *She counts the sins of all men there, and slays the red-stained horde—*
> *The ghosts of all the sins of men must know the whirling sword*
> *Of the Washer of the Ford.*
> *She stoops and laughs when in the dust she sees a writhing limb:*
> *"Go back into the ford," she says, "and hither and thither swim;*
> *Then I shall wash you white as snow, and shall take you by the hand,*
> *And slay you here in the silence with this my whirling brand,*
> *And trample you into the dust of this white windless sand—"*
> *This is the laughing word*
> *Of the Washer of the Ford*
> *Along that silent strand.*

There was silence for a time after Torcall Dall sang that song. The oars took up the moonshine and flung it hither and thither like loose shining stones. The foam at the prow curled and leaped.

Suddenly one of the rowers broke into a long, low chant—

> *Yo, eily-a-ho, ayah-a-ho, eily-ayah-a-ho,*
> *Singeth the Sword*
> *Eily-a-ho, ayah-a-ho, eily-ayah-a-ho,*
> *Of the Washer of the Ford!*

And at that all ceased from rowing. Standing erect, they lifted up their oars against the stars, and the wild voices of them flew out upon the night—

> *Yo, eily-a-ho, ayah-a-ho, eily-ayah-a-ho,*
> *Singeth the Sword*
> *Eily-a-ho, ayah-a-ho, eily-ayah-a-ho,*
> *Of the Washer of the Ford!*

Torcall Dall laughed. Then he drew his sword from his side and plunged it into the sea. When he drew the blade out of the water and whirled it on high, all the white shining drops of it swirled about his head like a sleety rain.

And at that the steersman let go the steering-oar and drew his sword, and clove a flowing wave. But with the might of his blow the sword spun him round, and the sword sliced away the ear of the man who had the sternmost oar. Then there was blood in the eyes of all there. The man staggered, and felt for his knife, and it was in the heart of the steersman.

Then because these two men were leaders, and had had a blood-feud, and because all there, save Torcall, were of one or the other side, swords and knives sang a song.

The rowers dropped their oars; and four men fought against three.

Torcall laughed, and lay back in his place. While out of the wandering wave the death of each man clambered into the hollow of the boat, and breathed its chill upon its man, Torcall the Blind took his harp. He sang this song, with the swirling spray against his face, and the smell of blood in his nostrils, and the feet of him dabbling in the red tide that rose there.

> *Oh, 'tis a good thing the red blood, by Odin his word!*
> *And a good thing it is to hear it bubbling deep.*
> *And when we hear the laughter of the Sword,*
> *Oh, the corbies croak, and the old wail, and the women weep!*
> *And busy will she be there where she stands,*
> *Washing the red out of the sins of all this slaying horde;*
> *And trampling the bones of them into white powdery sands,*
> *And laughing low at the thirst of her thirsty sword—*
> *The Washer of the Ford!*

When he had sung that song there was only one man whose pulse still beat, and he was at the bow.

"A bitter black curse upon you, Torcall Dall!" he groaned out of the ooze of blood that was in his mouth.

"And who will you be?" said the Blind Harper.

"I am Fergus, the son of Art, the son of Fergus of the Dûns."

"Well, it is a song for your death I will make, Fergus mac Art mhic Fheargus: and because you are the last."

With that Torcall struck a wild sob out of his harp, and he sang—

> *Oh, death of Fergus, that is lying in the boat here,*
> *Betwixt the man of the red hair and him of the black beard,*
> *Rise now, and out of thy cold white eyes take out the fear,*
> *And let Fergus mac Art mhic Fheargus see his weird!*
> *Sure, now, it's a blind man I am, but I'm thinking I see*
> *The shadow of you crawling across the dead.*
> *Soon you will twine your arm around his shaking knee,*
> *And be whispering your silence into his listless head.*
> *And that is why, O Fergus—*

But here the man hurled his sword into the sea, and with a choking cry fell forward; and upon the white sands he was, beneath the trampling feet of the Washer of the Ford.

II.

It was a fair wind that blew beneath the stars that night. At dawn the mountains of Skye were like turrets of a great Dûn against the east.

But Torcall the Blind Harper did not see that thing. Sleep, too, was upon him. He smiled in that sleep, for in his mind he saw the dead men, that were of the alien people, his foes, draw near the stream that was in a far place. The shaking of them, poor, tremulous frostbit leaves they were, thin and sere, made the only breath there was in that desert.

At the ford—this is what he saw in his vision—they fell down like stricken deer with the hounds upon them.

"What is this stream?" they cried in the thin voice of rain across the moors.

"The River of Blood," said a voice.

"And who are you that are in the silence?"

"I am the Washer of the Ford."

And with that each red soul was seized and thrown into the water of the ford; and when white as a sheep-bone on the hill, was taken in one hand by the Washer of the Ford and flung into the air, where no wind was and where sound was dead, and was then severed this way and that, in four whirling blows of the sword from the four quarters of the world. Then it was that the Washer of the Ford trampled upon what fell to the ground, till under the feet of her was only a white sand, white as powder, light as the dust of the yellow flowers that grow in the grass.

It was at that Torcall Dall smiled in his sleep. He did not hear the washing of the sea; no, nor any idle plashing of the unoared boat. Then he dreamed, and it was of the woman he had left, seven summer-sailings ago, in Lochlin. He thought her hand was in his, and that her heart was against his.

"Ah, dear, beautiful heart of woman," he said, "and what is the pain that has put a shadow upon you?"

It was a sweet voice that he heard coming out of sleep.

"Torcall, it is the weary love I have."

"Ah, heart o' me, dear! sure 'tis a bitter pain I have had, too, and I away from you all these years."

"There's a man's pain, and there's a woman's pain."

"By the blood of Balder, Hildyr, I would have both upon me to take it off the dear heart that is here."

"Torcall!"

"Yes, white one."

"We are not alone, we two in the dark."

And when she had said that thing, Torcall felt two baby arms go round his neck, and two leaves of a wild rose press cool and sweet against his lips.

"Ah! what is this?" he cried, with his heart beating, and the blood in his body singing a glad song.

A low voice crooned in his ear: a bitter-sweet song it was, passing-sweet, passing-bitter.

"Ah, white one, white one," he moaned; "ah, the wee fawn o' me! Baby o' foam, bonnie wee lass, put your sight upon me that I may see the blue eyes that are mine too and Hildyr's."

But the child only nestled closer. Like a fledgling in a great nest she was. If God heard her song, He was a glad God that day. The blood that was in her body called to the blood that was in his body. He could say no word. The tears were in his blind eyes.

Then Hildyr leaned into the dark, and took his harp, and played upon it. It was of the fonnsheen he had learned, far, far away, where the isles are.

She sang: but he could not hear what she sang.

Then the little lips, that were like a cool wave upon the dry sand of his life, whispered into a low song: and the wavering of it was like this in his brain—

> *Where the winds gather*
> *The souls of the dead,*
> *O Torcall, my father,*
> *My soul is led!*
> *In Hildyr-mead*
> *I was thrown, I was sown:*
> *Out of thy seed*
> *I am sprung, I am blown!*
> *But where is the way*
> *For Hildyr and me,*
> *By the hill-moss gray*
> *Or the gray sea?*
> *For a river is here,*
> *And a whirling sword—*
> *And a Woman washing*
> *By a Ford!*

With that, Torcall Dall gave a wild cry, and sheathed an arm about the wee white one, and put out a hand to the bosom that loved him. But there was no white breast there, and no white babe: and what was against his lips was his own hand red with blood.

"O Hildyr!" he cried.

But only the splashing of the waves did he hear.

"O white one!" he cried.

But only the scream of a sea-mew, as it hovered over that boat filled with dead men, made answer.

III.

All day the Blind Harper steered the galley of the dead. There was a faint wind moving out of the west. The boat went before it, slow, and with a low, sighing wash.

Torcall saw the red gaping wounds of the dead, and the glassy eyes of the nine men.

"It is better not to be blind and to see the dead," he muttered, "than to be blind and to see the dead."

The man who had been steersman leaned against him. He took him in his shuddering grip and thrust him into the sea.

But when, an hour later, he put his hand to the coolness of the water, he drew it back with a cry, for it was on the cold, stiff face of the dead man that it had fallen. The long hair had caught in a cleft in the leather where the withes had given.

For another hour Torcall sat with his chin in his right hand, and his unseeing eyes staring upon the dead. He heard no sound at all, save the lap of wave upon wave, and the suss of spray against spray, and a bubbling beneath the boat, and the low, steady swish of the body that trailed alongside the steering oar.

At the second hour before sundown he lifted his head. The sound he heard was the sound of waves beating upon rocks.

At the hour before sundown he moved the oar rapidly to and fro, and cut away the body that trailed behind the boat. The noise of the waves upon the rocks was now a loud song.

When the last sunfire burned upon his neck and made the long hair upon his shoulders ashine, he smelt the green smell of grass. Then it was too that he heard the muffled fall of the sea, in a quiet haven, where shelves of sand were.

He followed that sound, and while he strained to hear any voice the boat grided upon the sand, and drifted to one side. Taking his harp, Torcall drove an oar into the sand, and leaped on to the shore. When he was there, he listened. There was silence. Far, far away he heard the falling of a mountain-torrent, and the thin, faint cry of an eagle, where the sun-flame dyed its eyrie as with streaming blood.

So he lifted his harp, and, harping low, with a strange, wild song on his lips, moved away from that place, and gave no more thought to the dead.

It was deep gloaming when he came to a wood. He felt the cold green breath of it.

"Come," said a voice, low and sweet.

"And who will *you* be?" asked Torcall the Harper, trembling because of the sudden voice in the stillness.

"I am a child, and here is my hand, and I will lead you, Torcall of Lochlin."

The blind man had fear upon him.

"Who are you that in a strange place are for knowing who I am?"

"Come."

"Ay, sure, it is coming I am, white one; but tell me who you are, and whence you came, and whither we go."

Then a voice that he knew sang:

> *O where the winds gather*
> *The souls of the dead,*
> *   O Torcall, my father,*
> *My soul is led!*
> *   But a river is here,*
> *And a whirling Sword—*
> *   And a Woman washing*
> *By a Ford!*

Torcall Dall was as the last leaf on a tree at that.

"Were you on the boat?" he whispered hoarsely.

But it seemed to him that another voice answered: "*Yea, even so.*"

"Tell me, for I have blindness: Is it peace?"

"It is peace."

"Are you man, or child, or of the Hidden People?"

"I am a shepherd."

"A shepherd? Then, sure, you will guide me through this wood? And what will be beyond this wood?"

"A river."

"And what river will that be?"

"Deep and terrible. It runs through the Valley of the Shadow."

"And is there no ford there?"

"Ay, there is a ford."

"And who will guide me across that ford?"

"She."

"Who?"

"The Washer of the Ford."

But hereat Torcall Dall gave a sore cry and snatched his hand away, and fled sidelong into an alley of the wood.

It was moonshine when he lay down, weary. The sound of flowing water filled his ears.

"Come," said a voice.

So he rose and went. When the cold breath of the water was upon his face, the guide that led him put a fruit into his hand.

"Eat, Torcall Dall!"

He ate. He was no more Torcall Dall. His sight was upon him again. Out of the blackness shadows came; out of the shadows, the great boughs of trees; from the boughs, dark branches and dark clusters of leaves; above the branches, white stars; below the branches, white flowers; and beyond these, the moonshine on the grass and the moonfire on the flowing of a river dark and deep.

"Take your harp, O Harper, and sing the song of what you see."

Torcall heard the voice, but saw no one. No shadow moved. Then he walked out upon the moonlit grass; and at the ford he saw a woman stooping and washing shroud after shroud of woven sunbeams: washing them there in the flowing water, and singing a low song that he did not hear. He did not see her face. But she was young, and with long black hair that fell like the shadow of night over a white rock.

So Torcall took his harp, and he sang:

> *Glory to the great Gods, it is no Sword I am seeing:*
> *Nor do I see aught but the flowing of a river.*
> *And I see shadows on the flow that are ever fleeing,*
> *And I see a woman washing shrouds for ever and ever.*

Then he ceased, for he heard the woman sing:

> *Glory to God on high, and to Mary, Mother of Jesus,*
> *Here am I washing away the sins of the shriven,*
> *O Torcall of Lochlin, throw off the red sins that ye cherish*
> *And I will be giving you the washen shroud that they wear in Heaven.*

Filled with a great awe, Torcall bowed his head. Then once more he took his harp, and he sang:

> *O well it is I am seeing, Woman of the Shrouds,*
> *That you have not for me any whirling of the Sword:*
> *I have lost my gods, O woman, so what will the name be*
> *Of thee and thy gods, O woman that art Washer of the Ford?*

But the woman did not look up from the dark water, nor did she cease from washing the shrouds made of the woven moonbeams. But he heard this song above the sighing of the water:

> *It is Mary Magdalene my name is, and I loved Christ.*
> *And Christ is the son of God, and Mary the Mother of Heaven.*
> *And this river is the river of death, and the shadows*
> *Are the fleeing souls that are lost if they be not shriven.*

Then Torcall drew nigher unto the stream. A melancholy wind was upon it.

"Where are all the dead of the world?" he said.

But the woman answered not.

"And what is the end, you that are called Mary?"

Then the woman rose.

"Would you cross the Ford, O Torcall the Harper?"

He made no word upon that. But he listened. He heard a woman singing faint and low far away in the dark. He drew more near.

"Would you cross the Ford, O Torcall?"

He made no word upon that. But once more he listened. He heard a little child crying in the night.

"Ah, lonely heart of the white one," he sighed, and his tears fell.

Mary Magdalene turned and looked upon him.

It was the face of Sorrow she had. She stooped and took up the tears. "They are bells of joy," she said. And he heard a wild sweet ringing in his ears.

A prayer came out of his heart. A blind prayer it was, but God gave it wings. It flew to Mary, who took and kissed it, and gave it song.

"It is the Song of Peace," she said. And Torcall had peace.

"What is best, O Torcall?" she asked, rustling—sweet as rain among the leaves her voice was—"What is best? The sword, or peace?"

"Peace," he answered: and he was white now, and was old.

"Take your harp," Mary said, "and go in unto the Ford. But lo, now I clothe you with a white shroud. And if you fear the drowning flood, follow the bells that were your tears: and if the dark affright you, follow the song of the Prayer that came out of your heart."

So Torcall the Harper moved into the whelming flood, and he played a wild strange air, like the laughing of a child.

Deep silence there was. The moonshine lay upon the obscure wood, and the darkling river flowed sighing through the soundless gloom. The Washer of the Ford stooped once more. Low and sweet, as of yore and for ever, over the drowning souls, she sang her immemorial song.

ABOUT THE EDITOR

C. **S.R. Calloway** is a prolific writer across a multitude of mediums and genres. His horror novels include *Desiderio*, *The Ungodly Hours*, and *The Veil and the Shade*. In addition to creating, curating, and editing the entire HORROR HISTORIA anthology, he is best known as creator and showrunner of the award-winning series *Pretty Dudes*. Calloway currently lives in Los Angeles with his Venus flytraps Betsy, Bootsie and Itsy Bitsy.

CHANCECALLOWAY.COM

HORROR HISTORIA presents your favorite frightening classics:

Dracula
Bram Stoker

The Elemental Trilogy:
The Boats of the "Glen Carrig," The House on the Borderland, & The Ghost Pirates
William Hope Hodgson

Frankenstein
Mary Shelley

Innominato: The Wizard of the Mountain
William Gilbert

The Lancashire Witches
William Harrison Ainsworth

The Phantom of the Opera
Gaston Leroux

The Picture of Dorian Gray
Oscar Wilde

Satan's Signature: Jekyll and Hyde, the Invisible Man, and Other Mad Scientists
Robert Louis Stevenson, H. G. Wells, and others

She
H. Rider Haggard

Wolf/Man: A Collection of Werewolf Classics
The Door of the Unreal & The Undying Monster
Gerald Biss and Jessie Douglas Kerruish

and more…

www.ingramcontent.com/pod-product-compliance
Lightning Source LLC
Chambersburg PA
CBHW011549190726

48287CB00010B/2808